# THE
# RIGHT
# GIRL FOR THE JOB

THE
# RIGHT
# GIRL FOR JOB
THE

## KAREN MCGOLDRICK

Deeds Publishing | Atlanta

Published by Deeds Publishing in Athens, GA
www.deedspublishing.com

Printed in The United States of America

Cover photo by Leila Moore; cover design by Mark Babcock and Matt King
Back cover photo by Emma Gustafsson

Library of Congress Cataloging-in-Publications data is available upon request.

ISBN 978-1-944193-76-8
EISBN 978-1-944193-77-5

Books are available in quantity for promotional or premium use. For information, email info@deedspublishing.com.

First Edition, 2016

10 9 8 7 6 5 4 3 2 1

This book is dedicated to my teachers, both human and equine. You made me better and that is reason enough to get up in the morning and try again.

# Prologue

MARGOT

*"Good, Lizzy, and now the half-pass from center line to the coun-*ter-canter and a flying change at M."

*The half pass was more sitting today and jumped to the side with good air time and a front leg that marked the beat of each stride nicely with a bit of a lift through the knee.*

*Where in the world did that come from?*

*I watched for something to correct.*

*I could see her smoothly set the mare up for the change, which was expressive and uphill.*

*I found myself looking at Lizzy and Winsome as if for the first time. I finally found my voice.*

"Beautiful, darling, now medium down the long side and then down centerline and the same to the left."

*I was just directing traffic today.*

*When did Lizzy get to be that good?*

*When I saw her in the hospital bed she struck me as too young, too frail, too sweet for this hard life. I even wondered if she would leave. Well, that question had been answered.*

*We have all silently agreed to rewrite history, to allow Frank and his "connections" to provide a quiet and unfettered justice, while ostensibly we pretend it was all an accident.*

*At first, after the "accident" Lizzy seemed to stagger around and we were worried, but I can see now that she's turned some invisible corner. She has regained her balance. When she lets go of fear and doubt and rides what she feels, she looks like a pro up there. And that is why she is here after all.*

*Lizzy is now completely one of us; the walking wounded, determined to make a life with horses; to make a life with us, understanding we do take care of our own.*

*And now Lizzy is riding better than ever, but so is Deb, and so is Emma. And so, too, is Ryder.*

*They are my work to showcase, just as my horses are my work to showcase and by God I have soldiered on, making beautiful horses and beautiful riders, no matter the losses, no matter the sadness, no matter the pain. And so will Lizzy.*

*The alternative, to let fear be your master, well, that is too terrible.*

# 1. Paradise

LIZZY

*We practically needed crossing guards for all the bunnies hopping all* over Equus Paradiso North, here in Peapack, New Jersey. We'd had a lot of rain this summer and the grass was lush. Maybe that's why there had been a bumper crop of bunnies.

Winsome and I were the last to go today and my workday was basically done. It meant I could linger with my mare, so I was hand grazing Winsome after her shower.

I had led her out under the shade of a big tree and watched as she greedily ripped at the grass and rhythmically chewed away, grass falling out of her mouth as she took another bite.

As we stood there, the bunnies began to appear, one, two, three, and then four. They didn't seem to mind me being there. It felt fairy-tale-magical, like I was some kind of Snow White and soon I'd have bluebirds landing on my finger.

Winsome pulled up something stalky, roots and all, covered in wet earth, and paused in her grazing to vigorously rub the dirt off the roots before working it up and into her mouth. Her eyes had gone unfocused. For a horse, this was the height of happiness and relaxation.

The bunnies grazed along with Winsome, quietly searching for the best little bits down in the grass. Some bunnies were small and some were larger, little white tails flipped up when they were alert but then slowly relaxed back down as they explored, mostly crawling but adding occasional leisurely hopping.

One sat up on his haunches and listened for a distant threat. His eye was large and round, his coat brown with flecks of gold that almost turned him a camo-green. Winsome and I did indeed live in paradise. The time had arrived when, like the bunnies, I had grown less skittish. I belonged here, and even with all the work involved, I could take time like this to look up from my labors, scan the horizon for distant threats, and not seeing any, relax and breathe.

A fine mist started falling, and I had to tug hard to get Winsome's head up out of the grass.

She reluctantly followed me in. I put her in her stall and slipped off her halter and then she put her chin up on my shoulder. This was her way of begging for a scratching between her jawbones. As usual, as I scratched away, her chin got heavy on my shoulder to the point I could hardly bear it, while her eyes half closed and grass and spit slid out the side of her mouth.

"OK, precious."

I gently pushed her chin off my shoulder, gave my shoulder a rub, and then took another moment to scratch her withers vigorously and let her return the favor with her top lip on my hip. Then I gave her a pat, and backed out the door, sliding it shut.

I turned around and almost yelped in alarm. There was a man standing not five feet away. He looked surprised, too. "Sorry to scare you."

I couldn't help but feel this intruder had no right to be here. Heck, we had a coded gate.

He stuck out his hand and smiled. "I'm Anthony Cavelli, and you are?"

My brain was doing a search. Nope. Never heard of this Cavelli. I used my best secretarial voice. "Can I help you?"

He was some thirty-something guy wearing pressed jeans and a white oxford shirt with shined up moccasins.

He looked around at the barn. "Just looking for my mother. The place looks great. I haven't been out in ages."

Well, that changed things. This had to be one of the sons; one of two Cavelli sons who had disappointed his parents by taking absolutely no interest in the family business.

I didn't say anything for a moment. I hung up Winsome's halter and finally extended my hand for a shake. He clearly did have a right to be here. Of course he would have the gate code. I needed to be polite to the guy. As soon as he gripped my hand I realized my nails and fingertips were filthy from scratching Winsome.

He looked me in the eye and smiled. "Sorry again to have startled you. I didn't get your name."

I forced a smile. "I'm Lizzy."

Here was a guy that was nothing like his father, Frank Cavelli. Frank was big and loud with a paunchy belly, and entirely relaxed in his demeanor, and this guy was nothing like that. Frank would never have snuck up on a girl like that.

Instead Anthony Cavelli had a resemblance to his mother, Francesca. And that was a strike against him.

I guess he was good looking in a polished kind of way; a good haircut and a membership at an expensive gym kind of way.

As he released my hand I saw him glance down at my filthy hand and nails. "Lizzy, yes, I've seen your name on the payroll, nice to meet you and match a face to a social security number." He glanced again around the barn. "Mother said she'd be here."

I shook my head. "I think you're out of luck, Francesca left hours ago. She rides in the morning. She's always gone by now."

But just as the words left my mouth, here came Chopper and Snapper, Francesca's advance guard of Jack Russells. They were flying at high speed. They had seen Anthony and there were squeals and butt-tucking as soon as they reached him. They ran circles and zigzags and then jumped all over his pressed jeans.

He leaned over and put his hands out like shields. "No! No! No!"

It was useless. Chopper, the rough-coated one, was using Anthony as some kind of trampoline. He was jumping up high and then punching off of Anthony's legs with all four feet, springing off of them in almost a back flip, and then doing a wild butt-tucking circle, and zooming back again for more. Finally, Anthony squatted down and both dogs squirmed around his knees, still making little squeals that diminished into whimpers as he petted them into a calmer state.

And then Francesca was there. "At least the boys are glad to see you, Chess." She made no move to embrace him.

I was confused by her use of the word "chess."

And then Anthony started sneezing. Repeatedly. Finally he stood up and pulled a handkerchief from his back pocket.

"Chess," Francesca said, in a scolding voice I knew well, "You know you shouldn't be here. You're allergic to everything here, you know that."

"I'm fine. I took my meds; that should help for the day. Dad wants me here. Let's get started."

"Really you needn't bother."

His pleasant smile never wavered. "Mother, I am trying to be helpful, and Dad said it was OK. C'mon."

Francesca narrowed her eyes and looked directly at me and then back at her son. I got the distinct impression she didn't like her son making time with the help, then with a little sniff of disgust, Francesca turned on her heel and left.

Winsome hung her head out over the yoke gate of her stall, hay hanging out of her mouth. She was probably hoping that someone had a peppermint in their pocket.

"Chess" put his hand up and touched her funny moth-eaten blaze.

"He's a beautiful animal, Lizzy. Is he one of my mother's?"

Before I could answer, Winsome blew her nose loudly, dotting Chess's white oxford shirt with green hay slobber.

He backed up a few steps as Winsome returned to her hay, disappointed in all of us. Chess looked down at the splatter on his shirt front and wiped at it with his hands. I braced myself for a Francesca-like cutting comment. Instead he bit his lower lip as if suppressing a laugh.

I couldn't help myself. I started laughing. "I'm so sorry. Winsome is *my* mare, and yes, she is beautiful."

"Does that mean he likes me?"

"No. It means SHE had a tickle in her nose."

He chuckled, and it struck me that his laugh sounded just like his father's. He brushed off his shirt and then indicated with his thumb towards the office.

"I'd better catch Mother while I have the chance. Nice to meet you, Lizzy."

I watched as "Chess" walked away. What a weird nickname. He was probably captain of his high school chess team ... a nerd supreme; but at least a smart person. A little part of me became intrigued. But he was Francesca's son. I tried to shake his name right out of my head. It was time to go take a shower.

I walked up the stairs to the barn apartment that I shared with Ryder. Tonight Ryder and I would be walking up the hill to Deb's barn cottage to eat homemade Ratatouille over brown rice with Deb and the newest addition to our staff at the farm; Natalie. All the veggies were from Deb's own garden behind the mare barn; grown in the soil fertilized from the poop of our own horses.

Natalie had survived more than I would ever know. There were a lot of things we just didn't talk about. Deb had taken her under her wing after Francesca had brought her out of hiding out west at a dude ranch. Nat, who had once done the advanced young rider division, was a damn fine horsewoman though, and good with the babies, so it wasn't just charity. Plus, Deb's feral cats had soon accepted Nat. To Deb, that beat out a fancy resume. The two of them had become like sisters.

When Ryder and I started up the hill, I noticed two cars parked in front of our barn. Francesca's familiar black Mercedes, and a small white BMW. Chess, the nerd son, was still there.

At Deb's I grabbed a chipped white bowl off the counter and took my turn ladling the colorful Ratatouille over the brown rice and then went outside to sit with everyone. Deb had lit Citronella Tiki torches around the yard so we could eat outside without being eaten. The New Jersey mosquitoes were enormous, and along with the bunnies, we seemed to have a bumper crop. I slid into my chair next to Natalie.

I gave Nat a friendly little punch on her arm. "Hey, Nat. Man, this looks great."

Despite everything that had happened, Nat still looked like a jolly pixie. Like Deb she was petite yet muscular with light brown hair and a smattering of freckles. She was about my age, in her early twenties, but much more worldly. Nat had known what it was like to hit rock bottom, yet she always was laughing or singing, and always entirely un-self-conscious.

Nat had just taken a bite and closed her eyes and leaned back in her chair. "Ambrosia. God, Deb sure can cook!"

I pulled my chair closer to the table, and had my first bite. Natalie was right. But, the food was really hot, so I couldn't speak, and I rolled it around carefully in my mouth, blowing and waving my hand around.

We now had a brand new outdoor dining table and chairs to sit in. In fact Deb's cottage was sporting a lot of new furniture, thanks to

Frank and Francesca. It was a far cry from the single broken down lawn chair that had previously been Deb's only outdoor furniture.

Ryder joined us and our little party was complete.

Deb didn't have to feed us, but she seemed to enjoy cooking, and we enjoyed eating her cooking, and somehow it had become a routine every Wednesday night to eat at Deb's. If we volunteered to bring anything we were turned down.

But, I noticed that Natalie had begun to help produce the meal. Even if it just meant that she chopped things up. Natalie had also been helping out around the house. Gradually Deb's barn apartment had become clean and the magazines and books were now in stacks and on shelves rather than sliding off of every table and chair seat, and the cat hair was at least kept to manageable levels.

Deb was having a go at contact lenses again, and I noticed her eyes were watering. I turned to her. "Contacts bothering you again?"

"No. Maybe a little. Nat peeled some hot onions tonight. They got to me."

"Well, they don't seem too hot now. This is delicious."

Deb straightened up suddenly. "Nat, you forgot your bread."

Nat wrinkled her nose. "Deb...No."

Deb announced, "Natalie is learning to bake bread."

I laughed. "Nat, Deb is domesticating you!"

Ryder had said nothing but was now smiling and shaking her head in disbelief.

But Natalie didn't seem to think it was funny, and pointed her fork at Ryder. "A person's gotta' eat, and I don't see either of you leaning over a hot stove."

I looked at Natalie and smiled. She had softened since moving in with Deb. Even her sharp sense of humor was less cutting these days. Maybe she had even gained a few pounds. Plus, Nat and I had discovered that we both loved to read novels, and Nat had turned me on to an alternate reality series. It was a great way to unwind and relax and talk about something other than horses. Unlike Ryder, who was only two weeks away from traveling to the North American Young Riders Championships in Lexington, Kentucky, and looking thin and pale with nerves strung tight. I knew she was not sure of a gold medal anymore. She had tasted defeat during her struggles riding Petey.

We all chowed down in earnest for a minute before I remembered my news. "Hey, I met Anthony Cavelli."

That made an impact. Everyone sat up. Deb spoke first. "You mean Chess was here? He never comes here."

Natalie and Ryder spoke at the same time. "Chess?"

I explained, "He introduced himself as Anthony, but then Francesca called him Chess. He was here to see Francesca."

Deb looked truly surprised as she flipped her long blonde braid over her shoulder. "He'll always be Chess to me. Anyway, he's allergic, and I mean really scary allergic, to all animal dander. He had asthma as a kid. Very serious."

I realized then what had happened back at the barn. "Oops. I shook his hand after giving Winsome a big scratching session. My hand was really filthy, too."

Deb's eyebrows went up. "Poor guy. He must have needed a Benadryl after that."

I grimaced. "He did start sneezing like crazy, but that was after the dogs jumped all over him."

Now Ryder leaned in. "Francesca has a son?"

Deb held up two fingers without taking her eyes off of me. "Two sons, Frank Jr. lives out west with his wife, and I haven't seen Chess in ages and ages, though he doesn't live too far from here. He and his mom butt heads a lot."

As did most everyone with Francesca.

Natalie chimed in. "Single? Good-looking?"

I turned my head. "Yeah, I guess. He looks a lot like Francesca." Then I turned back to Deb. "Why do you suppose he's here now?"

Deb shrugged. "Margot will know. She knows all." She got up and brought back a slightly browned loaf of bread and Nat started to apologize. "I thought it should be a little brown on top, but I waited too long to take it out."

Deb broke in. "It will be crusty."

And we all ate it and it was "crusty" but still good. As we complimented Natalie I could tell she was proud of her new skill.

The sun set and our talk turned to horses and riding theory and an analysis of all the top European riders and horses that were making the news. Even with the Tiki-torches, we were soon swatting at mosquitoes, and I was scratching at my ankles. But I hated for our meal to end. The talk was as delicious as the meal, but Deb began to rub at her watery eyes, a definite no-no with contact lenses. Under the table I gave Ryder a little kick, and we both pulled our chairs back from the table at the same time.

We washed up our dishes, put our bottles into Deb's new recycling bin in her laundry room, and Ryder and I started our walk back down the hill to our apartment over the main barn. I had a full stomach and a deep feeling of contentment, until Ryder started talking.

Ryder lifted one corner of her mouth and tipped her head with interest, "Did you say Anthony was married?"

I turned my gaze back to my feet. "I don't know, Ryder, and I guess he goes by "Chess" although that's sure a weird name, but I'm guessing he was a chess player in high school or something."

She probed. "How old a guy?"

I snorted. "Too old for you."

Ryder kept it up. "I'll bet he's single."

I looked back up to see if she was serious. "You're probably right. Any girl that met Francesca would run for the hills."

Ryder scrunched up her face, and spoke emphatically. "*I* like Francesca."

I snorted again. "Yeah, you would, but that's 'cause you're her little 'mini-me' suck-up."

Ryder's voice got snappy. "Hey, if she wants to adopt me, I'm willing. Besides, I like guys that are older than me. The guys my age are too immature."

The tone of my voice rose to meet hers. "Maybe you should marry her son then so you can start calling her 'Mother.'"

We stopped and looked at each other suddenly horrified, but laughing anyway, then she gave me a little punch in my upper arm, though not as gently as the one I had delivered to Natalie. I guess I deserved it for calling her a suck-up.

I rubbed my arm. "Ow. That hurt! How'd you like a punch back?"

I kept rubbing my upper arm, and she began dancing around me with her fists up but giggling. "Come on Grandma...come and get me."

That was it for me. The girl who liked men who were "mature" was acting like a grade-schooler, and sadly, I was quickly degenerating into one myself. In a wink, I was transported to the after school fight-zone behind the playground. I took the bait. I growled, "OK then Miss High-Horse Couture, I'm going to pummel you!"

When I made a move toward her she darted around nimbly. I barely tagged her shirt and she took off running, and she *was* fast. I sprinted after her, but couldn't close the distance. Ryder was a true athlete.

She stopped and taunted me, gesturing with both hands, curling her fingers in a backward sort of wave to come and get her. "Where are your circus moves now?"

That momentarily stopped me: Low blow. There was something cruel about Ryder. She was violating our unwritten rule; all that had happened was to be forgotten and not spoken of. I tipped my head and studied her, regaining my composure, because I realized this teenager was still jealous. Gorgeous Marco, the circus trainer, had chosen me, not her and I *had* learned a few circus tricks. One of those tricks had saved my life. In the dark of night, in a moment of crisis that was the stuff of nightmares, I had remembered what Marco had taught me; how to swing up onto a horse's lowered neck to mount. I shook off the memory of that night, and focused on the memory of Marco's dark brown eyes and rich musical voice. Of course she would be jealous.

I relaxed for a moment and Ryder put her hands down, and so did I. She must have known she had crossed the line.

She said, "Uncle?"

I took her nonchalant pose as a cue to sprint; it was the only way possible for me to catch her. But I had to stop suddenly with a bad stitch in my side and leaned over groaning.

Ryder walked back to me. "You OK?"

"Yes, I think I just made myself sick using the word "Mother" and Francesca in the same sentence."

Ryder smiled wickedly. "Nope. You made yourself sick pigging out on Ratatouille and bread. You can really pack it away."

I grimaced again, and tried some deep breaths and the stitch started to ease. I was skinny enough, but Ryder never let me forget that she had been a model and was pencil thin. She and Francesca were almost transparent they were so damn thin. Ryder only ate organic and watched every morsel that went in her mouth and was "holier than thou" about it, too. She wasn't done either.

Her mouth was in a twisted smile. "Carbo-load like your friend Nat there and it will take a team effort to zip you into your white breeches."

And without even standing up, I tackled her.

# 2. Loyal Guardian

*Gorgeous Marco, who had taught me so much about horses as well as* teaching me a few circus 'moves' had indeed moved on. But we still kept in touch. He sent me small video clips of his newest routine he was working on for the circus with his two Andalusian stallions, Bernardo and Caruso. He had started doing more Roman riding with them, standing on both of them at the same time. And now he had added small jumps. He even worked them in an open field, side by side, their manes and tails flying behind them as he let them gallop. It never failed to move me.

In another clip he had both horses lying down in a field of small yellow flowers. He sat cross-legged on the ground leaning against Bernardo's barrel, while Bernardo and Caruso calmly nibbled on the flowers.

I wished I had such inspiring video clips to send back. I didn't. But I did send photos, mostly of Winsome. Ryder snapped a shot of me crouching next to her as she was curled up napping in her stall. I was giving her a peppermint. Her ears were up as I smiled into the camera, my cheek pressed against her cheek. I liked it so much I used it as my profile picture on my Facebook page.

But I had performing of my own to focus on. And I had to let my thoughts of Marco be stored away or I would never be able to sleep.

And sleep was precious. I watched the clip of the Roman riding one more time, sent Marco a short message, and turned out the light.

Sleeping had finally become easier. Sometimes I woke up in the night, with a pounding heart, ready to fight an invisible foe. I never held the image from my nightmare in my mind's eye long enough to see it clearly. There was no doubt where I had been, or who I had been ready to fight, but also no doubt where I was, tucked safely in my bed. And I usually drifted back to sleep.

By day, Patrick, the monster who had tried to destroy Wild Child and Margot, and had very nearly destroyed me, was never mentioned. And when he managed to intrude into my thoughts I fought him back into a dark corner. He did not deserve any of my conscious thought. He was a nothing. No; less than nothing.

But a nothing who had been all too real.

I had not told anyone about my dreams. We never spoke about the near disaster of that night. Everything on the surface was back to the normal, usual routine; though at times I sensed Margot, and sometimes Frank, watching me thoughtfully.

I woke up the next morning to the sound of my cell phone's alarm. Even after all this time, I still had to drag myself out of bed in the morning. I would never be a morning person.

I don't think Ryder would ever be one either because our morning routine never contained friendly chit-chat...ever.

No matter how much I loved this life, and loved this farm, the job was unrelenting. All those eager eyes were on me as soon as I opened the door from our apartment stairs into the barn aisle. They whinnied; they banged on their doors, as they did every morning, desperate and excited to begin their day with a scoop of grain in their feed boxes. No translation was needed to know what they were saying. "Feed me! Feed me!" They never took a day off from eating, and pooping, and peeing, and needing to go out and come in and, of course, be exercised and trained. I was the waiter, I was room service, I was the masseuse, I was the beautician, and I was the personal trainer.

I had finally accepted that Ryder's silence toward me was not personal. She rolled her eyes when I cooed and baby talked to the horses. She was way too cool for that. But I was not. Chirping to my horse charges helped me get my blood moving, so I greeted every horse with sweet talk as I dumped grain.

Two stalls that had been full were now empty, and I still felt a pang as I rolled the cart past them. I was still missing Kiddo and Petey, who had gone back to their owner, Cara.

The day they left had been an emotional day. Cara had cried as she was reunited with Kiddo. She had hugged Kiddo around his neck and then fed him a crème-filled oatmeal cookie and gave him a coke to chase it down.

And I had cried, too, as Kiddo happily followed her up the ramp of her horse trailer. He paid no attention to me, but tugged at his hay net, contentedly ready for his ride. Such are the good-byes we say to our horse friends. I knew I probably would never see Kiddo again. It hurt.

Petey loaded up alongside Kiddo. Ryder seemed unaffected, but I didn't buy her casual act. She had to feel sad. She had changed Petey for the better, at no small cost. It had not been smooth sailing. But now he was a high-scoring Third level horse on his way to the FEI. It just wasn't going to be with Ryder. Although Ryder didn't cry, she had gone up to her room and closed her door. I let her be, but I cried enough for both of us.

With them gone, our main barn was down to just Wild Child, Hotstuff, Papa, Winsome, and Lovey.

And I was worried about Lovey. Francesca had recently earned her USDF Silver medal (by a slim margin). Margot wanted her to stay at the Prix St. Georges and Intermediare 1 level and work on improving her scores before making the big jump up to Intermediare II and the

Grand Prix. But I could tell Francesca was impatient to move up and there was a problem.

Lovey was what was called a "small tour horse" and would not be able to move up to the Intermediare II and the Grand Prix level. For that, Francesca would need a different horse.

He had been "Saint" Lovey for Francesca. He did his job without complaining about Francesca's rough hands and stiff joints. Francesca never showed any affection for Lovey. I felt he at least deserved a permanent place in this barn. I always gave him an extra carrot and a good grooming to let him know that he was valued. He worked hard, and when his session was done each day, I wanted him to feel safe and to rest. Horses are prey animals. They are hardwired to save their energies for flight by recognizing safety. Perhaps safety was always an illusion for us as well as our horses. But, if it was an illusion, it was one I wanted to create.

I had long ago noticed that when horses in a herd lay down to nap, one trusted soul is usually left standing guard. Even when horses in the barn are down resting in their shavings there always seems to be at least one left standing. That one horse is the guardian.

Because of me, while I groom at least, I hope they can relax and save their energy.

I am a guardian, too.

I pushed the feed cart back into the feed room. Ryder and I had an hour to relax before we had to begin grooming and tacking.

I poured myself a cup of coffee with flavored creamer. Ryder prepared her healthy breakfast of blueberries and yogurt with wheat germ and who knows what else sprinkled on top; the breakfast of champions.

I reached for my bagel and saw Ryder raise an eyebrow. I knew what that eyebrow was saying; 'White breeches.' I pulled a steak knife out of the drawer and sawed the bagel in half and put half back in the package.

The day began to roll along in its now familiar rhythms. Alfonso began the turnout, dragged the arena, and then began mucking. I got Hot-stuff ready for Margot. Hotstuff was now her number one mount, and the USEF National Young Horse Championships were in her sights as she currently was ranked number two. The top twelve would be invited, so Margot's position was assured absent a calamity. The championships would be at the end of the summer in Chicago.

Before then Ryder would be going to the North American Advanced Young Rider Championships in Lexington, Kentucky, which was Margot's current focus, since she had been named the Chef d'equip (team manager) for our region, replacing the now-banished Patrick.

Wild Child had been Margot's number one ride each day. One day, when I had Wild Child ready for Margot, Deb had taken the reins instead. When I asked, Margot had said that she had come to the conclusion that Wild Child was just too hard on her body, and that he needed a younger rider.

I was surprised how affected I was by her pronouncement. Wild Child had been purchased specifically for Margot to get her back into the High Performance League, and as sort of a "stuff it" to Dennis, Margot's old boyfriend.

The Dennis break-up happened before my time. But I got filled in by Emma, who had been the one to school me in all things Equus Paradiso when I had first arrived down in Florida. Dennis, Margot's boyfriend, had run off with Margot's then-working student, Sophie. When Dennis tried to buy Wild Child for Sophie, Frank swooped in, outbid Dennis, and Wild Child went to Margot instead. I guess Wild Child had been Margot's consolation prize. But, the purchase was made without Margot's knowledge or consent, orchestrated by Emma, and paid for by Frank. Emma had confided to me that Margot had given Dennis up without a fight. It appeared to me that if Wild Child had been Margot's consolation prize, she had just given her prize away. That shook me.

I knew it wasn't rational, but somehow I felt it was my fault. Margot had been on the verge of winning a grant to compete in Europe when everything had gone to hell. And I had been in the middle of that hell. I understood that my feelings were not rational. Still, it pained me.

Gaining the ride on Wild Child was a great opportunity for Deb. It had been a very hard spring for Deb, too. She had lost her great horse Regina, and had worked tirelessly to save the foal. She deserved this. Riding Wild Child would allow Deb a shot at the "big arena." Of course, the ride on Wild Child's was not really Margot's to give away. The horse belonged to Frank and Francesca Cavelli, and ultimately they had been the generous ones by agreeing. That impressed me. Their dream had included Margot, not Deb. Heck, Deb and Francesca hadn't even been speaking to each other until recently.

Francesca was a person who was hard to like. But she kept surprising and confusing me with things like that. For some reason, even Francesca's generosity made me uneasy.

I snapped Hotstuff into the cross ties. His black coat had only a little sunburn, it was slick and tight. He loved his grooming sessions. His giant ears drooped to the side, and his eyes rolled around in his head as he yawned and did his morning yoga stretches.

I was used to his goofy routine. "Go ahead, big guy."

He walked his front legs out in front of him. He had huge shoulders and long legs. Then he rocked back on his haunches and did his "downward dog" with a long protracted groan, straightened up, and finished his routine with his own special move. He crossed his front legs, scratching one leg with the other before standing on all fours again.

I gave him a pat. "Hotstuff, you are the strangest horse I've ever known. But I mean that in a good way, bud."

I walked back to his shoulder and he twisted his head around to look for his peppermint, giant ears now up. "OK. I've got one right here."

The wrapper made a crinkle sound that made Hotstuff lick his lips.

I began his grooming by picking up his front right hoof and cleaning it out, and then I picked up the right hind hoof, but he pulled it away and did one more stretch out behind himself, accompanied with more sound effects, and then politely placed his foot back in my hand.

"All done, buddy?"

Hotstuff was as sweet and kind a horse as Wild Child was cranky and unforgiving. Hotstuff and Margot always seemed to love their time together, and even though he had springs in his toes and bounded over the ground, Margot always said he was easy on her body. I almost resented the comparison. It was like comparing your children. I knew Wild Child would never be easy in any sense of the word, impressive as he looked.

I got Hotstuff tacked up and then waited for Margot. And waited. Finally she came down the barn aisle.

Margot was her own golden light, and it wasn't just because of her blonde hair, always pulled tightly back into a low bun. She was important. And we all knew it, people and horses alike.

"Lizzy, darling, sorry to be so late, there was road work and our little bridge was blocked. Go ahead and hop on him and take him to the arena and walk him around. Francesca wants to talk to me."

I felt a flush in my cheeks. I'd never sat on Hotstuff. "You want me to sit on him?"

Margot smiled at me. "Why not? He's only four, but really he's the safest horse on the farm."

She turned and headed to the office. Hotstuff watched her go and then pawed once and leaned forward against the cross ties as if to draw her back to him.

I stroked him gently on his neck. "No worries. You and I are going for a walk."

I ducked into the tack room to put on my boots and grab my helmet. Once dressed, I led Hotstuff to the indoor and parked him in front of our extra tall mounting block. Even with Margot's long stirrups and the tall mounting block, it was a long way up. He stood like a rock.

I patted his neck. "Good boy."

Then I gathered the reins and gave him a touch of my leg and we were off.

It was like sitting on some other species; maybe a giraffe. His giant ears were a mile away, set on a long neck. His walk was eager and his entire body undulated with each step, his head and neck bobbing up and down. It made even Winsome's good walk seem small. When I turned to look behind me there was not nearly as much horse behind as in front, and it sloped away in a steep angle. We walked around for about ten minutes.

Margot's voice startled me. "He must feel vastly different from Winsome."

Margot had walked in without making a sound. I turned him towards her, but she waved me away. "No, go ahead and trot a little. Have a feel of him."

I asked, "Can I shorten my stirrups?"

"Of course, darling."

Once I got organized I picked up the reins and touched him again with my legs, and he sprang into trot.

Each stride bounced, but Margot was right, his trot was easy to ride. Although he was narrow as a fence rail, his ribs still found the inside of my boots and my legs hung down in a way that made me feel secure and low in my center of gravity. He reached into the reins, creating a soft traction to the bit that also felt secure. And he stayed in one trot tempo; steady as a metronome.

Margot began to coach. "Bending lines, Lizzy. Hands together and low and quiet, just let him do it without too much interference."

I began riding serpentines.

"Yes. He looks wonderful, darling. It's so nice to see him go."

I looked over at her and smiled.

"Now some canter-trot transitions on the circle, just easy and steady, that amount of power is just fine for warm up, not more."

I wanted to weep with joy. This was awesome. Hotstuff promptly jumped into canter with exuberance. He also felt joyful.

"Good, now forward and back on the circle. Yes. Lovely. Change direction. Do it again. Yes. Good, Lizzy."

I felt in sync with the rhythm of his strides, and fell into a sort of happy trance. Too soon, Margot got my attention; time to stop. So this is what a world-class horse felt like.

"OK. Well done, darling. But now I must take him away from you. You need to get Wild Child ready for Deb."

I was nodding, and yet feeling a bit like I had just cheated on my precious Winsome.

"Thank you, Margot. That was a treat."

"Every ride on Hotstuff is a treat. I can't wait to sit on his little brother, too. Deb said he has been easy to start, even easier than Hotstuff."

I went to fetch Wild Child, with a guilty smile stuck on my lips.

But Francesca caught up with me, looking serious. "Lizzy, come see me after you finish up today. I have something to discuss with you."

I was immediately anxious. "Can I have a hint?"

I could tell she was already thinking of something else. I was dismissed with a curt reply. "No. We'll talk later."

Francesca never felt the need to explain herself.

So I had to carry that around for the rest of the day. Francesca was an expert at creating dread. I tried not to let it affect me, but still, she had dampened my spirits from my ride on Hotstuff.

I tacked up "Shark-face." Wild Child and I had become like an old couple. We loved each other, but we still had the same petty arguments each day. But no matter how much he told me I annoyed him, and that he didn't like at least one hundred things about me, he tolerated me better than pretty much anyone else.

And he knew I was good for a peppermint. He was totally addicted. He could change his facial expression from sour to ecstatic with the crinkling of a peppermint wrapper. Putting on his bridle used to be a battle but now when I held it up he always gave me a low whinny.

I was preoccupied with buckling his noseband when Deb appeared. "How's the old man today?"

Deb flipped her braid over her shoulder. She was wearing her contacts again. It made her look younger. The summer had splashed freckles across her nose. Her arms were lean and ropey and her breeches looked a size too big for her. She may have been a good cook, but she burned it all off and then some.

I put my hand across the bridge of his nose to steady his head as I rubbed his face with a damp towel, carefully wiping out each nostril. "He's his usual cranky self."

He stood perfectly still, not happy exactly, his nostrils wrinkled and his ears half way back and his mouth a small tight grimace, but he tolerated it.

I can't say whether he remembered that I had saved him and that he had saved me. But I think he considered that he owned me in a strange way. That thought made me smile to myself. Such is the arrogance of stallions.

Deb had no problem giving him a good kick in the pants when he forgot his place. And she refused to be impressed by his hormonal displays. He was a little wary of her, too. She might have been tiny but he recognized that she was formidable.

"Hey, Deb, Francesca wants to talk to me about something at the end of the day. She's being her usual dramatic self. Do you know of any sins I may have committed?"

Deb was looking at Wild Child, examining him. "Nope. Not a clue."

"I got the feeling that maybe I'm in trouble."

Deb stepped forward and pushed a keeper up on his bridle.

I was still fretting. "Maybe it's about her son? Francesca seemed annoyed that he was chatting with me. In fact, she seemed pretty annoyed with him, period. Do you mind asking Margot? She always knows what's what."

Deb gave me a casual nod, her mind completely focused on the big glowing chestnut stallion in front of her. Wild Child was the only thing that mattered to Deb at that moment.

I grabbed the dangling curb chain and turned it until all the links lay flat and smooth and counted to the third link, carefully slipping it onto the hook.

"Let me give him another spritz of fly spray, Deb, and then we're all done."

I put the finishing touches on my grooming job and handed him over to Deb. His ears were up and he followed her just as he used to follow Margot. They both had a job to do.

Later, when Deb came back, Ryder was finishing tacking up Papa for her lesson, and I was sweeping. We never really finished sweeping and dusting, so I hung the broom on the wall and took a rein.

Wild Child had a nice sweat on his neck and lather between his hind legs. Deb looked happy with the boy, so I asked a question I knew she would like answering. "Was he good?"

Deb gave him a friendly swat on his butt as I walked past her and turned him into the grooming stall to untack. Her smile dimpled and her head tilted as she looked at him, shaking her head.

"That boy's a hunka-hunka burning love!"

Ryder scowled, pulling her ear buds out. "He's what?"

Deb said, "C'mon Ryder, it's an Elvis Presley song. You've never heard of Elvis? Wild Child's got the moves. Just like Elvis."

Ryder's voice was smart-ass dismissive. "Uh, whatever Deb; it doesn't make any sense."

Deb just shrugged. "Elvis could make the girls swoon with a shake of his hips. Look him up on Youtube. Lizzy gets it, don't you, Lizzy?" And she smiled her great dimpled smile.

I laughed and nodded, my fingers busy taking care of our hunky boy.

Deb was watching intently as I unbuckled the throatlatch, the noseband, and unhooked the curb chain. I put my left hand on Wild Child's nose and carefully lowered the bits out of his open mouth so they wouldn't hit his teeth. He opened wide and didn't even try to nip. He seemed content.

I changed the subject. "Did you ask Margot what's got Francesca upset?"

Deb looked disappointed to stop talking about Wild Child. "Relax, Lizzy. It must be about Chess. He's helping Francesca with the books. He's an accountant. Margot said to be nice to him and make him feel welcome. I think she feels sorry for him."

I was immediately relieved. "Glad to hear it's not me. Margot feels sorry for him?"

Deb raised her eyebrows. "Maybe we'll have him up for one of our Wednesday night suppers."

That got Ryder's attention and she piped up. "I think that's a great idea."

I looked over at Ryder. She was sounding over-eager, just as she had with Patrick; another older guy Ryder went for because of his 'name'. And Patrick was not just older, but as it turned out, plain evil. I sighed audibly, thinking of the absurdity of her interest in someone she had never even met; just because she knew he came from money.

She knew exactly what I was thinking and flipped me the bird. Since I was pulling the saddle off of Wild Child there would be no tackling her now. So I let it go.

When my turn to ride finally came, I had a great lesson on Winsome. All in all it had been a fine day. I even saw some of Francesca's ride on Lovey and thought she had ridden better than usual.

I was hosing down the wash rack and Ryder had just gone up when Francesca found me. Her voice stern, "Lizzy, come to the office please."

I told myself that she didn't scare me anymore. I hadn't committed any great offenses. I also knew I wasn't about to be fired. But my tensing up was reflexive anyway. Why the drama had to be directed my way, I couldn't say. I took my time finishing cleaning the wash rack and neatly coiling up the hose, stalling as much as I could before heading to her office.

I gently knocked on the door and slipped in as soon as I heard Francesca's voice. I stood right by the door.

Francesca was sitting at her large mahogany desk, surrounded by stacks of papers. She looked up, peering over designer reading glasses. "For heaven's sake, Lizzy, you look ready to bolt. Come in and sit down."

As soon as I sat in one of the upholstered armchairs that faced the desk, Chopper was in my lap and Snapper was standing up with his paws on my leg, checking to see if there was room for two.

Francesca pulled off her readers. "Push them down, Lizzy."

My voice sounded weak. "No really, it's fine."

There was something reassuring about having a warm body with a steady heartbeat on my lap. I began to stroke Chopper's wiry coat and he turned a circle and then settled. Snapper gave up and hopped up on the other upholstered chair, settling into his own nest of pillows.

Francesca scowled. "He's ruined that chair." She leaned back, pushing her rolling chair away from the mess of papers. "I need you to put in a couple of extra hours for me in the afternoons. You don't have Kiddo on your schedule anymore, and Deb has Natalie to help her now, so you should have a lot of time on your hands while you're still on company payroll."

My shoulders dropped as I released tension I hadn't even been aware of. "Sure, Francesca. Not a problem."

And then she casually tossed off another sentence. "Oh, and it needs to be our secret."

Now my tension was replaced by dread, cold and heavy, that settled in my chest, and I couldn't think what to say.

Francesca looked annoyed at my response. "Good grief. Don't look so stricken. We will be spending the late afternoons over at Claire Winston's. They have a horse over there that's Grand Prix, and I simply want to sit on a Grand Prix horse. It's an opportunity. Anyway, you will need to groom for me. But no one needs to know about this yet, is that understood? I've chosen you for this job because you have proven your loyalty. You should be pleased."

I nodded up and down, wondering how Francesca could possibly pull this off.

Despite my efforts at self control, I babbled, "You don't think Suzette will be talking to Ryder about this? They are back on friendly terms, you know. Or Claire might say something. What about Frank? Does Frank know?"

Francesca put up her hand to silence me. "Lizzy, that will be enough! I will take care of all that. Your job is merely to groom, and not say anything to anyone, and that means everyone. You are just the groom. Is that clear?"

It was clear and I got it. She had shut me down by reminding me of my place. The 'help' was getting uppity again. I nodded and dropped my eyes, staring into the shiny bright eyes of Chopper, who licked my nose. I answered her quietly. "Sure."

"Good. We'll go over tomorrow at 4:00 sharp. Ryder can do dinner chores without you. I'll let her know."

Francesca was nuts. Ryder's antennae would be up. I interjected softly, cautiously, while I stroked Chopper. "She'll want to know why."

Francesca smiled her thin devilish smile, answering confidently. "Ryder is riding my horse in two weeks in Kentucky. She knows what to focus her attention on right now." Francesca returned her eyes to her papers, pulling her readers back down. When I did not move she gazed back over the lenses at me. It was a clear dismissal, and so I stood up, sliding an unwilling Chopper to the floor with a thud.

The interview was over, and I was dismissed. Francesca was right about one thing. Ryder might not respect Francesca as a rider, but she respected her mightily for the power of her pocketbook and all it could provide for a talented young rider who didn't even own her own horse.

# 3. The Chosen One

*Francesca was right.*

No one asked me where I was going the next afternoon. But I still felt sneaky. On the other hand, I was curious to go over to Claire Winston's barn. Ryder had been over several times to visit Suzette, her teammate for the Young Rider Championships, but I had never been. Francesca had left written directions, with a note to put them into my phone. I wondered if I should eat the paper once I had done that task. One thing was clear, we wouldn't be traveling over together.

It was only a right and a left and a right, down small winding roads, not more than a five minute drive. I pulled up to gates similar to ours, with just as many blooming beds of annuals mounded in dark mulch, and a brass farm sign embedded in the stone columns; "Two Left Feet". It was a cute name and made me smile.

I keyed in the code and the large iron gates swung away from me. Claire Winston's farm was on a ridge road with a brilliant view down a gently sloping hill. The barns were like ours too, with old stone on the bottom and timbers above. Horses hung their heads out of windows and dozed in the dappled sunlight that filtered through mature trees. I walked through an arched central hall with a two-story open timbered ceiling. The barn aisleways stretched to my left and right. I continued walking straight through to gaze down a green bank with a paver stone path that led to the outdoor arena. The arena had little evergreen bushes cut into the shapes of horses in levade and piaffe placed along the sides. The topiary reminded me of Disneyland. Next to it on a slightly lower elevation was the indoor. It had been dressed up too, with neatly rounded low shrubbery that ran along the stonework. Large windows had been opened up for the summer.

I turned around and walked back into the barn; deciding to explore while I waited for Francesca. I went from stall to stall, admiring and cooing to the horses. I knew that Suzette, who had previously been Patrick's advanced young rider, had taken over the training duties since Patrick's departure. There were a lot of empty stalls. The interior of the barn was as over the top as the outside, with polished brass fittings and black wrought iron. The center aisle lighting was provided by black iron hanging chandeliers. I stepped into the bathroom and admired the fancy fixtures and granite. When I came out, Francesca was waiting for me. Her arms were crossed and her tone was business-like. She uncrossed her arms and gestured down the aisle.

"Lizzy, let me show you where to find everything, so you can manage on your own. The afternoons here are quiet so it will just be me and you, but Suzette and Claire's numbers are posted in the feed room if you ever need them."

I nodded, trying to look equally business-like. We strolled down the aisle and she opened a door with a polished brass galloping horse for a doorknob.

"Here's the tack room."

I had never been in a tack room before that had an oriental rug on the floor. All the saddle and bridle mounts were dark lacquered wood and polished brass. The counters were granite and the tack cleaning sink looked like something out of a design magazine. I envied the boots lined up on a shelf. If they were Suzette's, then someone was spoiling her. She had five pairs… patent leather, light brown, maroon, a black pair with a thin topper of leopard print, and one that looked sort of like alligator or something. I reached out to touch it.

Francesca's voice was disapproving. "Lizzy, please. You have a job to do here."

It was hard to focus. I sounded breathy. "Look at all those boots."

Francesca sighed. I winced. "Sorry."

Francesca put her hand on a saddle hanging on a rack and looked at me intently, not trusting that I was all there.

"Here is Johnny's saddle and here is his bridle. Can you keep them straight?"

I mimicked her by touching the saddle. "Sure."

Francesca turned and continued the tour. "Polos are communal. They are in this drawer."

Francesca pulled opened a large sliding drawer that looked like it was built for holding about a gazillion cans of soda, but instead held polos. You pulled polos from the bottom and put the clean ones in the top. Brilliant. I was nodding, and Francesca kept checking on my level of attention through earnest looks.

"Saddle pads from here. Put the dirty ones in the hamper here."

More brilliant storage designs. I couldn't help but sound impressed. "This is so smart."

Francesca grimaced and I wondered if she minded being one-upped in poshness. Her voice sounded weary. "Follow me. The brushes are in the grooming stalls."

I followed Francesca into the set of three side by side grooming stalls with half partitions between the horses. They had rubber floors that had the farm logo somehow stamped into the middle; it was the profile of a horse making a flying change of lead, set inside a circle, the left legs fully drawn, and the right legs in outline. On the top of the partition were built-in trays filled with grooming supplies; every kind of brush and lotion and potion for hair and skin and hooves.

"Follow me, and I'll show you which stall is Johnny's."

So I trekked after Francesca to a stall that said "Johnny Cash" on the door.

In the stall stood a tall bright chestnut with four white legs and a broad white blaze. They didn't come flashier than that. "Wow, Francesca. He sure has a lot of bling doesn't he?"

I turned and looked at Francesca. She was staring through the bars at the horse, and I could see the corners of her lips turn up. She looked strange. "He's my first real Grand Prix horse," she said, with reverence in her voice.

I almost choked on my words, incredulous. "He's yours?"

Of course, she didn't answer me. She was busy giving directions. Orientation was not over. "Get him out and tack him up. I have a few things to tell you about him. It will help you in your job."

So I grabbed his halter off the hook and went in. He made big eyes at me but then pushed his head into the halter and followed me politely out of the stall and into the grooming stall.

"Johnny Cash? Francesca, I think I've seen this horse before."

Francesca ignored me. And then I remembered. "Francesca, this is the horse that was second in the Brentina Cup at Gladstone, right?"

The Brentina Cup was an elite competition at a modified Grand Prix level for under-24 year old riders.

Francesca shrugged her shoulders as if to say, "so what?"

I didn't mean to sound so perplexed. "You own Johnny Cash?"

Francesca wasn't going to say more. "Just do your job, Lizzy."

This was confusing and mysterious, and I cautiously probed. "But why is it a secret?"

"Lizzy." And now Francesca sounded firm; like a parent calming a fretting child.

So I buttoned my trap, and began to groom. Surprisingly, Francesca went and fetched his tack, something she never would have done at home. I was standing behind him combing out his tail when she returned. "Lizzy, be extra careful with his tail. He needs every single hair. He's been showing with a wig and I hope we can grow enough tail to eventually do without."

I scoffed, "A wig? Are you serious?"

Francesca replied, "Not every horse is blessed with a tail like Hotstuff, you know."

I took a deep breath. "OK."

Francesca watched as I arranged his square pad, then his fleece half pad, and then his saddle, pulling the saddle pads gently up into the gullet of the saddle so they couldn't bind at his withers. I put the girth on loosely, just like I always did. I could feel Francesca's eyes on me throughout, judging me as I performed tasks that I had done just fine every day back at the farm.

As soon as I reached for the bridle, Francesca reached into a little brown bag and pulled out a small mound of little white pebble-shaped stuff.

"Here, feed him this when you bridle."

I held out my hand. "What is it?"

"It's sugar-coated paraffin. All the top barns use it, and besides, he likes it. It coats his teeth so he won't grind them."

"OK."

That was a new one for me. But hey, if all the top barns used the stuff, I knew Francesca would be all over it. I fed Johnny the pebbles, and then slipped on his bridle. Francesca leaned in to watch me buckle the noseband.

"Lizzy, one more hole."

I felt the urge to elbow her away.

"OK." I reminded myself to stay cool. I was going to have to endure these afternoons for however long it took for Francesca to bring Johnny Cash home to her own farm. I really didn't understand why she was keeping this a secret. I know if I had Johnny Cash I would want to show him off. He was a cool horse.

I gave the girth one more snugging up and led the big guy down the paver stone path into the arena while Francesca trailed after us.

The arena had European-style shredded felt footing and extra large mirrors lining the far end. In the entryway was a three step extra-tall mounting block, and on both sides of us were stairs to elevated seating areas. Francesca was going to need that extra tall mounting block. She was very stiff, not very tall even though she had nice long legs, and this boy had to be 17.1 or 17.2 hands. Lovey was maybe 16 hands with his shoes on.

I led Johnny up to the mounting block. He tipped his head and looked at it with big eyes and then puffed at it as if he thought it was not to be trusted to stay inanimate.

I pulled down the stirrups and checked the girth one more time, and then threw the reins over his neck and walked to the "off side" to hold the stirrup so Francesca wouldn't pull the saddle off center when she mounted. I noticed that Johnny was still tense.

And then I waited and wondered what the heck was keeping her. Finally I poked my head under his neck and saw she was taking her gloves off. "Francesca?"

"Lizzy, please get on and walk around for me while I run to the ladies."

"Sure." I totally understood how nerves instantly activated your bladder. I only had on my clogs, no gloves, and most importantly, no helmet. But, clearly Francesca and I were not going to have a discussion. She had already turned her back. And off she went.

So I got on.

At least he wasn't too wide, just leggy. I looked at myself in the mirror. Lucky Francesca is what I thought. He was striding around the arena in big ground covering steps. But, he still had his eyes bugged out, and kept tipping his head and stopping to examine the shadows cast on the sand by the low sunlight slanting through the windows.

I could feel that this horse had an internal throttle that was set on high. I knew Francesca was over mounted just by feeling his walk. But soon she was in the doorway, and when I looked over at her I could see that strange look in her eye again. She was admiring her new horse.

"Go ahead and trot and canter him a little for me."

And so I picked up the reins, which were double reins as he was in the full bridle. I hadn't ridden in a full bridle since Rave. I tried to slip the curb rein a little longer than the snaffle rein so it would not come into play too much but instead hang a little loose.

I put my leg on to trot, and Johnny lurched forward. I got a whiplash as I was left behind the motion. This boy was eager to move. I sat up straighter. Oh dear. You really had to ride this guy. His big bright chestnut ears were pointed forward on high alert, and as we passed the door he almost hung in the air and then scampered a little to the inside, but then he went back to work. But he was still looking for something to spook at. He wasn't anywhere near done.

Francesca began coaching me. "Ride him more forward, Lizzy."

I said nothing but thought to myself…"Yeah boss. Let's see you up here." Meanwhile, my clogs were hanging off my heels and my socks were working their way down my shins.

But I put on my leg again and posted a huge trot around the arena and tried not to think about all this weirdness. Instead, I tried to do a good job on Johnny.

Francesca barked, "Now some canter transitions."

I put him on a circle and cantered, the stirrup leathers of the saddle now pinching and chafing my calves right through my breeches.

Now she was yelling. "Do some lengthenings down the long side."

This was crazy. But I followed orders. And as he warmed up, at least he relaxed and began to sweat.

I decided to sit the trot and ride some bending lines, but as soon as I did, Francesca called for me to stop.

"Lizzy, I'll get on now."

Now that he looked safe, I was being excused. I got it. "Sure. OK."

I made a transition to halt, and then looked in the mirror. It was square and he stood like a soldier, ready to salute, my socks were now past my heels and bunching under my instep, but I tried to ignore it. I was sincere when I commented. "What a cool horse, Francesca!"

I dropped the reins and gave him a pat with both hands on either side of his neck and then slipped off and led him back over to the mounting block.

Francesca stood on the top step waiting for me. I had to take one moment to pull my socks back up. I also had to rub my calves. My skin was burning. I sidled Johnny up into his parking spot and this time his eye was soft and he was relaxed. Francesca was now eager to step into the irons.

Off they went. Francesca watched herself in the mirror and she once again had that strange look on her face. Her lips were gently upturned, but she wasn't smiling exactly. She was looking at her reflection, but I thought she was somewhere else in her thoughts. I think I understood what she was feeling as she reached down and petted Johnny's neck: She had a crush on Johnny Cash.

Francesca gathered up the reins and put Johnny into piaffe while never taking her eyes off her image in the mirror. She sat up extra tall, picked her hands up way too high, and put her legs too far back, with her heels too high.

But I kept my mouth shut.

He piaffed like a machine anyway.

I knew Francesca felt like a million bucks.

Then she went to the middle of the arena and did a pretty awful walk pirouette. But it didn't matter, she was digging it. She walked forward and picked up a canter and then turned a canter pirouette.

It was not bad. Not at all. Johnny must have been on auto-pilot. Francesca was still riding someone else's training. I knew that. I doubt she understood what was happening.

Francesca proceeded to walk again and then she picked him back up and made it about one time around the arena in a big flashy sitting trot before walking again.

She picked up the canter and did a diagonal of one-tempis. Francesca knew the aids, and I realized it was because of Rave. He had been a one-tempi machine, teaching them to me as well as Francesca. The ones were good, too. This guy could do it all it seemed. Francesca cantered a circle in front of me then she halted, gave the horse a pat, and gently dismounted, a little stiff, but clearly satisfied.

"He's quite rideable. Lizzy, you can take him now."

She pulled off her gloves and gave Johnny a pat on the neck. Then she stood back and looked at him a moment with her head tipped.

I knew she was pleased as punch with him. Who wouldn't be?

I chimed in. "He's fantastic, Francesca."

In a matter-of-fact tone, she answered, "I know."

Francesca seemed relaxed. And I thought maybe, just maybe, we could talk. I pressed my luck. "I don't understand why you don't bring him home."

"All in good time, Lizzy." Her eyes never left Johnny.

I tried again by asking, "I'd love to know the plan." But the spell was broken. Francesca turned and looked at me, recognition in her face; she was once again addressing the help.

"Give him a bath and rub down his legs with brace. Tomorrow we do this again."

And then she strolled off with a swagger.

Francesca was finally getting to do the Grand Prix tricks, the very reason she had started this entire endeavor. She was clearly enamored with this big chestnut horse. I think this was the happiest I had ever seen her. But maybe that was because she was scheming. Some people, people like Francesca, are happy only when they are scheming.

It made me think that Margot needed to go ahead and just give her what she wanted … the ride on a Grand Prix horse like this one. I know Margot wanted Francesca to become more proficient, but maybe that was never going to happen. Francesca needed to get as close to Grand Prix as she could and the clock was ticking. And this was probably going to be it. I didn't think it could last without Margot riding the horse, too. The longer the horse went with Francesca as the sole rider, the worse the horse would go. Margot always said the horses can only go as well as the rider can ride, that the "trainer-effect" would fade as the horse was limited and actually impeded by his less talented rider. Surely Francesca had heard Margot say all the things I had heard her say? I knew riding a few tricks in isolation as Francesca had done today was not the same thing as riding an entire test under the stress of a show environment.

Could that be what Francesca was planning?

The very idea made the hair on the back of my neck stand up. But maybe it was just a chill from getting all sweaty and then standing here. Whatever her plans, I knew I would only be fed tidbits of information on a "need to know" basis.

I gave a tug on Johnny's reins. "C'mon, big guy."

Johnny lowered his head and walked next to me back to the barn. He towered over me. No one in their right mind would have thought to pair this big horse with old, stiff, featherweight Francesca. But apparently he had caught her eye at Gladstone and she had fallen in love, and I guess she and Frank could afford him.

I could imagine how the conversation between Margot and Francesca must have gone.

Francesca I am sure told Margot she wanted to try him, and Margot said it was the wrong horse. And then Francesca disagreed … and bought him anyway. Because she loved him at first sight, or something like that.

On the upside, maybe I would get to sit on him some more. In any case, his care was my responsibility now. And I had been instructed to keep my mouth shut about him, too. That last part was going to be a tough one for me. The CIA would never have recruited me. I needed my buddies; my Deb and my Natalie. I couldn't imagine not telling them about this horse. I hoped Francesca would soon come clean.

I drove home with burning calves, wondering how I would manage a shower. But when I pulled through the farm gates I noticed HIS car was there again. Drat.

I thought I could just slip in quietly. Nope.

Francesca's office door was open and the light was on, throwing a sliver of light across the dimming light of the barn aisle.

"Hey, Lizzy."

Chess Cavelli opened the door wider. The desk behind him was scattered with papers and two laptops were open.

I tried to muster a friendly tone.

"Oh, hi!"

He looked as clean and groomed as the last time I saw him, wearing a button down shirt and jeans. I noticed his alligator belt was as expensive looking as the boots at Claire Winston's. His hand was on the doorknob, "I didn't startle you this time? Good."

"No, I saw your car."

"I heard you pull in. The time has really gotten away from me, and I just realized I'm starved. You want to get a bite to eat?"

I looked down at my filthy shirt, my stained breeches with the sagging socks. "Thanks, but I'm filthy."

"Just a deli. Doesn't matter how you look. Otherwise I'm eating by myself again."

I tried to think of more excuses. "It's nice of you but really..."

"C'mon. My treat. I'll even spring for dessert."

I really did not want to go. But on the other hand, I was hungry, and he was paying. Plus he sounded so much like his father, who was always offering free foodstuffs to the farm folks.

I looked at my watch in a slightly irritated way.

"I won't keep you long. I know you guys start early in the morning."

I sighed. "OK, sure. Should I go get Ryder, y'know, the other working student, to join us?"

He smiled gently. "Another time maybe."

I was stuck.

Chess ducked into the office and grabbed his keys.

I was going to have dinner with Anthony Cavelli, AKA Chess. Alone. Ryder would have fun with this later, at my expense.

We went to a local deli that stayed open for dinner. He ordered a cup of matzo ball soup and pastrami on rye. It was one of those sandwiches that had about a week's worth of meat on it.

I had ordered a tuna melt. It was hot and gooey and in my first bite the cheese pulled out of the bread and hung out of my mouth inelegantly. I peeled it off my chin and stuffed it back into my mouth. It was a first rate sandwich, but messy, just like the rest of me.

"Here Lizzy, let me get you another napkin."

"No, it's OK. It's delicious. I was planning on a shower tonight anyway."

He laughed politely while I wiped my chin. But then I could tell he was still staring at my chin.

"I didn't get it?"

"Here." He held up another napkin.

I took it from him and wiped down my chin and lips, making sure I covered all possible dribble territory. "Surely it's gone now?"

"Yes. You got it."

I took another bite but now I was self-conscious and slightly irritated at him. Why did he have to look so clean?

Besides being so clean, he was a fidgeter. I think he was doing something annoying with his foot or leg under the table, like he was keeping time to music that only he could hear. It was especially noticeable since there was now too much silence while we both ate.

I punted. "So, how long do you think you'll be working on the farm books?"

He cleared his throat and took a sip of his vitamin water. "Don't know yet. Dad wants me to sort things out, and then maybe help make a business plan. I've got to be sure we meet all the tests the IRS uses to determine a business is legitimate."

I felt wary, "That farm has got to be a legitimate business."

He sighed like he had heard that line before; probably from Francesca. "How so?"

"Well, for one thing, look at all the people the farm supports."

He nodded in agreement, "That's true. But that's not one of the tests the IRS uses."

I didn't mean to sound defensive. I shouldn't kill the messenger. He was trying to help. I just wish he would stop jiggling his foot or whatever it was he was doing. I grabbed my pickle with my fingers and took a bite. But I had noticed that he had specifically mentioned the IRS.

There was another lag of silence. I couldn't think what else to say. Mercifully he thought of something.

"So, Lizzy, I thought since I know next to nothing about horses and what goes on at the farm that maybe you could show me around and explain things to me. Beyond the finances and numbers, I mean. It'll help me."

I answered quietly into my sandwich. "Francesca should do that."

"I suggested that. She told me to ask you."

"Me?" I couldn't hide my surprise.

"Yeah. She said not to bother Margot or Deb and that Ryder is getting ready for some important horse show, and that Natalie is too new."

Francesca had made me the chosen one, again. I was not sure whether I should be flattered or worried about that. I decided to try for upbeat. "Sure then. I guess. What would you like to know?"

"Well, I know a little bit, having seen my mother dive into this stuff when I was in high school, but then I was off to college and didn't pay much attention to it. Plus, with my allergies I was never encouraged to hang out much with the horses, even though I did enjoy it. My spare time was all about tennis. That's my sport, or was. But, now if I'm going to be of any help, I think I need to understand things better."

I swallowed my bite. "Tennis?"

He grinned, "Tennis. You know, racquets, tennis balls, all that."

That made sense. Tennis players wore white, didn't they? "OK. Maybe I can help."

"Okay. Good. First off, why dressage? I know you guys do some fancy steps and all, but I don't really have a grip on how dressage is a sport, like horseracing, and the Kentucky Derby, things like that. Seems more like horse dancing to me."

I think he saw me deflate a little. How to explain dressage to an outsider? I hadn't had to do that for a very long time. I lived in a rarefied world where I didn't have to spend time with "civilians."

But there he sat, cutting up his Matzo balls with the edge of his spoon. I shook my head but forged ahead.

"The word dressage is French. It means training. It's a system of training horses, that's pretty much it."

He wasn't going to let me get away with that cursory an answer.

"C'mon, it's got to be more than that. People spend a fortune on breeding these horses, and after that a fortune for coaching. And then you spend another fortune to go to competitions where you don't even win any money. What's that all about?"

This was not going to be easy.

"Well, I just gave you the short version."

"That's great, but I'm going to need the long version. Hey, you want dessert?"

I was a sucker for dessert, but it was going to cost me. I looked back over the menu while I answered. "Sure, but I'm afraid I haven't been very successful in the past explaining this stuff to non-horse people."

"They have great eclairs here. You like eclairs?"

Then I laughed. He sounded just like his Dad. Maybe Chess wasn't so bad. To Frank Cavelli food and drink were always the first order of business. I always liked that about him.

I was thinking of his Dad when I answered. "I love all things sweet."

He smiled. "I'll try to remember that."

Oh God. That sounded like flirting.

He got up and made an order at the counter and then came back. "Okay, I'm ready for my tutorial."

"OK. Let me think. Okay, you've heard of the Lippizzaners."

He shook his head no.

"The dancing white horses?"

His eyes lit up in recognition.

"Yes. Disney made a movie right? Patton saved them from the Russians at the end of World War II? Terrible movie. Mother has it at home on DVD."

"Yes, and yes it was a terrible movie. But of course I loved it." I felt a small victory. We were smiling at each other. I had a foothold here. I launched my lesson, shifting into teacher-voice.

"OK, so those horses are like a museum quality version of what we do. They are preserving the tradition of dressage from the Baroque period. They do all the same exercises we do plus some more movements that we don't do. They do leaps and kicks that we don't do. The horses in the famous Spanish Riding School in Vienna, Austria are all purebred from the same small gene pool of that era. The people there dedicate themselves to preserving the same bloodlines and the exact same system of training. So it really is like a living museum. They consider it a sacred trust. You touch a Lippizzaner and you touch history."

Chess was nodding. "Okay."

He was still with me, and actually seemed interested, so I kept going. "We do a modern sport version of what they do. The modern "sport horse" isn't anything like the small compact Lippizzaners in the Spanish Riding School though. With selective breeding we've bred huge athletic gaits into the sport horses. The horses just keep getting more and more extravagant."

He still looked interested in what I was telling him. His eyes narrowed in what seemed to be intense interest and for a moment I could see Francesca's face.

"Mother seems to have bred a slew of them."

Surprisingly, I found myself sticking up for Francesca. "Your mother has bred some incredible horses."

His eyebrows went up. "That's good to hear. But she doesn't seem to sell too many of them. And when she does, she does it at a loss."

I waved his comment away like a bothersome fly. What did I care about sales prices? It was the horses that mattered. I was getting enthusiastic now.

"Have you gone up the hill to see the new foals? Have you seen Habanero? He is special. And what about Hotstuff? He's ranked number two in the country right now in the four year olds."

His toe was tapping out some new beat against the floor, and his index finger tapped the edge of the table once like a cymbal marking a crescendo. The tuneless tune had clearly come to a finish. Here was a man who had made some sort of decision.

"No, I have not, but you can take me up there and show me what is special about these horses."

I smiled through my big bite of éclair. The custard was the kind I liked, eggy and flavored with vanilla, with chocolate icing that was clearly homemade and not too sweet. I would be coming back. I grabbed another napkin before answering.

"Each one of those horses is a distinct individual."

"So they have personalities, do they? I've never really known a horse even though Mother has so many of them. To me they've always been livestock."

I had never thought of horses that way. Livestock seemed to relegate them to old westerns about cattle drives, to nameless masses.

I was frowning. "Livestock? I guess I've never thought of them like that before. They are much more than livestock. They each have a character, kind of like a dog, but not exactly. The point is we get to know them intimately."

He tipped his head. "I've never had a dog."

I was incredulous. "Really?"

But his voice was matter of fact, "Remember...bad allergies as a kid. The dogs came into the family after I was gone from the house."

"I'm so sorry. That's really sad."

"Not at all." He shrugged off my pity. It was pity. I couldn't imagine a life without animals in it.

He got business-like as he asked questions about employees vs. working students, and what each of us did each day as part of our duties. He asked how long a working student was likely to stay, and then asked where Emma had gone and what she was doing now. And I answered all his questions as best as I could.

He was a good listener. And when he dropped me back off at the barn I realized I had not asked him a single question about himself. But I had many. Like why he was suddenly so interested in learning about the horses and dressage.

Ryder had closed her door when I got back. I popped open my laptop, logged in, and entered in my new e-journal some notes from my weird day. And then I thought about Johnny Cash. I imagined him standing in his stall over at Claire Winston's palatial barn. I could imagine Francesca staring at him though the bars of his stall.

And I suddenly understood why he was being hidden away. It wasn't just Margot who would not approve of her new purchase.

It was her numbers-crunching accountant son ... and just possibly Frank. This was a potential mess of immense proportions.

And Francesca had just put me smack in the middle of it.

# 4. Power Through Relaxation

*I was just about to pull Winsome out of the crossties for my lesson when* Francesca walked up to me and started to say something about "our appointment."

At the same time, Ryder was leading a sweaty Papa in. She took a sideways look at Francesca but said nothing.

I hated secrets. I hated walking into a room and having the chatter die down. When people are whispering I am just ego-centric enough to assume they must be talking about me. I wondered if Ryder felt the same way. I felt guilty.

Francesca moved in a little closer and turned her back dramatically to Ryder and stage whispered to me. "See you at four."

Then she turned on her heel.

I realized my shoulders were now somewhere up around my ears. I tried rolling them around and shrugging them up and down. No use. Ryder was looking curious as she stripped the bridle off of Papa and slipped his halter on.

I thought she was giving it a pass, and I began to lead Winsome out of the barn.

But no.

Her voice sounded like Eeyore's… world weary. "What have you done now?"

Inwardly I smiled. Ryder assumed I was in trouble with Francesca… again.

"Thanks for your concern, Ryder, but you know I live to please Francesca, I'll make it right."

I loosened myself up with another shoulder roll and headed for the arena.

Margot sat on the viewing stand, talking on her phone. I thought for a moment about Francesca and her secret, and wondered why she had chosen me to keep it. It was not fair to make me keep a secret from Margot. Francesca knew that I was here because of Margot. I had not come to Equus Paradiso to work for Francesca. But, Emma had explained to me on day one, that if Francesca was not happy, we could all be out on the street. I had never forgotten that.

Still, Francesca knew that Deb and Natalie were my close friends. Ryder, on the other hand was a bit of a loner, and would have been the natural choice for Francesca's partner in crime. But, she hadn't chosen Ryder. She had chosen me. I needed to be careful, since I knew if I let slip anything about Johnny Cash, Francesca would hold it against me forever. I tried to shake it off, brush my thoughts to the side, but my feelings of being ill-used by Francesca were making me angry.

My lesson time was my precious time with Margot. I would not allow Francesca and her drama to steal the joy from this precious time. I couldn't stop thinking about it. I was having trouble shaking it off. Damn Francesca. So, I imagined a tiny "Francesca-devil" sitting on my shoulder. Mentally I created a pair of celestial tweezers that pinched her firmly by the waist and flung her out a window of the indoor arena. That did the trick. I cracked myself up, suppressing a grin, and my shoulders dropped about two inches as I picked up my posting trot.

As usual, Margot said little during my warm up. I did my trot figures and leg-yields in rising trot and then my canter-trot-canter transitions. Winsome blew her nose and shook off her cobwebs.

Winsome was not big and scopey like Hotstuff, or a splashy Grand Prix horse like Johnny Cash, or some visually stunning god of horses in the way Wild Child was. She was only 16.1 with a feminine face and a funny moth-eaten blaze. She was light-footed enough but would never have the scope or athleticism of the big-time horses that competed internationally. But, she was beautiful, and she was mine. Owning her was important, my emotional anchor. I couldn't exactly say why that was so. It just was.

When I took my walk break, Margot got out of her chair, going into teaching mode.

"It's important to teach piaffe before passage, but now that you have a start on piaffe, I want you to begin searching for the doorway into passage."

I nodded, all business, even though I had the urge to chatter back in excitement.

"Let's pick her back up."

So I took up my reins and once again re-settled my mind.

Margot continued. "Begin with the walk-trot-transitions. Take no more than three steps of walk. Feel the trot contained within those walk steps, no sleep-walking. Keep them active."

And as I began, I tried to turn inward; to feel through my relaxed seat, my weight heavy on the back of my breeches, and my torso solid, the hind legs of my horse. Margot had awoken in me new awareness of the correct feeling of a thing called engagement. The horse had to learn to carry the weight of the rider over a strengthened "bridge" of back and loins to their pelvis, keeping the thrust of the hind legs under the rider and not pushing out behind the rider. The back has to lift and carry and not flatten or sag. The rider has to feel the difference.

Margot's voice began to narrate our ride. "Be sure the trot steps feel as though they begin behind you, like your first step of piaffe. Good. Now let the steps go forward into trot. Keep the neck soft. Don't allow the neck to stiffen from the push behind."

And I repeated the exercise until I could get the small active trot steps behind with a soft neck and then allow the trot to move forward. I tried for no more than three walk steps before trotting out again. This was a familiar exercise and a good one to make the shift from the warm-up phase of the session into the working-phase of the session.

"Now reduce the steps to only one or two."

Again this was a familiar exercise and I felt successful.

"Now almost walk but don't, and then trot out again. Keep the neck soft, the joints must stay relaxed enough to add the spring we are looking for. The neck is a good indicator of the tension. A neck that is relaxed and hanging straight between the reins indicates a soft and swinging back. Herm Martin always says that the neck is the part of the spine we can easily see."

Now I focused more on the relaxation than the power. Things went too far that direction, and Margot's voice was there.

"Ah, don't mistake lazy for relaxed. The trick is to create power through relaxation. Power needs positive tension, not slackness. Feel positive tension behind you, but softness in front of you."

So I tried to up the impulsion. I gave Winsome a "tap-tap" of the whip to remind her that this was work that required effort. I just had to find the right temperature ... too hot and she was tense and her joints lost all their springiness ... too cold and she was coasting. I needed to find simmer. With another "tap-tap" we were there. Margot approved.

"Yes. I like that, Lizzy."

It started to feel really good. Winsome became a little firm in my reins and her front end rose up in front of me. I could feel her become "four-square" like having all four tires equally inflated and she became fatter under my legs from her hind legs coming closer to my seat, expanding her ribcage. And at the same time, I felt like I had sunk deeper, feeling adhesive to my saddle. It felt great. It felt powerful.

Margot's voice was purring. "Oh yes. Now, leave out the walk steps. Trot, almost walk, trot, and now almost walk again. Keep her guessing, without losing the desire to go forward."

And then I felt it, a different sort of step. It was a tiny bit hesitant, as if she lifted off the ground and waited in the air to see if she should go more forward or make a transition back to walk.

"Feel it?"

I could answer honestly this time.

"Yes!"

"That was one step of a soft-passage. See if you can find that step again."

And I couldn't. I tried and tried. But it was like Deb's shy cat analogy. The more I tried to go after it the further it slipped away.

But Margot didn't scold me. "Now go out and make a medium trot."

Margot was telling me to change things up. "Now the half-passes, and search for that same bounce in the half-halts as you enter the corners."

Margot continued. "Enter the corner with a feeling of that almost walk step then go forward, bend through the corner, but leave the corner with a step of medium trot."

Winsome and I were soon drenched in sweat. I could look down and see lather under her reins and her veins standing up.

I glanced over at Margot. Her arms were crossed but her head was tilted. She was studying us. "Good job, girls. Rising trot and stretch. Winsome earned her carrots today."

I let the reins slip a little through my hands as I began posting the trot. Winsome felt like an elastic band as she reached down and out with her neck. Then I sat and she walked without my touching the reins.

I had a feeling of deep contentment. Winsome was tired, but I also liked to think she was content, and knew how proud and happy I was with her. These moments were what dressage at its best provided.

I kicked my feet out of the stirrups and Winsome and I had a leisurely stroll around the property. We headed up the hill past Deb's and waved at Natalie who was sitting tentatively on a round-bodied bay gelding walking around inside the fenced pasture.

It was my little friend Boingo! He stopped and lifted his head to examine us, letting out a high-pitched whinny, and tossing his head. I could hear Natalie laughing, even from a distance.

The barn was quiet as I put Winsome away, and since no one was watching, I put my boots and gloves and my helmet in my truck. If I was going to get on Johnny again, I was going to be prepared. Last night when the water in the shower hit my raw spots, it burned like fire.

I have to admit, as cranky as I was with Francesca for putting me in a spot, I was looking forward to seeing Johnny Cash again. I was hoping Francesca would put me back up on him.

When I got to Claire's barn it was dead empty again. I felt like a trespasser, but Johnny picked his head up as soon as he heard me and wobbled his nostrils. I wondered if he did that for everyone, or if he already understood that I was his new groom, the giver of goodies and massages. I dug in my pocket and found a slightly sticky puff peppermint to seal the deal.

I had a chance to study his long straight face and the big wide blaze that covered his nostrils and wrapped around his lips and under his chin. His blaze was almost as distinctive as Winsome's with an irregular chestnut splash breaking the white blaze right below his left eye. His nose and lips looked a little too pink, and the creases of his lips were cracked, like he needed sun block and lip balm.

He clearly enjoyed his grooming, and we continued warming up to each other. I searched his body with my soft rubber curry, finding the right spots and the right amount of pressure. Most horses love their wither area rubbed, but Johnny especially seemed to enjoy the top of his rump. He tipped his tail and leaned in. I went and got the mounting block so I could get more leverage. He was loving it. He stretched his neck out and rolled his eyes back into his head. When Francesca arrived he was covered with circular dust marks and loose hair. She shrieked. "My God, Lizzy, he's filthy!"

"Hi, Francesca. He asked for a massage. So, I gave him one."

Francesca huffed at me. "I need to get my ride in. If you want to give him a massage, come earlier."

I picked up the pace and quickly flicked the dirt off with the long bristled brush, and then sprayed fly spray on a towel and rapidly wiped him down. The currying had brought out the oils in his coat and he looked great, except for his nose. I grabbed the jar of Vaseline and began massaging it in. I caught Francesca's eye.

"We need some horsey sun block, Francesca. His nose is peeling."

Francesca stepped a little closer and squinted at his nose, and then stepped back again. "Anything else, Lizzy?"

I couldn't tell if she was mocking me, but I kept my voice businesslike. "Maybe some aloe cream, his skin is peeling. And I noticed a little fungus on his pasterns, too. How about some baby powder for after his bath? I want to make sure his skin is really clean and dry."

Francesca was silent. Did that mean OK? Or maybe I was just boring her.

I finished tacking up while she stood and watched. Before I put the bridle on I got up the courage to ask her point blank.

"Am I getting on today, because I brought my boots. I rubbed the stew out of my legs yesterday."

She lifted an eyebrow. "You would like that wouldn't you?"

It was classic Francesca bitchiness that only slightly irritated me. She needed me, and I knew it. "If I can help you by sitting on him, I'm happy to do it, I just don't want to rub my legs raw again."

Ha. Take that Francesca.

Francesca narrowed her eyes and then nodded. "Go get your boots."

Yesssssss. I probably trotted out to the car a little too eagerly. Francesca was right. I did like this.

Once I was dressed to ride, I gave Johnny his small handful of sugar-coated paraffin pebbles, tightened down his noseband, and then snugged up the girth.

He was even spookier than the previous day, screeching to a halt and carefully lifting his legs over the sunbeam in front of the entrance to the indoor. I put the stirrups on my hole and climbed up without asking. She needed him warmed up for her stiff old bones. She needed me to do it for her. So I did. And today I tried to own my warm up. He felt eager to work, lots of gas in the tank.

Warm up was about basics, and I knew Francesca would shriek if I touched any of the Grand Prix "tricks." Basics are the same, no matter what the level. The horse needs to loosen the muscles, get the blood pumping, and the joints well-oiled. Like loosening a rusty hinge, the horse must bend from side to side. The gaits need to be energetic with good ground cover, with the entire top line of the horse long and loose with a swinging back. Margot said that until you feel this, the ride cannot proceed to the harder exercises.

Margot had also taught me that you need to feel mental and physical relaxation. Johnny was wary of his environment. I could tell he needed his rider to provide his courage. I knew Francesca wasn't capable of that. But I was. I sat upright and kept my hips to the front of the saddle and my shoulders back. At the same time, I kept my muscles in my legs and arms and buttocks loose, releasing all tension between applying my aids so Johnny would feel my relaxation and realize there was no cause for concern. If he spooked, I guided him back to "true north" and ignored it.

As soon as he was swinging along, Francesca called me over. "I'll get on now." My fun had to end right where the good stuff began. But I walked and slid off and put Francesca up.

Francesca began her stop and start style of ride from trick to trick. I went to the corner of the arena and leaned against the kickboards to watch. If she thought she was going to get through a Grand Prix test like that, she had a wakeup call coming.

I could tell she was getting irritated. Finally she pulled up and snapped at me. "Why don't you say something useful, Lizzy, instead of standing there looking annoyed. I know you want to."

I felt attacked. It wasn't hard to feel that way around Francesca. But I tried not to sound as pissy as I felt. "What would you like me to say?"

Francesca glanced at the ceiling as if someone up there could see what a pain-in-the-ass groom she had to put up with. "Be a ground person, since you are clearly on the ground. You know enough by now to be able to give feedback."

I sounded like a four-year-old child whose feelings had been hurt. I hated that. "Okay."

Francesca shot me an exasperated look and picked up the trot and tried a steep half-pass. As she trotted past me she shot me a dirty look over her shoulder. "Well?"

I was on the defensive again. "Well, what?"

Francesca didn't sound mad now, now she sounded like a person on a mission. "I guess it was perfect. I'm so happy it was perfect. I'll be expecting a ten at the horse show."

Her sarcasm was duly noted. I said, "It wasn't exactly perfect."

Francesca was now playing with me. "I can't hear you. I'll do another. Speak up."

I took a breath. True to form, Francesca was going to find a way to make our sessions torture. She wanted the truth? Really? Clearly this was some kind of drill sergeant power trip. Time to just give her what she wanted. I gave it to her. Loudly. I inhaled deeply and let it rip.

I raised my voice for effect, "Ride the corner. You're sliding into it. Don't stiffen your inside leg in the half-pass, that's your bending leg. Sit more in the direction of the bend. More impulsion."

Surprisingly, Francesca said nothing. She made another attempt. I drew another deep breath and began narrating. "Better at the start. You need to relax your arms down and stop working so hard with your legs. He knows his job, so set him up and then relax so you can follow more."

My God. Francesca seemed to be listening to me.

Too soon she pulled up and took a walk break. She wanted my feedback? Well, I wasn't going to let her do her stop and start routine. I spoke up again, smiling to myself because I was now playing the drill sergeant. And she had asked for it. "Francesca, if you intend to make it through a Grand Prix test you will need to be much fitter. You can't keep stopping."

She wasn't going to take that comment passively. "He's bigger in his gaits than Lovey. I just need to work up to it. That's all. I'll get there."

I shook my head. "If you do that constant stopping, then that's what you'll train. Don't be surprised if he stops in the test, anticipating that little routine you do here. The test is only ten minutes but I haven't seen you go that long without stopping. Surely you can go ten minutes."

Francesca rolled her eyes and spoke down to me. "Little Miss twenty-something, you have no idea."

I replied, "Well, you asked for feedback, and I think you get so tired because you're too grippy in your thighs. I'd wear out fast, too, if I did that. You need to drop your stirrups and settle down into the saddle more."

"Enough." Now Francesca was mumbling regrets as she picked the reins back up and walked away. But I could hear her. She couldn't have possibly seen my grin.

When I got home I was bursting at the seams to talk to someone about pushing Francesca around the arena, but of course I wasn't allowed to. This was already killing me. Ryder was eating noodles at the table with her laptop open.

"Hey, Lizzy." She looked up for only a split second and then put her eyes back on her screen while she kept talking. "Chess Cavelli was wandering around asking questions tonight."

I stared at the back of her head as I replied. "He's doing the farm books and probably bored out of his mind."

Ryder was watching a video of some Advanced Young Rider from last year's Championships. She had probably watched it a dozen times already. She kept talking. "I invited him to come watch my lesson tomorrow. He's nice."

I shook my head, because I knew what she was doing, and I thought it was just silly and unrealistic thinking. The guy had to be around thirty. "Ryder, c'mon, he's way too old for you."

She looked up at me briefly and then back at her screen. "You don't have to like him. Besides, you just don't like him because he's Francesca's son."

I was suddenly really tired. So I poured a big bowl of cereal for my dinner and plopped down next to her. "And you like him because he is Francesca's son, and Francesca has lots of money."

She rolled her eyes again at me, looking like the teenager she was. "Uh, and I don't see how that should count against the guy."

And for once I had no comeback. Who the heck cared? Instead I spooned up my cereal, and then tipped the bowl into my mouth and drank the extra milk left pooling in the white ceramic bowl.

Ryder twisted in her seat and smirked at me. "Attractive. Now are you going to belch?"

She looked so young sitting there, and so clean and prissy. I was tired and filthy and feeling like she was once again baiting me. I couldn't resist.

"Maybe, or maybe something even worse."

"Gross. You and Natalie are just disgusting."

She shut the laptop and fled to her bedroom. I giggled to myself.

I was feeling cocky from pushing Francesca around the arena, and now I had actually dislodged Ryder from the sofa, and chased her into her room. I guess I shouldn't feel too proud.

I showered and typed a good long entry into my journal. I hoped to hell no one ever got a hold of my password.

And then I sent an e-mail to Marco. He was the one person I could tell about Johnny Cash and about being Francesca's ground person and how he would have been pleased that I had "manipulated the manipulator." It felt good to be able to tell someone. But I didn't tell him about my crude teasing of Ryder. I felt a little guilty about that.

# 5. Widgets

*When I rode Winsome the next day, I channeled Johnny. The bouncy* hesitation steps came and went and came again, not exactly at my bidding, but I stumbled around in the dark and grasped hold of the fleeting moments.

I heard Margot's voice, but I no longer saw her. I hardly saw the arena around me. Instead, I focused on my horse underneath me. I felt the up and down motion of her back, following the downbeat with my seat the way a boat follows a wave, not on top of it but part of it. No one from the ground could experience this inner journey; this feeling I had of power over her body, at the same time feeling that I had become an extension of her body. I was on an inner high. I felt that I could shape and direct her body in any direction. It felt great.

I had grabbed onto something new: power, exciting, exhilarating. With my feeling of power came a lot of responsibility, or maybe it was just fear of messing up. After my lesson, once I was walking around the field and relaxing, I had to mull over the past two days. I needed not to screw things up and behind my new-found bravado was a feeling of teetering on a knife edge, one moment feeling almost cocky over my new level of proficiency, and then the next minute feeling insecure. I was pushing the boundaries with Winsome, with Ryder, and with Francesca, too.

Ryder was hand grazing Papa after his bath, right outside the barn, when I returned. Chess was chatting away with her. He looked up and gave me a friendly wave.

Ryder said something and drew his attention back to her before I could make a polite wave back. I saw her turn around and show him the label on the back of her breeches. Of course they were Francesca's "High Horse Couture" design. And of course Ryder's tiny little bum looked great in them. They were the newest stretchy summer weight fabric in denim with a low rise. I didn't think Chess looked all that impressed, but Ryder seemed too oblivious to notice his impassive face. He pulled a little notebook out of his back pocket and scribbled something down.

After I showered Winsome and cleaned tack and started laundry, I was ready for a bologna, cream cheese, and spicy-sweet-pickle sandwich. It was my latest dollar store concoction and I thought it tasted great. Then, of course, I had my appointment with Francesca. Today I needed to get there earlier so I could curry up the dirt and scurf and have it all brushed off of Johnny before Francesca could see it and screech at me. She didn't seem to understand that bringing up all the dirt and dander and loose hair was part of the process of grooming. I wondered if the woman had ever groomed her own horse.

Ryder still had Chess attached to her hip when they passed the tack room door, leading Papa to his stall. In a moment they did a return stroll, sans Papa, passing the tack room again, this time headed toward the office. I poked my head out into the aisle to be friendly, tack sponge still in my hand. They didn't seem to notice me as I looked at their backs.

Ryder was saying. "You want to grab a sandwich? I know a good deli."

Chess answered her sweetly. "I can't today, but I'll definitely take a rain check. Thanks for taking the time to explain all about the young rider championships; very interesting."

Ryder was as animated as I ever saw her. Her eyes were bright as she replied. "I wish you could come watch us go in Kentucky, but you can still watch it live-streamed over the internet."

Chess looked impressed. "That's very exciting, Ryder. I just may have to do that."

Ryder twirled her keys and had a bounce in her step as she headed out to her little compact car. "See you later then."

Chess turned around and caught my eye before I could duck back into the tack room. Busted. I vigorously wiped down the tack room counter and put away the leather-balsam and refolded some towels and re-stacked them in the cupboard, anything to make-work and kill time. I wasn't going out in the aisle until I was sure he was gone.

And then,-there he was again, standing in the tack room doorway with a ledger in his hand. "Lizzy, do you mind translating this for me? Mother isn't here, and this bill is huge. I can't categorize expenses properly if I don't understand what they are."

I was still embarrassed that he had seen me listening in on his conversation with Ryder. But he didn't seem to care. Instead, he sidled up to me and handed me a vet bill. I took it from him and looked at the line item charges. Considering what it was for, I thought it was reasonable. I glanced up at Chess and noticed he was watching my face. He couldn't know the pain in my chest just looking at the bill, and remembering the night.

I handed him back the bill with a slightly shaky hand and started babbling. "This was for the foals. We had a mare die, not just any mare, but Deb's mare, Regina. Well I guess it was your mother's horse when she died. And we had little Fiddle left an orphan and then we had a dicey time getting the other mare to take her on. Then, Fiddle was a high risk foal, and then we had to supplement Sister, too." I noticed the blank look on his face, pleasant but not understanding what I was saying. "You didn't hear about this I guess."

He shook his head and furrowed his brow, but he also had a distracted look. I could tell he had no idea what agony we had endured.

Chess spoke almost to himself. "Mother's already lost money on these two then."

My face felt hot and my voice sounded shriller than I meant it to. "This isn't about selling widgets."

He smiled weakly and answered softly. "The problem is, Lizzy, I can't figure out how any of this is about selling anything."

Chess obviously did not get it. This was a business like no other. I tried to calm my tone. "You have to see them to appreciate them."

Chess drew out his words carefully, "Okaaaay. I'd like to meet the little widgets then. Can you walk me up the hill and show them to me?"

I had not asked for this. I turned my wrist to make a show of looking at the time.

Chess placed the invoice back in the ledger book and closed it before speaking. "If you have time, of course."

My bologna sandwich was calling me. But that was the only thing I had to do right now, and sadly it could wait. He was the boss' son, and Margot had asked, no, more like directed, that we be nice to him.

I tried not to let my annoyance show. "Let me load my pockets with horse treats. But I can't show you everything. Maybe if Deb and Nat are there they can show you around. It's really Deb's kingdom up there."

Chess' face brightened. "I'd love to see Deb! I always liked Deb."

Now I had a plan to hand him over to Deb. Things were looking up. "OK, then, and you need to meet Natalie, too. She's a lot of fun. C'mon."

I loaded up with puff-peppermints and we headed up the hill. But here came Deb and Nat driving down the hill toward us. They pulled alongside us and Deb rolled down the window. I noticed Deb had put her skinny little rimless glasses back on. She sounded genuinely enthused.

"Chess, what the heck? Long time, no see. What are you up to?"

Chess put both hands on the door frame, leaning toward Deb in a way I've only ever seen guys do. They gave each other a friendly hug as best as they could through a car window. It looked genuine. I could tell they were old buddies.

"Hi Deb, it's great to see you again."

Deb dimpled up, with a broad smile. "So what brings you back to the funny-farm?"

He pushed back off the door frame and laughed. "Doing the books. Someone's got to do the paperwork, you know."

I could tell Deb was genuinely glad to see him. "Ugh. Poor you. Life treating you good?"

"Ah, OK, I guess. I'm trying to be the dutiful son. Someone has to be. And you?"

She nodded. "Doing what I do." Deb pushed her glasses up her nose reflexively and looked concerned. "Got your inhaler with you? You know my barn is run rotten with cats."

Chess smiled back, "I'm not afraid of your kitties. Bring 'em on."

Deb tipped her head back and examined Chess through her lenses. "Well, you must be managing your allergies better these days, but, don't say I didn't warn you."

Then Deb introduced Natalie, who had been sitting there uncharacteristically quiet. To my chagrin, Deb invited Chess to our next Wednesday night gathering, which he accepted, farewells and see-you-soons were then exchanged. Off they drove with a pat-pat of the door frame from Chess and a wave of Deb's hand. And my bologna sandwich receded farther into the indefinite mist of time.

I hadn't thought about the cats.

We walked to the back field where the two mares contentedly grazed with the three foals. It wasn't yet time for them to come in, so when I unhooked the chain around the gatepost, the mares only picked their heads up for a moment before putting them back down in the grass.

All the rain had made the fields lush, and the mares were fat, even though the foals were still nursing, which often pulled mares down and made them ribby, but not this time.

Chess hesitated when I gestured for him to follow me. "Come on in." Chess took a tentative step through the gate. "You promise it's safe?" That made me laugh out loud. "Well, maybe I wouldn't go that far." Poor guy. He thought I was serious and froze on the spot.

I laughed and gestured again for him to come on. "I'm kidding, well sort of kidding. Horses are horses. They're big animals, but none of these are aggressive. It's not like one of those old westerns with the stampeding cattle. Don't worry, I'll look out for you."

Just as I spoke, here came the foals, ears up and tails up, galloping full tilt toward us. Chess came in and I latched the gate. I knew they would stop before running us over, but Chess didn't. I heard him inhale and exhale loudly, as if bracing himself.

His voice was gently sarcastic. "You're right, Lizzy, not at all like a wild herd of stampeding cattle."

I laughed because his Dad would have said exactly the same thing.

The foals broke to trots and then to walks and arched their necks, examining us. I pulled the plastic off of a peppermint and handed it to Chess. "Don't feed them any of your fingers, just the mint."

He spoke out of the side of his mouth. "Thanks, I feel so much safer now."

The foals crowded in, the two fillies, Fiddle and Sister pushing the colt Bazooka away and making me laugh again. "Girls rule around here, Chess. Zookie hasn't got a chance between the mares and the fillies. He's outnumbered."

Chess nodded. "Yep, just like growing up. Even with Dad and my brother Bobby, we were always outnumbered by my mother." He grinned and opened up a peppermint and put it in his palm with his fingers spread wide, and Fiddle got it first. "The boy's name is Zookie?"

"His name is Bazooka. Margot named him."

I gave Sister her mint and then gave her a friendly wither scratching.

"See, they all like to have their withers scratched. It's how they socialize with each other. It's co-grooming."

Chess's face brightened. "Like chimpanzees?"

Sister was digging it as I continued scratching. "Yeah, kind of like that."

He nodded. "Okay, I want to try."

I pointed to Fiddle. "Here, reach right there where the neck joins the back. See how the spine rises up? Those are called withers."

Chess said, "Yeah, I've heard of withers. Wither thou go-est, I shall go also, right?" He chuckled at his own lame pun.

Chess started giving Fiddle a proper scratching, and Fiddle was showing her appreciation with a protruding top lip, stretching out her neck and rolling her eyes around.

I bandied back at him, "Scratch her withers and she'll follow you anywhere."

Chess was still chuckling. "What's with the funny face?"

"Oh that's a happy face."

Fiddle started to return the favor by using her top lip to groom Chess's back. And Chess was looking a little nervous but smiling and seemingly enjoying himself.

"Is she trying to bite me or have I just been admitted to the pack?"

"It's a herd, and you're fine … I think."

Chess tried to lean away from Fiddle's mouth. "Lizzy? You promised to take care of me out here, remember?"

Fiddle disengaged and turned fully around and backed her butt into him.

Chess held both hands up. "One thing I remember is never stand behind a horse."

I was laughing again. "She just wants her butt scratched. Just keep scratching."

I had slowed my scratching of Sister so she had turned from my lazy hand and walked over to Chess, rotating around like Fiddle and backing her butt into him. Chess was scratching both fillies now, one with each hand. Zookie saw his opportunity and was tip-toeing in to me for his peppermint. I unwrapped it and fed it to him while giggling at Chess and the fillies. Chess was scratching both fillies like mad and they were rocking back and forth doing an odd sort of rumba.

He was grinning. "Look, Lizzy, stereo scratching!"

"Good job, Chess." I gave him the thumbs up.

I gave Zookie his scratchies and then finished with a big hug around his neck. Sister noticed, and she pinned her ears and shook her head at him; poor Zookie.

Chess was watching and not paying attention to Fiddle who had turned back around and nipped him.

"Ow!" He was rubbing his butt.

Chess looked only mock-angry. "She bit me. I thought we had an understanding."

I winced. "You OK?"

He nodded. "It was only a little nip, but it startled me."

The mares had now figured out that treats were being handed out and they were ambling our way with the authority of beat cops disbursing a crowd. They had cranky faces, and the babies backed up obediently and let them through.

With the big girls closing in it was starting to feel crowded. I gave the mares each a couple of peppermints and then shooed them away, and as they backed away the foals poked their necks toward us and began to tip-toe in for more.

Time to go. I gave my thumb a jerk toward the pasture gate.

"We can walk back out and I'll tell you about each one of the horses up here." Chess sidled back up to me, and as we walked he kept checking over his shoulder.

"Yeah. I'd feel safer on the other side of the fence."

I noticed though that the herd had gotten the picture and the mares were pushing the foals around, for no particular reason that I could see. I loved those mares. I loved those foals.

I said, "You could see that they are not widgets right? They are all individuals, with really distinct characters. The girls are really bossy, but cute though, don't you think?"

Fiddle broke from the herd and made a mad dash back up to us at the gate. She came to a screeching halt in front of Chess.

I laughed, "You see what I mean. I think Fiddle has a crush on you!"

Chess ran his hands over her big floppy ears and through her short curly forelock and then down her long black face, shaking her head a bit from side to side, sort of like you would rough-house with a playful puppy.

She was surprisingly quiet for it all. Chess now had this baby horse, big eyed and soft as a plush teddy bear, eating from his hands and begging for his touch. Fiddle had worked her charm on Chess, and clearly vice-a-versa.

We walked out of their pasture and I gave him a tour of the fields, quickly describing the residents, their ages and breeding, and a brief analysis of their finer points.

And I tried to give a quick description of the tragedy of losing Regina, and the drama of grafting Fiddle onto Sister's dam, "Glimmer." This time he did not speak of money or business, but listened quietly.

As we were walking back through the barn I turned to him to speak. "That's the tour. I hope you can appreciate a little bit more what goes into … uh … "

I noticed he was scratching his elbow first, and then noticed a weird blotchy red patch on his throat. It was practically ballooning in front of my eyes.

"Chess are you OK?" He turned his hand palm upwards and examined the inside of his forearm.

"Actually I'm breaking out in hives."

"Hives?"

He nodded back. "Hives. Thanks, Lizzy, for the tour. Your little widgets are cute and friendly even if I can't appreciate their finer points. I'll just need to take an extra antihistamine before I do this again."

We turned down the hill and he started walking faster.

I could see welts on the back of his neck now. I sped up, trying to keep pace with him, and feeling guilty. I shouldn't have had him scratching the foals. What was I thinking?

"Can I get you something?"

"Thanks, but no. I have all my emergency supplies in my car. It's my cross to bear. I'm used to it."

"I'm so sorry."

He stopped and turned, looking agitated. "Hey, don't feel bad. I asked for the tour. I enjoyed it, too. I would like to understand this business better, if it is a business. Anyway, I'll go grab my computer and papers from mother's office and finish up today at home. If I take meds and a bath in colloidal oatmeal it will calm it right down, but if I don't I'll be scratching all night long."

I shooed him away, feeling terribly guilty, and wondering if his hives were something serious. "OK. Sorry. Don't let me slow you down. Get going."

And as I stood there I began to understand why Margot would feel sorry for him.

# 6. Temporary Loss Of Balance

*I was sweeping the barn aisle, deep in my own thoughts, when Ryder's* disembodied voice floated out of the wash stall.

"Guess what? Chess is going to be with us at Deb's for dinner. Isn't that cool?"

I was thinking about how to respond as I swept my way down the aisle toward Ryder. She couldn't seriously think Chess was interested in her, could she? I sounded distracted as I answered. "I don't really care one way or the other."

The air was filled with the smell of menthol. Ryder was squatted down next to Papa; she held her hands flat on either side of Papa's cannon bone and briskly rubbed, moving her hands up and down his leg. I stopped sweeping and watched for a moment. I could tell Papa was enjoying it; his head hung low, his ears relaxed. But something struck me as odd about it.

"Lizzy, don't be such a wet blanket. It will be great to have a guy at the table instead of just us."

I knew I was scowling and tried to let it go. Why should I care?

I leaned on my broom and watched her gently smooth down the hair on Papa's legs. "Ryder. Liniment? That's new for you."

She ignored me, and kept her eyes down, then stood up and let him sniff her hands, which he did and then he lifted his top lip, sucking in the strange odor in what was called the "flehmen" response. Ryder put on her adult schoolteacher voice. "The flehmen response; I doubt you know why they do it. You'd have to read a veterinarian textbook."

I pressed my lips together and answered sarcastically, "Gosh Ryder, could it be because they have an extra organ called the vomero nasal organ, and the flehmen response is to push the scent deep into the skull to the organ. Did I get it right?"

"Uh, yeah, mostly." She had effectively changed the subject and made me defensive by challenging my knowledge of horses. At least I had been able to remember the vomero nasal organ. I was amazed at myself for being able to dredge that up. Ryder unclipped Papa and led him back to his stall.

The thought of her rubbing down Papa's legs still niggled at me. But I had to let it go. I was looking forward to my Johnny time. I packed my boots and helmet and gloves and spurs and even grabbed my favorite whip.

As usual, Claire Winston's barn was deserted when I walked in. I got Johnny ready and still no Francesca. So I went ahead and led him to the arena. It was a warm and still day and Johnny was more relaxed today. I went ahead and set the stirrup leathers on my holes and swung up. I walked around and around on a loose rein, waiting. No Francesca. So I picked him up and began to warm him up. I rode nice long lines with his neck a little low so I could feel him lift and swing through his back. Left and right, I changed directions, left and right again and again in large serpentine loops. He felt especially nice and loose today, not snorting at the mounting block or spooking. Next I rode the trot to canter and back to trot both ways until it was prompt and smooth. We walked. No Francesca yet. What the heck? I looked around.

I went ahead and picked him back up and sat the trot. I did some half halts. Wow. He felt awesome, uphill and bouncing over the ground and light in my hand. I did another Francesca check. No sign, so it was time for some fun while I had the chance. I did some long and forward half-passes. He was amazing. I hadn't felt half passes like his before, it was exhilarating.

And then I couldn't resist. I rocked him back and he hit the passage button. I looked around guiltily…still no sign of Francesca. I sent him forward across the diagonal. He knew all about what that diagonal was about. He turboed up out of the corner, rising in front of me and sinking down behind like a speedboat. I felt a flutter in my stomach. I was tasting forbidden fruit. I brought him back in the corner and looked all around me again. No Francesca. I walked and then did a few steps of piaffe…still nervous to be discovered.

I wondered if I could get away with a little canter.

But no. I saw Francesca come out of the barn. And I instantly walked and dropped the reins.

"He's all ready for you, Francesca." I probably sounded too chipper.

"Good. I just had a massage. Let's see if it was worth the money."

So I jumped down and put the stirrups back on Francesca's holes. I could tell when she started trotting that she was a little looser.

"You look good, Francesca."

She ignored me, and came through the corner and set up her half pass all wrong.

"Haunches leading, Francesca. Start over. Shoulder-fore."

She didn't even scowl at me. And she set it up wrong again. I raised my voice.

"Do it again."

She circled around.

"Lead with the inside foreleg. Do more than you think is right."

And she fixed it. It was a miracle.

"You got it!" I think I sounded incredulous.

Francesca finished the half-pass and began to pull up. I pushed my luck again.

"Keep going, Francesca." I shook my head in disbelief when she put her leg back on and kept going. Holy cow. Francesca was actually listening to me. I shut up and just watched. So many things were wrong with her riding. Where to start? I knew any eighteen-year-old girl could sneer and feel superior pointing out her mistakes. Instead, I tried to think about what words would help. Despite the stress she created in my life, oddly I wanted her to be successful on Johnny. I had to shake my head again to even believe the generosity of my own thoughts.

As much as it was impossible to like Francesca, I understood how much she wanted this. Enough to buy a horse she was told was not appropriate and hide him over at her friend's barn. Her stiff body and her attitude were always working against her.

It was hard to care about someone who had made it a point to make me uncomfortable; but here I was, wanting her to succeed. I didn't like Francesca, but I had stopped *not* liking her.

I credited Marco with helping me past that point. He had told me that if I knew "my hair was not green" then there was no reason to be hurt if someone said it was. His funny example stuck with me. I no longer gave Francesca the power to make me feel like a fish out of water. Besides, she needed me now. I was a knowledgeable and useful person. A tiny bit of power had shifted.

And I began to think that maybe I might be able to move her closer to her goals.

That felt good.

Just when I was about to yell out another encouraging, "Good!" Johnny surprised us all. A little squirrel had leapt onto the top of the kickboards, and Johnny spun around hard to the left and then scooted a few steps.

Francesca almost fell off over Johnny's right shoulder, but Johnny blessedly came to a standstill after his little scoot. His stood stock still with his eyes bugged out and that braced look that is not comforting to see. Francesca was sitting in front of her saddle, leaning on Johnny's neck with both feet still in the stirrups.

Francesca's voice sounded weak and wavering. "Lizzy?" I didn't understand why she didn't push herself back into the saddle.

I sounded slightly annoyed. "Francesca, why don't you get back into your saddle?"

She wiggled a little bit, but was firmly planted in front of the heavy thigh blocks of her saddle. She was still flopped over on his mane and was trying to use her hands to push herself upright, but I could see if he dropped his head now she would be a goner, sliding right over his ears into the dirt. Her chin was now buried in his mane.

Her voice then took on a note of urgency.

"Lizzy come here, NOW!"

Francesca could not see or feel what I could see and instinctively knew. Johnny Cash was frozen in fear, and that was not a good thing.

If Francesca panicked, then Johnny might panic. I suddenly envisioned a scene of escalating chaos and ultimate doom if Francesca got flung into the dirt. Francesca was no spring chicken; she was small boned without an extra ounce of fat. If she hit the ground with any force she would shatter like glass. I lowered my voice.

"I'm coming, Francesca, stay still. Whoa, Johnny, that's my good man."

He still had that "deer in the headlights" look about him. Cautiously, I walked up to Johnny. I fished into my pockets for a peppermint, and at the sound of the crinkly wrapper he relaxed, and gave up that braced look. I knew the real danger was now past. Now he was interested in the peppermint, the "killer squirrel" forgotten. He seemed content to stand there with Francesca sitting on his neck. Francesca sounded exasperated.

"Lizzy, forget about him. Help me."

I couldn't help myself. I started to laugh.

"Francesca, you really can't just push yourself back?"

Francesca positively growled at me. "My legs are stuck in front of these damn thigh blocks. Stop laughing and be of some use here."

So I grabbed her right knee and pulled. But I couldn't stop laughing. And then I walked around and grabbed her left knee and pulled. I still couldn't stop laughing. Francesca started to giggle, too. She was giggling!

Francesca finally got the strength to push with her hands, while I kept pulling on her legs. I finally saw part of the problem, the crotch of her fancy breeches were caught and stretched over the pommel. She finally reached around behind herself with one hand and pulled herself backwards by grabbing the cantle. We were both laughing harder now. Her breeches finally let go and she popped back into place. I had to lean over and gasp for air, I was laughing so hard.

I caught my breath and stood up and wiped my eyes. Francesca was still giggling when she said, "Lizzy, if you ever tell a soul I swear I'll fire you on the spot!"

I stroked Johnny's neck and wondered if she was serious. "My lips are sealed, Francesca."

I looked up at Johnny's big wide blaze, thinking of how he had frozen in place and waited out his panic. "What a saint he is!"

Francesca snorted. "A saint? Big old horse just melted down over a squirrel! Ridiculous."

I knew it wouldn't be Johnny's last spin. "I guess you better learn to keep your weight back, huh?"

I got the old Francesca back with an icy stare and grimly pursed lips. To her credit, Francesca picked him back up and finished her ride just fine. Another horse would have been shipped off to the sale barn; but not Johnny.

When Francesca finished her ride and handed Johnny back to me, she totally shocked me by cupping his muzzle in her hands and planting a kiss on the soft flesh next to his nostril. She looked back at me, and said, "Not a word." And then she ran her hand over her hair and headed to the parking lot, looking like a model walking the runway. The woman did have a certain presence.

I drove back to our barn, getting out of my old red truck and strolling lazily toward the barn apartment. The sun was sinking in the sky behind the clouds, making a rosy light. Instead of going up the stairs to the apartment though, I detoured to the tack room and gathered enough carrots to hand out treats to all the horses.

Wild Child got his first. He was King of the Barn after all. He wobbled his nostrils and came to the front as soon as he heard his name. He took his carrot all at once, and then pinned his ears. Even with his ears pinned he got his face rubbed, there was no chance of a bite with his face stuffed full of carrots anyway. I knew he liked his face rubbed even if he had to pretend he didn't. His half closed eyes told on him.

Then I gave Hotstuff his. And then next was sweet little Lovey. And then Papa. And I was about to go to Winsome before heading up the stairs. And then I didn't. I looked around me. No one was around. And I opened Papa's stall door and went in.

I handed him Winsome's carrot and then gave his withers a little friendly scratching. "Hey, Papa."

He was tall dark and handsome, always with a slightly worried look on his face. He munched his carrot with wrinkles over his eyes, turning to examine me, ears pricked.

"It's OK you big weenie. I just want to check something."

I ran my hands down his right side and squatted down. Then I closed my eyes and simply felt my way down the back of his cannon bone. Did I feel anything? Any heat? Any swelling? Nope. None. I heard myself blow out a breath as I opened my eyes.

I ducked under his neck and felt his nose gently bump my head. He was still worried and carefully watching my every move.

"I know, I know. I don't usually bother you. I'm probably being silly." I was still whispering and feeling guilty about what I was doing. I was treading on Ryder's carefully guarded turf. Before I knelt down I glanced once again down the barn aisle. But the coast was still clear.

I started again, running my hand down the left front. I always closed my eyes when feeling for heat or swelling in legs, since for some reason it helped me focus more on what I was feeling. I started at the top, right below the knee and went slow and light with my finger tip and thumb. And I stopped half way down. It was slight. Maybe it was nothing. But no; I did feel something. I started again at the top. I thought maybe there was a little heat, too, but it was barely detectable.

I knew right away that Ryder had found it, too. Of course that was what the liniment was all about.

Ryder had only one week left before she left for Kentucky for the Advanced Young Rider Championships. Or maybe didn't. I exhaled a little bigger this time as I got up and slipped back into the barn aisle. I went and fetched another carrot for Winsome, barely registering giving it to her.

Then I dragged myself up the stairs. Ryder was sitting at the dining table on her computer. My voice was soft, hesitant. "Hey, Ryder."

Ryder's was matter-of-fact. "Lizzy."

I started again. "Ryder..."

"Yeah?"

She finally looked up and narrowed her eyes at me, but before I could say anything she said, "Hey, what's going on with you and Francesca?"

"What?" Her question startled me.

"You've been gone every afternoon and Francesca told me to do evening chores without you. Therefore, I get that she is using you for some, ah, probably weird errand or task."

I hedged as best as I could, "Yup, you called it. And if I told you then I'd be signing my own death warrant."

I didn't even get a smile. Instead, she pressed her lips together and looked thoughtful for a moment. "Hmm. Weird. OK, fine by me, I guess. I need to stay focused on my show preparation."

I wasn't going to let her skillful redirection stop me this time. "That's what I wanted to talk to you about."

Now she looked irritated. "I stay focused all by myself, thank you very much. And all kidding aside, I don't want to hear any lectures from you about Chess."

I wanted to explode. Ryder had done it again. This time I was struck dumb as I marveled at how good she was. Instead of playing defense she was playing offense. The girl should be press secretary at the White House. I didn't know what to say next. In fact I couldn't form a rational sentence in my head.

My discretion had in fact vanished, and before I lost the topic entirely I just blurted out the heart of the matter. "Papa has heat and swelling mid-cannon bone. Left front."

At first Ryder narrowed her eyes, angry. "Lizzy, don't lecture me, I know my own horse."

And so I just kept going. "Does Margot know?"

Ryder said nothing.

I shook my head. "I didn't think so."

She picked her head up and looked at me, her eyes almost pleading. "He is not lame. He'll pass the jog."

I snapped back at her. "Ryder, it's not a matter of just passing the damn jog. If he's hurt himself and you keep training, he could make it worse."

Ryder had pulled herself erect, her jaw set. "Lizzy, he just has to go through the competition, and then he can have a long vacation."

I kept shaking my head. "Ryder, you have to tell Margot. You have to. Papa does not belong to you. It's not your decision to make."

"I've been planning to talk to Margot. I just haven't found the right moment yet."

I was gathering the force of righteous indignation. Ryder was lying. "The right moment is not after the competition, Ryder, it's tomorrow morning when she comes in. You're not being fair to the horse."

Ryder chewed her lower lip a moment, and then scowled at me. "I will."

And I did believe her now. For one thing, she knew that if she didn't tell Margot that I would. I softened my voice. I did feel for her. She had to be eaten up with anxiety over Papa. But then I had another thought, because clearly Ryder was well versed in all things veterinary, and always made a point to let me know it. Ryder probably knew what was going on.

"So, what do you think it is?" I asked.

She chewed on her lip a moment before replying. "Not sure. It's very slight. He feels just fine working, but I'm afraid it's his suspensory ligament."

"Bad?"

She shook her head, looking disgusted that I could even ask. I guess I should have answered from a vet textbook like I had about the flehmen response.

"God, Lizzy, why don't you stop reading your dorky novels and try studying something about, oh I don't know, horses maybe?"

I caught myself before I said something defensive. She was doing it again, going after me and deftly changing the subject. I had a weird sense of detachment as I saw the situation with brutal clarity. Poor Ryder, I had momentarily caught her off guard, but she had righted herself.

There was the Ryder I knew.

# 7. The Right Thing

*Ryder's face was pale with shadows under her eyes. I had a feeling she* hadn't slept much. She squatted down next to Papa's left front leg while he stood in the cross ties. I had one hand lightly on the halter, stroking Papa's face, while Margot stood to the side holding her coffee.

Ryder's voice lacked its usual edge. "I always check his legs, Margot. I mean, I wasn't sure at first. But, I am now."

"Darling, I know you do. It's probably nothing. Let me have a look."

And Margot and Ryder changed places. I don't think I'd ever seen Margot squat down, but she did. She felt down the leg just as Ryder had done. Then she reached under Papa and ran her hand down the other leg, and then back to the left again. I could see her lips tighten as she closed her eyes and her fingers hovered mid tendon on the left front. Clearly she had found the same spot that I had found.

Margot opened her eyes and looked up at Ryder. Her voice was soft; concerned. "Yes. Good job, Ryder. I think to be safe we need to have Doc come have a look. Let's skip our work today and wait to hear what he says."

Ryder's voice was also soft. "Okay."

I let go of Papa and turned to Hotstuff, who was ready for Margot. We were quiet as I unclipped him from the cross ties, slid off the halter which had been over his bridle, and handed him off to her. Margot's face was unreadable.

Ryder silently finished grooming Papa, gave him a carrot and then unclipped him to take back to his stall. The normal sounds of the barn suddenly seemed louder amidst our silence.

I didn't know what to say. But I tried to console her. "Ryder, it's going to be all right."

I was met by total silence. No correction, no slap down. In a way, I wished she had responded with her usual attitude. I tried to justify my optimism.

"It could be superficial. Then you could get back to work and go to Kentucky with a clear conscience."

Ryder's lips barely moved, and her voice was very quiet, but I heard her. "Nice little fantasy. I probably just wasted a year of my life for nothing."

I felt my teeth clench and tried not to overreact. I was determined to stay positive. "Ryder. You don't know yet. Just wait."

She walked away, leading Papa back to his stall. Maybe I should have kept my mouth shut.

When Deb came in I quietly filled her in. Even though Ryder had gone to the arena to watch Margot ride, I found myself whispering. "Left front, some heat and filling."

Deb squinted at me, taking it all in and shaking her head. "Poor kid. She must be sick. They're supposed to leave next Wednesday, right?"

I kept whispering. "Yes, and she looks devastated, like she already knows she won't be going."

Deb gave me a look that clearly said, "shut-up."

Ryder had walked back in.

Deb's sympathy was genuine. "Hey, Ryder. Sorry to hear about Papa."

Ryder looked right at me and blew through her nose. "The rumor mill sure started fast." She turned her attention to Deb. "Thanks, Deb. Doc's coming later."

Deb nodded. "It's in his very capable hands then. Doc's the best soundness guy around."

A dispirited Ryder answered her. "Yeah."

I noticed Wild Child had been following our discussion, and when Deb took his reins and tried to pull him out of the cross ties he balked.

Deb laughed at him. "Wild Child, y'know, sometimes it's not about you. This has nothing to do with you."

Remarkably, he took a hesitant step forward, glancing back at me as he went reluctantly with Deb.

I had to laugh, too. "You're fine! Really."

And I clucked and clapped my hands together and he sighed and relaxed and put his head back down, following Deb out of the barn.

Later that morning, a solemn knot of people stood around Papa for his exam, including Francesca. Deb had told me that our vet, who just went by Doc, was practically a local legend, and was especially known for his expertise in diagnosing lameness, not only that but he knew Papa well. Since Papa was not stoic, but a worrier and reactive, well, Doc would be able to take those things into consideration. He started with a passive exam. First he felt down the leg as we had done, and then he picked up the left front and palpated the ligament from the top, right below the knee all the way down, and around both sides of the fetlock joint where the ligament branched.

Of course he found the heat and swelling, too, and Papa jumped when Doc evidently hit the sore spot on palpation.

Next, he had Ryder take Papa to the indoor arena and put him on the longe line.

Doc, followed by Francesca, Margot, Deb, and me trailed after him in a silent parade.

Ryder began longing Papa to the left. He snorted and scooted away from her, throwing a bit of footing material into the kickboards with a thud that sent him into a nutty spell of bucking. Ryder reeled him in, soothed him with a few pats, and then sent him back out on the circle at a walk, only letting him finally break into a small trot once he looked calm. He appeared totally sound. I could feel my shoulders relax downward. Papa's left front was on the inside of the circle where I reasoned it had to be taking a greater load than the right front, and yet he was sound. That had to be good. I looked at Margot, and I looked at Deb, and then I looked at Doc. Everyone seemed to have on their poker faces.

Doc pushed himself off the kickboards where he had been leaning with his hands behind his back.

"OK. Let's see the other way."

Ryder brought Papa to a halt and then walked out to him, stroking his neck and then walking to the other side of him to reverse.

Again, Ryder made him walk the circle, and waited until he was quiet before asking for a small trot.

At first I thought he was going to be fine. He still looked sound to me.

But, Doc called out. "Do you mind making the circle smaller?"

And Ryder shortened the longe line.

But not enough to satisfy Doc. He called out again. "A touch more, Ryder."

Now she reeled Papa in onto a tiny circle.

And then it was there, ever so slight, but I could see it.

He was not regular with his front left now that it was on the outside of the circle.

Doc turned to look at Margot, and she shook her head at him. She said, "He never showed that under saddle."

He whispered his answer in a matter of fact tone. "It's amazing how a good rider who really has influence over a horse's carriage can cover it up. That's why I depend on you guys who feel it before anyone, including me, can see it."

And then I saw Margot and Doc exchange a knowing look.

He called out again. "Okay. That's good. Thanks."

Now he shifted to normal speaking tones that everyone could hear.

"So, Margot, I could start the blocks, but we all are thinking the same thing, right? So, I think we skip that step and ultrasound, and I'll pull a radiograph, too, to check the splint bones, just as a precaution."

Margot said, "Of course. Do you think there's any chance she's leaving for Lexington next week?"

He blew through his lips and answered softly. "Probably not. I doubt you'd want to risk it."

No one spoke as we put Papa back in the cross ties and Doc set up his ultrasound machine.

It was a simple and painless procedure, but Papa, being the worrier that he was, was given a light sedative just so he would stand quietly while the vet wet his leg down with a spray bottle of alcohol, and then ran the probe lightly up and down his leg. All the while the vet watched the screen on his machine. It was incomprehensible to me; just a lot of little black and white lines.

But Ryder and Margot watched the screen with looks of intense concentration.

Doc's brow was furrowed. He kept spritzing the leg, wetting it down, and going over and over it with the probe.

"There!"

He hit a button, which froze the screen. Then he fiddled with controls, aiming an arrow, and then hitting a print button.

"Not too bad, guys."

His cheery tone fell on deaf ears, but he was focused on his job, absorbed in the little gray and black lines on his screen. "So, see the frayed edges."

He pointed to things that made no sense to me at all. He almost sounded excited, pointing with the plastic cap of a needle. I could tell his excitement was from getting a clear diagnosis, as much as from establishing the extent of the injury.

"And look, right there? See how disorganized the fibers are there." He kept talking. "Ryder caught this in time. A full training routine could have resulted in permanent damage. I'm thinking rest and shockwave therapy will heal this up in pretty short order, of course ligaments can be slow to heal. But, if you had kept going, well, it's an overuse issue…very common. But this is so small you won't need to do stem cell. Let's start the shockwave today, and I'll leave you Surpass to rub in twice a day. Only walking for exercise…no turn out, and in two weeks I'll be back and re-ultrasound. That may be all we need to do."

The vet turned his attention to the obviously dispirited Ryder. "Young lady, I'm sorry about this, and I know it is a disappointment for you. But you'll have other chances. I saw you compete and was very impressed. And I don't impress easily. Do I, Margot?"

Margot shook her head. "No, Doc, you certainly do not."

Francesca asked Doc if he had time to pull a few Coggins tests. He was kind enough to agree. Francesca went to the office to gather all the out of date Coggins paperwork. Winsome and Lovey and Hotstuff were due. At least I would be splitting the farm call fee four ways with Francesca.

Margot spent a long time out at the Doc's truck over styrofoam cups of coffee talking to Doc as he copied information from the expired Coggins tests. I said nothing to Ryder, but left her in her misery. Instead, I went to Papa's empty stall and pulled his hay out so he wouldn't try eating it while sedated.

Soon, Ryder was slowly clip-clopping him toward the stall. It was a mournful sound; a dirge.

I walked around to the back of Papa, and watched Ryder carefully line him up so that he would walk straight into the stall without bumping his hip on the doorway, even if he should wobble.

She slipped off his halter, walked out, and slid the door shut.

Margot was walking toward us. Ryder stood in the aisle, Papa's halter still in her hand.

Margot put her hand on Ryder's shoulder. "Darling, you did the right thing. I'm proud of you. You could have tried to hold things together and push him through the competition. But, you put his welfare above your own." Ryder dropped her eyes, and Margot kept talking. "I have to notify USEF. They'll move someone from a reserve spot into your team slot. But I'm still the Chef d' equip you know, so we're still going. That means you, too."

Ryder looked incredulous, and started to speak, but Margot cut her off. "Darling, I agreed to be Chef d' equip because of you. Besides, you can learn a lot by grooming for and supporting the team, and it will only make you a better competitor next year. You'll also get to meet people. That can be very important."

Ryder was scowling. "Grooming?"

Ryder voice was pleading and sounding like the teenager she still was. "Margot, please don't make me go. Please. Not now. I had the highest average of anyone in the region. Grooming will be humiliating."

Margot's voice was firm, resolute. I knew Ryder didn't have a chance on this. "There's no shame in grooming. As a groom you will have a pass into the barns and to the warm up arenas. You can groom for Suzette. Not only is she our neighbor and friend, but now she's the strongest rider in our group. I'll enjoy having you along to help. I know you're miserable now, darling, but trust me on this one. You need to come. You're coming."

Ryder dutifully nodded but I knew at this moment Margot's request, no Margot's order, felt like salt on her wound. And I had set this in motion. I could only imagine how Ryder felt about me right now.

I led Doc to the stalls and held halters while he swiftly pulled blood for the Coggins from the jugular vein. He made pleasant conversation with me, barely looking at what his hands were doing. He pulled the cap from the needle, held it in his lips, while he pushed his thumb on the vein and made the puncture. Then he pushed the glass tube onto the needle and blood rushed in. Once he was done he wrote down the tube numbers and put the blood filled tube in his shirt pocket while I took the halter off and led him to the next horse. He was efficient. In a chipper tone, with three blood filled tubes in his pocket, he thanked me, told me it was nice to meet me, and wished me a good day. I wondered if those tubes ever leaked. I felt a slight bit queasy.

That night when Ryder and I walked up the hill towards Deb's, I noticed she had put on makeup. I resisted saying anything. Despite her totally depressing day, she obviously was looking forward to seeing Chess at dinner. She needed this. I got that. Even if Chess was a ridiculous crush for Ryder, a little male attention would probably be balm for her wounds.

When we got to the mare barn, Natalie greeted us, looking totally grubby. It was a relief to have Nat as a buffer between Ryder and me. My voice was overly cheery. "Hey, Nat!"

Natalie waved back. She stared right at Ryder, almost too long and hard before speaking. "Ryder, sorry to hear about Papa. You know, I ruined my own Young Rider Horse a few years back. I pushed and pushed until I broke him. I'll never get over it. It was on me, I should have known better. He was a great horse, but I was too damned selfish."

I resisted the urge to hug Nat. Ryder was stoically silent, but at least nodded to Nat.

Natalie bit her lower lip, and then briskly changed the subject. "Anyway, follow me. I want to show you guys something."

She walked around the end of the barn.

Natalie was one of those people that didn't get tan, she got freckled just like Deb. In fact her freckles had freckles, and they weren't just on her face, but across her shoulders and down her arms. Her brown hair was pulled back in a falling apart pony tail, her breeches had leather knee patches that were coming unstitched, and her tank top looked like it had been used by a horse for a snot rag. But she was smiling as we practically jogged beside her.

"I don't know what's gotten into me, but I saw these cool little bird sculptures in a store and I thought I could do something like that. Y'know people pay good money for them and I thought I could maybe even sell something."

I had no idea what Natalie was talking about, but Ryder and I followed her to where she had set up a couple of saw horses with a piece of plywood across them to make a work table.

On top of the table was a heaping pile of... junk.

Ryder scowled. But Nat was grinning like she was showing us something precious.

"Look at this stuff. Isn't it great? I found most of it at a flea market. And then Deb took me to one of those places where they salvage stuff from tear-downs."

I pawed through an interesting pile; an ornate key, some broken jewelry, old bicycle gears, a piece of bicycle chain, a couple of door knobs, a billiard ball, and old typewriter keys.

"An interesting pile of stuff, but I don't get it, Nat."

"You don't know it yet, but what you are looking at is a rabbit."

Ryder let out a guffaw. "You're kidding me, right?"

"Nope. I've been studying rabbits all summer. I've been taking photos and I've been sketching them. All I see anymore when I close my eyes are rabbits, and I see rabbits when I look at this stuff."

Nat's monologue was perplexing, but I wanted to be supportive. I reached into the pile and tried to find a rabbit somehow among the mess of junk.

I thought of my little friends grazing alongside Winsome, the gold flecks in their coat, the big round eyes.

I looked up at Nat, and she was practically vibrating with excitement. I didn't even know she was interested in anything artistic. Then I looked at the bronze doorknob in my hand. And I smiled at her.

"Ears up or ears down, Nat?"

Ryder looked at me like I was crazy, too.

But Natalie slapped me on the back.

"I knew you would get it, Lizzy. I got inspired by seeing Steampunk sculpture online. The sculpture, entirely from junk, well they call it repurposed items, is made into sculpture that's kind of from an alternate reality; like Victorian era meets Star Wars. Check out these old typewriter keys with the blue enamel. I want somehow to include a little tiny bit of color, kind of like my personal signature even though the rabbits blend into the grass; it will be my trademark when I'm famous. I think I'll need a soldering iron, some clamps and files, and a lot of thinking outside the box."

I picked up another piece of broken jewelry, multiple rows of filigreed chain, and ran them smoothly across my palm.

"This is lovely. I can't wait to see what you do with it."

"It's going to be so cool, Lizzy."

Natalie was singing some unrecognizable tune as she turned back toward the apartment, gesturing for us to follow. She interrupted her singing to recite our menu. "Deb made vegetarian lasagna and one of her great salads, and I made the garlic bread. I understand we have Chess coming; should be interesting."

We walked into an aromatic kitchen with Deb putting on an oven mitt to check on her lasagna. Deb was back in her little rimless glasses, and when she opened the oven door they steamed over, but Deb didn't seem to notice. They slid down her nose and she just peered over them. I greeted her.

"Hey, Deb; smells great."

She closed the oven door, looking satisfied. "Hi. I guess you heard we have company. I made an extra pan. Big risk here, cooking Italian with a Cavelli coming over. Oh, and I went ahead and invited Margot, too."

I exclaimed, "Oh, how fun!"

Margot didn't usually join us.

The kitchen was a mess. Natalie jumped in. "Hey, let me get a head start on clean up."

Deb looked surprised to find her countertops covered with dirty bowls and spatulas and vegetable peelings, some of which were on the floor. A stack of placemats was on the kitchen table with a fat yellow cat curled up on top, purring happily.

"Oh, yeah, thanks."

I looked at the fat, hairy cat. "Maybe for Chess Cavelli's sake I could…."

Deb's eyebrows went up. "Oh man, you're right. Thanks, that would be great, Lizzy."

I picked up the cat and carried it outdoors.

I was surprised when Ryder jumped in, too. "Hand me that broom."

Deb cheerfully said, "Thanks, Ryder."

We mobilized. Deb turned off the oven, and went to put on some of her old music…loud, and Nat couldn't help herself. First she had to rib Deb about her depressing music. She called it music to "slit your wrists by" and music for "navel-gazers." Regardless of the angsty balladeers that Deb seemed to favor, Natalie had learned the words, and she loved to sing along…really loudly! One of her favorite games was to get the lyrics wrong. But her lyrics were so much funnier than the real lyrics that she soon had us howling with laughter.

The group singing were called "The Indigo Girls" and they had been big in the 80's. They were singing their hit, *Closer to Fine* but Nat was belting out her own version of the chorus.

*I went to the drugstore; I went to the market;*

*I looked to the winos, I drank from the toilet.*

*There's more than one answer to this cop's questions, as I stagger a crooked line.*

*The more I sip this stuff out of a mason jar, the closer I am to bri-i-i-i-ine! The closer I am to bri-i-i-i-ine!"*

After a few repetitions we caught on to the new lyrics and joined in, even Deb. Before we had finished the last verse, Margot and Chess walked in and caught us and we collapsed in laughter. Margot was carrying a couple bottles of wine and Chess had brought flowers. The Indigo Girls were allowed to finish their last chorus properly. Margot winked at me as she put her wine down and gave Deb a hug.

"Darling, it smells wonderful in here."

I glanced around to check. No visible cats and the kitchen at least did not look unsanitary.

Deb's smile brought out her dimples. "All from scratch, Margot, even Natalie's garlic bread. We did use Cavelli pasta and tomato paste, though."

Natalie looked at the floor while Margot got to hear about Nat's new bread baking skills, then she left the room to turn down the music, and I suspect, change her clothes and clean up a bit. Ryder left to go light the Tiki torches so we wouldn't be eaten up by mosquitoes.

The room was a little too quiet all of a sudden.

My comrades had fled, and I had the same urge, but I couldn't think of an excuse.

Deb put the flowers in a vase and handed them to me. Relieved, I went outside with the flowers to join Ryder. And soon Chess had joined us, too. Margot and Deb were clearly having a conference.

We three had one of those, "how are you ... fine, how are you ... fine", type of conversations until Deb and Nat and Margot came out bearing food and plates.

Natalie had wet hair and smelled of soap. She reached across the table and gave Chess an enthusiastic handshake. "Hey there. Hard to believe Francesca was ever anyone's mother, but there you are!"

Chess was gracious enough to laugh and just said, "Here I am."

Margot asked for plates, and did the job of serving the hot lasagna. We passed the hot garlic bread (which was just the right amount of crusty) and the salad bowl went round with one person serving themselves while one held the giant wooden bowl. It was a few minutes before we settled into the meal.

Chess was the first one to bring up Papa. "Ryder, I am sorry to hear that Papa is on the disabled list."

Ryder drew herself up.

"Yes. Thanks. He has a very mild suspensory ligament injury. He'll be fine, but it means I'll miss the North American Championships."

Chess made a sympathetic face. "Oh, the Championships? I am sorry. Does the injury affect his value, y'know, on-going?"

Ryder's usual poker face fell away for just an instant. She glanced over at Margot, her voice halting. "I, well, I don't think so."

Margot leaned across the table and placed her hand over Ryder's, but with her eyes on Chess.

"Ryder here was so on the ball, Chess. Due to her vigilance it will probably only be a tiny blip on the screen, so no, it won't."

Chess dropped his eyes to his lasagna. "I see that Mother, well, Mother's company, carries medical insurance on Papa. Is horse medical insurance like homeowner's insurance where you don't want to make a claim but, y'know, save it for something major, or do we file for reimbursement even though this isn't major?"

We were all silent for a moment. I think Ryder felt Chess's charm fade. I felt for Chess. His questions made sense. I didn't know the answers either. Winsome was not insured. I couldn't afford it.

Margot stayed positive. "Well, we are obligated to report the claim to

the insurance company because the insurance company will exclude suspensory injuries on our renewal. The exclusion will most likely expire after
six months to a year when there's no recurrence. So, to answer your question, it's not like homeowners insurance, and yes, we should file a claim,
and then Francesca should get whatever reimbursement she is entitled to."

Chess wiped his mouth and nodded appreciatively. "Thanks, that's
good information. I'm just trying to understand how things work
around here. It's a lot to learn, and there's not much time to learn it."

Margot smiled sweetly at him. "So, I take it you're part of the
team now?"

He contemplated the question for a moment. "Dad would say yes,
Mother would say no. I'll stick around at least until I finish the farm
financials. That's what Dad asked me to do, at least, so far."

Just then Ryder blurted out. "Margot, I feel so bad about Papa. It's
all my fault!"

I looked at Ryder, trying to telegraph with my eyes…"NO, NO,
NO!" I did not want her to spill her guts to ease her conscience. Thankfully, Margot silenced her with a head shake.

"Now darling, that's just not so. Injuries happen. They happen in all
sports. Live and learn. In hindsight we should have been doing more
cross training with Papa, taking him out on the hill like we did with
Wild Child and given him more short breaks. The pastern can sometimes drop too far when they are fatigued, and Papa does have rather
long pasterns, so that's probably how the injury occurred. If we follow
Doc's orders, Papa will recover just fine."

Ryder lifted her chin. I was braced. She wasn't done.

"Margot, I wanted more than a perfect test; I wanted to blow them
all out of the water. I pushed him too hard. And now I won't even
be riding."

Margot exhaled, and spoke gently. "Darling, look at it this way, you
were so vigilant about checking his legs every day, you knew your horse's

"normal" and found that small amount of heat. You quite possibly saved Papa from a career ending injury."

Chess added, "And protected Mother's investment, very responsible of you."

I couldn't help myself; I cringed and shot him a dirty look.

Chess winced, and then shrugged apologetically.

I saw Deb and Natalie exchange looks.

"Sorry," he said. "I meant that as a compliment. Remember, I'm an accountant and a business guy, not a horseperson. So, I look at all of this as a business. Dollars. Cents. Depreciation. Amortization. Revenues. Deductions. And Ryder, when I say you protected Mother's investment, that's a very, very good thing. At least, it is in my world."

Ryder looked soothed by Chess's attention.

Margot laughed. "Poor Chess, I'm afraid as a pure business, Francesca has made a terrible investment in all of the horses and in all of us here, too. You've been away from all of this for so long now, you've forgotten how emotionally invested we get, and I'm afraid the drama never ends. I hope you don't mind us."

Chess smiled at Margot. "No, Margot, not at all. I get that this is everyone's passion." He then muttered, almost to himself, "But I'm the guy who has to figure out how to justify that passion as a bona fide business."

I found myself once again feeling sorry for Chess. There was a divide between those who were caught up in horses and those who were not, and looking across that divide at Chess was strangely familiar and discomforting. I spoke up. "I know the horse crazy thing can be hard to understand if you're on the outside looking in. A passion is an emotional response isn't it? And business, is well, just business."

Chess smiled sheepishly and scratched his neck, which did look a little pinkish. He pushed back from the table a little and smiled a little guiltily, putting his hands up in resignation.

"Okay, I promise to work hard at understanding. I do want to be part of the team here. I'm revisiting a foreign country, and I need to remember what little I knew about the culture. They say submersion is the best way to learn."

Margot reached across the table, placing her hand flat and leaning toward Chess. "Good, glad to hear it. And we'll try not to run you off! You just ask us what you need from us to do your job, for the team, and we'll do our best to help you. Right everyone?"

We dutifully nodded and made sounds of assent.

Blessedly, Natalie changed the subject to her art project, and even brought out her sketchbook which was full of fine pencil drawings of rabbits in every pose imaginable.

Her sketches were surprisingly very, very, good. Her rabbits almost hopped right off the page they were that detailed; almost photographic.

Chess brightened when he saw the sketches. I think he was relieved to talk about something other than horses.

# 8. Channeling Margot

*Ryder and Margot had gone to Lexington, Kentucky, for the North* American Young Rider Championships. Francesca had sprung for their airfare since our trailer could stay parked at the farm all week. I was left in charge of the show barn, which was not a problem. I enjoyed chattering at the horses without anyone looking at me like I had two heads. But more importantly, I was in charge of Papa. Right now he was our "special needs" child.

I had been giving Papa chopped carrots at feeding time, since Doc told us to take him off all grain while he was on stall rest. I chopped the carrots into about three inch chunks. The local grocery store sold 25 pound bags of organic carrots that looked like they were on steroids, extra fat and long, but hard to chop up.

Initially, I had tried slipping him just a "hush puppy" handful of grain when I fed the others, but he scarfed it down in moments. Then he would bang gently on his door and whinny, sure that he had been skipped. So, the carrots were my bright idea, they slowed him down, and kept him content. I chopped and sawed away with one of our steak knives until I had a good mound of them ready for the next feeding.

I also had the job of hand walking him in the indoor arena for twenty minutes twice a day while Ryder and Margot were at Championships.

Papa was already a handful just a little over a week into his lay-up, either prancing and pulling on me, or putting on the brakes or shaking his ears or pawing like he wanted to roll. I was nervous that he would further injure himself on my watch. I couldn't let that happen. So, I bribed and cooed or rattled the chain I had threaded over the nose piece of the halter. Walking was all he was supposed to be doing. There was no way of explaining to him that he needed to take it easy for the next two weeks, or until Doc gave us permission to do more.

There would be no paddock time for him to buck and roll and graze as it was too risky. He was frustrated. He didn't understand why no one put his tack on and let him do the work he was trained to do. He was one heck of a big boy busting at the seams with energy. Papa was always a worrier, but now he walked circles in his stall whenever any horse went out to the paddocks or to the arena. He had received his first shock wave treatment, and now we had to let time do its magic. I wished I could explain it to him. But he would just need to trust us like he always had. The tranquilizer was in the fridge. I hoped I wouldn't need it. Clearly, this had been a hard turn of events for more than just Ryder.

Once I had him safely back in his stall from his first walk of the day, I let the tension drain out of my body. Today would be fun. It would be just Deb and me in the main barn while Nat did the morning chores alone up in the mare barn. To have Deb to myself was a treat.

I got Wild Child out of his stall and began his grooming, which I believed he enjoyed, although I couldn't say for sure.

Wild Child had an image to keep up. He had to pin his ears and pull his lips back, making ugly grimaces. Mostly I ignored him, although sometimes he seemed to want a smack or two. Crazy. But he was not a horse to be ignored, and a slap on the neck seemed to elicit a softening of his facial features.

When I put my back into the curry he leaned into it, lowered his head and wiggled his top lip. That always amused me. *This* part he was clearly digging.

I always admired his brilliant copper-penny chestnut coat with gleaming layers of undertones that changed depending on the light. He had a huge stallion neck, arched and powerful, with a kite-shaped face, tomcat cheeks, and delicate muzzle, one that tempted you to stroke his velvet nose and look deeply into his large dark eyes. But, of course, he would never allow someone to be so intimate.

Wild Child did love peppermints, and thought of me as his personal Pez dispenser. For a peppermint he could put on the sweetest expression, fleeting though it was. Between the grooming and the peppermints, I think he saw me as a servant, and sometimes a member of his herd, but never his master. He would never be *my* horse the way Winsome was.

I finished up with the brushes and then carefully sprayed his tail with de-tangler, combed out his mane and tail, and oiled his hooves.

I had put on the polos when Deb arrived.

She gave a loud wolf whistle and Wild Child's ears swiveled forward as she yelled to him. "Hey, Hunk!"

Deb walked up and handed Wild Child a peppermint and rubbed his face while he took it. She gave him a vigorous wither scratching, raising dander and dust where I had made him slick and shining.

I shook my head. "There goes my great grooming job."

"Sorry, Lizzy. Hey, let's have some fun this week. I mean if we are going to get left behind we might as well."

I grinned. "Sure. I'm looking forward to it."

"Come watch my ride and be my ground person, and I'll return the favor when you ride Winsome."

"Cool."

So I headed to the indoor with Deb.

As usual, Deb had to light a fire under him. Wild Child was never exactly a "volunteer" for the hard work of dressage. But once he had his blood pumping he was an impressive sight.

Within about ten minutes of warm up rising trot, Deb was ready to put him through his paces.

"Hey, I want you to watch his canter half passes. Let me know if you think I have them too quick and hectic. I've been trying to get them quicker and more in front of me, but I may have gone overboard."

I watched Deb set him up out of the corner, and they started great. Deb had improved them and they had a much better jump up into the air.

"Wow, Deb. He looks much better."

With each step though, he seemed tenser and less elastic in the canter, his hind legs stepping short and too close together.

"See what happens?"

I yelled back at her. "Yeah, but at least now he's not throwing himself to the side like he used to do."

Deb pulled up. "He keeps me on my toes. I need a new plan."

I pressed my lips together and mulled over it a moment before speaking. "Seems to me that within the movement you need to be able to relax him, maybe even stretch his neck down, because you've basically lost the relaxation in his back."

Deb was nodding. "Yeah, but without losing his balance which was the problem in the first place."

My brain was in gear. "Margot always says that half pass and haunches in are the same exercise, but that haunches in has the support of the wall and half pass is performed on the diagonal line without the support of the wall. The wall supports the balance."

I could tell Deb was following my train of thought; she slowly drew out her reply. "Ye-ah."

I was rolling. "So what if, just as an exercise, you did canter haunches in along the wall, ask for more collection, and if he gets tight in his back you lower the neck to release the tension in his back, letting the wall act as support?"

Deb grinned. "You're smart, Lizzy. Let me try it."

So Deb began working in canter, shifting Wild Child into haunches in as soon as she left a corner. Then she experimented. She tried collecting the canter and then dropping his neck within the exercise, and then rode longer steps. At the end of each long side she straightened him and then rode through the short side.

I could tell she was concentrating hard, and Wild Child was working hard, too.

She changed direction, and the other way was even a little harder, and Wild Child did get tense and short in the steps on occasion.

Deb pulled him up with a pat and dug a peppermint out of her pocket before taking a walk break.

"That was a good one, Lizzy. I think he just needs to get stronger. I think he was avoiding the hard work before and now I won't let him and he gets tired and when he gets tired he tenses up, but I'm proud of how hard he is trying. I like your thought process though; you'll be a trainer yet."

I was speechless for a moment. Deb had just called me a trainer...well, a someday trainer.

Deb gave him a big pat on his shoulder and slid off. "Have you ever sat on him?"

"Just once..." Deb and I stared at each other, remembering my very close call.

"You need to sit on him again...and this time really ride him. You've earned it."

I looked over my shoulder. No one was around. I'd already pushed my luck on Johnny, but I was terribly tempted.

"Can I? Just to feel his gaits?"

Deb made a sly smile that made dimples appear and creased the corners of her eyes.

"Sure. Why not? Here, borrow my helmet."

Then Deb began to lengthen the stirrups.

"Maybe two holes?"

I was a lot taller than Deb.

Deb put her hip next to mine. "Probably."

I slipped on Deb's slightly damp helmet. It fit perfectly. Then I took the reins of Wild Child, the God of horses, and made my offering of a peppermint before mounting.

When I put my foot in the stirrup he tipped his head to have a look at me out of his left eye. I apologized, "Yup. Sorry, Wild Child. But, this time it's just for fun."

I stared down at his thick crest, the one that had lifted me up and held me on that crazy scary night, and then I patted his bright copper mane, the same mane I had gripped for dear life. But today my hand was flat and open. I didn't even have on my gloves. He was just as magnificent from this view as he was from the ground. I walked him over to where I could have a good look in the mirror of his entire profile.

I turned to look at Deb and she laughed. "I know, he's a hunk, but don't just stare at him in the mirror, make him move his big ass around."

I took up my reins and began to trot. Margot was right. He wasn't so easy on the body. In fact, I would say that anyone who could sit his trot would definitely develop six pack abs. His back moved a lot and I was lucky my stomach was empty.

But I pulled up my ribcage and sat a little more on the back of my bottom and we made a cadenced collected trot across the arena.

Deb hollered. "How's he feel?"

"Nothing like I imagined!"

"Are you nervous?"

"I'm fine as long as Francesca's not here."

And as I passed Deb she said, "Oh, hey Francesca!"

I just laughed.

Until I came back around.

Francesca really was standing next to Deb, and her arms were crossed.

I abruptly pulled up with a flash of hot panic hitting my veins. Francesca and I locked eyes for a moment. "Lizzy, I don't remember asking you to ride *all* my Grand Prix horses."

Deb tipped her head to look at Francesca, a little puzzled, but she wasn't going to let it stop the ride. "I just wanted to see how Wild Child reacted to Lizzy before I put you up."

I was too stunned to know what to think, but Deb wasn't going to give me time. She turned her attention back to me. "Make some shoulder in and long half passes; I want you to save some horse for Francesca."

I picked him back up, but the magic was gone. But I did what Deb asked, listening hard for whatever Francesca and Deb were saying to each other, but not being able to catch the words.

I did enough to satisfy Deb and walked over to receive what I expected would be a complete dressing down from Francesca. But it didn't come. She was eerily silent. I slid down and found another now sticky peppermint deep in my breeches pocket and gave Wild Child a face rub, which he tolerated.

Deb turned to Francesca. "OK, the opening act is over, your turn now. Now that we know he won't put you in the sand!"

Francesca didn't hesitate. Her face was stern with resolve.

"One hole down please, Lizzy."

I changed the stirrup while Deb held onto Wild Child, and as I ducked under his neck to go to the other side, I caught Deb's eye and she winked at me.

Once Francesca was up, Deb was all business and stayed just steps away from Wild Child and Francesca, keeping them on a circle around her. Neither of us trusted Wild Child to be generous to his owner. He cared nada about who paid his bills.

Wild Child, to my surprise, did not try to kill Francesca. In fact he deflated and was as lazy as could be. I could see that Francesca could barely make him move and was struggling hard to sit his trot. Wild Child was smart. He read Francesca as weak enough to be no kind of threat to him, but also no one he needed to mind.

But soon, Deb took the whip away from Francesca and led Wild Child over to the arena kickboards, right in front of the mirrors, where she proceeded to take back control of Wild Child, asking him to do piaffe steps (his specialty). Francesca could see herself in the mirrors and her face, still stern with concentration, also had a look of contentment.

When Francesca got off, Deb was beaming a big dimpled smile.

"I'll bet you never thought you'd get to ride Wild Child. But, I figure, you pay all his bills. You ought to get to sit on your own Grand Prix stallion, and with Margot away this was your chance. Margot protects you. She would be too afraid you would get hurt. But I know you wanted to sit on him, at least once."

Francesca looked thoughtful. She was buying it. "I appreciate that, Deb, and I do admire him, but you can have the ride. I don't envy you having to sit him. I see why Margot's given the ride away to you. You need a young back to manage all that motion. And I agree, Margot would not approve of you giving pony-rides on him."

Deb gave Francesca the same impish smile she had given me. "I won't tell if you don't. You and Lizzy both deserved having a feel of the ride, and it didn't hurt the big guy. Not a bit."

Francesca raised her eyebrow and pursed her lips. But then she nodded. "Well, put him away so I can have my ride on Lovey. I thought I would let Lizzy be my ground person today. It's good practice for her." And she turned and left.

Deb shook her head and gave me a slap on my back. "You seem to have gotten a promotion. I was supposed to teach Francesca today."

I was still trying to figure out what had just happened. "How the heck did you just pull that off?"

"You didn't hear me? It was an easy fix. I bought her silence with a ride on Wild Child. Wasn't he a lamb?"

"I heard you all right. You piled it high and deep and she bought it."

"Naw, I doubt it, Francesca is no dummy. She badly wanted a ride on Wild Child, that's all. I dangled it out there and she went for it. You did, too, by the way."

Deb didn't seem to notice that "old shark face" behind her was wrinkling his nostrils and looking quite disgusted by all of us. He nimbly reached over and nipped Deb on her thigh. "Ow!"

Deb swung her fist and missed, since he had immediately scurried backward, knowing what was coming.

I couldn't help but laugh. Wild Child knew exactly who to blame for the "pony rides."

Later on, after I groomed Lovey and handed him off to Francesca, it was time to change hats and head to the arena to be her ground person.

Francesca was trotting around on Lovey looking like less of a rider than she did on Johnny Cash. It wasn't Lovey's fault. He was petite and sweet, a plain bay with large soulful eyes set in a wide forehead with tiny pointed ears and a small brown velvet nose. He was the perfect horse for a small junior ... or a timid senior. It was not only his size, but it was because his gaits were not huge, and he never did a naughty thing. In fact, it would kill him to think he had done something wrong. He was what was often called a "packer."

I knew in Francesca's mind she was already finished with Lovey. She had moved on to her heartthrob Johnny, a huge bright chestnut, tricked out with white on every limb and a huge blaze on his face. Johnny was as big and flashy as Lovey was small and plain. Johnny had "bling."

I sat watching quietly. But Francesca wasn't having it. She trotted by and spoke as she passed. "Lizzy, for God's sake, wake up!"

I jumped to my feet as if I was going to salute or something, but my face was burning. Francesca had once again put me in a tough spot. I studied her seriously and wondered how much honesty she really wanted. I drew a deep breath. Time to test the water. "OK. You want me to correct your position? Because that's what I've been wanting to do for ages."

Francesca pulled up and turned in her saddle to glare. "Let's get this straight. I expect respect, although I rarely get it, but I also expect you to develop a professional attitude. You are here to become a professional, I presume."

Oddly, I felt calm when I replied. "Yes."

"Well then, be sure that what you say is said in a professional way, and that it is said only in my best interest. Any catty teenager ringside can tear riders apart. The professional knows how to make a rider better."

Francesca said the words, but Margot's voice echoed in my head. She had been the one who had spoken those exact words to me in the past, and I had just repeated them to myself yesterday. We were both parroting our instructor. I nodded. "Yes. You are right, and I apologize. "

Francesca gathered her reins back up. But I stopped her. "Wait. I think you should drop your stirrups."

Francesca threw the reins petulantly back down on Lovey's neck, and began pulling her stirrup leathers down from under the buckle guard then crossed them carefully in front of the saddle across Lovey's neck.

She looked pissed ... but she did it.

As she began trotting around, I tried my best to channel Margot, using her calm tone of voice, only omitting her "darlings". "Lower your center of gravity. That means letting go of all your negative tension. Tension, or any kind of stiffness, draws you up away from the horse. Shoulders need to hang lower. Hands lower ... let go of all the holding you do in your shoulders. It makes you carry your hands too high. Keep the classical line from the bit to the elbow. You tend to break the line upward. Relax back onto your buttocks instead."

I had crossed my arms and tilted my head. I was seeing some small changes. I kept going. "You have to let go and ride from relaxation and confidence. Lovey won't make a bad step. You have to trust Lovey. Now or never, Francesca."

Then I heard a whisper at my elbow. "Shit. Fools rush in where Angels fear to tread. Are you nuts?" It was Deb, shaking her head in disbelief.

I whispered back to her. "She asked for it."

"She doesn't really mean it."

I could see Francesca was still gripping with her knees. I called out, "Francesca, grab the pommel if you need to for a moment, so you can stop gripping with your knees. Pull them away from the saddle for a second. Let go! That tension is what wears you flat out."

Deb was looking at me, shaking her head again and smiling. "Who *ARE* you?"

Francesca couldn't take anymore and picked up the canter and headed across the diagonal, performing a line of sloppy tempi changes.

This time I shut up because I could see she was embarrassed that Deb had seen her working on something so basic as her sitting trot position.

I whispered back to Deb. "You think there's no hope?"

Deb looked at me and frowned. "None whatsoever. There is a line she just won't cross. To go there she'd have to be brave. Sometimes you just have to be brave. You gotta' leap through that ring of fire into the unknown. You gotta' be a little crazy to do it though, right? With horses you have to be willing to lose control to get control. I don't see Francesca loosening her grip on control. Nope. Not for a second. There is way too much deep-seated fear there."

And with that she slapped me on the back. "But hey, go for it!"

And that did give me something new to consider. Francesca was afraid. She was usually so busy scaring the hell out of the rest of us that I never thought of her as fearful.

But the truth about bullies was that they strike first because they are scared. But that didn't mean that a bully wasn't dangerous. I still knew Francesca could be dangerous because she still held all the power. I briefly considered that many dangerous dogs as well as horses were called "fear-aggressive." Those thoughts tempered the rest of the lesson. I became much more self-conscious. At the end of the session, Francesca asked me what I thought, and I told her she had finished looking much more "seated."

And, though Francesca considered me a full-time peon and some-time pain, she seemed pleased at the compliment. I sadly thought to myself that Francesca probably didn't get many compliments. Everyone here rode better than Francesca. That was just a fact.

Later, Deb gave me a great lesson on Winsome. And then we picked up Nat and headed to lunch. Of course, we didn't even think to invite Francesca along. And although I didn't mention it to either of them, I felt guilty. I knew if I had suggested it they both would have been shocked. We did not consider Francesca our friend and we excluded her without a thought.

Francesca was right; we neither respected her nor liked her. In fact, we loved to hate her. Making barbed comments about Francesca was a generally agreed upon pastime for the three of us. Ryder, to her credit, was the only one who usually did not join in.

*** 

I made my way to Claire's barn early. I had the evening barn chores to do since Ryder was in Kentucky and the horses would have to eat a little late, but I didn't want them to be too late.

Besides, it gave me time to warm up Johnny again. The day was warm and the air was still.

Johnny was happy and loose again today. He didn't do any of his dragon snorts. I even snuck in a little piaffe before Francesca sauntered over. She seemed more relaxed. I think she had felt successful in our lesson, and of course she had sat on Wild Child. It had already been quite a day.

Her voice was almost friendly. "Save some for me, Lizzy."

"Hey, Francesca. He's ready for you."

"Yes, I see that."

I hopped off and reset the stirrups. But once Francesca hopped on she immediately pulled the buckle down and crossed her stirrups.

I nodded at her and tried not to smile. "It helped didn't it?"

"Actually it was easier without them."

"That's great, Francesca. I think it's going to help keep you from getting so fatigued. You've got to ride in relaxation or you aren't going to make it through a Grand Prix test."

Francesca sniffed. "I'll probably regret this tomorrow."

"I have some Advil in my purse. God knows I live on the stuff."

"Yes, well, I expect you would, what with all the times I've caught you sitting in my flower beds."

Touche', Francesca. We both laughed.

And so we began.

Francesca was scowling and visibly sweating as she tried to begin work on the canter zigzags. Johnny knew the drill and was basically trying to do them for her, but she still managed to screw them up. Since I had seen Deb and Margot strategically work their way through the exercise (and Francesca had been there too, but seemed to forget it all now that she was riding), I stopped her to try to help her review it. "Hey, don't you remember how Margot broke this exercise down? Now it's your turn to do the same thing."

"Lizzy, just say what you mean."

I took a deep breath and channeled Margot. I even heard Margot in my head and simply had to repeat her. "Don't do the pattern from the test until you have control over each piece of the exercise. After the first half-pass, focus on being straight on centerline. You can't make a flying change if he's crooked, and you can't half-pass until you have made a straight change. The key is straight, straight, straight. Don't worry about the count yet. You can't expect to speed things up until you have more control over the balance. Remember Wild Child."

Francesca stared at me silently. I was rolling like I knew what I was talking about. I only had the kind of knowledge one gets from watching and listening. Doing was another matter entirely. I knew that. I was confident though that my words were the right ones because they weren't mine. "Ride toward the mirrors, quarter line to quarter line, and don't count. Just work on having him straight in and out of the flying changes."

Francesca picked up her reins and set her jaw and put Johnny together in a collected canter. She turned down centerline toward the mirrors. My arms were crossed and my head tipped as I continued to channel Margot.

And it was better.

"Sleep on that, Francesca. They'll be even better tomorrow."

Francesca couldn't see it, but I was incredibly impressed…with myself. I had just improved her riding. Without trying, without knowing, I was learning to teach. Margot had given me that, and Deb had given me that, and Marco had given me that, and of course the horses were always the ones to give the final exams. It was a brief moment of realization that maybe it was something I could become good at.

Francesca quietly put her stirrups back down and stretched Johnny out in rising trot, just like we always ended our lessons with Margot.

When she got off and handed Johnny back to me she looked really stiff, but happy. But she laughed and then said. "Quite a good impression of Margot, by the way. *Darling.*" She kissed Johnny on his muzzle, and sashayed toward the parking lot.

I wondered if she realized it was the best compliment she could have given me. Even if she knew that I had done as well as I had by calling up my "inner-Margot."

She turned and walked backward for a few steps, remembering something she wanted to say. "Lizzy. I've entered a show. I only need two scores at Grand Prix over 60% for my Gold medal. Margot will be in Texas the same weekend of the show, coaching Emma, so we can easily slip away."

She didn't wait for a reply, but turned back around and continued toward the parking lot.

I was rooted to the spot. It was too soon, way too soon. What was she thinking? I was going to need more than an "inner-Margot" to help her pull that off.

# 9. Walk It Off

*Frank Cavelli was coming down the barn aisle carrying a 25-pound* bag of carrots under each arm like they were weightless. Chess was trailing at his heels in his Dad's ample shadow with a small white paper bag in one hand and talking to the back of his Dad's head. Frank seemed to be ignoring him. I saw Frank's face visibly brighten when he saw me. "Lizzy, baby!"

And I felt the same way seeing his large frame lumbering toward me. I smiled broadly as he sang out to me. "The carrot express has arrived. Make room in the fridge."

I couldn't even see Chess now as he stood directly behind his Dad. "Wow, Frank. That's a lot of carrots."

"I am just following orders. Francesca says Papa is not allowed any grain and bored out of his mind and carrots are the only thing keeping him quiet."

I hurried ahead of him into the tack room and opened up the fridge, pulling open the crisper drawer. "That is so nice of you, Frank. Let's see what we can fit in here."

Frank put the bags on the floor in the tack room and I began ripping open the plastic on the first bag. I pulled out a gigantic carrot and took a bite. It was incredibly sweet and I think I sighed and closed my eyes for a second as I chewed and then took another bite. I exclaimed, "Good ones!" I realized then how hungry I was.

Frank's eyebrows shot up. "Whoa, slow down there, Lizzy. Don't you ever eat?"

I suddenly felt self-conscious. "Oh, yeah, sure I do, but Frank, these are the organic ones. They're much sweeter than the regular ones. You should try one."

I could see Chess was still standing behind his Dad, seeming to be finishing a conversation his Dad had already left. "Dad, I don't think you are listening, we've got to talk about the findings from the audit."

Frank shot his son a sideways glance. "Don't hoard the goodies, Chess. Look at poor Lizzy here. She's been forced to subsist on the horse's carrots."

Chess suddenly looked down at his little white paper bag, almost startled to find it. He looked embarrassed; his Dad after all had just been hauling fifty pounds of carrots. He handed it to his Dad.

I turned back to unloading carrots, slightly uncomfortable on two counts. For one I wanted to finish the carrot that was now discarded on the floor. Those first little bites had been a tease, and my stomach was grumbling for more. They really were exceptionally good carrots.

In addition, Frank had innocently hit too close to home. I tried to focus on unloading the carrots. The whole fridge would soon be packed with carrots, but I knew we'd go through them fast with Papa eating carrots for every meal and because I had indeed been helping myself to them.

It wasn't exactly a joke to me that I did take carrots from the horses to supplement my groceries. More than once I had made a meal from steamed carrots. I felt a little guilty, but only a little. Sometimes I ate their peppermints, too. And I had been known to hoard a slightly dirty handful of sugar cubes in my pocket for dropping in to my coffee or tea cup later. To be honest, if it weren't for Deb's cooking and what I snitched from the barn, I probably wouldn't be eating very well. Of course, Mom still sent a regular "care" box filled with goodies and a small check here and there when she could manage it. Thank God for Mom. I guess between all of my "sources" I managed OK.

I was also embarrassed to witness the Cavelli men fussing at each other. I wasn't sure what was going on but I sensed it was about money. The Cavelli's were rich; I guessed they wouldn't begrudge me a few of their carrots, and Frank was always thoughtfully bringing gifts of food. I think I was one of his favorite charities.

I suppose I should be used to being surrounded by extreme wealth by now. Except in moments like this, it usually didn't dampen my enjoyment of everyday life. Winsome and I were damn lucky to be here at all, I understood that, and I never minded working long or hard. But the saying that the rich are different was indeed true.

I think I had come to the place where I did not feel "less" when I was around very attractive or well-dressed people, even as I could still feel envy. And I was smart enough that I felt pretty good engaging anyone in conversation without feeling stupid. But even though I knew there were people out there with far less than I, I knew I was never going to be these people's equal. I would always have more in common with Natalie, who loved to spout her socialist slogans, than I would with the Cavelli family.

I understood that money did not make you any better than anyone else. But it gave you freedom. It gave you options. It gave you power. I would never trade my passion for horses for a passion for money. And yet. And yet. My lack of funds was a keenly felt discomfort that in this setting of wealth would never fade. I wanted to be here so I would just have to find a way to live with my damned insecurity.

Frank handed me the little white paper bag. I knew exactly where it had come from. Peapack had a wonderful bakery. Good old Frank.

He gave his son a slap on the back, as if to show him that this was the way you treated your employees, and to shut up already about the audit.

Frank said, "Lizzy… I stopped by the bakery. I bought the store out of lemon squares, and I only ate one myself, which required a tremendous amount of self-control. It will go straight to this big old spare tire around my middle, but I know you girls will burn it off and then some. But you can't live on lemon squares and carrots alone."

Frank's eyebrows shot up in mock exasperation. "What am I to do with you?"

Natalie would have blurted out "pay us better." But not me. Not to Frank. I took the bag and peered in, inhaling the sweet smell of lemon and powdered sugar.

"Oh Frank, these smell divine! It's sweet of you to bring us treats. I'll make sure that Deb and Nat get theirs."

He smiled at me sweetly. "I'll bring you girls steaks next time."

Just then Francesca walked in. Her presence always made me sit up straighter, sure she would put me in detention, or make me run laps or drop and do pushups. And she did run her eyes over me disapprovingly. I scrambled to my feet and closed the fridge door.

She had a different effect on her husband. They clearly had permission to break any rule with each other. I say this because Frank routinely swept her up in his arms with her protesting only half-heartedly. Today was no different. He was beaming at the sight of her. "Ah, there is the woman of my dreams!"

Frank took her manicured hand with drama and pressed it to his lips, inhaling deeply, and not releasing her hand afterward. I did notice the smallest of squeezes returned from Francesca. But otherwise she appeared unmoved and was soon all business.

Chess crossed his arms and rolled his eyes at me. You'd think he would be used to their performances.

Francesca was looking at the unopened bag of carrots still on the floor. "Only one? I asked for two bags."

"One is already unloaded my pet, and I 'm ready for my next assignment. I was thinking of stocking this fridge with a few other items."

Francesca was about to answer but Chess interrupted. "Mom, why haven't you answered my texts?"

Francesca shrugged her shoulders. "I don't look at my phone all day like you kids."

That wasn't going to put him off. "So, Mother, why is Two Left Feet, LLC sending us invoices for 'services rendered?' I can't back up a deduction with a loose description like that. And then there are bills from Texas. Do we *even know* anyone in Texas?"

Francesca gestured to Chess with a jerk of her chin toward me and turned her back. I focused on tearing open the second bag. But even with the whispering I heard every word.

"Chess, Emma has one of our young horses in Texas to train, show, and sell for us. I thought you knew that, but then again, you haven't taken any interest in the horses since you had that crush on Emma." It was almost like listening to Ryder, turning a defense into an offense.

Chess must have been mortified, and I felt for him. What bad luck to have Francesca as your mother. Yikes she could turn the knife. She was good. Chess shut up, and I realized she had never explained the invoices from 'Two Left Feet" the humorous name that was set in a brass plaque in the stone gates of Claire Winston's farm.

I knew those were Johnny Cash's board bills. And I also knew that I couldn't say anything about it.

Then she turned her back to her son too, their interview over. She and Frank started talking about tickets to the ballet. Chess shook his head, walked over to me, squatted down and reached into the second bag of carrots, silently handing me fistfuls. We filled up another crisper drawer and then the meat drawer. Then we left the remaining carrots in the torn bag, stuffing them onto a shelf. Chess stood up and offered his hand to give me a lift. "Here."

I took his hand and it was surprisingly strong with a firm grip and a tug that propelled me onto my feet. "Thanks."

He gave a little nod. And he held my hand and my eye. A funny buzz started in my fingertips and ran all the way down my arm and into my chest, which seemed to suddenly tighten. He still had my hand. I cut my eyes over to Francesca. I noticed she and Frank had stopped talking and were both looking at us. I pulled my fingers through his grip. The idea flashed in my head that Chess had just used me to take a stab at his Mother who would not approve of Chess fraternizing with the help. Well, well. Someone else could switch from defense to offense.

I dropped my hand and awkwardly wiped it off on the backside of my breeches. Francesca was staring at me now. I looked down at the floor and noticed my half eaten carrot, which I picked up. I was ready to receive my demerits when she asked, "Lizzy, have you taken Papa out yet for his walk?"

I drew myself up and forced myself to make eye contact. "Nope. Last thing left to do."

Francesca held my gaze, no flinching on either side.

"Well, get it done."

I answered pleasantly while muddling over her relationship with her son in my mind, which I imagined had to be toxic. "Sure thing."

I had to walk around both Francesca and Frank to get to the door and even though I was making a beeline, I could see Francesca cut her eyes to Frank with a grim look on her face, her mouth drawn tight with the corners turned down.

God, how I knew and hated that look. I had a feeling that Chess was going to get a piece of her mind as soon as I was out the door. On the one hand, it was a nice feeling to have a bit of male attention. I

missed Marco. And I knew in my heart that by now Marco had someone new. Well, someone new seemed to be interested in me, too.

That somebody, however, was the bitchy boss lady's son. Not good.
No way would I want to have to spend any additional time with that
dysfunctional family, even with the wonderful Frank around. The very
idea was creepy. So, I needed to nip the whole idea in the bud. Besides,
I think perhaps I had just been used as a walk on player in the Cavelli
drama. Blech.

Or maybe he really was attracted to me. Now there was an idea I
had to admit was a balm to my soul. To catch him looking at me with
that sort of interest, and feel the little buzz of his touch was well … nice.
Take that, Francesca. You may not think much of me; your hired help,
but your son does. The little incident preoccupied me while I fed Papa
my half eaten carrot. I slid into his stall and silently ran the chain
through the inside ring of his halter, up and over the nose piece, snapping it to the far side ring. Papa nervously munched his carrot but his
eye was on the half open stall door.

"Whoa, buddy." As soon as I slid the door all the way open, he
bounded out of the stall. I needed to come back to reality and pay
attention to my job. I grunted at him. "NO, NO, NO!" I had my right
elbow pushed into his shoulder and pulled his head toward my chest.
His big bay body loomed over me. I was land skiing sideways down the
barn aisle, steering blindly toward the indoor, leaning back on my heels
and hanging on with all my might as we crabbed sideways in a sort of
prancing jog trot. The indoor arena had two heavy half doors with kick
boards on the inside. I was determined to get the hell inside that arena
and close up the doors so if he did somehow get loose, he couldn't go
far. But I also was determined that Papa would not get loose from me,
no matter what, not on my watch.

He spurted into the arena. Whoosh. And then spun around to face
me when I dug in my heels.

"C'mon, Papa, whoa. Play nice. I just need to get these doors shut. Be a good boy."

Papa's ears pricked forward. His eyes were shining bright.

"That's my boy." I reached for the first door. "Easy. It's OK."

He reached his neck toward me and gave a little snort as I pulled the door slowly toward him. Normally something like closing the arena doors would be a nothing event. But Papa was frustrated with his new sedentary life and I could see him looking for a reason to blow off steam. I pulled a sugar cube out of my pocket.

"Here, see. No biggie."

He took the sugar cube, but with a distracted air. And it fell out of his mouth. And then I slowly pulled the second door shut. Papa ducked to the left, ready to bolt, but I was ready for him, and blocked him with my right hand up by his left eye.

I yelled at him. "NO!"

I then tugged on the chain shank hard. Wrong move. He stood straight up in the air. I was looking at his belly button. He seemed to stay up in the air a long time, and the shank was pulled all the way through my grip to its end, where I had tied a knot, thank goodness. I suddenly understood the saying of being at "the end of my rope." The knot was all I had, and it was barely there but digging into the last joint of my index finger.

The pain was sharp and fueled my irritation at him. "Papa, damn it get down here!"

Papa was a massive horse who could easily have gone bye-bye right that moment. But he landed his rear and stood there blinking at me with worry wrinkles over his wide eyes and with his ears pricked at me, looking very concerned. I just had to shake my head as I gathered myself and got reorganized. This hand walking business was getting dangerous. Horses were dangerous. I was shaking but I gritted my teeth and began marching around the kickboards with a prancing strung out massive fire-breathing monster at my side. It was like he had overdosed on some kind of speed.

I tried cooing to him. "C'mon, big guy, we'll get through this together. Walk it off, man, walk it off, walk it off."

I was leaning against his shoulder with my elbow, and he in turn was leaning against me. So, I did a "Natalie." I started singing.

*"Lean on me, when you're not strong, and I'll be your friend, I'll help you carry on, for it won't be long 'till I'm gonna ' need somebody to lean on. "*

I found the tune began to flow in my head, and more lyrics started coming back to me.

*"Sometimes in our lives, we all have pain; we all have sorrow, but if we are wise, we know that there's always tomorrow."*

That was all I could remember, so I just started belting out the chorus again. I began to settle, and then Papa began to settle, too. Pretty soon we stopped leaning on each other, and Papa's eye began to soften, his muscles relax, and he went from looming over me to walking beside me.

I just kept walking and walking and singing the same little bit over and over until I was too out of breath to continue. And then it just seemed incredibly quiet in the indoor. I began to tune into the noisy chirping of the little birds that flitted in and out. I never noticed before how many of them there were; it was like they were singing their little hearts out, too. Finally Papa and I stopped walking and just stood and listened. He felt safe enough to take him back outside where I let him crop grass and in the quiet I began to spot bunnies again, and up on the hill, by Deb's, deer brazenly stood grazing on the other side of the pasture fencing from the weanlings where the grass was rich from being unmolested by the horses.

By the time I got Papa safely back to his stall, I realized my finger was throbbing and pinkish and swollen. I also think it looked a tiny bit crooked at the end, but maybe I was imagining that. I went to the tack room and put some ice in a zip lock baggie and wrapped it around my finger, securing it with about half a roll of bright red vet-wrap, and then took some ibuprofen. It looked like some kid of freakish cast. That would have to do for now.

When I stepped out into the barn aisle, Francesca was waiting for me. "Lizzy, I'll be out to ride Johnny a little late today, but while you wait for me I want you to memorize the Grand Prix test."

I could tell she was in a foul mood. Maybe she and Chess had that unpleasant meeting I had predicted. I was cautious when I answered.

"Sure. Why?"

"Well, the weekend that Margot is in Texas for Emma's first CDI, there is a small horse show nearby."

Oh no, the horse show idea again. She couldn't be serious. I answered cautiously. "Okay."

Before I panicked I considered other possibilities. Maybe she wasn't going to enter. Maybe she would go as a non-compete and get a feeling for what Johnny was like away from his home farm. Maybe it was a recon mission where she could go watch the show; maybe check out the scoring of the Grand Prix. She did need to see what it took to score a 60%. The possibilities went through my head in a flash. But I said nothing. She hesitated a beat, and then continued. "…So I thought we'd take Johnny."

I blurted it out. "As a non-compete, right?"

She drew out the word. "Nooooooo."

She wasn't going to watch and learn. She wasn't going to take Johnny as a non-compete. The words, 'too soon, too soon' rang out inside my head like a chant. I blurted out. "Francesca, that's in like what, two weeks?"

Francesca lifted her eyebrows. "Time waits for no one, Lizzy."

Maybe she couldn't get in at such short notice. Yeah. That was probably true. Closing dates for entries were usually about four weeks ahead. I tried to sound casual. "I'm sure the closing date has passed."

Francesca made a twisted smile. "I made a phone call. We are entered."

She looked so satisfied, I mumbled back. "Oh."

Then she was narrowing her eyes, as if I was trying to get out of work or something. "So, memorize the test."

I didn't know how to say what I was thinking in a tactful manner. All I got out of my mouth was her name. "Uh, Francesca."

That was enough. She got it. "Lizzy, the reason I have this horse is to earn my Gold medal. And I know none of you think I am capable, but the point is, it is your job to help me do just that. Did I choose the wrong girl for the job?"

I sure as hell didn't want her exchanging me for Ryder. No way. I looked her straight in the eye, my voice soft. "No."

Francesca did not smile, she just curtly nodded. "Well, then. We start this afternoon, memorize that test."

And I tried to show the same businesslike manner. "Sure. Got it."

And then she seemed to notice my red vet wrap monstrosity. And her expression was more irritation than concern. "And for God's sake what is that, that, blob of vet-wrap doing on your hand?"

A sarcastic voice spoke inside my head, something about her strong maternal instinct, but I tried to sound matter of fact. "I hurt my finger."

Francesca was shaking her head, exasperated. "Do you need to go to the hospital?"

I shook my head, "No."

Francesca made a little sniffing sound. "Well then. Good. You'll need to take that thing off. You certainly can't groom or tack or ride in that get-up."

And she was on her way.

# 10. Lighten Up, Lizzy

*Deb came down for her ride on Wild Child. She stood by the cross ties,* putting a braid in her hair, winding the elastic round and round the end, and then flipping it over her shoulder before putting on her helmet. She gave me a breezy smile; her dimples on show, making her look mischievous. "Lizzy, let's screw dressage today."

I answered a bit warily, "What?"

"Go get your mare and let's go for a nature ride."

I smiled. This was classic Deb. Margot had made a schedule for us, but Deb was her own woman. One thing about Deb though, she was never dull, and there was always something to be gained by going with her flow. So I answered, "Why not?"

I ran and got Winsome while Deb plopped down in a chair. I gave Winsome "a lick and a promise," shaking the shavings out of her tail. Wild Child craned his neck around and gave her a wistful little "huh-huh-huh" with quivering nostrils. She wrinkled her nose and pinned her ears with a little twist of her head barging forward in her set of cross ties and emitting a high pitched squeal that made me step back and cover my ears.

Deb laughed. "Wild Child, don't even think about it, buddy. You make a move on her and she'll smack you into next Tuesday."

I was really surprised at Winsome. "Wow, Deb, I've never seen her so aggressive."

Deb was looking at Winsome and nodding in approval. "Mares rule and the boys need to remember it or pay the price. Nature insures that mares only are bred when they are ovulating. Interesting isn't it? Not ovulating; not allowing that boy within a country mile."

I stopped to look at Deb, and I thought she was the most self-confident woman I had ever known. She should be, she was also one of the most talented horsewomen I had ever known. But then I thought that real horsewomen couldn't be weak in any sense of the word. We had to be the leader of flight animals who were a thousand pounds plus. We needed to be physically fit, and also able to create emotional stability in ourselves to be effective trainers of our horses. I nodded thoughtfully at Deb and her information. "That's amazing. I think we horsewomen are pretty tough-assed, too. I'd say we're all pretty much Alpha-mares here."

She laughed back at me. "Literally, tough-assed for sure."

Well, that cracked me up. "Yeah Deb, my ass has toughened up considerably since coming here, in more ways than one."

Deb smiled gently. "Yeah, tough-ass or not though, don't discount a good man when you find one. We get a little too much girl drama around here sometimes if you ask me, and the guys help balance out that energy."

"It's been peaceful since Ryder's been gone though. I've enjoyed the break."

I squatted down next to Winsome and put on her sport boots. Polos got too wet riding through the grass. I could see Deb was watching, and approved of my choice, even as our conversation stayed on point.

Deb said. "That break is over. They'll be back tonight and there won't be any celebrating. It didn't go so well down there."

I walked around to boot up Winsome's other side. I hadn't said anything to Deb about the championships, but I had been following the competition closely online. I had avoided exchanging any messages with Ryder though.

I sighed. "Yeah, I know. I've been watching on the USEF channel. No team medal. But Suzette got the individual bronze and was our saving grace. She looked good doing it, too."

Deb nodded. "You think that's going to put Ryder in a better mood?"

I only had to think about that an instant. "No. She's going to be eaten up imagining how she would have been on the top step of the podium."

I saddled Winsome and then slipped on her bridle. Once I got the bridle on she started bobbing her head up and down eagerly and I couldn't get the buckles done. "Be still...dang... let me get you buckled up."

I had to wrestle her to get the noseband done. When I let go of the reins to pull on my gloves and strap on my helmet, Winsome started off to the mounting block without me. Miraculously, she did not head toward the arena. I don't know how, but she knew where we were going. I found myself shouting at her. "Hey, wait up, mare!"

I ran to catch up with her while I heard Deb clip-clopping behind me laughing.

Winsome was ready to move. She was wiggly at the mounting block and as soon as I had swung up she was eagerly walking. Winsome never did like the electric gates, so I let Deb get them. I think Winsome would always be a bit of a spook. She did not like things that moved magically on their own like the gates. Going through the open gates she scampered with her tail clamped down like the devil was after her. It was a relief to get out onto the road.

Wild Child was quite brave about some things. He loved his hill work. He was basically lazy and it was a nice change from the arena that he seemed to find refreshing. Deb had really connected to who he was. She had a different way from Margot, and unlike Emma, who had worked very hard to be Margot's clone; Deb had her own distinctive style.

She did not have Margot's elegance or presence in the saddle, but the horses responded well to her free-spirited yet no-nonsense demeanor.

Deb and I walked the horses side by side along the shoulder of the road, headed for the always open gate that sagged on its hinges. It led to our favorite field.

She called over her shoulder. "Let's do a little piaffe-y trot!"

She gathered Wild Child with a shortening of her reins and a bit of leg-aid and asked for a forward going piaffe-like trot. Wild Child bounced out a few steps before deciding himself that he had done enough. Deb delivered a sharp kick and he bounced out a few more, shaking his ears in protest. Deb teased him. "C'mon, you big galoot, shake your tail feathers!"

Winsome did a little jig behind him and Deb smiled at us over her shoulder before going back to walk and dropping her reins. "That looked good, Lizzy."

We slipped through the gate and turned left, up the hill along the edge of the field. Deb turned and gave me my instructions. "Here we go…trotting warm up and then we'll do a canter set."

Deb and I took up our reins again, and then got up into our jumping positions, breaking into trot and letting the horses chug along. Both of the horses were strong, leaning into the bridles and blowing in puffs every other beat of the stride as we found a steady tempo. They knew the canter was coming and damn it but we were torturing them by making them wait for it.

I bridged my reins and leaned my knuckles on either side of Winsome's withers as we settled into a pace. Wild Child covered more ground that Winsome and she had to really move to stay with him.

I held her behind Wild Child's tail so she couldn't pass him. I marveled at the two chestnuts churning up the hillside. Winsome was a darker chestnut, liver as it was inelegantly called, and she had some black marks in her coat, too; her beauty spots. Some black hairs also ran through her wavy tail. Wild Child was a bright copper chestnut, but they were both "W" line Hanoverians, that went back to the same famous sire. You could see it, too. Although Wild Child was huge and masculine, and Winsome was petite and feminine. The arch of their necks, the shape of their faces, the slope of their hips, and even the set of their tails; they were the same. And the breathing! Such drama. Every other beat of the trot was an accented, puff, puff, puff. Sometimes it seemed like a relaxed drum beat, and sometimes it sounded like a fire breathing dragon had been set loose. Today they were dragons; beautiful chestnut dragons... and we were wizards clinging to their backs.

Deb looked over her shoulder at me, her cheeks were red. "Ready?"

I nodded. The horses leapt into canter. Our rhythm changed from a puff, puff, puff, every other beat to a deeper longer purring that trilled through their fluttering nostrils. The wind whipped tears from my eyes, and my calves heated up with fatigue as I pressed down into my heels. This never ceased to be thrilling.

The great thing about our hill was its length. It was long enough that we always ran out of horse before we ran out of hill, so there was never any worry about getting run away with. It was all thrill and no fear.

At the top of the hill our horses were spent. All I had to do was sit back down and Winsome walked. Wild Child stopped so abruptly I had to steer around his big orange behind. The horses were happy to stand quietly and catch some air, their sides heaving, pushing ribs against our legs.

I kicked my aching legs out of the irons and let them hang. This was a great spot to stand and admire the green, green hills of the garden state of New Jersey. The horses seemed to do the same. I could also admire the God of horses, Wild Child, while Deb admired my pretty little mare.

"You have to breed her someday, Lizzy. I can't help myself, I'm a horse breeder. She's too lovely to leave out of the gene pool."

Wild Child might have been tired, but he stopped staring across the hillside and looked again at Winsome, clearly sharing Deb's opinion. It was time to get them moving again.

We sauntered down the hill, relaxed and chatty.

Deb said, "You going to show her soon?"

Even the thought of showing again put a flutter in my belly. "I doubt it. Margot hasn't said anything to me."

I could tell Deb did not approve. She was matter of fact when she replied.

"I'm entering my first CDI with Wild Child. They have an open show, too. Enter."

It sounded like an order.

I wasn't sure as I replied, "Oh, I don't know, Deb. That's a big deal show. Shouldn't I do one of the smaller shows instead?"

"Don't be silly. It will be fun. Margot's taking Hotstuff. It will be his last outing before The Young Horse Finals in Chicago. We three could have a blast."

I still felt uncertain. "I guess it's up to Margot."

Deb smiled. "In that case, I'll see that you enter."

But then, of course, I thought of the expense. "I don't have the money."

Deb shook her head. "Don't let that stop you. The Cavellis should cover that, but it will take a nudge from Margot; Francesca can be so stingy. You've earned it, for God's sake. Lizzy, you have to be that tough-assed woman we were talking about. You've just got to ask for what you want."

And there came the dimples. Deb managed to be tough-assed and cute all at the same time.

"Thanks, Deb."

"And speaking of tough, how'd it go teaching Francesca?"

I felt myself shrink down in the saddle. "OK, I guess. She did a little better."

"Frankly, asking to have you help her kind of floored me. No offense, Lizzy, but maybe she asked because she can't stand taking orders from me."

Oh, how I wanted to dish to Deb all about Johnny Cash. I hated keeping secrets.

I sighed. "It's just that she knows she can boss me around. She gets pissy with me and she knows I'll take it."

Deb blew air through her nostrils and answered in a voice heavy with irony. "Pissy? No! Not Francesca. Must be you."

I chuckled, but then I remembered what I really needed to talk to Deb about. "I can handle Francesca's moods, but what I'm really nervous about is Papa. He almost killed me yesterday. I can't wait to hand him back to Ryder."

Deb shrugged. "Just drug him."

"You said that before, but that makes me even more nervous."

"There's probably a tube of the gel stuff in the fridge. It's safer for both of you that way and you don't have to give an injection or anything. If he's not tranq'ed he might jump around and re-injure himself, but if he doesn't move enough, the knitting fibers of the ligament won't align properly. Better safe than sorry."

I lifted my eyebrows. "Yeah, or dead."

Deb smiled at me like I was being silly. "Yeah. That, too."

But my finger still hurt, and I was thinking about how I had been looking at his belly and his big steel-clad hooves had been above my head and then came back to earth not too far from my head, and I wondered if I should also put on my helmet. No. Deb was right.

I asked, "How much do I give him?"

"Just read the label. Start with a smaller dose and then if he's still too bright give a little more."

It was time for me to learn to use drugs.

I nodded back. "OK."

So, not such a big deal I thought. I would get Lovey all ready, and then give Papa his little "cocktail" then while he was chilling out, I could teach Francesca. When they were done, Papa would be ready for his walk and I would live another day.

I found the tube of gel in the fridge, just like Deb said. And it was easy to give; you set a little ring on the tube and pushed it into his mouth under the tongue. No prob.

Francesca was terribly distracted on Lovey. This was our last Lovey session as Margot and Ryder would be back tonight. I was thinking probably the same thing she was, which was how in the world she was going to pull off a Grand Prix test on Johnny when she really wasn't competent riding Lovey.

But I kept that to myself.

And when I had Lovey put up, and went for Papa I was really disappointed. He didn't look at all sleepy. I put on his halter and he was already dragging me to the door, ready to bolt out into the barn aisle.

I dug in my heels and pulled him around to face me. "Papa! You are not going to do this to me again!"

My finger began throbbing just at the thought. I knew it would be at least two weeks before it felt normal again. No way was I going to let him injure another one of my fingers today. I had seen some older grooms with handfuls of bent fingers before. I was not going to allow that to be me. I unsnapped the shank and walked out.

Clearly I had not given him enough tranquilizer.

I got the tube back out and twirled the ring a couple more notches.

When I put it in his mouth and pushed in the plunger he flung his head up, tossing the tube across the stall.

"Papa!" I wasn't sure if anything had actually gotten into the horse. I was stuck. I had to search for the tube in the shavings. And when I picked it up I noticed the little ring was missing, and the plunger was pushed all the way into the tube casing.

"Oh man. How much of this stuff got in, Papa?"

I went out and threw the empty tube into the trash, cleaning Lovey's tack and sweeping the tack room, wiping down counter tops, taking out the trash, waiting for the drug to have time to take effect. I was pretty sure that Papa had flung his head up before I could fully depress the plunger. I was probably going to still have too much horse to walk.

But when I got to Papa's stall he was standing with his head low. "Papa?"

No response.

My face flushed. Oh my God. He got that whole tube.

I went into the stall and clipped on the shank and opened the stall door wide.

"C'mon, Papa. Can you even walk? I gave the shank a tug and he walked forward, swaying in his hips."

"Oh shit, shit, shit."

I unclipped the shank, sliding the door shut and ran to the tack room to get my cell phone and called Deb. Good old Deb came driving down the hill with Natalie in the passenger seat. I had trotted out to the front of the barn to meet them, relieved to see that Francesca's car was no longer in her parking spot.

"Deb, please tell me he'll be OK."

"Chill, Lizzy." she said, the voice of calm. "Let's go have a look."

Natalie was grinning. "Just say no to drugs, Lizzy."

I rolled my eyes at her. I couldn't laugh at her lame joke at that moment. For one thing, I was the last person to use drugs on a horse and she knew it. I reflexively defended myself. "It was Deb's idea. It's just at first it wasn't enough, and then, y' know, by accident it was too much."

Deb peeked into the stall, where Papa was standing with his head hanging down. Her voice was breezy. "Take the hay out of his stall and come have lunch with us."

My voice was shaky. "He's going to be OK?"

Natalie was peering over my shoulder and slapped my on the back. "Lighten up, Lizzy. It's no biggie."

I looked back to Deb for reassurance. She was still watching Papa.

"Well, you could probably do minor surgery on him now, but sure, he's no more drugged than if Doc was going to do a hock injection. Just let him wake up a bit and then hand walk him later."

I felt the anxiety drain from my body. "Oh man, I feel so much better now."

So, I headed out to lunch with Deb and Nat. When we sat down with our sandwiches, Nat reached into her backpack and pulled out something and placed it in the center of the table.

I let out a gasp. "You did it!"

I picked up a small metallic sculpture of a rabbit, one ear up and one ear down. The ears were made of some kind of gears, the body, which felt heavy in my hand, had once been a door knob. It was made of sundry pieces of scrap, but in my hand was a rabbit, at once delicate and sturdy, realistic yet fantastical.

"Oh my God, Natalie. He is lovely."

"The problem is he took me so long to make, and I had to start over and over again. I need better metalsmith skills. So, I found this guy who teaches at the local community college and he's been really helpful. I have a lot to learn."

"Are you going to sell them?"

"Yeah. Little shop down the road says she'll take as many as I can make on consignment. She'll get a percentage."

Deb looked proud. "I told Natalie that she has got to make horse sculptures next. I think there are way more horse art buyers out there than rabbit buyers."

I had to agree with Deb. I was a bit awestruck when I chimed in. "Nat, you know horses inside and out. I'll bet you could do amazing horses."

There was so much more to Natalie than met the eye. She was a good horsewoman, but I thought she was a great artist. And she was an original. I didn't know anyone else like her. Or maybe I did. She was tiny, like Deb, and cut from the same cloth. There was no wonder that the two had hit it off; they could have been sisters, and each had the heart and soul of an artist.

"I am awed by both of you. You both are artists."

Deb looked puzzled. "What the heck?"

"You guys are different kinds of artists, but both artists; brilliant."

Deb gently shook her head, but Nat smiled and looked down on her little rabbit that sat in the middle of the table. She was proud as she should be, and almost amazed, I thought, at her own little creation. She loved it, too. I could see that.

But Deb was shaking her head. "I am no artist, but I think Nat's going to be famous one day. And we can say we discovered her. She poked Nat on the arm. "Hey, Nat, you going to remember us when you are a celebrated artist?"

"Oh sure, I'll remember you. I won't hang out with you then, but I'll remember you." We all laughed. Nat reached out and gently touched the rabbit. "It's a nice dream isn't it? I hope one day I can support myself. Maybe even own my own horse again."

I laughed because, of course, the dream of being a famous artist did not mean anything if it did not mean horses. We three smiled at each other.

Natalie got serious then. And Natalie never got serious. "I owe you guys my life. I'm not kidding."

Natalie had gently peeled back a corner of a bandage over an old wound. We did not need to talk about it. But it made a bond between us. It was time to go.

When we got back, Deb and Nat walked with me to check on Papa. He was awake and nosing around his stall looking for his hay.

I was flooded with relief. "Oh thank God, Papa!"

Deb slapped me on the back. "See, he lived."

"I hope Francesca didn't come by."

Deb shook her head. "Doubtful. Even if she did, she never really looks at the horses."

Nat joined in. "You know our lips are sealed."

I gave a deep sigh. "Looks like I can take him for a walk now."

Deb said, "And don't be afraid to use the tranquilizer again, just y 'know, adjust the dosage. And don't add more dosage too fast, let it work first."

"For sure. Thanks."

And they left, and Papa and I had a totally safe and relaxed walk around the indoor. I even let him graze for twenty minutes afterwards. And then I realized tomorrow he would be Ryder's responsibility again and I would be off the hook. There was a bright spot to Ryder's return.

# 11. The Arrogance Of The Present

*It was late when Ryder came in, but I was wide awake. I was en-*grossed in one of Natalie's hand-me-down novels. How could I not be wide awake since the novel's brave heroine had just fought off would be rapists in the wilds of the Scottish Highlands. But I didn't get to stay in the Scottish Highlands. Ryder was stomping around so loudly that the scene in my head stopped and started and stopped again. At first I tried to ignore her, but no, she was now dragging stuff across the floor. It sounded like she had killed someone and was trying to hide the body. I needed to go to the bathroom anyway, so l got up and padded out into the hall in my oversized tee-shirt, book in hand, and found her dragging a huge duffle bag into her open bedroom door.

I waved at her with my book. "Hey, Ryder."

She had a ball cap on that had the logo of the Kentucky Horse Park on it, and a polo shirt with the same logo on it; souvenirs; lucky girl. Her whole body was radiating tension and I took pity on her because I remembered my exhaustion at the end of a long day of travel after a horse show; it was a bone deep kind of tired.

As tired as she had to be, she was intent on dragging the huge duffle bag behind her through her bedroom door. As soon as she was on the bedroom side, she turned around to tug at it. Once it was all the way in she growled and gave it a sharp kick as if to punish it, but she only jammed her toe.

"Ouch! Shit!"

Ryder was hopping around on one foot, cradling the other foot in her hands.

She let out another angry growl. "Damn thing doesn't have wheels. What was Francesca thinking?"

Ryder scowled at me as I stood in her bedroom doorway while she gingerly put her foot down. That's when I noticed the "High Horse Couture" logo on her bag. It looked like Ryder had gotten all kinds of goodies, even though she hadn't ridden.

I exclaimed, "Ryder, that's a great looking bag. I wouldn't mind having a bag like that. But what the heck's in there? I mean you didn't have to pack much since you weren't riding."

Ryder scowled. "I got stuck with the team stall drapes and banners and the filthy tack room mat and they're sitting under all my clothes. Francesca had the drapes special ordered for the team, and we had to pick them up on our way out of town. It meant I had to check instead of carry-on. Look at this thing; duffel's a piece of shit. No wheels. Who makes travel bags these days without wheels? My back is killing me from dragging it up the stairs. You can have the damn thing if you want it."

I let her comment pass because I thought she probably didn't mean it. I continued to take polite interest in her return, even though my sore finger was marking my place in my book and Scotland was calling. I understood that the North American Young Rider Championships were a big deal. I put on an upbeat tone. "Well, so tell me about it."

Ryder still sounded pissed. "Suzette won the individual bronze with an okay test, but otherwise it totally sucked."

I knew Suzette's win must have been hard for Ryder. They were friends, but they were rivals, too. I held onto my forced cheeriness.

"I watched it on the USEF channel. Suzette did a good job, but you would have beaten her ride on Papa. I'm sure of it. With you on the team next year things will go better. You'll know exactly what to expect too since you were there this time."

Ryder was still scowling at me. I blabbered onward. "It will only make it sweeter next year. I mean, I'll bet you learned tons from being there, and the extra year will give you an advantage."

Ryder frowned. "Sure, Mary Sunshine, I learned how to groom and braid and hold onto Suzette's horse while she climbed up on the podium and got her flowers and medal. The thing is; I've been there before on my old horse and didn't medal. This time was going to be different. This time I had the horse-flesh and I had the coach. I watched all the rides. They weren't that great, even the California horses. I should have been on the top step of that podium. Instead I got demoted to groom."

It was embarrassing for me to hear her whine. She was acting like the poster child for bad sportsmanship. I am sure I sounded like a kindergarten teacher with my disapproving tone.

"Ryder."

She almost frightened me by erupting in a high whine that must have been waiting for a release. I felt lucky she had already kicked the duffel. I found myself drawing back, just a little, while she let it out.

"I would have kicked ass with Papa. We should have just gone. He could have rested up after the competition, but now I have to wait an entire year to have a shot at it. This is not what I planned. A year is a long time, Lizzy, a long damn time. I'm not sure I can take another year at this funny farm."

When she said "funny farm" it felt like a blow. I knew she didn't mean Margot or Francesca. She could only mean me. All I could do was say her name again, this time sounding hurt. "Ryder…"

She turned her back to me, the fury gone, and her voice small. "Right now I just want to go to bed."

My voice got softer too, "I'm sorry, Ryder."

Ryder mumbled, "Yeah. I'll bet you are."

I narrowed my eyes at Ryder. I WAS sorry; sorry for Margot. Poor Margot had just spent a very long time cooped up with a bunch of disappointed riders and that included Ryder, who hadn't even been competing. No team medals and even bronze medalist Suzette was probably disappointed she hadn't won silver. Margot had probably wanted to throttle the lot of them. I thought it would have felt good to throttle Ryder right about now. I felt my stiff and swollen finger, my trophy from hand walking HER ride, try and curl between the pages of the paperback.

Before I could find my inner half-halt I blurted out. "Look at you standing there with all your goodies, having your way paid in full, and horses given to you like a little professional. You lead a charmed life and you don't even see it."

Ryder sighed. I hoped I had shamed her, just a little. But then she pointed to my book. "Go back to your fantasy world, Lizzy."

I looked down at the cover art on my paperback, all hunky flesh and tartan. My cheeks went slack and prickled with a flush of heat. I roughly whispered, "Gladly."

I turned on my heel and fled for the safety of my room. I had sympathized, even hurt for Ryder, when Papa was pulled from Championships and she lost her chance to compete. Ryder was quickly losing that sympathy.

In the morning, Ryder went about her chores in silence, as usual, a virtual "do not disturb" sign hanging out. Once the horses were munching away I went upstairs and poured myself a big mug of coffee. I looked through the window down into the barn aisle. This was a great place to observe, and to hide. Ryder would have to work herself out of her blue funk without my interference. The guys filed in and turned on the Spanish language station on the radio; and the mucking and turnout began. I watched Winsome being led down the aisle out to turn-out. I got an interesting view of her back and wide hips covered with dark dapples. That sight of her beautiful topside was enough to give me courage. Winsome would have made a far better roommate than a sulky Ryder. Winsome was the girl that really mattered to me.

It was time to go tack up Hotstuff for Margot. I wanted to make him look beautiful for her. So I refilled my mug, which I knew would grow cold sitting on a shelf in the grooming stall, but I also knew I would still drink it, as long as there wasn't a fly or horse hair floating in it.

Hotstuff had been leading a life of leisure while Margot was away. Margot knew Hotstuff had stressful weeks ahead of him with one more show before he shipped to Chicago for the FEI Young Horse Championships, so Margot felt the break would be good for him. It takes a lot of courage to give your horse time off before a championship, but I had confidence Margot knew her horse. There would always be a temptation to over train. I had already learned a lesson through watching Margot carefully plan Wild Child's training so he would peak for Gladstone. Wild Child looked the best the second week of Gladstone because he had come home and lounged in the paddock, rolling in the mud, and resting. That took guts. In comparison, Papa had missed his competition due to an overuse injury.

Currently Hotstuff was ranked second in the country. Margot could relax, knowing they had secured their spot in the top twelve to be issued invitations. He was definitely going to the National Young Horse Championships. I assumed that meant I was going, too. Hotstuff and I were buddies after all, and I had groomed him for Margot at every one of his shows so far.

I fetched Hotstuff and clipped him into the cross ties. He was filthy. Time to do my magic.

I started by spraying his tail with de-tangler and then began what I considered my signature currying. I made it a vigorous one and by the time I had gone from stem to stern his black coat was covered with dust rings made by the round curry comb. I knocked the dirt out of the curry by whacking it against the wooden back of my body brush. I had a good rhythm, rub, rub, rub, whack, rub, rub, rub, whack. Then I took the stiff body brush, the one with the long bristles, and began the next step; short brisk strokes that flicked the dirt off his coat and into the air. Then I used the soft short bristled brush. And then the mitt with the fly spray on it, which left his coat glossy and clean. Then I sponged off his face, combed out his tail and stood back to admire my work. He looked great. Of course I was now covered with dirt and hair. Time to gulp down my cold coffee.

His giant ears pricked and he leaned into the cross ties, signaling that Margot was here. I think some of the horses, like Papa and Hotstuff, had learned the sound of her car.

She called down the aisle. "How are my darling boys?"

Papa let out a shrill whinny that I am sure was meant to let her know he had been terribly mistreated while she was gone.

"Oh my darling, Papa, you sound so very sad."

I looked for Margot but she had disappeared into his stall.

I let her be and started putting the saddle on her horse. Hotstuff began pawing and wiggling around while I placed the saddle. I tried to reassure him. "Shhh. Patience; patience is a virtue. She'll be with you next but you have to wait your turn."

Suddenly there she was. I still felt a little lift just seeing her. She looked as polished as ever, her hair shellacked into its prim bun, her make up carefully applied. Her breeches looked brand new. She had already put on her burgundy boots and they were polished to a high shine.

She was crooning cheerfully as she reached out to touch Hotstuff. "Hello my Hotstuff, my darling, my pet. I can't tell you how happy I am to see my boys, and of course you too, Lizzy." Margot pulled gently on Hotstuff's forelock and then rubbed his giant ears.

I was just like Hotstuff, bubbling with excitement to see her. "I am so happy to have you back, too. I missed you. Hotstuff missed you, and poor Papa is about to lose his mind. He doesn't understand why no one is riding him or turning him out."

Despite the immaculate hair and dress and make up, I thought Margot's eyes looked tired.

She nodded thoughtfully. "Well, maybe his ultrasounds will be good enough to start tack walking next week."

Just then Ryder walked up. "Hey, Margot. What should I do today anyway?"

Margot pursed her lips for a moment in thought. "Do?"

Ryder crossed her arms and looked annoyed. "Yeah. Who should *I ride?*"

Margot looked surprised. "Ah. Well, I'm afraid you're horseless at present, Ryder darling."

There was a short pause from Ryder and then a clearing of her throat. "Y'know, I was thinking that maybe this would be a good time to go home for a visit."

There was then a longer pause from Margot; long enough to make me uncomfortable. I turned to tighten Hotstuff's girth.

Margot's voice, so chirpy a moment before got quiet and firm.

"Ryder, we have the CDI coming up and then the Young Horse Championships, then Regionals, and then Devon, then possibly Nationals, and I am probably forgetting something else. There is no break until after Devon. Just because Young Riders has finished doesn't mean YOU are finished. Your job here does not end with your competition. We are a team, and you are part of this team."

Ryder nodded but then said, "Well, it's just that if I'm not riding..."

Ryder wasn't registering what I was registering. She was heading out onto thin ice. Margot was shaking her head almost in disbelief.

"This job you want, that you chose... of a life with horses... is not just about riding. You have those skills in spades, darling. But you must understand that riding is the smallest part of what we do. If you make it to the Olympics ... it will not just be because you can ride the socks off a horse ... no darling, it will be because you showed up for every long damn night when your horse was colicky. It will be because you did your time in the trenches to do the best for your horses and for everyone else on YOUR team. Right now that team means everyone here at Equus Paradiso."

Ryder had just gotten a big slap down. Probably had it coming from a long week of being a whiny pain-in-the-ass at Young Riders. I had no pity, even if witnessing it did make me squirm a bit.

Finally Ryder answered the only way she could have. "Yes, ma'am." But I thought Ryder's tone lacked remorse.

Margot must have thought so, too. She narrowed her eyes and after another pause she continued.

"Ryder, Papa may not be the horse that ultimately makes you famous, but he is your responsibility right now. Lizzy has been holding down the fort for us while you and I were off at Young Riders. Now it will be your turn. Lizzy is going to be showing Winsome soon, and you will be grooming for her and for Deb, and if Francesca wants to show, you will be grooming for her, too."

The mention of Francesca showing made me swallow hard. Francesca wanted to show all right ... Grand Prix on Johnny Cash. My heart did some thud-thudding as I though of the conflict of interest that Francesca had created for me.

Ryder wasn't done either. She looked Margot right in the eye, like her equal or something. "I don't mind work, Margot. But I should be riding something in lessons with you, that's my pay."

Margot's lips pressed into a thin line. I'd never seen Margot look like that. All I could think was, "Oh crap." But Margot did not yell; her tone remained measured. "I assure you that you have received more than sufficient compensation, but if you would like to give up your spot, I am quite sure one of the fifteen people who e-mailed me just last week asking for a position would be very willing to take it." I noticed there had been no "darling" this time from Margot for Ryder.

I left them staring at each other like two cats facing off in a back alley and went to the tack room to fetch Hotstuff's bridle. I felt sure that someone's wheel-less duffel bag was about to be repacked and dragged back down our stairs.

While l was hunkered down in the tack room, the terriers came busting in. I sat down on the floor and rubbed and scratched them, trying to listen in over their happy panting.

Francesca had joined Margot and Ryder. I expected Francesca had come in for the final kill. But I knew there would be no yelling. Voices were lowered and as hard as I strained to hear, all I took in were the panting terriers. When the dogs had been thoroughly scratched on their butts and then their bellies, they jumped up and ran out of the tack room.

I grabbed Hotstuff's bridle. When I got to the grooming stall, Francesca and Ryder and the dogs were walking away, but Margot was still there rubbing Hotstuff's ears. She stepped back to let me in.

I threw the reins over his head and unclipped him, slipping off the halter and hanging it on the nearest hook. I always had a peppermint for the horses as soon as they slipped the bit into their mouth. Hotstuff practically put his own bridle on in eager anticipation of his treat.

Margot went to the tack room and came out with her spurs on, pulling on her gloves and carrying her whip. She still didn't put on a helmet. I wasn't going to change her even though I never got on without one.

I expected that the topic of Ryder had to be raised. I chewed on my bottom lip, waiting. But Margot's tone was light. "Can you please come to the arena, Lizzy?"

I was always happy to be ringside when Margot rode. I said, "Sure."

We walked side by side and Margot slipped her arm through mine. She tipped her head toward mine and spoke in a conspiratorial tone. "I asked Ryder to get Wild Child ready for Deb, so you are free for a bit. We'll do Winsome together right after Deb is finished."

I slowed my pace and Margot turned to smile at me. I asked, "Ryder is still here?"

Margot's eyes twinkled. "Oh yes. Don't look surprised. Francesca will straighten her right out. Francesca is quite good at that actually, and she enjoys it, too. Plus Francesca is always a chess move ahead of everyone."

Another thud-thud from my heart, thinking that Francesca was also a chess move ahead of Margot. And I was a pawn in her game.

I sat down on the viewing deck of the indoor while Margot mounted and let Hotstuff have a loose rein in the walk. He was still the tall awkward and long legged baby I had first met down in Florida, but he had grown heavier over the summer, with a larger crest developing on his neck that helped balance his long head and gigantic ears. I could tell one day he would be stunning in a noble sort of way. He still needed to move before his beauty was apparent.

While he was striding out in walk and swinging his neck left and right having a gander at his environment, Margot finished up on the topic of Ryder.

"I am sorry that Ryder is so unhappy right now, and I can imagine she is not great company for you. She was no fun down in Kentucky, I assure you."

I stretched my legs out in front of me, and tried to sound reassuring. "It's OK, Margot."

Margot continued. "I have to remind myself sometimes that she is still a teenager. Poor little thing, she doesn't know the price of being in this sport yet. But honestly, if any of us knew how long and twisted our paths were going to be, with more downs than ups, we'd have been frozen in fear long ago. We'd never have taken the first step. I want to help her, but some of this has to come in its own way and time. Life has a way of sanding down the rough edges."

I nodded back. "I have a hard time understanding her. She's already worked out a detailed plan that takes her all the way to the Olympics. She's not embarrassed to say that out loud, which just slays me because it seems so arrogant, and she has a sense of urgency about it, too. Time that doesn't move her closer to that long-range goal is wasted time to Ryder. I do get that she's really frustrated that things didn't go according to her plan."

Margot had just passed by me and turned Hotstuff around to be able to look at me while she spoke. "Well, I had a plan, too. Then my Walter died. I can't believe how many years ago that was." Margot paused, and I could tell that just saying those words still caused her pain. Margot was usually so private, so guarded.

But she drew a breath and continued. "The thing is, Lizzy, you, my darling, have already experienced some seismic shifts and have endured. Those hard lessons do give perspective, don't they? Most of the time Ryder behaves as if she is much older than her years, but she is just a little girl, and a little girl having a hard time coping right now. You are much more patient." She paused for a moment. "For you and Ryder, being so young, a year is a long time. When you get to be my age, time passes much faster." She looked at me and smiled. "It seems like it was only a couple weeks ago you pulled into the farm in Florida for the very first time, driving in from Georgia."

I wasn't sure patience was what Margot was seeing. I couldn't quite put the right words together. But I tried. "I don't think I have patience. Maybe I just have no long term plan."

Margot looked surprised. "Don't you?" She halted Hotstuff and peered at me with interest.

I felt myself getting emotional. Something about Margot looking at me so intently made me feel her concern, and that concern made me feel weak somehow. I tried to gather myself to answer.

I answered, "Only a vague sort, one that includes you and Winsome. Beyond that, it's pretty fuzzy. I'm no Ryder Anderson. An Olympic goal is too big for me. I'm not sure where I fit in with dressage. The thing is, I'm not anything yet."

Margot let out a small, comforting, laugh, shaking her head. "Darling Lizzy, you don't have to know every step along the way. This is a great time in your life. You are young and your best rides are ahead of you. Just stay with us and learn. Those who think life is ever a settled affair are absolute fools. Remember this, Darling, nothing is ever settled until they pack the earth down over your grave. You understand?"

That did get a smile from me. "I think so."

"And Elizabeth," she had never called me by my given name.

"Yes?" I had a momentary feeling of fear.

She faced me directly, her tired eyes direct and unwavering. "I was quite serious when I told Ryder I get at least fifteen emails with videos every week from riders wanting to train here. But I am very well satisfied with my students. This is my team. You are a valued part of my team. I am pleased you are here."

At that moment I would have walked through fire for her. "Thank you," I said at last.

Her tone changed. "Good! Now, during my Kentucky trip I had time to think about all you girls, and you especially. Let's get you out to a show this summer. Deb is going with Wild Child, so let's get you in the third level tests with Winsome."

I knew Deb had been the one to get the ball rolling, but Margot looked so pleased with herself.

I said "Thanks, what a great idea."

And in my head I said, "Thanks, Deb."

Margot said, "I'll talk to Francesca about getting your entries in right away."

"Margot?"

"Yes, darling?"

"I looked Walter up on the internet and watched a clip of him schooling you on Maestro."

Margot smiled in bewilderment. "Where in the world?"

I smiled back. "Youtube."

She still looked astonished. "Of course, I know of Youtube, but I had no idea those videos are there."

I grinned. "It was awesome."

Margot's lips pressed into a small, satisfied smile. "You must send me the link. I realize the horses today make our horses of the past look heavy and coarse, especially Maestro. He was not as light footed and springy as what the breeders are producing these days. But, what Walter could do with him! I was just a puppet really. Walter could put me up after he rode and ride the horse through me. But I learned so much from that horse… and that man."

I couldn't help myself. I got in a dig. "Ryder mentioned that, about the horses being better movers nowadays. She watches all those old videos too, but all she sees are the mistakes and comments on stuff like the outdated tack and the old fashioned hard looking footing and no protective headgear, stuff like that."

Margot sighed and shook her head. "Walter used to say that the greatest arrogance of the present is to forget the intelligence of the past."

And she picked up the reins and drew inward. It was time to give Hotstuff her full attention. Time to stop talking. I took my cue.

And I sat back and watched while I let her words echo in my head.

"The greatest arrogance of the present is to forget the intelligence of the past." I wished I had a piece of paper, but I would commit it to memory and put it into my journal tonight.

Hotstuff stopped gawking and became all business, too.

She gave him 100% and he returned it. I think that was one of the biggest lessons of watching Margot ride; her intense concentration. No one would dare talk to her now. We all knew better. I had tried to copy her, calling it the "drawing of the curtain."

Later, when Margot gave me my lesson on Winsome, I felt a duty to give Margot my very best.

Margot had a knack for making me feel like a million bucks. Margot's students all rode so differently, as if she preserved our differences rather than trying to make us all alike. We were allowed to "bloom in our own pots" just as her horses all went the same, yet each had a separate charm of their own. At least that is how I saw it. In Winsome, I may have been riding a horse that was not International in scope or athleticism, but while I was riding with Margot I was never aware of it.

Margot's voice drifted past me like a gentle breeze. "Beautiful darling… gentle, gentle with your inside rein. Lightly lift the inside rein for right flexion, not backwards on the rein. Yes."

And then, "Add impulsion a drop at a time. Don't allow positive tension to tip into negative tension. Not more than you can keep swinging over the topline. Not yet, feel the moment… now. Yes, you did feel the moment, well done."

And then sometimes the arena was silent but for the rhythm of Winsome's breathing.

I might catch a glimpse of Margot as I passed; her arms crossed, her head tipped, studying Winsome and me. I might see her in the background as I glimpsed myself in the mirrors, her image a blur and yet essential to the picture.

When we got into a difficult spot in our work, we might walk and discuss strategy. Then we would come up with an exercise that broke things down into simpler elements. We then worked on the separate elements and slowly put the thing back together. Sometimes she would pick up on some infinitesimal detail that once understood made a huge difference.

Once we were working shoulder-in to renvers along the wall, which was in the second level tests, but also one of Margot's favorite exercises. So many people get twisted up in the saddle and pulled the horse's neck one way and then the other. Margot had me simply focus on weighting my seat bones. So for shoulder in right I focused on my right seat bone feeling heavier, and then when I shifted to renvers, I focused on weighting my left seat bone. It was such a small adjustment, invisible to the onlooker, but Winsome felt it, and I felt it, and it was a huge moment of revelation as Winsome switched from one bend to the other without any drift off the line of travel. It was a revelation to me that Winsome felt fully and clearly such a tiny weight aid. It also made me realize how heavy and overdone most of my aids had been. Poor Winsome. I had been yelling at her with my body, when a whisper would do.

Margot knew what to tell me because Margot was more than just a rider; she was a thinker and a teacher. Maybe she was even a better teacher than she was a rider.

I was already more of a rider than I had ever thought I could become, even if I had little show success so far. Ryder was also more than she was when she arrived. Though I wasn't sure she realized yet just how much more. For Ryder, unless she could put it on her resume' of "wins," it just didn't count.

Even though I could smack Ryder for her spoiled rotten attitude, I did understand that the world at large didn't really care about your personal growth.

Just like Ryder, it wanted the resume.

# 12. Wannabes

*In the late afternoon, I led Johnny to Claire Winston's elegant arena* and Francesca trailed after us. Johnny snorted at the shadows, just like he did every day. I got on at the mounting block to do the "pre-flight" check and warm up. The reason was unspoken but understood; it was to ride out the spooks and the tension so that Francesca did not end up on his neck again.

Johnny carefully stepped over the shadows cast across the footing as if they were solid. I intentionally kept my muscles slack. Margot had taught me not to get emotionally involved in a horse's problems. A rider needs detachment; coolness. I had also discovered that by letting go of my physical tension, my emotions could follow. Because of Margot's advice, I had learned to let go of a lot of things in order to ride well. Emotional detachment was critical. But it had been Wild Child, not Margot, who had taught me that horses do not follow weak leaders, and I had come to understand that emotionalism was a sign of weakness. Leaders needed to be calm, leaders needed to be brave, and leaders needed to be wise. Whoever sat on a horse's back needed to be the leader, and here I sat upon a spooky Johnny Cash. I was never one to be stoic about my feelings, so to cultivate detachment was a biggie for me. But with Wild Child I had learned to step up to the job and sitting on Johnny was another opportunity to cultivate that skill.

Emotional detachment did not mean that a rider was passive. Sometimes you had to be like the alpha-mare of the herd, who may make a correction with a bellow or swift kick, but followed it with unconcerned and quiet grazing. I needed to make corrections, but when they were done they must be done and forgotten. Johnny needed my leadership and he needed my direction and shaping, but mostly he needed me to lead with relaxation in order for him to find his own.

While I was musing over leadership and the head game that makes up a huge portion of the riding task, Francesca sat on the mounting block in the corner of the arena and tipped her head to watch, barking out things from time to time like a drill Sergeant. Each bark grated on my nerves, intruding rudely on my thoughts, and pulling me away from my riding, reminding me that this was all about Francesca and not about me.

Today Francesca planned to run through the Grand Prix test. She had already entered the show without even knowing if she could do the test. I think in her mind she had already won her USDF gold medal rider award.

Supposedly my job at Equus Paradiso Farm, according to my latest conversation with Margot, was to focus on working and learning. I need not worry myself yet with external measures of success. But here I was stuck in cahoots with Francesca who had felt the need to "go for the gold" behind Margot's back. Francesca was all about external success, her own that is, and Francesca signed my paycheck. Francesca had the right horse and the right clothes, and I guess she had the force of her iron will. Maybe that would be enough. But it made me deeply uneasy. I did not see a possible happy outcome. How could there be?

Francesca's voice intruded. "Lizzy, you are not focusing!"

She was right. "I'm sorry."

I tried my best to model Margot and draw the curtain, squishing my unease right under the seat of my breeches. I tried to pull my hips to the front of the saddle and sit down on my "back pockets."

She barked again. "For heaven's sake, what are you doing up there? Sit up and ride."

I always sat up, a hell of a lot better than she did, but I stuck out my chest a little to shut her up, and then I again tried to listen to what Johnny's body was telling me. Could I feel where his hind legs were? Was I sitting back enough in my saddle? Were my legs really relaxed and draped? Was I looking through his ears onto the line of travel? Did I let the energy flow through me unblocked? Was Johnny staying between my legs and reins, or was he drifting or falling through any of those parameters I set for him? As my mind began to quiet I started to feel connected to Johnny and Francesca melted into the landscape. We trotted bending lines and rode leg-yields, then did the canter to trot to canter until he was shifting through his gears smoothly and I had control of the line of travel. He was ready...meaning safe and relaxed...for Francesca. But when I made a transition to halt and was about to jump down she surprised me, waving me away.

"Run through the test, Lizzy."

I gaped my mouth open in surprise. "Me?"

Francesca was nodding. "Yes. I want to see how difficult it is for you."

I couldn't hide my disbelief. "I can tell you right now, it will be unbelievably difficult and worse than that, it will stink. I've never even shown PSG. I'm not sure it's even fair to Johnny to submit him to it."

I suppressed a sigh. I had come a long way in my riding since I started with Margot; far enough to know how much I still had to learn, especially about riding Grand Prix, which required a higher degree of balance from the horse and a whole new set of skills from both horse and rider. Riding Rave had been a gift, I understood though that it did not make me a Grand Prix level rider.

Francesca looked smug. "Don't be silly. I don't expect the test to be any good. Just do it. You memorized it as I asked you to?"

I was grimacing because it seemed both ridiculous and counter-productive. I wasn't the fool who thought she could pull off a 60% Grand Prix test practically overnight. I tried to explain, "I know the pattern, but that's not the same as riding it. I don't think…"

Francesca interrupted with a dramatic sigh. "You disappoint me. Most dressage wanna-bes would jump at the chance."

I gathered myself, stung. She seemed to relish calling me a "wanna-be." If she had meant to goad me into the challenge, she had succeeded. Heck, it was just for a lark, a game of pretend. Sure. I could do that. Why not? I nodded back at her. "You're right, Francesca. I love sitting on this horse. He's a generous soul to put up with us both. It's not a horse show. It will be a hoot."

She smiled her little tight-lipped smile.

I found myself giving her the same smile back. "You mind calling it for me? You memorized it too, right?"

I had thrown the gauntlet right back at her, but she was still smiling as she answered dryly. "If you feel you need it."

Touche' Francesca. I wasn't sure if I would remember, but I wasn't going to admit that now. I returned the jab. "If you haven't got it memorized yet, I can probably remember it." Margot's words seemed to strengthen my resolve. I was part of Margot's team. I am here because I belong here. And I was not going to let Francesca take that from me.

I put Johnny back together and rode away, turning my back to Francesca. It was time to give it a go, with or without a caller. I started my preparation with a few trot to halt to trot transitions, then woke his hind legs up even a bit more with a few piaffe steps. From Francesca's corner perch came, "Ring-a-ding, Lizzy…you have 45 seconds to enter."

Even though this was a lark, a joke, a bit of role playing, my stomach still did a flip-flop. I picked up the canter and headed down the centerline; missing it by about a meter, I sidled Johnny back to straight and then landed a halt at X. Not too bad I thought. At "C" I turned left and made a very modest extension across the diagonal while I thought about what came next...the steep half-passes. Not a peep from Francesca in the corner. I was going to have to remember the test.

The steep half passes felt impossible. Poor Johnny made it but they were flat and creeping sideways. We made the halt at C, and did a stiff-legged rein back and walked into the trot. I scored it all to myself...around 5.5. Not good enough.

Now the big boy part of the test was fast approaching. I made another modest extension across the short diagonal and then shifted into passage.

Good old Johnny. His passage felt wonderful...I looked into the mirror as I turned across the arena. I might as well relax and just enjoy the fantasy. He was flashy with his broad white blaze and tall stockings, especially the one that trickled up the front of his hind leg. And I loved the little splash of white on his tummy that was barely visible.

We shifted into a very modest piaffe. I counted off the steps...ten, eleven, twelve, now easy out. I could imagine Margot saying, "easy, easy, grow the steps, keep his back," because I had heard her say those very words to Deb.

And we went back into passage. And then it was time for the walk section of the test. It was a moment for me to think and review what was coming up next. Meanwhile, I couldn't get Johnny to stretch as he was supposed to do in the extended walk, he knew the passage was coming and was antsy. He knew the test, and passage was his best trick. We would have gotten a really low score for the walk. But who cared? It was soon passage time again and he jumped back into it enthusiastically.

Off we went into the second passage-piaffe-passage section. I wanted to admire myself in the mirror again as we turned across the middle.

But I only got a glimpse; there was no time to ogle at my reflection in the Grand Prix test.

I released him into the canter transition at E. The two-tempis were coming up next, and they magically happened. Good old Johnny. Then I did a very conservative extended canter across the diagonal, knowing the next section was a lost cause. I was now deep into foreign waters.

The canter zigzags had been a nightmare for Wild Child and Margot, and because of that I had spent a lot of time watching and learning about how to ride them, but I actually had never done them myself. As I had just said to Francesca, watching and doing are very different things.

I now demonstrated the truth of my statement. The zigzags were a complete disaster. I know because I rode them towards the mirror and practically smashed into my own image when the arena ended before my pitiful attempt at the exercise did. The strides of half pass between the flying changes were supposed to be 3-6-6-6-3-with a final flying change and turn right at C. I'm not sure what count I did. I'm just lucky poor Johnny didn't fall down as I pulled him suddenly to the right. I even squeaked like a mouse in alarm, while I thought to myself that I had just scored something like a 1. It was indeed "very bad."

There was no time to ponder the disaster, immediately it was time for 15 one-tempis.

I cantered almost to X before Johnny got the memo that I was asking for them. I think l squeezed in 7. No time to cry over missed tempis.

Down centerline to pirouette left, which I walked in the middle of and then managed to make a sucked-back flying change at X to a half walk and half canter pirouette to the right. At M it was back to trot and then R to V extended trot and blessedly down centerline for the last passage to piaffe to passage section to the final halt at G. It was a terribly abrupt halt. I collapsed onto Johnny's neck, laughing and petting him and apologizing all at the same time. Ridiculous slow clapping came from the mounting block set in the corner of the arena.

"Well, that was most informative." There was that tight little smile.

I sat back upright and tried to catch my breath. "Poor Johnny! I feel so guilty. And now he has to do it again." My ride had been ugly. But ugly or not, I had gotten though it.

She got off the mounting block and slowly pulled on her gloves like she was about to perform surgery. "Let me up then. We'll have another session of the blind leading the blind. I did see where you made some critical errors. I won't make the same mistakes."

This time I bit my tongue, but in my head I was saying, "Of course not, you'll make different mistakes, and plenty of them."

I hopped off and fixed the stirrups. Francesca got on stiffly while I plopped down on the mounting block. My body felt tight and I was surprised how wiped out I felt. I had totally over-ridden every step of that test.

She put Johnny on the bit and practiced the zigzags at the walk. She also did the steep half passes and pirouettes in walk. I knew she was mentally going through the test, her lips pressed together tightly, head down staring at Johnny's withers.

I didn't have to ring my imaginary bell; she picked up the canter and headed down centerline. Francesca kept Johnny's gaits small and slow, doing the whole test like he was wading through molasses. On the other hand, Francesca got through it about as well, if not actually better, than I had. I hated to admit it, but it was true.

I know neither one of us would have made the mark ...no Gold medal scores were happening today. But on the other hand, I was surprised at Francesca. Maybe she wasn't hopeless.

Francesca slipped off of Johnny, and I gave him a sugar cube. I was loosening his girth when I watched Francesca cradle his wide white muzzle in both her hands and press a red lipstick kiss on his nose. She looked quite pleased with herself.

"Tomorrow then, Lizzy. Tomorrow we make it a 60 percent."

I think Francesca was about as happy as I'd ever seen her. I was smiling back at her. "Sure, Francesca. And thanks. I had fun."

Francesca sounded a bit like Frank when she answered. "Well, well, well, I mustn't let that happen again."

I laughed. Francesca was a trip. Buried deep inside her wicked-witch persona there just might be a sense of humor.

She headed toward the parking lot with a backward wave. And I turned toward the barn, leading Johnny. He bumped into my back with that big nose of his as I abruptly came to a stop. All my happy feelings of good will disappeared. I had seen a flash of someone disappearing down the barn aisle. That someone had been watching us, spying on us. I knew that slender profile. Ryder.

Back at Equus Paradiso, that image of Ryder niggled at me as I slipped into the tack room and opened the fridge. Now that she had seen what Francesca and I were up to, what would she do about it? What would I say when I saw her?

I used my T-shirt as a basket, pulling it away from my breeches and piling carrots into it. I was going to have a mess of carrots for my dinner. With a little brown sugar and ginger and melted butter they would be divine. Maybe I wouldn't see Ryder. Then I could take the bowl of carrots to my bedroom away from Ryder and dive back into my book.

What was I thinking? I would have to see her eventually, and good offense was better than a defense. I was going to be proactive rather than reactive, and just come right out and tell her it was none of her business and to back off. Except that the closer to going up those stairs, the less sure I was. In fact, my mind shifted back to more important things, like my dinner. Did I even have any ginger? Brown sugar? How about steaming them and then slathering on butter with salt and pepper? Yeah. That would do.

As I trudged up our stairs, my feet got heavier and heavier. What did I care about what Ryder thought anyway? This wasn't my battle to fight. I was just taking orders wasn't I? Let sleeping dogs lie, right? Well then, I wasn't going to make it easy on her by bringing it up at all. She was going to have to be the one to bring it up. Or not. Honestly, I was hoping for the latter. I cradled my carrots in my stretched out tee-shirt and opened the door.

She was standing at the kitchen counter next to her dinner plate, which had a sandwich on it, and she was slicing up an apple. I tried to sound chipper. "Hey, Ryder."

Her voice was businesslike. "Hey."

I dumped my carrots in the sink and found a scrubby brush, turned on the cold water and began washing my carrots.

I heard Ryder's short derisive snort. "Aren't those for Papa?"

I knew she wasn't going to give me a pass on taking the farm carrots. I was ready, if a bit guilty when I replied. "Yes, but Frank knows I take some…he brought us some lemon squares, too. There's one for you in that bag over there."

I pointed at the bakery bag on the counter. She sounded world weary. "You eat crap, Lizzy."

The heat rose up in my face and made my scalp prickle. I was about to rise up in protest and defend myself. I stopped myself in the nick of time. What the heck just happened here? Where went my resolve about a good offense… proactive versus reactive? She was working me, dredging up the same old same old. Next I expected would be the line about white breeches.

So I buttoned my lip and sulked. I admit; also a really adult reaction. What had I been saying to myself about emotional detachment? Why could I manage it on top of a 1200 pound flight animal, but this teenager sent my blood pressure through the roof?

Ryder carefully wiped up the counter and then went to the table with her very balanced dinner and a bottle of water. Sheesh, I wanted to scream.

I chopped carrots. They were really fat and my knife blade was incredibly dull, so I had to apply a lot of pressure. Carrot pieces began to fly, some landing on the floor, one going so far as to make it to the kitchen table."

Ryder looked over her shoulder at me. "Hey! Watch it."

I went with it with a devilish grin and an attempt at humor. "Incoming!"

And another big chunk flew her way, landing in the middle of the table.

Ryder turned in her chair with annoyance. "Geez, at least make the pieces smaller."

I thought it was pretty interesting what great projectiles they made. What I needed was more precision. Ryder went back to her sandwich while I pondered how to improve my trajectory.

I rotated my chopping board a quarter of an inch or so and made the pieces bigger.

It took about four tries until I got a perfect shot right to the back of her head. I had a fleeting impulse to give someone a high-five or if I could have I would have spiked a football. Of course I just had to bite my lip.

"Ow, shit!" Ryder spun in her seat. "You did that on purpose!"

I couldn't suppress my giggles, as she narrowed her eyes at me.

"Sorry, Ryder. Let me try again." Ryder was shooting death-rays at me with narrowed eyes.

Ping went the next piece and hit her right on her nose.

She pulled her chair back and jumped up.

I was crowing, "Oh my God, I am good!"

Her fists were clinched. "Now you're really pissing me off."

I couldn't help but erupt in giggles, but clearly it was time to abandon my post and make a run for it. Ryder and I had reverted back to fifth graders. And I had been the one to initiate it.

Since I still had a carrot in my hand I ran downstairs and I went right on in to Wild Child's stall. Ryder, of course, did not follow me in. I knew she wouldn't.

I had a big fat carrot, and I began biting it into small pieces, feeding the tid-bits to a very surprised but happy Wild Child. All the horses had been disturbed, some even whinnied.

Ryder stood outside the stall. I was still softly giggling. "Sorry, Ryder, honest. It was just so tempting, especially after the jab about the lemon squares. I thought you would laugh, I thought it would break the ice, y'know?"

Ryder closed the door and slid the latch. "Hit and run with carrot chunks? Very mature of you. Good night, Lizzy."

I was impressed with her quick thinking. But, she really couldn't be serious about leaving me locked in with shark-face. Was she?

My voice was soft. "Ryder?"

She had begun to walk away.

Wild Child had eaten his carrot bits and now was making grumpy faces. He wanted his stall back to himself.

Ryder stopped and turned. "Y'know, actually I think this would be a good opportunity to have a chat."

Wild Child was pinning his ears and twisting his neck.

I took both hands and shoved him over to one side of the stall. "Give me some room, big guy."

He stomped his foot on the ground, but stayed against the wall, eyeing me with his ears back.

Ryder leaned against the stall front. "So what the hell was today about, over at the Winston barn?"

I spoke to Ryder, but kept my eyes on Wild Child. "You know I'm not allowed to say."

"What's Johnny Cash doing over there anyway, and why the heck would anyone let you two monkeys bang around on him?"

I frowned and glanced her way. "Can't say."

As usual Ryder was thinking of Ryder. "He'd be perfect for me, y'know, now that Papa is sidelined. I could do the Brentina Cup on that one. Get my gold medal while I'm at it."

I answered firmly, "You're not supposed to know anything about him."

Ryder's voice was equally firm. "Ah, but, I do."

My mouth dropped open. I couldn't help but sound accusatory. "You were spying."

She sounded matter of fact. "I was looking for Suzette."

I shook my head. "She's never there after four pm. You know that."

Wild Child made a little plunge toward me, but then retreated to his wall when I lifted my arm, snapped my fingers and commanded him to "get over!" He obediently stepped back against the wall, but did not look pleased about it.

I wanted out and I wasn't kidding now. "OK, Ryder, I'm sorry I launched carrot missiles at you; you're right, it was really immature of me, now let me out of here before Wild Child really gets pissed off."

Ryder nodded and put her hand on the latch. "Sure. But I think you need to make a case for me to Francesca."

I snapped back. "Not happening."

Ryder did the perfect evil-doer tsk-tsk-tsk and took her hand off the latch.

"Ryder! If you really want my help with Francesca, then you'll open that door now."

"Just kidding!" She put on a fake smile as she slid the latch open and backed away.

She tried to sound chummy again. "I could help you guys you know, whatever it is that Francesca is up to. But, now you will need to ask for it. You shouldn't be so secretive, especially when you know I could help."

I sighed in relief to get out, quickly stepping through the gap. Wild Child shook his head at me, plunging himself to the stall front, the victor. But then he turned his withers to me for a scratching. I sighed in relief and obliged, digging in with my fingernails. His neck stretched out and he wiggled his top lip.

Ryder had stopped to watch. "I knew all along he wouldn't hurt you."

I just scowled at her, gave Wild Child a friendly pat and slid the door closed and latched it.

I had my back to her when she said, "By the way, Chess is having us to his house Wednesday night for dinner."

I turned around, genuinely surprised and happy to have switched topics. "We're not going to Deb's?"

"Nope. He wanted to cook for us. Deb says he's a really good cook, too."

At least Chess had given the invitation to Deb, and we had all been invited. He was graciously paying a social debt. I nodded approval, "Nice of him. He's seems to be a decent sort."

Ryder crossed her arms. "I'll let him know not to serve carrots."

***

Wednesday night came too soon. I felt inexplicably shy standing with Deb and Nat and Ryder outside Chess' townhome as we rang the bell. My hand was getting sticky and hot holding the cellophane wrap around the grocery store flowers I had brought. I wondered if it was OK to bring flowers to a guy's house. Deb had a bottle of wine in each hand. I had put on lipstick, and right before Chess opened the door, Ryder told me it was on my teeth. So I had my finger in my mouth when Chess greeted us with open arms. He was wearing a blue striped apron with an olive leaf design that looked familiar printed along the border.

He was grinning ear to ear. "Welcome, welcome!" His town home smelled good, like fresh greens and spices. He gave Deb a heartfelt hug, while I quickly wiped my finger on the back pocket of my jeans. Then he waved us all in. "Come on into the kitchen, it's the heart of any house."

I was last in a line that followed him like a row of ducklings.

Chess had indeed made fresh homemade pesto sauce, and had a huge pot of boiling water sending up clouds of steam over his range-top.

He proudly showed us his mortar and pestle where he had ground up pine nuts and fresh basil and garlic. "My Nonna Cavelli was sure that all the world's ills could be solved with good cooking. I may not be as good as she was, but it's not because I haven't tried. This is one of her recipes."

He and Deb had an earnest discussion about fresh spices and pine nuts while he opened up the wine. I stood immobilized, gripping the flowers. Natalie had started opening his cupboards; helping herself to wine glasses and setting a row of them on the counter.

Natalie began pouring wine without asking, handing the first one to Chess and the second one to Deb. Ryder picked up her glass to be filled. And Natalie put a tiny splash of wine in it. "That's your limit, Ryder."

Ryder pouted, "Says you!"

Deb rolled her eyes, and then Chess noticed me and my tightly gripped offering. "Here Lizzy, let me take those."

Chess lightly touched my hand, which jolted me out of my trance. Once he had put the flowers in a vase, he gave us a quick tour of his home.

His town home was so clean you could have eaten off the floors, which were all bare hardwood polished to a shine. The furniture was angular black leather; the tables were cast iron and glass. The walls had framed posters from plays and movies, some current and some classics. Some were autographed. A small piano sat against one wall. There were no table lamps, but instead the ceiling had strips of little can lights. There wasn't even a light hanging over the dining table.

When we got to his bedroom, I hung back but still wanted to look. It was the same, bare floors with a built in wall of closets and drawers. A big TV was set on the wall like a piece of artwork with a leather sofa set at the end of the bed. An acoustic guitar leaned against one wall, right next to one of those tower style air purifiers that was humming away. The bathroom was all shiny granite and tile with a giant walk-in shower. Very sleek and modern and very, very clean.

The extra bedroom had been converted into a very well-organized office with two computers, three over-sized screens, a printer/fax/copier, and all the usual things. As with the other rooms, there was nothing decorative and no personal photos, although I didn't really look closely at the bookshelves.

We all made appropriate oohs and ahs.

Except for Nat. She was silent, and when we walked back into the living room, she gave him a friendly smack on his back, and then put her hand on his arm, speaking earnestly. "Chess, my man, there is nothing with a shape here. I mean it's all flat. No texture."

Chess tipped his head. "Why do I feel like you're about to sell me something?"

She took a swig of wine before answering. "What you need is a sculpture."

He smiled graciously. "Thanks, but I collect posters from plays and movies."

Nat winked and smiled broadly. "What you specifically need is one of *my* sculptures. For you I have a special price. It's called the 'special while Natalie is a little nobody slave of the Cavellis' deal.' But one day you will be glad you got in at the ground floor. Hey, you can even say you discovered me. Every artist needs a patron of the arts, right?"

Deb chimed in, "She's right, you know. Someday she *will* be famous."

And without thinking I added, "What this place needs is a woman's touch."

Deb, who was standing a little behind Chess, gave me a tiny shake of her head. Clearly I had drifted into forbidden territory. Later I would need to get the back-story. Later.

Chess nodded, and seemed to study one of the can lights before putting a happy host smile on his face. Then he excused himself for a moment to put in the pasta and came back with a glass of wine in one hand and a huge slotted spoon in his other hand.

"OK, Natalie. For the right price I'll bite. What do you think I need in here...for texture?"

Natalie strolled around his little living room with her wine glass in hand. "What's with this coffee table... it's like... barren."

Chess appeared to be seriously listening. He nodded, "I know but I like that there is room for wine glasses and even a tray of appetizers. It's very functional."

Natalie nodded back and looked around the room. "Functional. Good word to describe your crib. Functional. A little sculpture won't take much room."

Chess thought about that for a moment, then said, "OK, I could do that, but please, nothing too girly. No prancing ponies."

I felt a ridiculous giggle starting that couldn't be stopped. Everyone turned and stared at me. It just kept coming in nervous waves.

Chess was staring. "What? What did I say that was so funny?"

I had to sit down. Then I looked over at Ryder and she had a hand over her mouth and it was holding back her own giggles. It was catching, and it was all my fault. Nat started laughing and Ryder and I stopped restraining ourselves. We sounded like pre-schoolers.

Poor Chess, he still had such a serious expression. "What? What?"

I tried to spit it out. "Chess... it's just... you are wearing that apron."

And Nat added, "And waving around that spoon-thingy."

He looked genuinely affronted. "You don't recognize the apron? The logo design is from Mom and Dad's company, and it's the same olive leaf design the farm uses on all its stuff. And this…this…" He waved the spoon thingy around in the air, "is not a spoon-thingy, it's a special pasta fork from Mom and Dad's company. It's imported!"

We three were now hopelessly gasping.

Ryder whipped out her cell phone and took a photo. "OMG, Facebook material!"

She leaned over to show me the photo.

Chess pointed his fancy imported pasta fork at Ryder.

"YOU! You are officially cut off. No more wine for you. And I may have to confiscate that phone, too. And honest to God, if you put that thing on the net, I'll use my Mother to exact revenge. You don't want that."

Deb was sympathetically shaking her head. "Yup, Chess. They are a really mature crop. Sorry. And here you have opened up your home and made us a beautiful meal."

I managed to summon some restraint. "Deb, you are right. I'm sorry, Chess. Sometimes when I'm nervous I giggle. You with that apron and the fork, well, it just struck me as funny and I couldn't help myself. I am really sorry."

Chess put his hands on his hips. "Lucky for me, I am perfectly secure in my own masculinity, thank you very much."

And with that he affected a silly little sashay back to the kitchen; laughing a laugh that sounded just like his Dad's.

Deb let us have it, hissing at us. "Am I babysitting here?" She rolled her eyes.

We three gave her a chorus of apologies. And then Chess came back with a tray of marinated asparagus spears with strips of mozzarella wrapped in prusciotto. We had calmed down in a flash and managed to chit-chat like adults. They *were* delicious. Chess clearly knew something about food.

It wasn't long before we sat down to all white china with heavy angular silverware. The salad was served in a giant wooden bowl that we passed around, along with a huge long bread-basket of hot bread wrapped in white linen napkins.

Everything was impressively delicious, but conversation was slow to get rolling. We were on Chess' turf now. Instead of a mellow summer night swatting at mosquitoes and gazing over green fields, we were inside a small, almost sterile, space. I couldn't seem to lose my fish-out-of-water discomfort.

Natalie was a lifesaver. "So Chess, your apartment says a lot about you."

He nodded. "I guess anyone's personal space would."

Natalie reached across the table and grabbed the wine and refilled her glass. "Why no rugs?"

He nodded again. "Don't forget, I'm allergic to just about everything, not just horses. I have a housekeeper in once a week, and it makes it much easier for her to keep everything clean."

Natalie leaned back in her chair. "Oh. I get it now. No curtains either, none of those stupid foofy pillows rich ladies always pile all over every sit-able surface. I never understood those anyway. I guess all those things are dust traps."

Ryder nodded. "And no animals, so no animal hair. Not even a prancing pony sculpture." She was taunting me with that one, but there was no chance another giggle would pass my lips tonight.

Chess was still nodding. "I'd rather have a real one anyway."

That perked me up. "You're kidding me. You'd like a real horse? So it's not like you dislike animals or anything like that?"

"Lizzy, you know I don't. I love all animals...it's unfair really. My Mom always dragged me away from touching dogs and cats and horses, all the time stealing away to ride herself. Then, when I went off to college, Mom finally got the dogs she always wanted. I basically couldn't come back into my own home. So after I passed my CPA and landed a job, I bought this townhome halfway between my job and the farm."

Deb had been listening attentively, as we all had. "You were coming to the farm for awhile though. Weren't you getting shots then?"

Chess looked embarrassed. "Yeah. I gave it up though. It's a three-year deal, and at the start I had to go twice a week. When I stopped coming out to the farm, there didn't seem to be a reason to keep them up."

Ryder cringed. "I hate shots."

Chess looked at his wine glass and began to twirl the stem. "Ryder, you would do it in a heartbeat in order to keep riding. I'm sure of it. Besides, they weren't bad. But they made me sit for an hour afterward in the doctor's office in case I had a reaction, so it was a huge time commitment."

Deb nodded. "And Bobby doesn't have any allergies, does he?"

Ryder sat up straighter leaning forward. "Who's Bobby?"

Chess didn't miss a beat. "My older brother, Francis Robert Cavelli, Jr., Bobby to all. And no, he doesn't. He's got a wife now, Cheryl, she's terrific, and kids and dogs and cats and even hamsters."

Deb looked at us and provided backstory. "Older brother Bobby Cavelli. Good guy. Went into computers and moved out to Seattle."

Nat asked what I wanted to ask. "So why don't we have Cavelli grandkids on ponies out at the farm?"

Chess didn't seem to mind the intrusive question. "Well, for one thing, they live on the west coast, and for another thing, Mother and Cheryl aren't too fond of each other. So, we don't see much of them. The kids are cute though. He's produced an heir and a spare. There's even a little Francis Robert Cavelli the Third."

I finally found my voice. "I can't believe how little I know about your family."

Chess was not thinking about his brother though, he mused. "I've been allowed to start a trial of daily drops, every morning under the tongue. No doctor visits, less time lost."

Deb looked at him attentively, "Are you going to stick with it this time?"

He looked right at me even though he was addressing Deb. "Yeah, well, I will if I'm going to be spending more time out at the farm again. Mom and Dad need me to sort out the business and I have offered to put together a business plan that will pass muster. Of course I need to understand the business to make a logical plan. And I need to work that around my paying job. At Equus Paradiso I'm an unpaid volunteer." He mused about that for a moment. "Maybe that's why I can't get them, especially Mother, to sit down and focus with me. Mother may feel she's taking advantage of my time."

Ryder cut in. "That's not it, Chess."

He turned to look at Ryder, as if he had forgotten she was there. "I don't think you would understand, Ryder."

Ryder tipped her head, glancing slyly at me. "Chess, I think you are reading it wrong. Maybe your Mother doesn't want you around because she's hiding something."

If I could have kicked Ryder under the table I would have. Instead all I could do was shoot invisible laser beams from my half lowered eyelids.

Natalie looked gleeful. "Ryder has info. Spill it, Ryder. What new nefarious scheme is our twisted leader, um, sorry Chess, I mean Francesca, what is she up to now?"

Ryder was grinning. "Don't ask me. I'm the stupid teenager who got cut off at one ounce of wine."

I stepped in, feeling red faced. "Ryder, you are not old enough to drink. You don't need to punish Chess for that."

"I'm just trying to let him know that Francesca..."

And I jumped in again, taking the same tone as Nat, as if I wanted her to tell us all what she knew, because really she didn't know squat. "Yes, Ryder, tell us what's going on."

And there was a long beat of silence.

Nat glanced at me pointedly, and came to my rescue. Nat said. "So, is the farm in some kind of financial tangle?" Nat's normally cut-up voice was serious as she shifted her gaze to Chess and away from Ryder.

Chess exhaled. "Please, I don't want any of you to worry about things. You just do your horse things and I'll work on the boring numbers. And as to my Mother, she's always had enough ambition for all of us, so it won't surprise me if she's got plans she's not ready to share with me yet. Dad's a charmer, but my Mother is the one with all the drive. But like Margot said, we're a team on this, so if I find a tangle of sorts, well, I'll just sort it out."

Deb reached across the table and put her hand over Chess's. "Well, I for one am thrilled someone's on the team who can deal with those boring numbers. I feel good knowing you're here. Don't let your mother run you off. The farm, the horses, they are worth more than money."

"I know you love it here, Deb. I can't imagine that place without you and Margot and of course Mother and her precious horses and her hyperactive terriers. It's the life she's always wanted. It's just that she's so impulsive about everything. And then there's my Dad. I worry about him, too. He needs to lose weight and get some exercise. He loved being king of the Cavelli Empire, and he's never known how to stop working hard." Chess sighed. "We'll see how sustainable I can help Mother make the farm as a business."

Deb gave Chess' hand another pat, and then reached for her wine. "You keep taking those allergy drops, Chess. I want you to be able to sit outside with all of us and look down that green hillside at horses grazing in the fields. I want you to be able to have a cup of coffee early in the morning up there with a purring cat in your lap. And someday, someday, I want to put you up on a horse, so you can feel a bit of the magic."

Chess pressed his lips together. "I'll do the coffee, and maybe even someday the horse thing. Not too sure about a cat in my lap though. Cats are the worst, you know."

Deb raised her eyebrows. "So I've been told, but they are almost as fascinating a creature as a horse, and good for your soul."

Chess rose. He held up his hand. "I have homemade Panna Cotta, Nonna Cavelli's recipe. How many coffees?"

We all raised our hands. I felt myself take a normal breath and my shoulders relax.

The conversation had moved on and Ryder had not revealed anything. But when I looked at Ryder she was staring at me with a look that said, *I have something over you. I have power.*

# 13. Plenty To Chew On

*"Here."*

Ryder threw a thin envelope at me like a Frisbee.

I slapped it between my palms, making a neat catch while it was still airborne.

"What's this?"

Ryder barely parted her lips.

"New Coggins are back. Francesca said you want to show Winsome, and you haven't set up a file so she can't enter you electronically. If you want her to pay for your entries, you've got to get it set up for her STAT."

I was almost dumbfounded. "Francesca is going to pay my entries!"

Ryder was shaking her head. "Yeah. You can thank Margot for that. I don't understand it myself. Winsome is your horse, not hers, but hey, take it. Better get your account set up before she changes her mind. Your entries will be late as it is."

I frowned. "I've never done that before. Can you walk me through it?"

Ryder harrumphed, shaking her head. "Download the signature page, then sign it, scan that, and the Coggins test, and then create your permanent file with all your membership numbers, and don't forget to put Winsome's numbers in, too. Then Francesca can pull it up and make out the entries, adding her credit card. It's a piece of cake. Even you can do it."

I ignored the dig. My voice was hesitant. "I'll have to use the farm scanner/copier."

Ryder was narrowing her eyes at me. "Uh, yeah? What are you afraid of? Francesca hasn't killed you yet."

I shook my head. "I'm not scared of Francesca. I just don't want her watching me while I fumble around with her office equipment. I annoy her enough as it is."

Ryder still had her eyes narrowed, but she added a crooked smile. "She left. But Chess is still down there. I'm sure you can play dumb and he'll show you how to do it."

I started to object. But I didn't. I wondered if Ryder was still trying to get his attention…and failing. So, I went with it.

I raised my eyebrows and smiled. "Not a bad idea, Ryder. He's the kind of person who would probably do it all for me if I asked sweetly."

She did look mildly annoyed, but then again, she always looked that way. She didn't answer but shrugged and turned and headed for her bedroom.

I stepped into the kitchen and opened the drawer and pulled out a knife. I carefully slit open the envelope and pulled out the new Coggins, tossing the envelope into the trash. Once I had it electronically in my files and made myself a few copies, Francesca would need to keep the original in her office files. The original always had to stay with the horse.

I tromped downstairs, laptop and cable and Coggins in hand, genuinely looking forward to finding Chess at work in Francesca's office. I knocked gently on the door. No answer. Then I slowly opened the door to find the lights off and the room empty. Bummer. But I spotted the scanner/copier/printer humming against the back wall. I looked for and found the spot to connect my laptop and got to work.

First I downloaded and printed the signature page from the website. Then I switched to scanner mode. When I lifted the cover, there was a document in there. I set it to the side and without too many hiccups managed to scan and save to file my Coggins and the signature page. I could finish the rest of the process upstairs. I closed my laptop back up and tucked it under my arm.

And then I picked the document back up that had been left in the scanner. And I looked at it.

The room suddenly seemed very quiet, and I had the feeling that I needed to ditch the thing before someone walked in and caught me.

The thing was headed, "IRS Reconsideration" and it was addressed to an IRS office in New York. I knew I should not read the thing. I should not be seeing the thing. But, I read the first paragraph anyway. It was asking for the IRS to reconsider their findings from an audit; an audit of the Farm that had a balance owed with a lot of zeroes.

I put it back into the scanner and shut things down. I had the feeling I should back away slowly. I was aware of my heart beating, of the sound of my breathing, and even turning the doorknob and releasing it back to shut the door with a click that was unreasonably loud.

Was my future here as shaky as my hand? I put a stopper on my thoughts. It was none of my business.

The next day Francesca had Ryder pull everything out of the tack room drawers and scrub and re-organize. Ryder was doing the work with what I thought was an unusual show of energy and false enthusiasm.

I saw Emma's old label gun on the counter top with a fresh roll of dark green tape loaded. Ryder was to re-label all the freshly organized drawers. Francesca had stolen some of the ideas from the Winston tack room. We now had a nifty soda pop dispenser drawer to store our polo wraps.

I had finished the horses for the day, put away the dirty tack amongst Ryder's project clutter, and was hosing down the wash rack when Chess stopped by. After greeting me he lingered. I turned off the hose and coiled it neatly on the hook and then wiped my damp hands off on my breeches.

He nodded at my neat wash rack. "Looks like you've finished in time to join me for lunch. My treat."

I shook my head. "I can't keep letting you buy me lunch."

He smiled, "Sure you can. It's worth it to me to have your company."

I tipped my head toward the tack room where Ryder was bumping things around. "Should I ask Ryder to come?"

Chess mouthed a quiet "no." "I thought it could just be us, I mean, if you don't mind. I need to, um, get some more background on farm expenses, that sort of thing."

Chess looked a bit awkward and even boyish standing there. But he was not a boy. Chess was a lot older than I was. He appeared to be about Emma's age, which had to be mid-thirties.

I realized I would enjoy my lunch more without Ryder. "I don't mind, but I do feel guilty depending on you to pay."

Chess smiled again, and it seemed genuine. "Lizzy, don't. I know how hard you work, and I know what you're paid. I'm looking over the books, remember?"

I snorted through my nose like a horse. "Well, that's embarrassing. But yeah, I accept then. Just let me tell Ryder."

I poked my head into the tack room. "I'm off to lunch."

Ryder was sitting on the floor with cleaned drawers standing on their ends in a semi-circle around her; label gun poised and ready to spit out another strip. She looked up, taking in the fact that Chess was right behind me. She squinted and waved the label gun at Chess.

"Ah, Chess, just what are your intentions with our Miss Lizzy there?"

Chess put up his hands, and Ryder turned the plastic wheel, going click-click-click, and then two handed the label gun and aimed it at Chess.

Chess played along, putting on a syrupy version of a hick accent. "Ah swear, Miss Ryder, my intentions are honorable."

Ryder lowered her label-gun and nodded. "They'd better be, Mister. We don't want any more circus clowns breaking hearts in this town."

Chess lowered his hands, but raised his eyebrows, clearly confused. "Uh, okay."

I rolled my eyes at Ryder, annoyed, and turned to leave. "C'mon, I'm ready for my free lunch."

Ryder couldn't resist, and shook her head, tsk-tsking. "Lizzy, you know there's no such thing. No such thing."

I might have felt a tiny bit annoyed. But I am ashamed to admit, a tiny bit smug, too. Chess wanted to have lunch with me and leave the teenager behind. Not only that, there *had* been a "circus-boy." I still felt a twinge when I thought of him. But, at this point the twinge was not so much painful as it was wistful. What a dream that circus-boy had been. I smiled inwardly.

As we walked down the barn aisle, Francesca opened her office door and stepped out accompanied by her flank guards; Chopper and Snapper. I felt like I had been caught stealing something. But Chess stayed relaxed.

"Mother, we're just heading out to the deli. You want me to bring something back for you?"

I knelt down and made the two little terriers squirm and pant with happiness by delivering vigorous butt scratchings.

Francesca watched for a moment with a tight-lipped smile before turning to her son. "No. But, Chess I thought you would be heading to the city by now."

He smiled back at her. "You'll be happy to hear I'm back to the city tomorrow to earn some money. But I have a lot left to do here. So I thought I'd make a day of it."

Francesca tipped her head to consider. "I hope you're not bothering Lizzy. She has a full-time job."

If that was supposed to make Chess flinch, it didn't.

"Mother, even Lizzy needs to eat. I won't keep her long."

I rose and took a look at my nails. Not too bad. Francesca managed to keep her dogs amazingly clean considering they were always rooting around in the dirt.

Francesca cautioned me. "Lizzy, don't be late. I don't need to remind you that we have a standing appointment."

I nodded back curtly, in a way that was sort of a salute. "I won't be."

Chopper and Snapper trotted out to the cars with us, peed on Chess' car tires with wicked grins and lolling tongues, and then trotted back down the barn aisle, back to Francesca.

Chess was on the wrong side of the car and missed it. Francesca's little henchmen had made a statement. Better to let it go.

Chess and I got our fat deli sandwiches and sat down. I tried chit-chat. "So, how's it going?"

Chess cut his pickle with his knife. I'd never seen anyone do that. Then he sighed.

"It's complicated."

I studied my sandwich, deciding to press it down with my hand so I could eat the giant thing neatly. I answered without much interest. "Yeah?"

"Yeah." He was staring. "Lizzy, why don't you quarter that?"

It occurred to me that I hadn't washed my hands after scratching the dogs. I wondered if that grossed him out. It didn't bother me.

He reached for his knife and I held up my hand. "I can handle this. Tell me about your work. I mean what you're doing for the farm."

He speared a bit of pickle and popped it in his mouth. "Just trying to clean up the books and stuff like that. It's all pretty privileged information. Besides, you know Mother and Dad. Very private about stuff."

I nodded. "Your mom's ... ." I tried to think of an inoffensive word, "Strong-willed person to work for, and always secretive, even about simple stuff when there's no reason to be that way. But not your dad. Your dad's a charmer. Not only that, he's been really kind to me. I love your dad. I mean that. I can believe he was a great salesman. He could probably sell ice to the Eskimos. We all owe him a lot."

Chess was now tucking in to his sandwich, but he looked thoughtful, too. He waited to get a sip of his drink before speaking.

"Dad deserves a lot of credit, but he and Mother built an empire from a corner Italian grocery because of Mother's ambition, not Dad's. The fact is, Dad would give away the store if someone asked for it. Take the sale of the business. When he sold the business to these young guys he only took 25% down and the rest was supposed to come in cash installments. He should never have done it. Never. Too little down, too much financed. Except these guys' parents were old friends from back in the 'hood. Mother was against the terms. He should have listened to her on that one. Five payments in, the cash stopped coming. The new owners simply are overextended and killing what Dad and Mother spent their whole working life to build." He stopped talking and looked me square in the eyes. "Oh man, I've said too much. Please don't repeat any of that."

I was shocked. But, I had a flashback image of a very tired Frank during the foaling season. He had been gone a long time, and had said something about trying to help the guys who had bought his company. At the time it just sounded like Frank being the good guy that he was, and being helpful. But this...this was a new angle. Frank was trying to save himself, possibly to save all of us. I quickly figured if the new owners failed and the business went under, well, Frank would likely never be paid.

I chewed my sandwich slowly...thinking before softly speaking. "Don't feel bad, your Dad already said something to me that hinted at that. But, I thought you being here was about an IRS audit."

Chess narrowed his eyes. "Why would you think that? And what do you know about the audit?"

I fessed up. "Because, I found something called an IRS reconsideration letter in the printer in the office. I wasn't snooping. Really. I just wanted to make copies of Winsome's Coggins and there it was. I didn't even read it, well, not all of it."

Chess exhaled slowly, then leaned in and also lowered his voice. "Damn. I was making copies and got a phone call on my cell, then had to go outside because I didn't have enough signal strength inside for the call. Mother would be so pissed at me if she knew I had left a copy sitting for you to find. See, all this financial stuff is critically important, but not your problem to solve. But, at least you get an idea of what I'm up against. And why I'm anxious sometimes."

I probably looked panic stricken. Chess looked worried, too. "Now can you see how important it is that I can prove this farm is a legitimate business? It's an IRS audit of a horse farm. The IRS hates horse farms. It's my job to convince them to change their minds about *our* horse farm."

I whispered back. "It might not be my problem to solve, but I can still worry. Can the IRS take assets to pay back taxes?"

Chess took a bite of his sandwich and mulled over my question. "Well, sure, but..."

"Wouldn't that mean the farms, the houses, the horses, the trailers, the cars, everything?"

"Lizzy, I don't think it will come to that." Chess was trying to reassure me.

My food was suddenly very dry in my throat and as I tried to swallow, it tickled. I reached for my soda. Now I was choking.

Chess looked concerned. "Are you okay?"

I nodded but was still coughing. I covered my mouth with my napkin, pushing my chair back. He looked like he was going to stand up. I motioned for him to sit. This was embarrassing. I focused on taking another sip and staying quiet, hoping for the cough to calm. I stared at my lap and waited. When I dared to look up, Chess was looking at me, concerned. "I hope that wasn't my fault."

My voice was raspy. "No, no, something just went down the wrong way."

"Maybe you should take another sip of your drink."

"Yeah. Thanks." The sip helped, and I cleared my throat, my voice less raspy this time. "What does your dad say about all this?"

"You know my dad, the eternal optimist. He says he's been through far worse than this. He's working to help the new guys turn the business back around by focusing on what's worked in the past. He's getting the young Turks back on track, but said that the company got too big too fast. They jumped into new lines, like gluten-free and all organic, and paid people more than they were worth. And, he likes to say that it takes time to turn around a battleship."

I nodded as if I understood. But this was all way beyond me. "And the IRS audit?"

"He has every confidence that I will defend the business status of the farm. That is, the tax lawyers and me. And I don't want to let him down. It would kill me to let him down. But Mother is so damn secretive; it makes everything a lot harder. What was Ryder hinting about the other night anyway?"

I wasn't sure how to answer that, but I tried making light of it. "So, Ryder was right in that the price of the "free lunch" is snitching on your mom?"

Chess snorted. "No, of course not." He looked exasperated. "Mother and her schemes and dramas; she'll sort things out to come out the winner. I know enough about her to know that. Nope. I can't waste too much energy on whatever it is Ryder's darkly hinting about. So feel free to keep Mother's secret, whatever it is, as long as it doesn't involve spending money we don't have. I'll probably figure it out anyway, but probably not until she wants me to." He smiled.

I tried to reassure him. "Well I don't think it has anything to do with the audit or turning around your parent's old company, so you should probably not worry about it." I felt bad about being so glib. What Francesca was doing did indeed involve spending money they didn't have; a lot of money.

We ate in silence for a while. I was chewing things slowly, both on my sandwich and ideas that drifted unformed in my mind. I needed to chew slowly so I wouldn't embarrass myself by choking. I needed to think slowly so I didn't make stupid assumptions or say things that were embarrassing.

Chess broke the silence. "I've got to stay focused on my paying job for the next week. But the week after that, I want to take you to the city. That is, if you want to."

I sounded surprised. "New York?"

He nodded his head and smiled. "Don't look so afraid. I'll make sure we get out alive. I've got two tickets to a Broadway musical."

"It's just that, I've never been."

"You've never seen a show on Broadway?" Chess seemed surprised.

"I've never been to New York. I mean the city."

Now he looked shocked. "Never?"

I suddenly felt like some country rube and it made me a little defensive. "The world doesn't revolve around New York City y'know. It just never has appealed to me."

"Well, Manhattan has its own charms. I'll just have to convince you. It's a date then?"

I found myself tipping my head and pulling at my earlobe as if it suddenly itched. How could I get out of it? Did I want to get out of it?

"I'll have to check if we have a show that conflicts. I have to get up so early on show days."

"I know that. That's why I got weekday tickets."

I was still pulling at my earlobe.

Chess laughed. "What? Do I have to ask Ryder's permission? She was pretty funny back there."

I laughed. "No way. She'll be green with envy though. A Broadway show would be right up her alley. She thinks of herself as being quite the sophisticate."

"Well, she'll have to get over it. I have only two tickets and I am taking you."

I couldn't help but grin. I had just been asked out on a date. "Okay then. I accept."

\*\*\*

By the time I got Johnny Cash into the arena at the Winstons', the sun was low on the horizon and casting long slanted shadows across the fluffy euro-felt footing. Johnny stepped carefully over the shadows, lifting his knees and hocks as if stepping over cavelletti poles. I watched in the mirrors and found something earnest and endearing about how he navigated the shadows. I knew in time he would settle and trot normally. Francesca came sauntering down the hill, pulling her gloves on. Would she ever find it endearing? I thought of her helplessly sitting on Johnny's neck. We had laughed and laughed, but I knew it could happen again. And if she ever came off, I knew she wouldn't be laughing.

I made a walk transition and hopped down. "He feels great today."

I led Johnny to the mounting block, and she stiffly mounted, gathered the reins, and sorted herself.

"Great? I was watching from the barn. He is a slow study about the shadows, don't you think?"

I gave him a pat. "No. He's not slow. I think that's just how he's made, Francesca. Some horses are more careful than others. He probably would have made a great jumper. He wouldn't have touched any of the fences."

Francesca pursed her lips. "Hmmmm. Either that or he would have refused to jump anything."

I shook my head. "He's too much of a 'try-er' and just as honest as they come. But he's a spook that's for sure. You'll have to be able to deal with it because whatever you get at home is probably a fraction of what you'll have to deal with at the shows. You've shown enough that you already know that though."

Francesca didn't correct me. In fact she looked thoughtful. "Lovey is exactly the same at the shows as he is at home."

I almost snorted. "Lovey is a one-in-a-million. But remember how Rave was? Oh my God, he dragged me around and was ridiculous on the first day. He was a bull until he settled."

Francesca was silent.

I lifted my eyebrows, realization sinking in. "You did show Rave, right?"

The look on her face said it all, even though she remained silent. If she had tried to show Rave it clearly had not gone well. In fact, my getting to ride and show Rave was most likely the result of things *not* going well. Francesca was delusional if she thought showing Johnny Cash at Grand Prix was going to be like showing Lovey.

I looked straight at her, but her eyes were staring at Johnny's withers. I'm sure I couldn't hide my disbelief. Did she think horses were some kind of machine?

"Francesca, he's not like Lovey. It might take awhile to get that gold medal. There's nothing wrong with that. I hope someday to earn all my rider medals, even my gold medal. But I know it will take years. And I love grooming Johnny and being your eyes-on-the-ground, but..." And then I said what I'd been wanting to say since day one. "This sneaking over here makes me really uncomfortable. I keep feeling like we're going to get busted. I mean this could take a long time. I expect this could be a year or two."

Francesca looked back at me, affronted. "Don't be silly. I could get this knocked out in two shows. Once I have my gold medal, I'll simply put the horse back on the market and all will be well. It will be fait accompli. A win-win for all."

Those words "on the market" knocked the air right out of me.

Francesca scowled. "Don't look so shocked, Lizzy."

I blurted out, "But you adore this horse!"

"Yes, but in a way he's just on loan. Like a leased car, I suppose."

I scowled, confused. "You don't own him?"

"High Horse Couture owns him."

I was confused and frustrated. "But you're High Horse Couture."

Francesca was starting to lose patience. "I am. Sort of. It's business, Lizzy."

Now I was getting the picture, and I'm afraid I sounded accusatory. "You used the company money...the money for producing breeches...to buy yourself a horse?"

Francesca just narrowed her eyes, her voice calm. "I made an investment with company money. And I will put it right back as soon as he is sold. And like I just mentioned, this is my business, not your business."

I blurted out, "Francesca, you're already under audit," and immediately regretted it.

Francesca's voice got softer but more intense. "How in the world would you know that? Have you been snooping around, or has my son the CPA been blabbing?"

My face felt hot. I had just dragged Chess into it. I was ashamed of myself. "Chess didn't say anything. I saw a piece of paper in the copy machine but I wasn't snooping. I just needed to make copies of my Coggins, for my entries. I didn't read it, I just saw it."

Francesca inhaled, clearly affronted. "Entries that I just paid for, by the way. You want my help paying for shows, and I want your help earning my gold medal. I'm doing more than most farm owners would for the working students, but I expect more in return. Anyway, High Horse Couture is NOT under audit...only Equus Paradiso Farm."

I kept my trap shut, but I knew this wasn't right.

Francesca gave herself a shake and then laser beamed her narrowed eyes back at me. "You will keep this to yourself. Just help me get my gold medal and this will all be behind us. Am I understood?"

What could I say? "Sure."

Francesca picked her reins back up and walked away. I had a job to do. I drew a deep breath. She had taken on an almost impossible task. The Grand Prix test was by design a difficult test not only of the horse, but of the technical proficiency of the rider. Francesca may have known her theory inside and out, and she may have known how things were supposed to look, but she was not loose or relaxed enough in her mind and body to influence the horse in perfect rhythm. Instead, her stiffness seemed to tamp down his natural buoyancy and drive a barrier between herself and Johnny. Not only that, but if she did come off, she could hurt herself, and maybe Johnny. What then?

I watched her slow progress around the arena. Johnny was way too constrained. How could it be otherwise? Horses go as they are ridden. The longer I watched, the more depressed I became. Could Francesca ever be up to the task? Was there a secret way to unlock her tension, the tension that was inextricably part of who she was? I was in too deep and Francesca was in dreamland. Dreamland? I inwardly harrumphed. That was what I was always being accused of being...unrealistic. But I didn't want to be like Ryder, trying to squash Francesca down. I hated that thought. When Francesca kissed Johnny Cash on his nose she had revealed something about herself in front of me. There was a heart in there. And she wanted to live the same dream that I did. That was something to chew on.

What could I do? Francesca chose me for some reason, but how could I make a difference in her riding?

I thought about the time a really good dancer had twirled me around a dance floor. We had really covered ground. I danced like I knew what I was doing. It was fun even though I was breathless when I finished. I think that guy could have taught me to dance as well as he did, in time. I felt certain about that even though I never did take up dancing. Dancing had been exhilarating and very satisfying. I thought that sort of exhilaration and satisfaction should be the way the horses feel at the end of a ride, too.

What made that dancer so good, and so able to direct my steps? He was balanced enough to change my imbalance, and confident in his steps and direction, and gave me that confidence too, just by holding my hand and touching my waist. He was firm but gentle in his touch. Touch. That was a big part of it. The quality of touch must start with who you are, it's embedded in your character, but could only become as controlled and yet gentle as that dancer's through the mastery of the dance.

No beginner is able to be controlled in their touch, and no beginner was really able to be gentle. This took time through mastery. And even though Francesca was no beginner, I doubted there was enough time left for Francesca to find the level she desired.

I think I was on to something, though, when I thought about that dancer taking me for a whirl with just one hand in mine and his other hand on my waist. Just by touch he had me dancing. Maybe what the deeper level of what the dressage term "connection" was had to do with touch. Riders touched the horse in a lot more places than dancing partners. We touched our horses with our seat in the saddle, the touch of our legs on the ribcage and the touch of our hands through the reins to the mouth of the horse. We could give more than directions with our touch. But in nature the only creature that would place themselves where we place ourselves would be a predator. And yet they come to trust us.

Still, we could give courage from this place on top of the horse, a place where he can't even see us. We do it with our touch. We could give confidence and comfort. But, without a certain level of mastery, that positive emotional message got lost. Without meaning to be, riders were inadvertently abusive, causing discomfort and confusion or becoming a burden that our horses, our dance partners, had no choice but to endure. Some horses seemed to endure it better than others; like Lovey.

But when it did work, it was miraculous. Sort of like that dancer whirling me around. In fact, because of the sensitivity of horses, the impact was much greater than the holding of a hand and a touching of a waist. But when the riding was not good, when the emotions were negative ones, the impact was just as great in the wrong direction. It made sense to me that as prey animals negative emotion is the most important emotion horses needed to detect. They may be domesticated, but survival instincts never domesticated. They picked up the negative much quicker than the positive. An especially "flighty" animal like Johnny was constantly on alert for a reason to flee. Francesca's connection would be a source of increased worry for whatever horse she was riding, but especially for a horse like Johnny. I'm not sure Francesca understood this. And I wasn't sure if she could.

I sat down in the corner on the mounting block and momentarily put my head in my hands. It was all too much for me ... Francesca and her schemes; Johnny and his temporary status; the sinking ship that I called home ... Equus Paradiso Farm.

My silence was not lost on Francesca. She broke my train of thought. "Lizzy!"

I drew a deep breath. "Yes."

"Back to earth please, the show is next weekend." She halted Johnny next to the mounting block, staring down at me.

"I'm sorry, Francesca. Next weekend? And then you tell me that

Johnny will get sold. And then there is the money stuff. I'm feeling overwhelmed." I surprised myself by hearing my voice wobble.

Predictably, Francesca didn't soften up. Not one bit. "Oh for heaven's sake. No one is dying, and you still have a roof over your head. The gamble is all mine, these are my poker chips on the table."

I felt heat prickle at my cheeks. I stayed silent, but I was thinking to myself that Francesca was betting my chips, too. And Margot's and Deb's, and Nat's and the guys ... and the horses. And what about Frank? Dear sweet Frank.

Francesca sniffed. "Honestly, between you and Ryder I have had enough working student drama lately. I suppose having had sons and not daughters I'm unused to female theatrics, but maybe you two are my penance. I do appreciate that you get attached to the animals, but which horses I keep and which I sell is above your pay grade. This is a business; my business. I cannot keep them all, which I feel sure Chess would tell you as well. Your rainbow and unicorn thinking gets really tiresome."

There was the charge again. I was all rainbows and unicorns? She was the realist? Of course she had made some valid points. The IRS did not care about the best-friend status of our horses. But I had seen the lipstick smears on Johnny's white nose. I think she was the one with Grand-Prix-sized delusions.

I tried to stay calm. "Are you telling me that I have nothing to worry about?"

She leveled her gaze at me. "I'm telling you to worry about the things I pay you to worry about. Clearly my son hasn't helped in that regard."

Chess. I owed him for my earlier slip. How could I help dig him out? I forced a little smile. "Don't blame Chess. He seems like such a nice guy, and I know he's working hard. I like him. Actually, he's asked me to go to a Broadway play."

Francesca rolled her eyes and grunted. "Wonderful. It's Emma all over again."

What did she mean by that? "What?"

She was barely audible when she said, "Working students really are the low-hanging fruit." Then in normal tones said, "Anyway, can we get back to work please? And this time, do pay attention. Time is of the essence."

I answered, "Of course." Francesca's jabs stung, but I had to pull myself together. I admitted to myself that my musings about her had not been kind either. But, at least I never said them out loud. No rainbows and unicorn thinking from me; no more deep musings on dancing and dressage. I needed to sharpen my skills as Francesca's man-on-the-ground, and try to separate my job from my sometimes intense discomfort and dislike of Francesca. Francesca was going to have to make some big changes in her riding if she intended to look the part. Johnny was a super horse, but no unicorn. She would need to ride better than she ever had before. I took a big breath. I thought to myself; be professional. Be kind. But be real or things will never change.

I drew a deep breath and squared my shoulders before saying, "Francesca I don't want you to be mad at me, but this is what I see ... you might not realize it, but you're pulling on your curb rein, and your spur is locked and loaded, you're rubbing the hair right off his sides. All that pressure is shutting Johnny down. You're going to have to find a way to let go of all that tension if you want Johnny to move like he can move. You need to think about being softer, gentler, more elastic in your touch. If you can loosen up your body, he'll relax. You'll give him more confidence and you'll get less spooking. Not so much grip."

It didn't seem to register. She shot me a withering glare that was visible all the way across the arena. Maybe some of it sunk in, or maybe grip was the only kind of touch Francesca really understood.

# 14. Francesca's Gift

*Francesca came down the barn aisle with a cheap cardboard pet carrier*, the terriers hopping up and down alongside her.

She called out, "Lizzy, Ryder, come take this hell-spawn from me, please!"

I jumped forward and grabbed the carrier just as I saw a tiny little cream colored leg poke through one of the ventilation holes. The carrier weighed almost nothing.

I put the carrier on the ground and started to open it. "Oh Francesca, what is it?"

Francesca looked horrified. "Don't you dare open that."

Margot walked over, pointing at the little leg sticking out of the box and now waving around frantically. "A kitten? But you hate cats, not to mention that we already have a pride of them up at Deb's."

Ryder put down the brush she was using on Lovey and came over, too. A little pink nose poked into the hole now, and then I heard the sound of shredding.

Francesca had a note of panic in her voice. "Lizzy, take it up to the apartment now! It's been making that noise all the way here and I was terrified it would get loose in my car. Imagine the bloodbath that would be."

193

Francesca turned to Margot. "I got it for rodent control in the girls' apartment since the terriers don't go up there to hunt." Then Francesca turned back toward Ryder and me. "But, don't you dare let it down here or I am sure the dogs will kill the thing."

Margot looked puzzled. "I didn't realize there was a rodent problem, but why not ask Deb for one of her wild kittens?"

Francesca turned back again to Margot. "Because I was told the wild ones won't stay indoors. Besides, evidently cats are territorial and any from Deb's would simply run back up the hill. This foreign kitten will claim the apartment as his territory. Or at least that's what the woman at the store told me."

Margot frowned. "We've never needed a cat up there before now."

Another long shredding sound came from inside the box. Francesca widened her eyes; she did look scared. She waved both hands at me.

"Shoo! And Ryder, go to my car and take all that cat stuff up to the apartment. Kitty litter is ridiculously heavy."

The shredding continued all the way up the stairs and I barely got into the apartment before the little cream colored kitten had almost its entire head crammed through an enlarged ventilation hole. Its ears were stuck back to its head and its eyes were squinty and elongated with mostly white showing. It wriggled its head and looked pretty freaked out. Actually, it was reminding me of Jack Nicholson in the movie *The Shining*.

"Oh my gosh, you wild little thing, don't panic, don't panic! Wait a sec, just wait and I'll get you out properly."

I set the box on the floor while the kitten pulled its head back into the box and the shredding sound changed to ripping sounds and then thumping sounds. Clearly it was now using its teeth and its whole body rather than just its claws.

I got the box open and snatched it firmly by the scruff of its neck. Luckily it went limp, so I cradled it against my body. It was trembling and I could feel its heart thump-thumping.

"Wow, you are one scared little baby." I tried to get a good peek at it. Cream colored, but with peachy toned ears and paws. And as I stroked its chin it looked up at me with stunning ice-blue eyes. "And you're beautiful, too."

Francesca had to have paid money for this kitten. I knew enough to know this was not your basic domestic short-haired kitten. It looked like a Siamese. Instead of dark points though, it had pale orange points and a pink nose and pink paws and the most beautiful blue eyes that were now focused directly on my face. I cupped the little face in my hand and kissed it lightly on top of its head.

"You are just precious." It answered me with a couple of loud plaintive meows. For such a tiny thing, it sure had a big voice.

Ryder came in toting a heavy jug of litter with a bag of kitty chow under her arm. "Francesca has officially gone off her rocker. This is just more work for us."

But I was smitten. "Oh Ryder, come look. He's beautiful!"

Ryder peeled my fingers from the kitten and pulled it away from me. Then she held it up at arms distance to examine it while the kitten meowed loudly in alarm. "This is a flame point Siamese."

Ryder then scruffed the kitten, placed it on its back along her forearm, and pulled back the tail and said, "And your he is a she."

I said, "How can you tell?"

She said, "See the little slit right under her tail? That would be female. Toms have a round opening further away from the anus."

My jaw dropped, both impressed and irritated at how rough she was with the poor little baby, and I pulled the kitten back away from Ryder. But I was impressed that Ryder immediately identified the sex and breed. "Ryder, the poor thing has been traumatized; give it back." I nestled it back up against me and said, "Looks like Francesca has bought us a fancy purebred kitten to be a mouser. That's so nuts."

Ryder nodded her head in agreement. "Damn straight it is. I've got another load to bring up. Since you're so taken with it, I'm putting all the supplies in your room."

I protested. "Ryder, don't you think a mouser is supposed to have the run of the apartment?"

She grimaced. "I don't want it pooping and peeing in my closet and in my shoes."

That seemed like a dumb thing to say. "I've never had a cat do that. Cats are naturally very clean. I've had cats before."

Then she smiled knowingly. "Have you ever had a Siamese cat?"

I shook my head. "No, but cats are cats."

She was looking quite smug. "Sure they are, and since I can tell you're already attached, it's all yours." And she headed down the stairs.

I snuggled the tiny kitten up against my chest and peered down into those amazing crystal blue eyes that stared intently back at me. The little thing was relaxing and starting to purr. It took one little pink paw and gently touched the end of my nose. I felt a surge of love for this tiny little thing. I said to the kitten, "Well, that's settled then. I feel lucky to have you since you are the most beautiful kitty I have ever seen."

Ryder came back through the door with a litter pan and a bag. As she passed she shook her head and said, "Well, Merry Christmas in July to you then." I was still cooing to the kitten as Ryder disappeared into my room, dropping all the supplies with a thud. And then she left.

Once she was gone I shifted into a higher pitched sing-song voice…the kind you reserve for babies. "Just ignore Ryder; she's always grumpy like that. You are just the prettiest kitty I've ever seen. Yes you are. Yes you are. I'm going to set you up in my room, but this whole apartment is for you OK?"

The kitten made a series of funny little meows that sounded like they ended with a question mark. I kept up our little conversation. "Yes, I am your new adoptive mommy. Now I'm going to set you down, but you stay close."

I set the kitten gently on the floor, picked out a couple bowls from our kitchen cabinet, and headed to my room. The kitten put her tail up like a flag and followed. She stopped in the doorway.

"C'mon in, little kitty."

She coyly rubbed her chin on the doorjamb.

"I know, it's modest, but its home."

The kitten watched me set up the litter box and the little bowl of food and water. That was that. It was time to go back to work. Of course, the kitten tried to follow.

"No, no, no, little one. You know those terriers will make a snack out of you. I think I'll shut you in my bedroom just like Ryder said."

The kitten was so fast trying to scoot after me that it took three tries to put the kitten on my bed and get out and shut the door without almost smashing the thing between the door and the jamb.

Later, when I rode Winsome into the arena, Francesca was strolling around on a loose rein cooling down after her lesson. I couldn't wait to tell her about the kitten. I was truly enthusiastic.

"Oh my God, Francesca, the kitten is gorgeous! I got it set up in the apartment.

Ryder said it's a purebred kitten. That it's a flame point Siamese. Did you know you bought a Siamese cat for a mouser?"

"Really? Well, I just went into the pet store at the mall and I picked it out for its blue eyes."

I was still bubbling. "Does she have a name?"

Francesca was now looking faintly amused. "I didn't ask."

Francesca had picked it out for its blue eyes. That was certainly a surprise. I wondered if Francesca was really as charmed by the little kitten as I was, but just was not going to admit it.

I offered, "Do you want to give our new little girl a name?"

Her lips curled in a crooked smile. "Why not? Margot always gets to name the horses. I think I'll christen the cat."

I waited a few beats then asked. "Any ideas?"

She grinned. "Yes. How about Wheezer?"

I liked it. "Oh, that's cute, Francesca. It sounds like the name of the rock band, or the character from that old movie *Steel Magnolias*, y'know, the character played by Shirley McClain."

Francesca lifted an eyebrow. "Whatever you say, Lizzy."

And with that she turned Lovey to the gate and strolled out of the arena. I guess the name Wheezer must come from something other than the movie. I guessed it was a nickname for the name Louise. Wherever Francesca got it from, it was cute. I had a new little pet named Wheezer, and if she was a bad little kitty I could call her by her proper name, Louise. The thought made me smile.

The next day I woke up to a gentle pat on my nose. Wheezer was staring calmly into my half opened eyes. Her crystal blue gaze seemed to hold so much intelligence.

"Good morning, baby girl." I gave her a rub on the side of her cheek, and she returned the favor with a head butt to my chin. She smelled good. Sort of like lavender. I marveled at her delicate frame, how weightless she seemed as I picked her up. She must be very young.

I don't know how, but kittens come pre-installed with litter box know-how. While I got dressed she scratched around, went potty, and then worked awfully hard to cover it up. She made a real mess of sand all around her box in the process. I was going to have to do something to improve that situation.

Just like the night before, Wheezer followed me around the apartment with her tail straight up, periodically meowing her little question marked meows. We seemed to be having a conversation.

"This is breakfast time for us."

"Meow?"

"This is where I make the coffee."

"Meow?"

Ryder was sitting at the table eating her breakfast of champions: stone cut oatmeal, blueberries, flax, and walnuts, with some kind of magic protein powder from the health food store sprinkled over it.

For some reason I found her bowlful a nauseating sight. I needed coffee.

Wheezer was winding herself around my ankles, meowing her little questions while I measured out the coffee.

Ryder looked annoyed. "Damn Siamese cats never shut up!"

I smiled because that was about the most I'd ever heard Ryder say in the morning. "Ryder, she got you to talk. You never talk in the morning. Good little Wheezer."

Even though Ryder sneered up at me, she was silent. One sentence was all I was going to get.

Before I went downstairs I scooped out her litter box, and checked her water and food bowls. She cheerfully followed me around the apartment, asking her questions, tail up like a flag.

Ryder had her hand on the door, ready to head down to the barn. "I closed my bedroom door. Please don't open it, okay?"

I nodded. "Of course, Ryder, but she is using her litter box. I don't think you have any reason to worry."

Ryder only grunted.

I looked down at Wheezer while the door closed behind Ryder. "What is she so worried about? You are a perfect little angel."

Wheezer put her little pink paws up on my legs and stretched and yawned. I scooped her up and put my nose right on top of her head. The smell wasn't lavender after all, but more like baby powder, a very clean smell for sure.

Wheezer, of course, wanted to follow me. I finally realized I would have to scoop her up and toss her into the apartment and then quickly shut the door. I hated to do it, but on the other hand I needed to go to work. Actually, I was flattered that the little kitten had bonded to me.

She was sweet and seemed unusually smart for a cat. I loved her chatty meows. Plus, she was so pretty.

When Francesca showed up I was gushing as I tightened up Lovey's girth for her to get on for her lesson with Margot. "I just love Wheezer, Francesca. You really picked out an incredible kitty. I think she's trying to speak English. Each series of meows is clearly a question she's trying to ask me. It's so cute. You should come up and see her.

Francesca seemed interested. "I did think her eyes were extraordinary."

I agreed. "Oh me, too! They really are the most amazing blue. I've never seen anything like it before. I just love her already."

And then from down the barn aisle Ryder yelled out, "Damn cat! Cat's loose. Lizzy, grab the cat."

Trotting down the aisle toward us, tail in the air and talking nonstop came Wheezer.

Francesca shrieked. "She can't be down here, the terriers!"

And as if summoned from thin air, here they came like missiles trained on my little Wheezer.

Even though Wheezer was short-haired, her coat instantly went electric. She spun around and arched her back, frozen for a moment on the spot. Her guttural yowl, long and loud, made the hair on the back of my neck stand up. She hesitated only a split second, and then was off like a shot.

I had made a rush for her, but she flew up the wall like Spiderman, not stopping until she made it all the way to the rafters, where she finally stopped, balanced on a narrow support beam, staring down below her.

The terriers looked pleased with themselves. They circled under the kitten, still yapping. Ryder had caught up to me.

"Damn cat shot out of the door the moment I opened it. Lizzy, you need to shut the thing in your room."

I shot back at Ryder, "Well that defeats the purpose, Ryder. She's supposed to be rodent control for the apartment."

Francesca squinted up at the cat and then back at us, clearly annoyed. "Be quiet you two. How the hell will we get that thing down?"

All three of us, plus of course the two terriers, stood with our heads tipped back, staring up into the rafters.

Wheezer began to pace and meow her little question, which was evidently the same one Francesca had just asked. I offered, "We would need a really tall ladder."

Ryder rolled her eyes. "For crying out loud, you guys. It's a cat. She'll get down."

Francesca raised an eyebrow. "Ryder, I know nothing about cats, nor do I want to learn. But I still don't want the terriers to kill it."

I looked at Ryder like she was a heartless monster. "Ryder, it's a tiny little kitten."

Ryder sounded exasperated. "Have either of you ever seen a cat skeleton in a tree?"

Francesca and I were silent for a moment while her odd question sunk in. When I got the gist of it, I realized she did have a point.

I shook my head "no" while still not quite believing her. "But then how come firemen come and get cats down out of trees."

Ryder blew through her nose in annoyance. "Hell if I know. Boredom? Community relations?"

We three were still looking up at Wheezer, along with Chopper and Snapper who had stopped barking but had their mouths open and tongues hanging out with gleeful wagging tails.

And Wheezer had stopped talking, too. But she was leaning down staring intently at the dogs with her crystal blue eyes wide open.

Then, while we all stared, she turned around on her beam, hung her little pink butt over the edge, and proceeded to piss. She made a direct hit onto Snapper...the smooth coated one, which sent him into a barking frenzy. Chopper joined him and all hell seemed to break loose.

Francesca screamed. Poor Lovey scampered backwards and I had to trot toward him in order not to lose hold of his reins while cooing at him. I wanted to let him get some distance from the mayhem, but not get away from me either.

Francesca was screeching at Ryder. "Grab Snapper. Ryder, grab Snapper. I'll grab Chopper."

Francesca made a lunge for Chopper, but then put her hand on her head. "Shit! That little devil got her piss on me, too!"

Ryder grabbed Snapper, but he twisted his head around with his teeth bared. "Ouch. Damn it, Francesca, Snapper bit me."

Ryder jumped back and was examining her finger and then yelling at Francesca. "You're going to have to get him yourself."

Francesca had grabbed Chopper by the collar and his back paws dragged along the barn aisle as she crabbed sideways, swinging her arm and snatching at Snapper who was twirling around in excitement, evading her grasp. She finally got a grip and then bent in half; she dragged both dogs, twisting and hopping, toward her office. They clearly were not ready to leave their prey.

Francesca yelled over her shoulder, "It can rot up there in the rafters for all I care. I'll leave the dogs in the office for now, and I'll come get on Lovey as soon as I wash the cat urine off myself and my dog. Oh, my God, it smells."

I led a worried Lovey back to the grooming stall to calm down and wait for his rider.

I cooed to him, "Poor Lovey, that was unsettling, but you have nothing to worry about. It's just a tiny kitten up in the rafters."

I got Lovey settled and then I walked back to Wheezer. I stared up and she stared down. She seemed content for the moment.

And then she asked her question. "Meow?"

And it made me laugh. "I don't know how, okay? But you're going to have to get yourself down."

And then she got up and paced back and forth on her beam, and I got a full paragraph of meows. She stopped again and gazed down at me intently. "Meow?"

I shook my head. "Well, I can promise you this little girl, the fire department isn't coming."

# 15. Training Or Untraining?

*Ryder was right. When I returned to the barn that afternoon after* helping Francesca with Johnny, Wheezer was waiting for me at the door to the apartment.

I felt a rush of happy relief seeing her. I squealed, "Oh, baby girl, there you are, safe and sound."

I scooped her up and tucked her under my chin, breathing in her sweet scent. Her "meow, meow" couldn't drown out the happy sound of her purring. I carried her into the apartment. Ryder was sitting at the table with her laptop open.

My voice was full of enthusiasm, "Ryder, you were right. She got herself down, brave little girl."

Ryder growled; "Instead of Wheezer she should be called Whizzer. Man, she let loose a stream on Snapper and Chopper, and even got Francesca."

Instead of being angry though, Ryder had a twisted grin on her face.

I grinned back, and gave Wheezer a kiss on her soft little head, drawing in another deep breath. I looked over her head at Ryder.

"I love the way she smells...kind of like lavender, or baby powder. You want to smell?" I stuck the kitten under her nose. But Ryder held up her hand.

"Ick. No. Take her away. It's probably flea and tick powder."

That momentarily deflated me. "Oh…I hadn't thought of that."

Ryder rolled her eyes. I reflexively sniffed her head again; flea and tick powder for baby kittens couldn't be toxic, right? I rubbed under her chin with my index finger and remembered the scene with her perched high above us in the rafters. In my mind I imagined the scene we did not get; firefighters…good looking ones climbing up to rescue little Wheezer, and handing her to me. I would be so grateful I would bake cookies or some such and deliver them to the firehouse. I smiled at Ryder while I spun out my fantasy. I said, rather dreamily, "Too bad we didn't get to call the fire department."

Ryder had turned back to her computer, but she looked up, slightly annoyed. "What?"

I grinned. "Just to have some hot guys to look at."

Ryder shook her head. "No guarantee they wouldn't send out the old guys with beer bellies."

But I had to disagree. I had thought about that already. "Nope. Not to go up a tall ladder after a kitten. They'd send one of the younger guys on that little errand."

Ryder and I spent a moment in silence…imagining. And then she grinned. "I could let the kitten out again tomorrow?"

And for once we laughed together.

\*\*\*

The next morning Wheezer woke me up again with her soft little paw on my face. Her little pat-pat-pats were gentle yet persistent. As soon as I opened my eyes the talking started.

"Meow, meow, meow."

She followed my every step, participating in all my morning routines, tail carried like a flag. I couldn't help myself, my heart flooded with an indescribable love for this lightweight bit of cream and orange-tipped fluff. Behind those ice blue eyes I detected a surprising intelligence. Or maybe I was just being silly.

This time when I left the apartment, I shut her in my bedroom. I figured eventually

Wheezer would learn her boundaries and could have the run of the apartment. She certainly didn't need another close call with the terriers; at least not until she got big enough to fend for herself.

But as much as I loved my new little Wheezer, I still had a job to do. I decided that today when it was time for Francesca to have her lesson with Margot, I would ask if I could watch. After all, Margot knew her riding better than anyone. Maybe I would pick up some insight that I could use to carry over to her Johnny ride. I knew Margot wouldn't mind, but I also knew I had to clear it with Francesca first.

Francesca squinted at me, as if I had some nefarious reason when I asked her. She said, "So glad to see you taking interest in my lessons with Margot. Think you might actually learn something?"

I stood my ground. "Of course. But Margot *should* be the one teaching you on *Johnny*."

Francesca looked over her shoulder while hissing at me. "Shhhhhhhh!"

I drew an exasperated breath. "Francesca, no one is listening. I'm asking if you want me to watch your lesson on Lovey. I'm no Margot, but I *am* trying to help."

Francesca was silent for a few beats, examining me with narrowed eyes, as if she were administering some kind of x-ray examination. But I was getting used to her. My knees no longer went weak under her gaze.

Finally she said matter-of-factly, "Do you want me to succeed, Lizzy? Do you really? Think before you answer."

I found myself nervously curling my fists, picking my nails of my ring fingers with my thumbnails. I stifled a knee-jerk defense. But I was soon nodding. "Francesca, I'm not always as good at what I do as I would like to be, in fact I've learned that failing seems to be part of my process. But, I always try to do my job well. It's a source of pride for me. I think I'm improving as your ground person, but I think I can learn more by watching Margot train you. Right now, your success is part of my job. So, yes, I do want you to succeed."

Francesca released me from her x-ray gaze, and I sensed that she approved. She said, "Good. See you in the arena then."

Later, when I walked into the arena to watch, Margot looked over at me. "Hello, Darling, everything okay?"

"Yes, fine. Is it okay if I watch?"

"Of course." She patted the chair seat next to her.

Francesca was doing the same warm up we were all taught, rising the trot and making easy bending lines and long straight lines. But even on Lovey, her hands posted up and down with her body, a sure sign of a stiff rider. I waited until Francesca was at the other end of the arena to ask questions. Even then I kept my voice low.

I whispered, "Francesca wants so much to improve, but her riding position seems to stay the same. I know she's trying hard."

Margot placed a hand on my knee and leaned toward me. "Darling, all the desire and all the effort in the world doesn't change reality, does it? Not everyone can attain the same skill level, can they?"

I whispered back, "So, how do you handle this, I mean, as a teacher?"

Margot looked back at Francesca trotting around, and spoke from the side of her mouth. "You learn to compromise. You must, otherwise you aren't really being fair or kind. I ask myself what can I give a student so they can make the most of what they do have. I try to set them up for whatever success they are capable of achieving. Do be sure, though, to leave room for happy surprises, because darling, sometimes they do surprise you."

Then she winked at me and put all her attention on Francesca. "Francesca, lengthen that curb rein. Now sitting trot, darling. Just
easy small trot steps that you can manage until your hips loosen. Ride
straight ahead, very slight shoulder-fore, that's too much angle. Now
address each corner as an exercise. Half halt right before the corner so
he enters the turn uphill in his balance. Now exit the corner by adding a
drop of impulsion. Good. Look in the mirror. Is he straight? Now look
at yourself. Are you straight? Do you look relaxed in your shoulders and
low in your center of gravity? Ah, see? Your shoulders do need to drop,
don't they?"

I waited for a gap of silence before I whispered again to Margot.
"There is so much that goes into being successful in dressage. It seems
to get more complicated the more I learn."

Margot made a "Harrumph" noise and kept teaching. Clearly I had
stated the obvious. Francesca meanwhile began to make some bad half
passes. Margot kept her voice friendly.

"Francesca, darling, no movements quite yet; to be spot on in your
timing you still need more relaxation. More relaxation in your muscles
and joints will allow you to influence Lovey in a more harmonious way,
rather than disrupt the rhythm and tempo of the stride. For now, just
relax your legs and arms and do nothing. Just hang out a bit. We'll add
more impulsion and more exercises slowly, step-by-step."

I thought to myself: letting go of tension; Francesca? I doubted
that was possible for her. I shook my head and whispered to Margot.
"Francesca will never have "feel," will she?"

Margot tipped her head, while keeping her eyes on Francesca. "Feel
is perception, timing, and coordinating the aids. Do you think those
things can be taught?"

I thought about it a minute, then quietly answered. "I guess perception requires awareness. You can raise awareness, sure. But some people
just don't seem as sensitive, or aware as others. I don't see why timing

can't be taught. Clearly though, some people are not as coordinated as others."

Margot kept her eyes on Francesca. "Ah, but Lizzy, remember that Francesca was a dancer. In fact, she can still dance better than you or I, and she can put both her hands flat on the floor and pull her head against her knees. I certainly can't do that. Food for thought isn't it?"

Margot had my brain clicking. I said, "And to interpret the music with their bodies like they do in dance…and yet maintain their form…that must take sensitivity along with a mastery of technique."

Margot smiled. "Yes, darling. Now you are thinking. But, of course, the muscles and turn out for ballet are totally different, opposite really, from what we need. She's had to make huge changes in her body to do this."

I stopped talking and watched as Margot began to make more demands on Francesca. "Transitions now, darling. Smooth as you can make them, rather than abrupt. They don't have to happen at any particular letter in the arena. No one is putting numbers on them. Ride for the best feeling you can produce with the least amount of effort in your body. That's why it's okay to make mistakes here at home. You must feel both ends of the rope to find the middle."

After a few minutes I finally saw Francesca begin to merge with her horse. Her face even relaxed its expression. Margot smiled at me to be sure that I noticed, then she patted my knee. She was showing me something important about teaching and learning.

Margot spoke again, almost to herself. "George Morris says that every moment you are interacting with your horse you are either training or un-training him. It's the same when you teach riders. Each time you teach, you must ask yourself, did I train or un-train my rider today, and be brutally honest in your answer."

I answered, "People are just so…complicated. I think horses are much easier than riders."

Margot nodded, "Maybe, but they are also captive. Not so our human students. I am sure many horses would change riders if they could."

I giggled, and then nervously looked to see if Francesca had noticed. Nope. Phew.

Margot sighed. "I do find the horses a lot easier to read. They are quite forthright, with no hidden agendas, no secrets." Margot briefly caught my eye in a way that made me uncomfortable. It was a relief to watch her focus once again on Francesca. I stopped asking questions.

*** 

I had put Lovey away and was sweeping when the terriers earnestly marched down the barn aisle, tongues hanging out the sides of open mouths. They seemed to be looking for me in particular because when they found me they stopped and stared, and even seemed to sniff the air.

I stopped sweeping. "What?" I leaned on my broom handle and they continued to stare. I realized I was carrying the scent of their prey.

"It's the kitten thing, isn't it? Don't chase her and she won't pee on you. She won round one but there better not be a round two...got it?" Chopper sat down and licked his lips. I felt my loyalty was being called into question by the scruffy little terrier-ist.

Francesca walked down the aisle toward me and when she got close she stage-whispered to me. "Lizzy, we'll do Johnny an hour later today. Deb needs you to lead the youngsters on a hack off the property, although I don't see why." Of course, it wasn't a request, it was an order, and I anxiously wondered what horse I was supposed to ride on this little adventure.

"Francesca, we need a Kiddo-type horse for that. Who am I supposed to ride?"

"Deb suggested Lovey, but he's done enough today. Besides, I can't remember ever taking him down a trail. I told her you would ride Winsome. You take her out all the time."

I mildly protested. "Yes, but she's not exactly a packer. Actually, she's a bit of a hot number."

Francesca waved me away. "Surely you can manage. Besides, Deb says they've been hacking the babies all over the farm in the afternoons and they've been stellar."

I nodded my head, but was still uneasy. Winsome was great fun to hack out *alone*. Hacking out alone was not the same thing as hacking out in company. Even alone, she was only fun once we got past the damn gate. That gate and I had a history. I let out a deep sigh. I did not have a choice.

That afternoon, Deb and Natalie and Ryder hacked down to the main barn on the three bambinos. I was tacked up and ready for them. I had been busy in the afternoons with Francesca and Johnny, and had not seen these guys hacking around the farm together. They were, of course, adorable.

Deb was mounted on Habenero; fondly known around the barn as Pepper. He was one of Regina's foals, and since her death there had been an unspoken agreement that he was a keeper. While his big brother Hotstuff had been claimed by Margot, and Deb went along with the line that Pepper was for Margot; I wasn't convinced. To my way of thinking, the bond had been made. He was Deb's.

Pepper, like Hotstuff, was tall, narrow, and jet-black, but with an unusual broken blaze. The blaze started on his forehead and stopped right above the noseband in a weirdly straight line. Then it started back up again and finished as a large snip between pink tinged nostrils.

Ryder was riding the chestnut Quester. He too was tall, but chunkier than Pepper and had a perpetual wild look in his eye.

Natalie was on little Boingo. Boingo was the brother of Bounce, who had been my ride down in Florida. Boingo was a carbon copy of Bounce. He was solid bay, round bodied, and a scant 16 hands. He had a cresty neck like a stallion, but his face was delicate with large soulful eyes and tiny ears that almost disappeared in his shaggy mane and wild bushy forelock. There was something terribly attractive and yet naughty looking about him. He reminded me of the kind of bad boy you wanted to date but would never dream of marrying; a punk. Yeah, it was right that Natalie was riding him. They were made for each other.

I had a plan in mind for Winsome. I would lead her to the gate, let it open while I hung on, and then get on her when I was safely out on the road. I was careful to fake confidence, and I called out to my friends enthusiastically.

"Hi, guys!"

Deb was smiling and cracking up already about something. "Hey, Lizzy. This should be fun."

I smiled back, "Oh, man, you're an optimist. I really miss Kiddo."

Natalie interrupted, "Stop your jawing and get on, girlfriend. Boingo wants to get moving."

I gestured toward the gate. "Not until I get her through the horse-eating gate." I tugged on Winsome's reins and led her toward the gate, but she slowed down and got big-eyed. "Now listen here, Winsome, you and I are the leaders today. The bambinos are depending on you to demonstrate grown up horse behavior. Got it?"

The three bambinos got bunched up in a nervous line behind her. I braced myself, tightened my grip on the reins, and pushed the button that opened the electric gates.

Winsome was stock still, head up, and ears pricked. I was congratulating myself on my brilliant strategic move. But all that went to hell as soon as the gates began their slow swing toward us. Boom. Winsome spread her front feet wide, pounding her hooves against the pavement in a spook-in-place, which was better than spinning and running off, or would have been had my right foot not been directly under her left front hoof.

I was yelling and pushing on her shoulder with both hands. "Ouch, damn, get off my foot!"

Hooves were clattering behind me as the knot of babies startled and bounced around on the blacktop of the driveway. I finally got my scratched up boot out from under Winsome's hoof.

Natalie yelled out. "Direct hit, Lizzy. That's going to hurt."

And I answered, "What do you mean going to? Shit, shit, shit."

And then Ryder growled. "Keep moving, Lizzy, or there's going to be three more of us yelling obscenities, and this time they'll be directed at you."

I hobbled through the gate, checking out the damage to my one and only pair of boots. My eyes were smarting with tears, but it was "suck it up Buttercup" time for Lizzy, once again. The young horses got out on the road with me, and I looked hopefully for a piece of fence line to sidle up against to mount, but then thought of the pansies and mulch and beautiful sod grass that I could damage. Francesca would probably examine the shoe prints and present me with a bill to repair the damage. Nope. I grabbed a hunk of mane and put my foot in the stirrup and pulled myself up on Winsome while she fidgeted nervously. I know she had no idea that she had just mashed my foot, but I did know she wanted some distance between her and that gate.

Deb began to organize us as the foursome fidgeted and weaved and bobbed down the road. We headed toward our magical field and conditioning hillside.

Deb took charge, directing and educating us in young horse field-training. "Nat, Ryder, go in front of us, side by side. It helps to put the insecure horses in front so they don't get anxious about getting behind. The lion always eats the trailing horse, right? If they balk, Lizzy and I will lead them past the scary object. Eventually we can do some field exercises out here to build fitness and confidence. I consider this part of their 'equine good-citizen' training. All horses need to learn to hack out by themselves and in company. Their new owners will appreciate that we took the time to teach them.

I watched from behind while Quester swung his head from side to side with googly-eyes. Meanwhile Boingo was periodically snorting at the ground. It was quite a thought that although these three had been born and raised right here, they had never stepped beyond these gates. They had lived a sheltered life. This was a big day.

Next to Winsome, Pepper was alert yet calm. I smiled, recognizing the same trusting personality as his big brother, Hotstuff.

I said to Deb, "Pepper is an old soul, isn't he?"

Deb just smiled and stroked his neck. We were walking close together, side-by-side, so I reached over and gave him a pat, crooning, "What a good baby you are."

In a flash, Winsome pinned her ears, pulled her lips back, and with a twist of her neck, threw her hips into Pepper. Luckily she did not actually kick or bite, but the threat was strong and clear.

Deb had quickly gathered her reins and brandished her whip toward Winsome. "Hey! Watch her, Lizzy, she is jealous!"

I was embarrassed. "Sorry, sorry. I sure didn't see that coming. Margot would kill me if Winsome hurt Pepper."

I couldn't dwell on it because Quester and Boingo had come to a screeching halt and were accelerating backwards toward us.

Deb was back in charge. "C'mon, Lizzy, time to take the lead."

Pepper was watching his two buddies and was frozen to the spot. Winsome, God bless her, did her new job and marched on ahead, surprising me by calmly walking over the fast food napkin that had terrified the babies. Behind me began a chorus of clucks and tapping whips followed by a scrambling of hooves against the pavement as the group made it past the dangerous paper napkin. Natalie and Boingo jetted past me, with Boingo's head down, hopping off his four hooves like the old skunk cartoon character Pepe LaPew.

I would have been hanging on for dear life, but not Nat. She bounced on ahead, yelling "Yee-haw!"

Deb yelled. "For heaven's sake, Nat, don't encourage him!"

I breathed a sigh of relief when we finally got off the road and turned through the sagging old wooden gate.

We turned left and Deb reorganized us back into our pairs along the edge of the field. When we were on an uphill grade, Deb called out. "Let's have a little trot side-by-side. You two start first so we have space, I don't want to run up into your butts, and I'm not sure Pepper's brakes will work out here."

I must have looked horrified. Deb turned to me. "Don't worry, Lizzy. These guys may be young and green and barely under our control, but in this heat they'll wear out really fast."

I got up in my jumping position and gathered up my reins. Winsome was on the muscle, pulling, begging me to let her loose to pass the young punks who dared place themselves in front of her. Deb was right, she was jealous. She didn't seem to feel the checks I gave with the reins, or the "whoas" and 'wait, wait, waits" I crooned to her. Instead every fiber in her quite fit body was saying, 'turn me loose in canter, Mom, I can take these guys.' But I kept her in trot, frustrated. Meanwhile, my foot was taking my body weight while I stood up in my irons. It was throbbing. Deb, as usual, was right, in that the babies were soon walking and panting, their necks wet with sweat. I let Winsome trot past the leaders before I walked, her ears pinned back against her neck. She kept her ears pinned and her eyes darting from one bambino to the others the rest of the trip around the field, taking turns making faces at each of them. Not one dared to challenge my little mare. They gave her space and averted their eyes, showing submission to the alpha mare.

The flies were now our main problem as they were drawn to the hot sweaty horses. I slapped several deer flies on Winsome as we strolled, leaving spots of blood on her neck and on my gloves. Boingo caused another scene as a big black horse fly landed on his croup, which sent him off on another, much lazier set of crow-hopping. Natalie deftly reached behind herself and smacked the fly mid-buck, and Boingo immediately ceased his hopping, let out a heavy sigh, and then almost fell down while he stopped and twisted himself into a pretzel to rake his teeth over the insect bite.

Soon we were back at the gate, and a flock of butterflies took flight in my stomach. I turned to Deb.

"I don't guess my strategy of getting off to push the button was a great idea."

Deb nodded. "Appears that way to me, too."

I grimaced, "If I hand her to one of you guys to hold, she'd only kick your horse."

Deb only nodded.

I took a deep breath. "I'm going to go for it."

Ryder called out, "For God's sake, Lizzy, don't fall off. It could scare the babies."

I tried to ignore Ryder's asinine remark, gritted my teeth and inched my wary mare up to the keypad and quickly pushed in the code. I looked over my shoulder to check on the bambinos. They were standing quietly, resting hind legs, swatting at flies with their tails, and periodically shaking the flies off of their faces; funny how you can take in so much in a glance.

Of course once the gates began to move, Winsome did her duck and spin. But I was ready this time...I thought. She had spun to the right, but I had shortened the left rein and had a firm hold of it. What I didn't count on was the sideways hopping she added to the spin. I don't know why, but suddenly I had time to analyze my chances of finding my way back into the tack. Time slowed down and I realized my only option was to find a good soft landing. I remembered the deep mulch. It was far preferable to the black top. I let go, and heard the air leave my lungs as I landed on my back.

I lifted my head in time to see that at least this time Winsome headed through the gates and straight into the barn. The babies followed in a reckless clattering of hooves.

Ryder still managed to say dryly as she passed next to my mostly prone body, "That went well."

I sat up and watched Deb peer down the barn aisle. "I think she put herself back in her stall, Lizzy. Are you able to go after her?"

I stood up, slightly out of breath. "I've got to do something about that damn gate!"

Deb ignored me. The bambinos were looking wild eyed again and restless. "Lizzy, if you're okay, I mean really okay, then we need to get these guys put up."

I hurt all over. But I nodded. "Yeah. Go take care of your guys. I have to go help Francesca now."

Ryder piped up. "You want me to go?"

I looked right at her and thought "bitch" but said, "No Ryder, but gee, thanks for the offer."

Then with a slight crack in my voice I looked at Deb. "Deb, Winsome has got to knock this shit off or it's going to be the end of me."

The horses began to move off, but Deb nodded her head and said, "Of course, I'll be happy to help you."

And Nat said, "Me too, Lizzy. I can cowboy with the best of them."

And then Ryder said. "Just let me ride her. I can fix that little problem for you."

And off they trekked as I turned to retrieve my horse, who I found happily eating hay in her stall with all her tack as unharmed as she appeared.

And damn it, I thought, as much as I wanted to just let go and cry into the neck of my horse and let someone else solve my problem, I also knew I did not want anyone else to solve my problem.

I wanted to be a horse trainer, didn't I? Margot had said that each day you rode you had to ask yourself if you had trained your horse or rider that day or un-trained them.

There was no denying the brutal truth.

I managed to get through my Francesca and Johnny session without incident or explanation, but my foot throbbed and my finger was still sore and my body was quickly stiffening up.

I knew I needed to head off my aches and pains with a good slug of ibuprofen. I had amassed a collection of small bottles from the dollar store. My bathroom drawer rattled with them when I opened it. One by one I opened the little bottles. I looked like a drug addict desperate for a fix as I pulled out cotton and shook out what I could find, throwing the empties into the sink. Four little orange tablets got swallowed down while I kept pawing through the drawer. Empty. All of them. I gathered my refuse into a pile and tossed it into the little step can next to the toilet. That would be enough to get me through the night. But the idea of tomorrow morning was frightening. I knew I would wake up feeling a hundred years old.

I found Ryder in the kitchen pulling a bottle of water out of the fridge. She had her purse slung over her shoulder.

"Ryder. Where are you headed?"

She turned and raised an eyebrow. "Why?"

"Could you please stop and pick up some ibuprofen for me? I desperately need a hot shower and some food and then an early night, and since you're heading out already…"

"Yeah, sure." She started to leave.

"Wait. Let me get you some money." I did a stiff shuffle to my room and came back with a five dollar bill, practically stuffing it into her bag. "Thanks, Ryder."

She gave me a wave and left. A long hot shower was in order.

My little Wheezer waited outside the shower, kneading the bath-mat and purring. She did the same thing while I ate my dinner, and when I finished my ice cream I put the bowl on the floor and watched her lick it clean.

I went to bed with Wheezer curled up in the bed with me. She gazed at me with her ice blue eyes with what seemed to be adoration. I stroked the top of her head with my index finger and listened to her relaxed and rhythmic purring. It was good to be worshipped by some-thing with a heartbeat; even if it was just a kitten.

# 16. A Punch And A Tickle

*I woke up feeling just as I expected I would. I ached from my neck and* shoulders all the way down to my buttocks and I was still limping from Winsome stepping on my right foot. In addition, my Papa injuries to my right hand were still a mild sort of sore; putting a kink in my second finger that would most likely never straighten. In short, I was beat up, and could not remember the luxury of not hurting somewhere in my body.

Ryder was eating her breakfast of champions, when Wheezer and I found her. "Hey, Ryder. Did you get my ibuprofen?"

She looked up at me with a blank face. "What?"

I repeated myself, "The ibuprofen."

She frowned, "Oh, sorry. I totally forgot." She got up and returned with my five dollar bill in her hand.

I took the money slowly, and watched as she sat back down and spooned another mouthful of blueberries and whatnot into her mouth. She didn't even look guilty.

Her disinterest in my pain made me feel especially sorry for myself. I said, "Ryder, I really need something. Do you have anything?"

She did stop chewing, and looked thoughtful, finally saying, "Nope, but I saw a huge bottle of aspirin in the feed room. You know, like from a warehouse club. They must have been bought for some horse."

I sighed. "I guess aspirin is aspirin. I'll go get some." I started for the door and then as if in a grand gesture of caring, Ryder piped up again. "Be sure and eat something and take a full glass of water with it. That stuff will tear up your stomach."

I stifled a sarcastic tone. "I'll do that. Thanks."

The aspirin helped, and as the day progressed I loosened up and was able to do my job. I kept tabs on the clock and continued to dose myself every four hours.

By the late afternoon I had consumed a bunch of aspirin and my tummy was beginning to complain while I was warming up Johnny for Francesca. I periodically burped a hot fizz. When Francesca appeared ringside, I was more than happy to slide off of Johnny and hand him over to her.

After Francesca mounted, she watched me limp over to the mounting block.

She looked slightly amused. "Have you been messing up my landscaping again?"

I winced, wondering if she was guessing, or if someone had told on me. I looked up at her confident expression. She knew. Damn Ryder. "Sorry, Francesca."

Her mouth twisted. "Hospital?"

I sighed. "No. Just bruises I think."

Francesca rolled her eyes and shook her head, as if I was falling off just to annoy her. "Lizzy, you need to stop doing that."

I sighed again, realizing that Francesca, in her own cracked way, was trying to be sympathetic. Still, I am sure I looked incredulous. "Uh, ya' think?"

Francesca gathered her reins and with a shrug rode away. I sat on the mounting block and stewed in my own fizzing-hot juices while Francesca began her warm up. I did seem to fall off more than anyone else at the farm. When Johnny had spun around with Francesca she had at least stayed on, which I supposed made her feel superior to me. This thought pissed me off. Maybe if my saddle had knee and thigh blocks the size of pool noodles like Francesca's I could have stayed on the top side of my horse; not only that, Johnny hadn't gone crow hopping off like Winsome. He had stood like a statue for her. My next burp scalded my throat. I was a stew of hurts, simmering in a big pot of hot bubbling resentment.

I was thinking how Francesca had the arrogance to enter a show this weekend with almost no time to prepare for it. She seemed to think she could buy herself that gold medal: Outrageous. I knew I was the better rider, but I would never have done such a stupid thing. I wondered how she would handle her big wake up call; the one that was surely coming. I suspected it was going to hurt a hell of a lot more than my collection of bruises.

Margot would be leaving in the morning for Texas to coach Emma at some big important show, so Francesca was going to "go it alone" and slip in her Grand Prix debut while the cat was away. She was jumping the gun and too stupid to realize it. Except of course, she wasn't exactly alone. I would be at her heels, doing her bidding. I slumped over, miserably staring at Francesca and Johnny with my chin in my hand. I yearned to be with Margot and Emma. I could be grooming for Emma this weekend. I should be with them, not Francesca. I had groomed for Emma before. Yeah, she was neurotic, but not mean. I wish-wish-wished I could be with them. I realized that I missed Emma. My eyes glazed over and I stopped watching Francesca.

This would be an important weekend for Emma. Margot would be helping her make a big step up with her client's stallion this weekend. The stallion sounded wonderful. I had never seen him in person. But Emma was stunning on any horse. There would be a lot on the line. I expected tensions would be high. Emma had been hired to ride and compete "Fable" due to Margot's recommendation. The owners had taken a gamble on an up-and -comer rider for their prized stallion.

Both Emma and Margot had to please more than just judges. They both answered to the horse's owner. That was who must be pleased at the end of the weekend, regardless of the outcome. Owners kept our world turning. That would always be true. I never thought of that before coming to work here. I know now that things that look easy and rosy from the outside rarely are what they seem.

Francesca was my "owner." Performance pressure was a way of life. I needed to get over it. I sighed.

I looked back at Francesca. It was my job to do my best by her, even when I thought what she wanted was just not possible. Even if at this particular moment I think I hated her.

One of the things I hated was that she made me feel like a bad rider by association. If she went down centerline looking like hell, I knew I was going to feel like hell.

When I watched Emma or Margot, I felt pride by association. In both cases, I didn't deserve it; I hadn't earned it. God, I was a sick puppy, wasn't I? My thoughts didn't soften my feelings toward Francesca. I just added self-loathing to my loathing of her.

It's hard to be kind and empathetic when you feel like hell. I called out. "Francesca, I think you need to drop your stirrups." It was mean spirited. But, I convinced myself it was the right thing for her to do. I had pledged to Francesca that I would help her succeed. I had listened to Margot's advice about making compromises. I knew as I said it that my motives were not pure, but I said it anyway.

She scowled, "My hips really don't need the punishment."

I shook my head. "It's the best way to loosen them up."

She stopped and took her feet out of the stirrups and crossed her stirrups over the top, carefully flattening the leathers in front of the saddle. "This will hurt tomorrow."

I smiled wickedly. "But will it require a trip to the hospital?" I was now skating a bit too close to the line. But thankfully, Francesca's lips twisted into a thin crooked smile. And she gathered up her reins and got back to business.

By crossing her irons she had taken away the crutch of the stirrups. She still looked tight, with her hip angle between the front of her groin and top of her thigh too small. The purpose of stirrups was to relieve the stress on the hips by allowing the ankle and knee to share the job of shock absorbing. I had taken that away, and put the total load on her hips. Somehow Francesca's biomechanics were always a bit off, and her joints were almost always too frozen. As I watched her struggle to sit Johnny's big stride, I felt myself soften just a tad toward Francesca, and own the guilt. I was probably making Francesca hurt.

But just enough to be good for her, right?

I didn't want to cripple her, but a little bit each day could only help, I rationalized. After about ten minutes I told Francesca to stop and put her stirrups back down.

I tried to sound like Margot. "You probably should begin every day like that. Gradually over time it will help. But, things take time, usually way more time than we think they should."

Francesca huffed at me. "What do you know about time? You're a little twenty-something. The fact is, Lizzy, that often the best time to act is already behind you. But I'm wasting my breath on you. If I'm around we can talk more about this in about twenty years. What I need to do now is run through the test without any stopping or do-overs."

I nodded, not even trying to digest what she had said. "Sure."

She picked Johnny back up, talking over her shoulder. "And don't just sit there licking your wounds, or trying to make my body hurt as much as yours. Do your job and give me feedback."

Oh my God, Francesca was totally on to me. Was I really that easy to read? Now I felt especially vulnerable. I nodded, feeling drained by my hurts, both physical and emotional. Francesca, that skinny little tyrant, was always pulsating with energy, hidden agendas, schemes, plots, and a wickedly sharp intelligence. She no longer intimidated me the way she used to, but she still struck me as some sort of unexploded bomb that, though basically dormant, could still be lethal. Honestly, I knew I was no match for her.

I gave her a play-by-play commentary of the ride, trying to keep my voice flat. "Drifting off the centerline before the turn."

"Lacking impulsion."

"Too constrained."

"Missed corner."

"Short in neck."

And so on. I made a comment for every movement, just like a judge would. To her credit, it was an improved effort. The entire test was still too constrained and the zigzag was still a disaster, but it was better. And after her final salute, I saluted her back. She looked pleased with herself and with Johnny, who had not spooked a single time today.

Francesca dismounted stiffly and gave Johnny his now routine red lipstick kiss on his white nose, regardless of his beads of sweat and puffing flared nostrils. When Francesca did that little gesture, it sure made it harder to hate her. She loved her wicked little dogs, and she loved this spooky horse. Both the dogs and the horse were never completely under her control. That was something to ponder ... later. She was motioning to me.

"Lizzy, get off your bum and come take Johnny."

I jumped into action and immediately felt my back catch. "Ow!" I hobbled over with one hand on my back, bent over like an old person.

Francesca shook her head and commanded, "Hot bath with Epsom salts and lots of ibuprofen. I plan on doing the same thing. Otherwise I'll be gimping around just like you."

I slowly straightened up and looked Francesca straight in her unsympathetic eyes.

She shook her head in disgust. "Lizzy, I performed sometimes with blood in my toe shoes. It's only when you sit still and your muscles get cold that it catches up with you."

I felt a catch in my throat. So, I just nodded. Francesca was so darn easy to hate, but in moments like this, I couldn't hate her, or like her either. She just left me drained and confused.

She gave Johnny's face a caress. "Tomorrow then?"

And I managed a, "Yes. Tomorrow."

***

The next day, as soon as Margot was off to coach Emma in Texas, Francesca put me in high drive. She wanted me to hook up my old red truck and two-horse tag-along trailer to take her and Johnny Cash to the show.

What a shock. No traveling in style with the four-horse and big-assed dually truck with the farm logo on the side. Nope, we were going incognito. But, while Deb and Natalie seemed unaware that I had gone AWOL with my truck and trailer, there would be no keeping it a secret from Ryder.

She found me winding down the jack that lowers the trailer onto the ball of the hitch. She had her hands on her hips, watching as the trailer made a satisfying and loud drop. I had aligned it perfectly. Ryder nodded, and then walked back to the rear tire to pull out the wheel chock. She chucked it nimbly into the bed of the truck.

Then she looked right at me. "She's already entered the 'Hill and Dale' farm show?"

I examined my hitch. "Ryder, you know my lips are sealed or my ass is grass."

Ryder snorted. "I could say something here about your ass and the mulch stains on your breeches. But, I won't."

I kicked the lock that held the collar back on the side of the coupler with the back of my heel; maybe harder than I needed. The collar slid forward with a pop.

I spoke softly through the side of my mouth. "Thank you very much for showing restraint."

I pushed in the cotter pin that secured the collar in the locked position. Then I plugged in the electrical, and clipped the safety chains onto the body of the hitch, checking the emergency brake cable. Deep breath. I re-examined it all, check, check, check. It was always a marvel to me that this fragile link between my truck and my heavy steel trailer was all that kept my soon-to-be precious cargo connected to me at highway speeds. I used the edge of my boot to roll the wooden block of wood that had been supporting the hitch's post toward me, picked it up, and heaved it into the bed of my truck. Then, since Ryder was still hanging out, I put her to use.

"Ryder, stand behind the trailer and help me check my electrical."

She crossed her arms and strolled to the back.

I started the truck and yelled out the window. "Left blinker?"

"Check."

"Right?"

"Check."

"Brakes?"

"Check."

"Running lights?"

"You're good."

Ryder walked up to my window, putting her hand on the big towing mirror. "Be sure and check for wasps' nests before you load up."

I frowned. Why was Ryder being so nice? "Thanks. I wouldn't have thought of that."

She looked so serious. "Y'know, when trailers sit…check your tire pressure, too."

Ryder never was this genuine. I asked, "Are you worried about me?"
I thought she looked grim. "You realize this will be a total disaster.
And Francesca won't take any responsibility for it."

I didn't answer. She continued. "Francesca's about to get slammed
by the judges. Dot your I's and cross your T's so the fall-out doesn't
knock you totally flat."

I faked enthusiasm. "Oh my God, Ryder, you do care."

Ryder rolled her eyes, looking exasperated. "Don't flatter yourself.
It's more like I just can't stand watching the amateur hour. Besides,
when she's in a bad mood we all suffer."

I gave myself the luxury of a long beat of silence. And then I said, "I
know what I'm doing, Ryder, but thanks anyway."

And I put the truck in gear, and drove straight to the gas station
that had the air pump for fifty cents. I pulled it around to all four tires,
having to wrestle it to its full length while the timer clicked off my
fifty cents worth. They were all low. Two dollars later I was good. Good
and cranky.

And when I got it back to the farm and opened up the trailer, sure
enough, there was a line of mud daubers along the interior roofline, and
a honeycomb of small papery nests. Buzzing waspy things chased me
right back out. I emptied three cans of jet insecticide spray on the interior, and then knocked the saturated nests out with the broom handle.
I swept out the dead bug bodies, feeling out of sorts that Ryder had
been right.

Francesca arrived and walked up the ramp, sniffing as she examined
the interior. "Smells terrible in here."

I nodded. "Bug spray."

Her nose wrinkled. "I guess I'm slumming it this weekend."

I caught myself. She owned a fancy trailer, but had told me to hitch
up my relic. I shook my head. "Truck is gassed up, trailer's hitched, air
in the tires, and no bugs in the box."

Francesca continued to examine the interior of my trailer, running her finger over spots of rust and scratched up padding along the walls. She walked back down the ramp and began to examine the exterior. I followed at her heels. She stopped abruptly and wheeled around, using an accusatory tone. "Where is the tack room?"

I laughed. "Francesca, you've seen my trailer before. I trailered Rave, remember? I don't have a tack room."

She wailed. "Where will I put all my equipment?"

"I can take the mucking stuff and the hay and grain in the bed of the truck. You can cram some of the stuff in the cab of my truck, but otherwise it goes in your car."

Francesca almost moaned. "I don't know how people do this."

I crossed my arms. "You want me to unhitch and go get the dually and the four-horse?"

She seemed to be considering my offer, but then gave a dramatic sigh. "I will just die if Claire sees this rig, but no. This will have to do. You can put my tack in my car, but be sure not to get it dirty."

Francesca followed me over to Claire Winston's farm. No one was there. Francesca still looked anxious to get loaded and out of there before we were spotted.

I spread towels out on her leather seats before packing her stuff. Then I schlepped the hay and feed and muck stuff, stiffly climbing up and down into the bed of my truck. Traveling, even with just one horse, was a pain in the ass. My back ached, and then it was my groin, and then it was my hip. I was feeling old for 24. Then it was time to get Johnny ready to roll.

I groomed him and put on his tall padded shipping boots, snugging the four wide Velcro straps across the fronts. He walked with exaggerated goose steps all the way to the trailer, but loaded up like a champ. I dropped down the tail bar before going around to secure the trailer tie at his head, then was careful to bend my knees and lift the ramp like a seasoned weight lifter to spare my back. We were good and ready to hit the road. I did my last visual check of the hitch and started the truck, putting it into drive and easing Johnny smoothly and slowly into motion.

But after about two feet of progress Francesca scared the heck out of me with a rap on my window. "Wait, Lizzy, wait. I forgot to give you his wig."

I had hit the brakes too hard, even though we were barely moving; Johnny rocked the trailer, and then commenced pawing, clearly annoyed. I lowered the window and Francesca thrust a chestnut tail wig at me. It landed in my lap. I picked it up. It was clearly real and had to have come off a cadaver. Icky. I frowned at Francesca. "What am I supposed to do with this?"

Francesca scowled. "Never mind now, keep two hands on the wheel and your eyes on the road. No texts or phone calls."

I rolled my eyes. I probably looked like Ryder. "Yes, ma'am."

Francesca got into her car, and then beeped at me to get a move on. As I drove, my hands at ten and two, I tried not to look at the chestnut tail lying on the truck seat next to me. But I couldn't help myself. It was creepy. It had a knot at the base, with a loop of nylon rope coming out of it. I couldn't imagine how you attached the thing to the horse's real tail.

As soon as we had gotten moving, Johnny had been quiet in the trailer. It was a short trip to Hill and Dale Farm. We soon turned off the four-lane and began to wind our way down shaded two-lane roads. GPS is a beautiful thing; since we had made so many turns I was totally turned around. I spotted small directional signs staked into the ground with arrows that read "Horse Show" that directed us for the last few turns. The final arrow said "Stabling."

This would not be like the big shows that I had done with Equus Paradiso. This show was small but well known in the area since "Hill and Dale Farm" was a family farm that had existed through multiple generations. The farm ran the local pony club and had hosted many schooling shows for years, but had added recognized horse trials, and then recognized dressage shows.

Even after the expense of upgrading their cross-country jumps, and adding stabling and new footing, I understood that the competitions still had been a life-saver for the farm, bringing in needed income.

It sure was close to home and convenient. I was wishing I had brought Winsome. It would also be a good place for the bambinos to get their feet wet. What an adventure that would be. We could show and still sleep in our own beds.

Francesca zipped around me in her Mercedes with a wave. She was leading me to our stalls. I pulled up behind her, putting on my brake, and stepping out. Francesca instructed, "Stall A-12, Lizzy. That one." She pointed.

It was time to go through the routine that Emma had taught me well. The first order of business was to prepare the stall for Johnny. I needed all the stuff in the bed of the truck. Muck cart, buckets, muck fork, mounting block, tool box, fan, hose, nozzle, and bale of hay.

Next job was to inspect the stall for nails, and sharp edges, then open and spread the bags of bedding that we had purchased from the show and were stacked and waiting for us in his stall. Hang the fan, hang and fill buckets, which always seemed to include slopping water all over my legs. Of course, Francesca had left me to go to the show office and pick up her packet.

Meanwhile, Johnny was hanging his head out of the trailer door, called the "escape door." It was built for people to escape the trailer, not God forbid, a horse. He was wild eyed and snorting like a dragon. Every now and then he popped his head back in and commenced pawing, which rocked the entire trailer. I sighed. This old fool was clearly going to be a handful, but he was just going to have to hang on until I was ready for him.

Francesca returned and walked over to the trailer, looking a bit freaked out. "Lizzy, for God's sake, get this horse out of the trailer instead of fussing around with housekeeping."

I tried to smile, realizing Francesca was nervous and clueless. "I can't unload until I have a stall ready to put him in."

I looked back again at Johnny. He was fired up. He was sweating and his big white nose was blushing pink with flared nostrils. I was going to have to think this one through. I looked at Francesca. "You want to take the front end or the back?"

Her face was a blank page. Yep. She was clueless. "What?"

"You want to get in the trailer with him and back him off, or you want to get the butt bar?"

She looked shocked. "I am most certainly not getting in that rust bucket with him!"

No surprise there. "OK, I'm going to go lower the ramp, but then I'll need you to stand back there, and lower the butt bar. I'll go in the trailer with him and back him off, but you'll need to guide him off the ramp if he gets crooked."

"Lizzy, this horse has experience. He's not one of the babies."

I sighed. "Right now he looks ready to explode. Just don't lower that butt bar until I say so. Please."

No reply. But at least she walked over and positioned herself by the ramp. I looked at her carefully manicured hands, with unchipped red polish, and sighed. Then I looked down at my lead shank. No knot. I quickly put one in and pulled it tight.

"Lizzy, this horse needs off NOW!"

"Just a sec." I slipped into the trailer, cooing to Johnny. He settled, finally standing on all fours, and I slowly ducked under the chest bar. He curled his neck and touched me gently with his big pink nose, somewhat calmed, but his eyes were still wide.

"Okay, Francesca. You can drop the bar, but be careful. He looks wired."

Rather than drop it slowly and quietly, and with one hand on Johnny's hip, Francesca let it go, and then got the hell out of the way. Coward.

"Bang" went the bar, steel against steel, and I was pulled right off my feet as Johnny went into reverse gear, sort of like a rocket launch. The shank went through my fingers until they caught on the knot. Of course the shank caught against the already damaged second finger on my right hand. But no way was I letting go. Instead I reached zero gravity, making about six moon walking steps ala' Neil Armstrong down the ramp and into the parking lot. Mostly. I had one kneeling moment in a fresh and very wet pile of Johnny's poop before the tension in the lead shank popped me back up and into the air.

My finger was screaming, but I was laughing as I said to Francesca, "Well, that went well, don't you think?"

Francesca did not smile. "Next time you get him right off that trailer instead of fussing with the stall."

I didn't have the nerve to argue with her. Francesca seemed unaware that she was the one who scared the already nervous poor horse with the banging butt-bar. Plus, she could have easily gotten to the show early and prepared the stall for me, or, sent me over to do it. Besides who knew Johnny would be so claustrophobic? But I bit my tongue.

Johnny was still big eyed and leaning into the halter as I led him into the stall. I pulled off the front boots, and looked into the aisle to ask Francesca to hold him while I pulled off the rear boots. No sign of her. I pulled the door almost closed and carefully pulled the back boots off, trying to keep the Velcro from being too loud when I pulled. Then I turned him loose and watched him circle and pee and push his nose down into the shavings and pull in all the strange odors. He tossed his head in full circles and then stood up on his hind legs and peered over the top of the stall, looking for his neighbors. I smiled and hung up his halter on the rack I had hung on his stall front. He knew what was what. That horse knew he was at a show. He was indeed an experienced show horse. But that did not mean he would be placid like Lovey. He was pumped.

I finished the unpacking while Francesca rummaged through her packet and did whatever it was that Francesca did. We hadn't brought any of our farm signs, nor did we set up a tack room. We were flying under the radar today. My right knee of my jeans was soaking wet and reeking of the grass-like smell of fresh manure. But I didn't mind. I tidied up our barn area and then went to clean out and park the trailer.

When I returned, Francesca had put a clean towel over the mounting block we had brought and was tracing her test in the air with her bright red fingernail.

I peeked in at Johnny who was now munching his hay and looking much more settled. "You ready for me to tack him up?"

Francesca pressed her lips together and frowned at me. "Did you remember to bring your boots?"

I knew for a fact that she had not asked me to pack my boots. I'm sure I looked annoyed. "No. Was I supposed to?"

With a tsk-tsk she changed course. "Well, then, just hand walk him first."

I nodded. "Okay."

"But put the wig on first. We can't have him seen with two different tails."

I am sure I looked annoyed. "Francesca, I don't have a clue how to do that."

Francesca fished around in a tote bag and handed me a zippered case. "This came with him. You kids can find anything on the internet. Your smart phones are practically grafted onto your anatomy."

I unzipped the bag and looked inside. There was one of those wooden handled rug hooks, chestnut 'braid-ette' rubber bands, and a roll of chestnut colored tape that reminded me of electrical tape. I nodded, "Okay. I'm game."

I grabbed my phone and Francesca was right. There were a couple tutorials on Youtube. I watched it three times, fast forwarding through the easy parts. And then I put it in. Piece of cake. I gave the tail a few shakes and a fluffing with my fingers. It looked luxurious.

I walked Johnny around the farm and the arenas, and boy did he look important. And by extension, I felt important. He looked like a big fish in this rather small pond, outclassing the horses around us.

But you don't earn prizes for being led around. When I got back to the stalls Francesca was dressed to kill. She had on her burgundy boots, and dark tan breeches of her own design, topped by a crisply tailored white shirt. Her schooling helmet was a deep brown with tiny crystals set in a stripe with gloves to match, right down to the crystals.

I quietly tacked him up in his stall, then pulled him into the barn aisle to oil his hooves and give his stunning tail one final fluffing. When I got Francesca up they certainly looked the part. High Horse Couture had arrived at Hill and Dale farm.

I walked ahead of them to the warm up arena, and Johnny followed, head held high, no longer anxious, but proud and keen to go to the arena. Francesca was doing her best to look confident. There was no hesitation as they entered the warm up arena. I grabbed a great viewing spot along the rail. Then Francesca began her warm up routine. I could feel the other railbirds come to attention. They were wondering who the hell it was. And I tried not to notice them, but keep my eyes on Francesca. I recognized some little inner lift in myself. It was hope. Hope that somehow Francesca was actually going to pull this off.

When Francesca trotted past me, I said, "He looks great!" And I could see her make her little tight-lipped smile. She shifted to sitting trot and began to gather Johnny and put him through some of the test movements. Johnny was full of power, yet under her control. He was putting extra cadence into each step of trot, putting his heart into it. Francesca was unfortunately still pinching with her knees to steady herself, but Johnny didn't let her stop him. He was putting on a performance to impress the other horses; he wasn't going to let Francesca get in his way. I was almost laughing, but kept a lid on it.

Francesca shifted to the canter work, turning some really impressive pirouettes in the middle of the arena, reminding me of ice skaters moving to the middle of the rink to do the advanced spins. Francesca moved out of a good one, and clocked off a great line of two-tempis, Johnny flicking his impressive tail to accent each change. And then I noticed.

His tail was growing. My face felt instantly hot. It was like my old Barbie-doll with the button on her stomach that you could push to make her pony tail longer. I gestured at Francesca to come on over, but she was in the zone. She headed for her one-tempi's. Flick, flick, flick, flick. There would be no stopping her until she had done the required fifteen. I squeaked out her name. "Francesca."

No response. I held my breath, willing the damn wig to stay in, and hoping everyone else was too self-absorbed to notice. As soon as she finished the line I belted out her name. "FRANCESCA!"

Thank God she turned her head. I gave my head a directional jerk, and she made a transition to walk and strolled over on a loose rein with a puzzled look on her face.

"What a super ride. Don't you think that's enough for today? We don't want to leave the best work in the warm-up arena, right?"

Francesca narrowed her eyes and sidled Johnny snuggly along the rail, a definite warm up arena no-no. She whispered. "What?"

I leaned close, stage whispering, "Wardrobe malfunction." Francesca was, as usual, clueless and just stared at me. I stage whispered, "Fashion emergency" followed by a deep sigh. Nada recognition. So I just said one word, "Tail." The lights came on.

She barked, "Oh, for God's sake." And Francesca headed for the barn. I trailed after Johnny who was walking in a self satisfied way, bobbing his head, content that he had put on a good show.

But I felt like I needed to hold a jacket over his ass. The knot at the top of the wig was visible and the falsie was hanging down about four or five inches longer than his wispier real tail hairs. I had failed as a horse-tail-stylist. I kept my eyes on my feet when we passed anyone.

Once Francesca dismounted, there was no place to hide. She was pissed. "For crying-out-loud, how long did I go around humiliating myself?"

I crossed my heart, "I swear it was only right at the end."

Francesca looked crushed. "What an ass I made of myself, I thought they were looking at my wonderful horse and my riding."

I began a stream of nervous giggling, spitting out my words. "They were! I promise, you guys looked amazing out there. I mean like I have never seen you before, Francesca. That's what people were looking at, I swear it."

She pulled off her bedazzled gloves and slung them to the ground. "Lizzy, they were staring because my horse was losing his hairpiece!"

"Francesca, that's not true. C'mon, you know you had the railbirds right from the beginning. Johnny was trotting like he was at the World Equestrian Games."

I saw her eyes soften. And her lips pressed into her thin smile.

I unbuckled Johnny's noseband, and unhooked the curb chain, and he bumped his big slobbery lips into my hip, poking his nose against my pockets and pricking his long ears. I pulled out a couple disintegrating sugar cubes, and let him continue to slime up my body parts and tickle my palm with his long nose whiskers.

Francesca wagged her red fingernailed index finger in my face. "That will not happen tomorrow. Got it?"

I was still suppressing giggles. "Yup. Message received. It was pretty funny though."

Francesca was trying to sound fierce, but I could see she was having to fight for it.

Me? I gave up trying to suppress my giggles. I was almost breathless.

Francesca was amused too, but she still warned me. "Do better, Lizzy, or we'll see who has the last laugh, meanwhile, this never happened. You understand?"

I took some deep breaths to get control of my giggles, but then nodded obediently.

Luckily, Francesca was smiling when she turned and primly walked away.

Then it hit me. The absolutely worst part of the amazing growing Barbie-doll tail incident was that I couldn't tell anyone about it.

# 17. Snatching Victory

*I watched the tutorial multiple times. What the heck? I had done it* just like they showed. You made a tight little braid at the end of the tailbone, and after braiding about three inches down you secured it with a rubber band. Then you took the rug hook from underneath the braid and pushed it through the braid near the end of the tailbone. Then with the rug hook you caught up the loop at the top of the fake tail, pulling the loop back through the braid. Next, you simply pulled the braid back through the loop on the fake to secure it. Done.

Except that it hadn't worked. There was nothing to keep the darn thing from working its way down the braid as the fake tail was rather heavy and Johnny was very bouncy.

I tucked Johnny's fakey under my armpit and reattached it trying to make the braid very tight, and adding a second rubber band right under where I had pulled the braid through to help keep it from sliding down. And then I remembered the roll of colored electrical tape in the little zippered bag. They hadn't showed that in the tutorial. Of course! I wound the tape over the loop, squeezing it tight. That had to be the missing piece.

I was determined that Johnny would not have the amazing growing Barbie-doll tail today. I had also put tight and uniform braids in his mane, his tail looked full and fluffy, and his coat and white face and legs were sparkling clean. I had picked out a saddle pad and polos that still had that brand new look. I had been the groom extraordinaire. As soon as I had all his tack on, I pulled him into the barn aisle and put on the finishing touch by polishing his hooves.

My work was done. He looked stunning.

Francesca didn't look so bad herself. She cut an elegant figure dressed in her tailcoat. When you are as skinny as Francesca and you have a good tailor, well, her jacket fit perfectly. Plus, I had her boots polished to a mirror shine.

I pulled down the stirrups with a smart snap, and grabbed our mounting block, dragging it over to Johnny. I held tightly to Johnny while stepping to the "off" side of the horse in order to pull on the stirrup so the saddle wouldn't shift. Once Francesca was up, I helped pull the tails of her coat out from under her seat, arranging them neatly. We did not speak, but I could see she was nervous. Francesca was licking her lips. She never did that. She drew her shoulders back and gathered her reins. And then she gave Johnny a squeeze with her calves, and they headed for the warm up arena.

I called out to her retreating figure. "I'll be right there, Francesca."

In my head I said a small prayer that the dressage gods would grant her a 60% today. When I thought of the work Francesca had produced in the warm up yesterday, I was cheered. It could happen, under the right circumstances. If a judge was in a happy mood, and perhaps understood that this little woman supported a lot of us, and this detail of earning the Gold medal meant a lot to her, maybe they would not be averse to a bit of score inflation. Even though Johnny was capable of much more than a 60% if Francesca stayed out of his way, he couldn't do the test by himself. Margot had often said to me that a horse never can go better than the rider can ride.

I grabbed a bottle of water and a towel and headed to the arena. I glanced up at the sky. It was filled with puffy white clouds, but it was already getting hot and the air was thick, promising a truly muggy afternoon. As I walked through a patch of grass, I disturbed gnats and they rose in a small cloud.

The FEI classes are not usually held first thing in the morning, but in the heat of summer, with an amazingly high humidity level, the little show had put the advanced horses first, which was a kindness since those horses work the hardest and are usually the most heavily muscled of the competitors. Johnny was no exception.

But it was not the time of day we usually rode him. I got nervous when I saw the low sun was casting slanting shadows of each fence post across the track of the warm up arena. Johnny noticed, too, and as he entered the arena he tipped his head and snorted. Francesca wisely moved away from the offending line of shadows.

Francesca took a few minutes to loosen up and begin to ride in a way that was anything close to effective. But she had plenty of time to shake her show nerves; almost too much time. She stopped and started, and then stopped and started again. It seemed like a long time before I gave her a ten minute warning. But those ten minutes went quickly, and then I waved her out so I could hand her some water and take off Johnny's polo wraps, and give her boots a swipe.

I took back the empty bottle from her. "You know the test. You need to say it to me?"

She licked her lips again. "No. I know it."

I nodded. "You have a plan for before the bell rings?"

Francesca frowned. "Not really."

I locked eyes with her. "What would Margot tell you right now?"

Francesca looked thoughtful. "She'd say to test him to make sure he was listening; to be tactful so I didn't rock the boat, but to still be definite."

I smiled. "Sounds like she is here in your head, even if she's not here in person."

Francesca smiled her tight little smile, and for once it seemed genuine. The ring steward turned to us. The previous rider had saluted. It was time to go in. I watched Francesca organize herself and her reins and then ask Johnny to walk, and then trot in. I clenched my teeth and leaned against the rail. There was nothing else I could do now.

Francesca had barely gone down one long side when the judge blew the whistle. Drat. I had hoped Francesca would get down the other long side. She still had 45 seconds before she had to enter, she could still do it, but instead she stopped, and picked up the canter, heading down the centerline.

It was a good entrance, nice and straight and landed softly in a square halt. I felt my spirits rise and thought, "Good for you, Francesca."

She trotted promptly off and made a good turn and a rather conservative extended trot. The transitions were fairly good and I was proud of her two good corners.

But then I noticed that down the long side of the arena were the same shadows Francesca had avoided in the warm up arena. Except now she couldn't avoid them. I had a very bad feeling, even before they came out of the corner, and felt my fingers grip the top rail of the fence I was leaning against.

The way Johnny came out of the corner reminded me of Wiley Coyote in the old cartoons. He seemed to stop in mid-air to process the shadow he had already stepped on. When Johnny came to earth, he was teetering over his splayed front legs, nose in the dirt, butt high, examining the next stripe on the ground, looking as if he thought one more step would send him over the side of a cliff. Then he did a quick duck and turn, not unlike the one that had previously put Francesca up on his neck. Thankfully, Francesca stayed in her saddle this time. But she could have been a flea on his back for all the influence she now had on him; a very well dressed flea.

Johnny next scooted a few steps to the side, turned back toward the striped long side, lifted his head, and made the equine danger call through flared nostrils. "Whoooof- whooof!" It immediately set off a ripple of whinny's from the surrounding areas. Along with his vocalization, he lifted his tail in all its glorious fakery and with an arch in his neck unloaded loose manure. He then did another twirl and headed toward the out gate in a world-class passage trot. I wasn't sure Francesca would be able to wrestle him back before the exit, but as he spotted some other ghost that only he could see, he came to a stop. Francesca turned him toward the judge and offered a hasty salute...a request to be excused...and the judge stood up and nodded her assent.

As soon as they made it past the little white competition boards, I stepped forward and grabbed Johnny by a rein, digging my elbow into his neck and pulling his nose toward me to slow him down. Looking up at Francesca I offered, "That was just unfortunate."

She said nothing. Poor Francesca's face was sweating and pale, her lips pressed together.

I tried to sound sympathetic. "Hey, let's take him back to the warm up arena and see if we can get him over those shadows out there."

She looked down at me like I was insane. "What? No! Let's pack it up and go home."

Now I was the one looking at her like she was insane. "But Francesca, we have a class tomorrow."

She gave me a look that silenced me. "It's at the same time of day. We'll have the same problem, and it won't be fixed by tomorrow. I had no idea of this spooking problem when I bought him. This changes things."

I was still holding on to Johnny, but looking up at Francesca as we crabbed sideways toward the stabling. "Oh, Francesca, we can work through this. I can help."

She still looked at me like I had two heads, her voice slightly shaky. "You? You think you can fix spooking? You're the working student who keeps falling off her horse every time it spooks. I think not."

Ouch. I let go of Johnny and stopped walking. Francesca and Johnny picked up the pace, leaving me standing there. What was the point? I was a sucker for letting myself get dragged into this. The whole ship was probably going down and no one else was concerned that I might drown. I needed to save myself, and I had no plan.

Someone touched my elbow, and I spun around. I was surprised to see Ryder. I said in a dejected voice, "You saw?"

Ryder was not smirking for once. "Didn't want to miss it."

I sighed. "Johnny doesn't like shadows."

But Ryder wasn't buying it. "Went around for his last rider, didn't he?"

I frowned, "Ryder, that's not fair."

But Ryder shook her head, "Johnny was spooky for her, too. But, she figured out how to put that bit of nerve into the work. She channeled it into brilliance. You want to ride those big powerful movers, you have to be able to cope with the sensitivity that comes with it. You have to be able to ride them through rings of fire."

Ryder was looking into my eyes. I was thinking of Winsome as much as Johnny. Francesca and I had the same problem. I looked down at my shoes and mumbled back to her. "Yeah, rings of fire. I've heard that before."

I looked up toward the barns, and Ryder did, too. She tipped her head in that direction.

"Better go catch up with her or she'll blame you. In fact, if she's running true to form, she's up there blaming everyone but herself. She's likely formulating a lawsuit against the seller for non-disclosure."

I nodded my head. "And I get to spend the next hour alone with her."

Ryder blew through her nose. "Naw, I'll bet she dumps him on you and drives off in that Mercedes, leaving you to do the grunt work."

I was about to agree, but then remembered. "She can't. I don't have a tack room in my trailer. She can't leave until I shower Johnny and clean the tack and pack up her car."

Ryder smiled. "Well, I won't offer to stay and help out then. No way I'm letting her catch me here. See you back at the farm."

I took one last look at Ryder to see if she was kidding. She had a sly look on her face, a cocky stance, and her arms folded across her chest. But, something told me she really would have stayed and helped tote and carry if Francesca wasn't around. At that moment, I wasn't annoyed with her. Instead I waved good-bye and broke into a jog toward the stables.

There was absolutely no reason to rush. Francesca was stuck until I packed her car, and I needed to take care of Johnny first, so I expected she would have to cool her jets or even offer to help me finish up. But did she offer to bathe her horse or clean the tack? Instead she attended her wardrobe and then fretted, having a fit when another groom tried to make pleasantries with me. "Lizzy, this is not an ice cream social; I want you to pick up the pace."

If only Margot had been there. Margot had forced me right back into the arena after my humiliating elimination with Rave. And here was Francesca fleeing with her tail between her legs. What a coward.

But I did not have Margot's authority to demand Francesca go work it out in the warm up arena. I had no confidence that Francesca was even capable. And Francesca was right that Sunday's class was scheduled for the same time, and unless the day turned cloudy, we would have the same shadows to deal with. She had no intention of repeating today's fiasco.

So, it was with a heavy heart that I schlepped Johnny's tack back to Francesca's car, carefully placing towels down on her seats first before loading them up. What would become of him, the horse she daily kissed on his big pink nose?

Meanwhile, Francesca kept her own counsel, and didn't dare chip the polish on her nails to help pack.

I still needed to pull out Johnny's braids, and the wig from his tail, where it hadn't budged, not that it mattered anymore. Francesca saw me start work on it, but stopped me.

She made a tight little shake of her head. "No. Not now. Do that back at Claire's." I saw her glance around. She was still tight as a tick with anxiety.

So, I put on Johnny's shipping boots, and loaded back onto my trailer a braided and sweat-marked horse, something I would never have done. I drove home slowly, mindfully, feeling like we had left the show grounds sporting a white flag of surrender. It was all wrong. I resented leaving that way. It was not the way any good horseman would proceed.

As soon as we got to Claire Winston's, I put Johnny in the wash stall to take care of his needs first, but Francesca had me leave him there and get a cart to unload her car. Then she was off. Not a word of thanks, or a "see you tomorrow." No discussion of what the next step would be.

I had the luxury of time to bathe Johnny, and pull out the braids and the tail wig. Then I cleaned the tack and started laundry. Maybe it was my imagination, but Johnny seemed depressed, too. I tried to make it up to him, feeding him carrots and peppermints and telling him that he was still a good boy. For him, the scary shadows were long forgotten, and our low spirits were a puzzle to him. He was a good horse, no, a super horse, and he had already proven himself as a dressage horse. It was Francesca who needed to step up to the challenge. Francesca should have let me help her ride through it. But, she had scoffed at my offer.

And then I thought bitterly, she had a point. I *had* fallen off my spinning spooking mare twice at her electric gates. Why would she think I could fix her problem? I was hobbling around, sporting a bent finger, and downing ibuprofen like they were candy.

But I had learned from Wild Child, who had bullied me and scared me half to death, that sometimes your biggest failures lead you to your greatest successes. All it takes is a resolve and a willingness to fail your way to success. Naively perhaps, I thought Francesca could do the same and I could help her, if she would just let me.

I drove my truck and trailer back to Equus Paradiso, and as I pulled up to the gates I pushed my remote and watched Winsome's evil nemesis, those darn electric gates, begin their swing away from the truck. I thought the opening gates were elegant and inviting; for a human that is. Winsome thought they were sneaky and unpredictable.

I looked up at my remote that was clipped to my truck's sun visor and the light bulb in my head switched on. Why the heck hadn't I thought of it before? I could use the remote control to train Winsome to go through the gate. Horses could learn things a few different ways, one of them was desensitization. Another was pressure-release. I could simply let her watch it open and close, and open and close, at a safe distance; working our way closer as she relaxed, and finally get her quietly through the gates once she was desensitized. By making her walk toward the gate until she felt pressure, then backing up one step until she felt the removal of pressure, I could use the principle of pressure-release, too. If I added the positive reinforcement of peppermints, well, I hit up three different modes of learning.

I had felt depressed and exhausted. But suddenly that was forgotten. I couldn't wait to get my trailer cleaned and put away, unload the bed of the truck, and get it swept out, so I could go train my horse. I worked now at a good clip.

Once I was done, I grabbed the remote off my sun-visor and headed to the tack room to stuff my pockets with peppermints. I stepped into the barn aisle and called out, "Winnnnnsome."

Man, I loved that horse. She poked her head out through the yoke opening, hay hanging from her mouth, nostrils rhythmically fluttering in greeting in a low rumbling whinny. Of course, several other horses mugged me along the way to her stall, demanding a peppermint, but I ignored them, and made my way to my girl as quickly as possible. I slipped her halter on over her ears and snapped the clip on the throat-latch. She followed me eagerly out of the barn, her head tugging down-ward, expecting to graze. But I turned the wrong direction.

"Not that way, girlfriend. Let's head toward the great beyond."

Her steps slowed down and she gave a tug back toward her grazing spot as if to correct me. "Nope. Sorry."

I reeled her in and faced the gates, but we weren't anywhere near them yet. I pulled the remote off my belt, and gave it a push. It must have had a good strong signal because even at this distance the motor immediately began to hum and the mechanical arms began to retract into their sleeves, pulling the gate toward us. At this distance she mere-ly lifted her head, and pointed her ears, going rigid in her body and expanding her nostrils to take in a good deep breath, widening her eyes. I placed my hand on her neck. The muscles were hard, but she hadn't fled. This was good. I was feeling smart and encouraged.

I unwrapped a peppermint, which she snatched from my hand quickly, immediately refocusing on the mysterious gates, which fin-ished the sixty-second open cycle. They hummed as they were pushed back out, the arms expanding until the gate clicked securely shut.

I fed her another peppermint. And then did it again. She merely snorted this time. I stuffed another peppermint into her.

"Good girl, Winsome. You are going to get this."

I waited and waited for her muscles to soften, for her eyes to soften, and for her to get bored and tug at the rope, begging for grass. And then I stepped her forward toward the gates; pressure and release; time again for pressure. I pressed the remote again, expecting her to begin to relax more quickly with the repetition.

Instead she began to get worse instead of better. I could feel the panic begin to rise in her in the stiffening of her muscles and the high carriage of her head and a slight rocking back onto her hindquarters. But I held on and waited the sixty seconds for the gates to begin to close. I was ready for her. She threw her head down and tried the old duck and spin maneuver that had caused me problems, and I *almost* got my foot stomped on. But I had leaned against her neck for support and pulled my foot back in the nick of time.

Clearly there was still some line that I could not cross. But I had to go near it or I was never going to get through those damn gates without risking another fall. I had heard Herm Martin say to take your horse and yourself out of the comfort zone, and into the achievement zone, but stay away from the panic zone; easier said than done. Horses could go into the panic zone in the blink of an eye. But it was wise advice.

Winsome was relaxing again, tugging at her rope, and eyeing the green grass.

"No, sweetie. If we can't manage those gates, how will we manage an awards ceremony or the flags or the water trucks or all the other crazy unnatural things that you and I will see at a horse show? How will we go through those proverbial rings of fire if we can't even go through the farm gates?"

She pushed at my hand with her nose, begging for another peppermint. But I waited until I pushed the remote and the gates were in motion before giving it to her. She was quieter this time. And I thought we were both getting bored, which was a positive sign.

My lower back was starting to ache. It had been a long and discouraging day. My bent finger twinged every time I gripped the lead rope. My neck was in knots, and my stomach was feeling empty. And if I let my mind go there, well, as usual, I would need to pee. But I was determined to snatch some kind of victory from the heavy burden of defeat. I was going to walk her through those gates, even if it was by moonlight. I had to fail until I succeeded. I had to listen to my horse, apply what I knew to be true, and inch by inch fix this.

I stepped her three steps closer and pushed the remote. I needed to watch my horse and come up with the right action. Watch the reaction to the opening gates; wait; reaction to the closing gates; wait; reward; wait for relaxation; step closer; repeat. Step by step, inch by inch. We were going through those gates.

Now the bottom of my feet were aching and burning. My stomach felt hollow. I really did need to pee. I was determined to stay emotionally neutral. I searched my mind for platitudes. "Do not get too attached to results." And "things take the time that they take." And, "you get the chicken by hatching the egg, not smashing it." I was trying to become a Zen master in one easy lesson.

I am sure that Ryder would have gotten out the longe whip and we would have been through the gate by now in a brisk trot. She would be saying, "Patience has limits, but you take it too far and its cowardice." Maybe after two falls from my mare I *was* a coward. Or maybe I was being smart.

I brought Winsome three more steps forward, and watched passively as she took one step back. I shook my head at a Ryder who was not there. I did not want Ryder or her methods, effective as she could be, to be what fixed this. I did not want Deb or Nat or anyone else to fix this. I wanted to fix this. And I wanted to do it my way, with my horse's cooperation, and without wrecking my body any more than it was already wrecked.

It seemed like an eternity of stuffing peppermints into her, and reciting truisms like mantras. I slowly sucked on one of the mints, easing my stomach, and benefiting from a small sugar lift. When I ran out of positive thinking quotes, I began searching my head for an appropriate song. I chose *Waiting is the Hardest Part*. I only remembered a few lines but it didn't matter. I sucked on the peppermint, sung a few words, and hummed the rest. I inched Winsome forward and then hit the remote. I was ignoring her and enjoying my song while I unwrapped another mint. For me.

An amazing thing happened while I was singing and sucking my mint and ignoring my horse, and it took me a moment to notice. Winsome took the next three steps all by herself before I asked. And then she kept going. We walked all the way up to the gates, and she reached her nose forward and touched the mechanical arm with her nose. I fed her a peppermint. Next, she did another remarkable thing. She reached forward and scratched her nose on the arm, and then bumped my pocket for another mint, which I hurried to unwrap and give her. I backed her up a few steps and hit the remote.

She watched with interest, but not alarm, and when they were fully open she almost rudely pushed me for a peppermint.

I forgot my sore back and neck, my sore finger, my empty stomach, and all my bodily functions. I was a horse trainer. Or maybe my horse was the trainer here. Margot always said the horses were our most important teachers. In any case, the victory was sweet, and warmed my sore body from my empty stomach out to my extremities, drawing a couple tears from my eyes.

I stroked her neck. "Good girl, my smart girl, my fine, fine, fine, girl."

I calmly walked her through the gate, and before the sixty seconds could end, turned her around and walked her right back through the gates, and back into the barn, and then directly into her stall. Then she got a vigorous wither scratching and the last peppermint in my pocket.

Score one Lizzy. This day I was the victor, and no one could take that from me. Francesca thought I was not able to fix a spooking problem. I had something to prove to myself before I could possibly prove it to Francesca.

Tomorrow I would try it mounted.

# 18. Small Victories

*I went to bed eager to wake up and go at it. But of course I could not* sleep, thinking about what I would do tomorrow to get Winsome through the gate mounted. When I finally did get to sleep, the demons came out.

I was in a dark stall with Winsome this time instead of Wild Child, and my heart was pounding, my breath quick and short. I could not see Patrick, but evil pervaded the stall. Winsome was backing up into a corner, eyes showing white. I knew it was up to me to save her. But I was almost blind in the dark stall and had no weapon. And then something grabbed me from behind, an arm across my throat. I jumped so hard that I woke myself up, and stared into the darkness, still blind. I was used to these dreams, although they came less frequently these days, but they still filled my bloodstream with adrenaline.

I stretched my arms wide and felt around the bedspread, finding Wheezer, and pulling her close up under my chin. She stretched under my fingers, her little body taut and long, and then softening and curling into a ball. She still smelled of lavender. I loved the smell so much that I decided then and there to buy a lavender fragrance and apply a drop of it to the top of her head on a regular basis so she would always smell this good. Lavender was said to have a calming effect. Maybe that's partly why Wheezer had a calming effect on me. Soon she was purring. She was my precious tonic. Francesca would never know how much I loved her little gift; how much this tiny animal had already come to mean to me. She was another heartbeat; one I could hold close to my own. She did not care about anything but being safe and loved. And she had attached herself to me. My heart beat slowed. I fell back into a dreamless sleep.

When I woke up, I lay in bed, picturing riding Winsome through the gate with ease, and tried to hang on to the image as I started my day. The one and only person I wanted to discuss my strategy with was Deb. I did not want to share my plan with Margot. I instinctively knew Margot would tell me to have Deb ride my horse and fix it for me, and if that's what she ordered, then I would have to follow orders. I got the feeling that Margot was always trying to take care of me, protect me. But I didn't want that. I would not tell Margot.

Deb, God bless her, would understand that this was my horse and my problem to fix. I would seek her advice. But the job was mine to do. My level of anxiety over this gate problem was almost embarrassing to admit to myself.

So, when Deb came down to ride Wild Child I was able to briefly talk to her, my back to Ryder, my voice low. "Deb, I have some questions for you."

Deb was busy pulling on her gloves, her whip tucked under her arm. "Yeah?"

I licked my lips and glanced briefly over my shoulder at Ryder. "Can I walk with you to the arena?"

She nodded. "Come on."

We strolled out of the barn toward the indoor, and I told Deb all about my success using the clicker. I was proud. I told her today I was going to take the clicker and clip it to my belt and continue the lesson mounted. I was expecting her to congratulate me, to reassure me that

I was over the tough spot and now it was going to go smoothly; that I was a good and creative horse trainer. She did dimple up while she listened. Those dimples always made her look younger than she was. I figured those dimples were a good sign. I knew at least I amused her.

Deb was a better horse trainer than me because she had so much more experience, and also because she seemed almost part horse. She was some kind of crazy animal psychic. Deb knew I valued her opinion, and in turn, she always took me seriously. So, I felt that the respect went both ways, and I knew her input would be thoughtful, helpful, and always on my side. Deb never had any other agenda. She wanted me to be successful.

She stopped Wild Child, jiggling the bit to get him to stand quietly. He was confused by our stopping, and pricked his ears at me, watching and listening. "Lizzy, that sounds good. But, don't assume that Winsome is going to connect the dots right away."

I shifted from one foot to the other. "What do you mean?"

Deb tucked her whip back under her arm, as if she needed both hands to explain to me.

"Well, when you lead a horse past something, you are leading much like an older horse leading an inexperienced horse. Just like when we took the bambinos out on the trail. Remember how you and I rode behind Quester and Boingo, so when they balked and spooked, we could take the lead? And when they did, and we took the lead, they followed us, right?"

The image of the bambinos appeared in my mind. I answered her thoughtfully, "Yes."

Wild Child was getting impatient; he stamped his foot and shook his head. Deb rattled his bit before continuing. "When we get up on their backs we are no longer leading them. We are driving them. That's a big difference. They can't see us; we disappear from their line of sight. They can only feel us and sense our intentions."

I had never thought about this angle before.

Deb continued. "We sit where a predator, for instance a mountain lion, would attack, and when we press our spurs into their sides if they are already afraid, their instinct is not to go forward, but instead it activates the prey survival instinct. Imagine claws or teeth pressing down into their sides. Instinct would then make them try to force us, the predator, off their backs and run away to safety."

I frowned. "Deb you make us sound cruel…and stupid. Who ever decided that legs and spurs would be forward driving aids? They weren't thinking about the predator/prey thing were they?"

She laughed gently. "There is nothing natural about riding horses. And as a system of training, well, legs, the whip, and spurs have worked pretty well over the millennia regardless, once the horse is thoroughly trained. That's the key phrase though, 'thoroughly trained.' Horses aren't stupid, they learn that we are not predators, and they learn the system of aids for going forward."

I nodded. "You're right there; they aren't stupid. Mine seems smart enough to keep making a fool out of me."

Deb chuckled. "You're not alone. When things go wrong they can go wrong at a high rate of speed."

I nodded in agreement. "I have got to stop having those near-death experiences."

Deb's dimples made a brief appearance again. "You have to feel whether your application of the driving aid is going to trigger panic, or if it will go "through" and they are going to respond the way you have trained them to respond. That's what that term "thoroughness" refers to. You need to develop an instinct to know where you stand. The smart rider feels what is possible at that moment and waits, if that's what is the right thing to do. It takes patience, but also good horse-sense. The not so smart rider doesn't feel or wait, and gets hurt."

I nodded. "Yeah, and right now I pretty much hurt all over."

Deb was not smiling now. "What I'm saying is that just because she is leading through the gate, which is great by the way, you have to realize she has to learn something slightly different now. She has to be brave enough to go through that gate without a lead. She has to be in front of you. In her mind, she has to go first, even though you are on top of her. Ultimately, she has to be so well trained that she gives you a forward reaction without question. But, she's not there yet. It's up to you to make her courageous."

I took a deep breath. "But what if she is still afraid?"

Deb smiled her great smile again, her dimples even deeper this time. "Oh, she'll be afraid. There is no such thing as courage without fear. Step by step, you can do it. Winsome can do it. Be ready and be patient, but persistent. And feel when the time is right to wait, and when the time is right to push. Ride strong when you need to be strong, and passive when you need to be passive. Be smart, but don't give up until you are successful. I have faith in both of you."

And then she turned her back and walked on... Wild Child following with a bobbing head and pricked ears. Off to the office, where the two of them would focus only on the work at hand.

Deb's input had made me a little nervous. I was as ready as I was going to be, but my eager confidence had dissipated, and continued to evaporate as the day wore on.

The moment of truth was fast approaching. The barn was quiet, the training day done. I had been told by Francesca that Johnny had the day off. I assumed that Francesca was still licking her wounds. But for now, I had my own challenges. I clipped the clicker to my belt and mounted up.

As soon as I turned Winsome toward the gate, she balked and stiffened. This from the horse who by the end of the session yesterday had marched up to it and touched it with her nose? Was her reaction my fault? Had my nerves already triggered her nerves?

My cheeks went hot. Deb had told me this was not going to be a slam-dunk. But I had still harbored hope. Winsome was making me anxious and we hadn't even begun the lesson. In a flash I saw myself falling off, a picture I tried to banish from my mind's eye right away. But it was too late. I had seen it clear as day.

I drew in a deep breath, and felt my limbs flush with weakness. "There is no courage without fear." That's what Deb had said.

Winsome was bolted to the ground. I waited. And waited, chewing my lip and thinking how my aches and pains had turned me into a coward. Everyone else seemed so brave. Were they ever afraid? What about Natalie? She always seemed unafraid, even on a bouncing bronc-ing Boingo. She was brave, wasn't she? But maybe she wasn't afraid because she was crazy. Nat was a happy and fun sort of crazy, but she was nuts. She said to me once that she considered each new day a reprieve from the governor on a death sentence. She was crazy in a way that only someone who had once given up on life and been resurrected could be. I was not that crazy.

And then there was Ryder; she never seemed afraid of anything. How I remember her wild ride around the farm on Petey. I know I could never have done that. But Ryder wasn't afraid because she was young and thought she was bulletproof. She had something to prove to the world. Ryder was jet fueled on ambition, and underneath that ambition I sensed something else, a sort of anger. I was not angry, or ambitious, or certain of my own abilities.

Nope. I was not like Nat, and I was not like Ryder. I was just plain-old-vanilla afraid.

I was all too aware these days of how fragile I was. At night my demons reminded me that we all were under death sentences, that the horses were not the only creatures who feared predators. I also did not want the humiliations of wearing Francesca's damp, dark, mulch on my breeches ever again. Mulch on my backside would be a dead give-away that I had fallen off, again. Shit, I hurt in my body but the truth was that I was embarrassed. I did not want to hear one more crack from Francesca about messing up her landscaping. I was tired of being the only rider at Equine Paradiso who fell off her horse. It was time to step up and fix this problem.

"There is no courage without fear." I drew another deep breath and shortened my reins. Time to be courageous. I was a good distance from the gate, pretty much where I had been when I had started the work in hand. It was time.

I pushed the clicker that was clipped to my belt. There was a moment of stillness as the motor whirred and the arms of the gate began to retract, pulling the gates toward us. Winsome brought her neck high, her ears pricked, her nose extending toward the gates as if to focus better. I felt an opportunity, that sense that Deb had asked me to listen for, that I could apply my legs and that the training would hold. I did. It did. And she responded as she had been trained to respond.

Winsome walked forward tentatively. I felt another flush, another weakness through the bottom of my belly right down to my toes curling inside my boots. Neither one of us was brave ... no, but we were moving forward anyway.

I knew the gates had a sixty second delay once they came to the fully opened position. We had started from a long distance, and step-by-step we made our way along the paver driveway. Clip, pause, clop, pause, clip, pause, clop, pause. She was going, so I did not want to add pressure, but in my mind the second hand was ticking. The last thing I wanted was for the gates to begin to close before we could get through. Once we were inside the sensors, the gates would stop and then reopen ...it was a safety feature.

Clip, clop, clip, clop, clip, clop, clip, clop, and we had made it. The gates were still open when we crossed the threshold. I leaned forward to pet her neck.

"Good girl, Winsome, good girl!" And I was still bent over when the gates began to close.

Winsome suddenly dropped into a crouch, like a football player ready for the kick off. It felt like the ground had dropped away from us. I heard the clatter of her hooves as I suddenly saw Francesca's paver stone driveway in intense detail. There were bits of mulch stuck down in the seams, and the color was not quite as uniform as it appeared from up higher. I made a hasty pact with myself right there that, by God; I was not going to fall off. I somehow flung my shoulders back over my hips as Winsome launched herself down the road, and then spun around to face back toward the gates. She was doing her dragon call, and my heart was pounding, my hands shaking.

"There is no courage without fear."

I sat passively as she stood like a marble statue, her head high, her tail flagged, her nostrils flared. I waited and waited, listening to her body, waiting for the signal that I could put my leg on again.

I turned my head and looked down the road, hoping that no traffic was headed our way, and Winsome broke her gaze from the gates, and followed my eyes. She looked around as if finally able to see more of her environment than just the gate. It was as if a spell had been broken.

That was weird. I turned my head and gazed down the road the other way, focusing on a beautiful large oak. And she turned and looked where I was looking.

So, then I looked over the gates, up the hill toward Deb's. And again she followed my gaze.

The moment was now. I hit the clicker on my belt, still staring up the hill toward Deb's.

When the gates began to move, she broke her gaze away from the hill for just a moment to take in the gates, and then she looked back up the hill, and all by herself marched through the gates.

I was stunned. But also emotionally exhausted, my body limp as overcooked spaghetti.

I slid off on wobbly knees and fished a peppermint out of my pocket. It was Margot's words that came to me then. "The horse is our most important teacher."

I had not fixed the problem tonight. But, I knew I was well on my way, with a new trick up my sleeve; horses followed rider focus. Horses knew, could sense, where we put our attention, and I could redirect their attention with something as simple as my eyes. That was a powerful tool.

I slept like a baby that night, and the next day my brain was percolating with new ideas on riding and training spooky horses.

Francesca was avoiding me. When she came for her ride on Lovey, she walked past me as if I was invisible. After spending so much time with each other, I felt that I deserved at least a "good morning." So, when she returned from her lesson, I stepped forward to grab Lovey, cutting Ryder off.

"I'll take him, Ryder. I know you're still finishing up in the tack room." Ryder wasn't buying it. She squinted at me and furrowed her brow. But, she also turned her back and let me take Lovey.

"Francesca, are we back on schedule this afternoon?" Francesca just glared at me.

I continued, "He's had two days off now. That's enough time off, don't you think?"

Francesca surprised me by walking over to one of our tall director chairs and pulling it up across from the wash stall, sitting down, and crossing her legs and arms. She never had done that before. "I have a lot of business to take care of today."

What a crock. She had to know I wasn't buying it. I kept moving, taking off Lovey's bridle and slipping on his halter, but as I hung his bridle on a hook and stepped around to unbuckle his girth I nodded to Francesca, and then changed the subject. "Guess what I did last night?"

Francesca sniffed. "Do I want to know?"

I smiled and pulled off the saddle. "I rode Winsome through your gates and did *not* fall off."

Francesca tipped her head and smiled her tight little smile. "Small victory that."

I had hoped for a laugh at my expense, and even some glimmer of camaraderie between us. I squatted down and began unwrapping Lovey's polos, but kept talking. "Francesca, my hands were trembling, and my legs felt like jelly, but I did it. And I'm going to do it again tonight. In fact, I'm going to do it every night until I can be sure that I'm never going to fall off going through your gates ever again."

Francesca started to swing her booted leg. Something I had never seen her do before. Suddenly, I saw her son. Chess was a fidgeter, but Francesca was usually too self-controlled to fidget, but here she was, foot going up and down in a steady rhythm. And the resemblance was striking. She had to get my not so subtle point. Suddenly she jumped up out of her chair.

"OK, Lizzy, four o'clock. Don't be late."

And she was off, leaving me with a smile on my face. I was getting damn good at "manipulating the manipulator." I knew Francesca was at heart competitive.

I was actually looking forward to this afternoon. I had ideas of stuff to do with Johnny. I knew I would have to sell my ideas to Francesca first. And I couldn't help it but at this moment, I kind of liked Francesca. Banish that thought! I laughed at myself.

Chess came into view coming down the barn aisle walking toward his mother. He and Francesca stopped and exchanged a few words, and he gave her a peck on the cheek, then they parted. He was headed straight for me. I turned my back and put my attention on Lovey.

He called out cheerfully, "Hi, Lizzy!"

I greeted him cheerfully enough in return. "Hi, Chess."

I turned on the hose, and let the water get just the right temperature for Lovey. He liked it hot, even in this summer weather. If I got it too cool he would fidget and paw, but when it was hot, he stood still and hung his head, even allowing me to put the shower right between his eyes and behind his ears.

Chess made a little noise to get my attention. "Just wanted to remind you we have a date."

The word "date" made me cringe and look around quickly to see if anyone else had heard the word. I kept my tone light. "We do?"

He nodded. "You are not getting out of it. The tickets are in my wallet. Wednesday night, front and center mezzanine level of the St. James Theater. You're going to love it. And then we'll meet up with some of my buddies for a few drinks after the show."

I did not want to be "on a date" with Chess Cavelli. But what to say? "Chess, that had to cost you."

I had turned off the shower, taken the scraper to Lovey, and with quick flicks was shedding water off his coat. The water flew and Chess stepped back.

"You said you had never been to a show, or even into the city. That needs fixing. You're going to love it. There's nothing like Manhattan."

I sounded like an ungrateful bitch. But, I also did not want to send the wrong signals.

I grabbed a dry towel and began to rub Lovey's face. This was his favorite part. Lovey lowered his head and tucked his nose up against my tummy, wetting my shirt. I made sure to dry out the inside of each ear, something that always made him roll his eyes and yawn. He was a happy little guy.

Chess was watching. "Is that one Mother's?"

"Yes. Isn't he adorable?"

Chess pondered that a moment. "Not sure I can think of a horse as 'adorable.' But, in any event, he clearly likes you."

I squatted down and began to dry his legs. If you didn't keep them clean and dry they developed skin fungus almost overnight in this hot humid weather. I looked up at Chess, finally allowing our eyes to meet.

"And I like him, too. In fact, I would say that it's more than just "like." Lovey is as honest a horse as they come, the kind of horse you can count on every day.

Chess nodded. "I guess we won't be selling that one, will we?"

I laughed, because he kept coming back to dollars and sense. "Chess, just stop it! When you find a horse this honest, this kind, this intelligent, well, only a fool would let him go."

He shrugged his shoulders, and then reached with his index finger and lightly stroked the velvet-soft skin between Lovey's nostrils. Lovey didn't react at all; he was looking snoozy after his workout and shower.

Chess seemed to think I had just said something amusing. "Kind of like the difference between the kind of guy you have a fling with and the kind of guy you marry?"

I laughed out loud and said, "Yeah, Lovey would be marriage material for sure." Then it occurred to me, "Hey, you're not sneezing."

And his eyebrows went up surprised. "Y'know, you're right. I don't even itch. I started the drops, maybe they're helping."

I stood up, threw the towel over my shoulder, and smiled.

"I'm taking Lovey out to hand graze and dry off in the sun." I expected Chess to follow me out and chit-chat, but instead he just nodded and started to turn and walk away, talking over his shoulder.

"I'm picking you up Wednesday afternoon at four, that gives us time to grab a quick bite before the show. We'll eat light, because we'll have something after the show as well. You won't regret it, I promise." Chess turned around and was walking backward.

I looked at Chess, and our eyes met. And I had to look away quickly. I was going to go on a date with Chess Cavelli. I knew this was dangerous territory. But I was going.

I answered, "Okay. I hope I don't have to dress up too much. My wardrobe is really limited."

He paused, "If it helps, I'll be wearing a coat and tie. I know it's old school, but I like to dress up for the theater."

Of course I had nothing but riding clothes, jeans, and one tired old sundress, but I guess I could cobble something together.

And then he said one of those guy lines that made my stomach do a flip-flop. "You always look great to me."

\*\*\*

Deb took me to the round pen and showed me where the poles were stacked. They were old and the paint was peeling off them.

She asked, "You really can't tell me what you're up to?"

I sighed. "Man, you'd be the first person I'd tell if I thought I could get away with it."

Deb looked amused. "Don't say a word then. But, I'm happy to help you load these into the back of your truck. How many?"

I rubbed my chin, thinking. "Let me take four."

Deb and I each grabbed a pole. Then we walked back for two more.

We both wiped our hands on our breeches after loading them in the bed of my truck. Deb asked, "Anything else from my collection?"

She seemed to have something in mind. So, I took the bait. "What do you recommend?"

Deb flipped her long braid over her back and then tipped her head, studying me.

"I've got a piece of plywood, and one of those blue plastic tarps. Should we throw those in the back, too? And you're welcome to some traffic cones. Just on loan, mind you."

I wasn't sure yet what I was supposed to do with any of it, but clearly these were all useful tools to Deb.

"Sure. Why not?"

I'm sure I was breaking all sorts of rules at the Winston's very fancy "Two Left Feet Farm." I drove my old truck as close as I could get to the indoor arena and put on my riding gloves to unload the truck. As soon as I finished I put my truck back in the parking lot and checked the grass to make sure I hadn't left any marks.

Then I set up the poles for trotting cavelletti, measuring off about four and a half feet between poles. I put the cones up like a gate over X. Then I put the piece of plywood down in the arena and covered it with the blue tarp. I stood back and had a look at my littered arena. Yeah, it looked like building refuse at a landfill.

My body was aching and my finger still hurt. But, somehow I did not have time for my aches and pains today. I was a woman with a mission.

I got Johnny out and since I was getting behind schedule I figured he was going to get just a "lick and a promise" for his grooming today.

Francesca still hadn't arrived when I led him down to the arena. Or I guess I should say "tried" to lead him to the arena.

When we got to the entrance, he slammed on the brakes. And when Johnny lifted his neck and went into the danger pose he was one magnificent creature, and I was an insignificant ant lost in his shadow.

"Yeah, buddy. I totally screwed with your arena. Sorry."

And I did as Deb would have advised. I waited. There was no chance of success while he was in the panic mode. I had just rattled his world. His home arena, usually scary enough with rogue squirrels running on top of the kickboards, now had been defiled with building materials.

"Listen up, Johnny. If Francesca can't get around a dressage arena with shadows, she can't get her gold medal. If she can't get her gold medal, you will be looking for a new home. Even with the lipstick kisses, her love is conditional. That's the honest truth."

The spell was broken. He twisted his head and poked me with his big white nose. I fished a peppermint out of my pocket. I had to get the plastic wrap off of it, and put it in my mouth to tear it off. Before I could catch it the plastic floated off in the breeze. I shook my head. I was now a litterbug, along with my other sins. He happily took the mint.

And I was able to lead him into the arena. I tackled the tarp first. He was, as expected, terrified. But I worked on one foot and then the other. And I finally got all four feet on the tarp, with his body rigid and his nostrils flared. He arched his neck and looked down at the tarp and snorted.

I was so focused on what I was doing that I never saw Francesca walk in. And when I finally did notice her, she was standing in the entrance with one hand over her mouth. When our eyes met, Johnny launched himself off the tarp. But I hung on. I figured he had earned a break and another mint. I walked him over to Francesca.

I expected her to chew me out, to tell me that I had no business messing up Claire's arena, or presuming to "train" her horse. Not that she looked happy with me. But, she looked thoughtful and then when she spoke it was stern, but not angry.

"Would you like to explain?"

I was only slightly rattled. I certainly had expected her to question me. "I've been having success with Winsome and I had an idea how to help Johnny..."

Francesca didn't let me finish. "I don't recall promoting you to trainer."

I was not going to get wobbly. I had a point to make, but I lost the thread. Instead I blurted out, "If I have to wait for you and Johnny to conquer your fear of shadows on the sand, and squirrels, and God knows what else, well, Francesca, I'm afraid it's not going to happen."

Francesca's arms were crossed, her lips drawn into a hard thin line. She said nothing. My mouth was working faster than my brain. I couldn't find the emergency brake.

"I'm doing whatever I can to help you get that damned medal. And if it means I have to ride Johnny over balloons in front of a marching band I plan to do it, for Johnny, and for you."

Oh, my God. What had I just said? Where did that come from? Balloons and a marching band? And the worst part was I said I was doing this not just for Johnny, but for Francesca. That could not be what I meant. I did not mean to say that. But it was too late. I dropped my gaze and studied my boots because I sure as hell could not stand the laser beams of Francesca's glare.

I was met by a long silence. And then Francesca surprised me yet again by waving me away.

She sounded impatient as she said, "Get on with it, then."

I think I detected a hint of a smile. I wanted to laugh out loud. I was ridiculous; this was ridiculous. The arena looked ridiculous. But I had just effectively made my case. Now I had to deliver results.

I managed to put Johnny back on the tarp, and then lead him through the cavelletti poles and between the cones. He was wary, but he went.

Francesca was getting impatient and bored. She had been sitting on the mounting block but now stood up.

"Well, it's no good to me if you are just leading him; get on."

I did not question Francesca, because this is where the rubber hit the road. Or Lizzy hit the sand; one or the other. I snugged up the girth, buckled my helmet, and led him over to the mounting block and got on.

Remembering Deb's wise words about leading versus driving, I made Francesca walk ahead of us first. Johnny cautiously followed. I made him stand on the tarp and fed him mints, cooing and praising him.

Then I had Francesca move away and I walked him through the cavelletti and between the cones without a lead. Then I trotted him through the cavelletti, and headed for the blue tarp. The first time he came to a screeching halt and then tip-toed cautiously over the tarp.

But as I looped back and forth over the tarp he settled. I made a transition to trot. He did it. I made a figure eight back and forth over the tarp. Then I got brave and cantered him over the tarp. He was cautious. But he went. Finally, I trotted through the cavelletti, picked up the canter before going over the plywood covered by the blue tarp, then added a flying change after the tarp to change direction, making a transition back to trot before heading back over the cavelletti to repeat the exercise. Johnny's hoofs made a nice "tattoo" drumbeat as we hit the plywood, and his breathing was now relaxed and rhythmic, his back swinging and his steps bouncy. I was having fun.

I cannot quite describe how good I felt. I pulled Johnny up and dismounted, making a big fuss over him.

I was pleased with myself when I said, "Your turn, Francesca."

She looked shocked. "What? No. This is for your pleasure, not mine."

I was incredulous. "You want that gold medal? Because this is all for nothing if you can't ride through this kind of thing."

In a temper, she grabbed the reins and marched herself over to the mounting block. Johnny was tired. I could see this was going to be a cakewalk now and I hoped Francesca would feel the benefit.

Once Francesca had walked quietly over everything, I encouraged her. "See? Go ahead, Francesca." She did it. She trotted and cantered through my little obstacles like nothing.

I had to bite my lip. I wanted to crow. She didn't praise me, but I could tell she was happy with herself. Johnny got his lipstick kiss and I got my marching orders.

"Lizzy, get this stuff out of the arena and take it back to the dump where you found it before Claire sees it. And be sure we didn't leave weird marks in the footing that tells on us either."

I couldn't help myself. "Sure, Francesca, I'll take care of it, don't worry. I'll put it all back at your place where I found it. 'Course, I've never thought of your place as a dump."

She looked as if I had just hit her. I would need to come up with some new stuff for tomorrow; maybe umbrellas. Maybe those balloons I had mentioned. I didn't know anyone in a marching band. But, anything I could find on the farm that would surprise and rattle Johnny and Francesca would do just fine.

This was going to be lots of fun.

# 19. Cinderella

*Natalie leaned over my shoulder, tapping on my laptop. "See what you* gotta' do first is find the wealthiest zip code. That's where the best thrift stores are."

I couldn't believe I was taking shopping advice from a female welder. But, Nat was serious. She was lecturing me intently, so intently that I would have considered it bad manners to not listen respectfully.

She tippity-tapped at lightening speed, until she landed on an address. "Bingo. That's where we're headed."

I twisted in my seat to focus on Natalie, my mouth hanging open. "Why do you know this?"

She tipped her head. "Lizzy, I may be a member of the proletariat, but it doesn't mean I don't know how to fake it among the ruling classes."

I shook my head. "Nat, this is not about class struggle. I just want to look nice for my night at the theater."

Nat smiled again. "Everything is about class struggle." Still leaning over my shoulder she pulled out her phone and took a screen shot of the open laptop. "So, shake a leg. Cinderella's going to the ball."

I grimaced because the idea of letting Natalie play fairy godmother couldn't possibly end well, but Natalie was a force to be reckoned with. It seemed easier just to go with it. I closed the laptop and grabbed my purse.

The thrift store was huge. Natalie grabbed a grocery cart as soon as we came through the doors. I trailed behind her as we headed straight for an entire wall of dresses hanging on a sagging rack. The dresses were arranged by color, and the majority of the dresses were black. I just stood back while Nat threw dress after dress in the grocery cart until the cart was heaped. Then we headed to a line of women waiting for a dressing room.

While I waited with our cart, Natalie went looking for shoes and shawls and who knows what else. I looked at the women in front of me. They looked like normal people. I'm not sure what I expected.

When it was finally my turn, I realized I had on totally wrong underwear. Trying on dresses in a sport bra and bike-short-style underwear takes a bit of imagination. And then there was the floor. It was old, worn and grimy linoleum. I had to be able to keep my clogs on. No way was I standing on that floor.

I started the tiresome process of pulling and tugging and half way pulling up zippers before stripping and hanging stuff back up. They were all awful. Then I heard Nat outside my door "Hey, let me see."

"Natalie, only when something actually fits."

"C'mon, Lizzy, crack the door and show me. It's boring otherwise."

So I picked out something totally ridiculous from the pile. It had to be a reject from some high school prom night. It had such a low neckline that my sport bra was all you could focus on, and then it had a dropped hemline and a ridiculous poufy skirt. Of course, my white legs and clogs added to the picture. I opened the door, standing in my basic farm hand stance."

I pouted like a fashion model. "How you like this little nightmare?"

Nat was camera ready, and the flash went off. She whooped, "Priceless!"

I slumped against the grubby walls in mock despair while she snorted in barely suppressed laughter.

I wailed, "I'll pay you money to delete that."

She ignored me and handed me yet another black dress, this one with a faded dry cleaning tag sticking out of the neckline. She was grinning. "I got a feeling about this one."

There wasn't anything special about it. But it was tailored with a boat neck in the front that scooped lower in the back. When I touched it the fabric felt nice. It was kind of stretchy. I unzipped the long zipper in the back and silently closed the door.

I stepped into it and knew right away. I got it about three quarters of the way zipped up. It followed the contours of my body, hugging my waist. I opened the door and Nat was holding a pair of black patent pumps with spikey heels, and a little black clutch bag.

Her mouth fell open and then she softly whispered, "Wow. My job here is done."

Although I expressed anxiety about walking in such high heels, Natalie insisted. They were pretty, even though there was a scratch on one of the shiny patent leather heels. We even found a wrinkled pink shawl, soft as silk; Natalie was gleeful over the find, calling it a "Pashima."

The best surprise was the label in the dress; Dolce and Gabbana. That gave me a little rush. Score. The dress was nine dollars and nine-ty-nine cents, the shoes five ninety-nine, and the clutch, that had a stained lining and the wrinkly shawl, were only three dollars each.

Natalie was now heavily invested in my night out. She made me call her before Chess came over so she could take my picture. It had been such a long time since I had played "dress up." It was silly, but also felt like college again, and I was having fun. I put my hair up in a twist, add-ed some earrings, and even put on mascara and lipstick. I had bought some super sheer black stockings, which covered up my pale legs.

Even Ryder told me I looked good.

Regardless of the fact that I was not interested in Chess romanti-cally, when I opened the door and saw the way he was looking at me, I had a happy thrill.

His praise felt genuine. "Lizzy, you look lovely. I love the dress. You look so, so ..."

And he did not get out another word. I had to stop myself from telling where the entire outfit had come from. Nat had told me she would come down the hill and personally pummel me if I breathed a word of it to Chess. So, I just said, "thank you" and I grabbed my "pashima" all ironed smooth, and my little black clutch, and pulled the door closed behind us.

***

Walking in impossibly high heels takes concentration, and strong ankles. If I kept my weight on the balls of my feet, I felt stable. But if I relaxed too much on my heels, well, I was wobbling on top of those little spikes. When Chess offered his arm, I was glad to take it. I could tell he had slowed his stride to accommodate my mincing steps. Wearing these high heels was like volunteering for a temporary disability, even if they did make my calves look curvy.

We had parked in a garage with a valet, and had to walk to a restaurant. Chess had no idea of the challenge that presented to me.

I looked up at Chess; he was wearing a jacket, yet looked crisp and cool. He glanced back at me and then up. "What do you think about the "canyons of New York?"

I hung on to Chess's arm as I took in the scene. The sidewalks were crowded, the streets jammed with taxis. And the buildings on either side of us so tall that other than the store fronts and the doorways, there wasn't much I could see. The sky was almost blocked from view.

I answered him truthfully. "I don't know what to think. I feel very small right now."

He nodded. "I think that's a pretty typical response."

I continued. "And a bit off balance, too."

He answered, "Yes. It's a huge shift in perception."

I smiled, "Especially in these high heels."

And Chess kept a deadpanned expression. "I wouldn't know about that."

I smiled. "I hope not!"

And then we both were laughing.

We went to a tapas bar in "the Village" where we ate tiny bits of delectable food on really large square plates. Each tasty morsel was decorated with colorful drizzles and even flowers.

Oddly, we did not talk about Equus Paradiso Farm. We did not talk about Francesca or Frank or Margot or Deb or horses or dogs or cats or Chess's allergies. Chess was not Chess the accountant son of the owner untangling the finances of the farm. And I was not Lizzy the working student sweaty and covered in horse slobber.

We talked about our other selves. We talked about books and movies and places we had been. Chess was well traveled. He had been to Europe, and I had not. But I had been an English major, and a lover of history and thought of these places as settings for grand stories. I told him I wanted to see them someday for myself.

I had almost forgotten that I was more than a rider and trainer of horses. That, in addition to a dressage wanna-be, there was a Lizzy who loved to read and to travel in her mind to far away places; that there was a Lizzy who could take pleasure in a nice dress, as petty as that sounds.

Soon it was time to go to the play. It almost felt like an interruption. We left the restaurant and Chess commanded a cab to our curb with confidence. Sitting side by side in the back seat I noticed for the first time that there was something "open" about his face. He did look like his Mom, but without the sly reserve of Francesca. The inner coil was not wound as tight. Here was someone who was enjoying the moment without judgment. I found I had relaxed in his presence.

He reached over and gave my hand a squeeze. "Did I tell you how beautiful you look?"

I smiled back, realizing that his comment had not made me uncomfortable, that indeed I liked hearing it. I said, "I think so. Did I tell you how good you look tonight, too?"

"No."

"Well, you do."

We pulled up right in front of the theater, and Chess came around and opened my door and gave me his hand. I threw the end of my pink Pashima over my shoulder with a bit of a flourish and grabbed my little clutch bag. Here I was like some red carpet actress stepping out of a cab in New York City, to go the theater. I was already having fun, playing a role. I just had to be careful not to ruin it by toppling off my heels.

We went to a little bar inside the theater lobby and Chess ordered wine, and I whispered to him to get me a pretend drink. So, I got some club soda with a little sliver of lime. People came up to us to chat with Chess who introduced me. I was astounded that people here knew Chess. They always extended a hand to shake my hand, which I hated to do. My hands were pretty calloused, but at least I had filed my nails.

I still had a hold of his arm as I whispered to Chess. "Why would anyone know you here?"

He answered matter-of-factly, "Mom and Dad have season tickets, and since they know I love the theater, I usually get to use them. After a lot of years, you start seeing the same faces."

Chess tipped his head and focused on me. "Are you tired of standing?"

Actually, the balls of my feet were on fire. "Do I look like I'm in pain?"

He smiled, "No. But standing in those heels probably feels like an athletic event."

And he graciously led me to our red crushed velvet seats in the beautiful old theater. It wasn't a grand theater by any means. But it was a genuine Broadway theater. When the lights went down and the music started up, I was transported. It was a raucous musical parody about a rival to Shakespeare, with lots of campy humor that had both Chess and me giggling. I glanced over at Chess several times, and found that he was looking at me.

After the show, he left me in the lobby while he ran around to the stage door. It turned out he had a friend in the orchestra.

In a few moments he had returned, and once again offered me his arm. He brought a cab over to the curb with a gesture and we were heading back to the village for a nightcap.

We made our way back to Greenwich Village, to a club where Chess's buddy played in a house band. It wasn't on street level, but was a "cellar" club. Chess explained to me a bit of the history of the area. This street, MacDougal, was evidently the epicenter of a lot of Greenwich Village history. During prohibition, the area had speakeasies protected by gangsters, then later featured jazz clubs, beatnik hangouts, and folk music artists. It was also an area of "off Broadway" play houses, although NYU now had taken over some of the buildings.

I never liked bars, but the smoking bans made the clubs much more bearable for me than they would have been back in the day, although the noise level was a bit much.

Chess led me to a tiny round table awfully close to the stage. A bunch of guys were milling around on stage fiddling with equipment. Chess's buddy saw him and waved. He was tall and skinny with close-cropped hair. I wondered if he was an accountant by day like Chess. I am not sure if I was supposed to see, but the guy made eyes at Chess in a way that clearly referred to me in some oblique way.

For a Wednesday night, the size of the crowd was impressive. The music got started, and I leaned back in my chair to enjoy it, although it was too noisy to chat without straining my voice. Chess was nursing a beer, and I had ordered my usual fake drink.

After a few songs, the tall guy pointed at Chess.

"C'mon up, man. We haven't heard 'Moon River' for a while. No one does it like you, Chess."

I sat up and must have looked surprised. Then the guy spoke right to me.

"She doesn't know. Ah man, he used to play with us all the time. Chess, I promise, piano's been tuned."

So, Chess shrugged and then turned to me. "You mind? I promise only one song."

And Chess got up and took the spot at the keyboard in the back, pulling the mike up to his mouth and saying, "Ok, I'll start it off and hope I don't screw up; it's been awhile."

And then he said, "One, two, and three."

And a voice I had never heard before almost stunned me with its richness. Even the other bar-goers fell silent.

*"Moon River, wider than a mile, I'm crossing you in style some day.*

*Oh dream maker, you heartbreaker,*

*Wherever you're going, I'm going your way…*

The drummer and the guitars backed up Chess' piano in a soft way, letting his voice carry and linger over the notes.

His voice was strong and clear and sweet. He was confident as all get out here in the city, singing and playing in public. But then why should I be surprised? Francesca had been a dancer. The Cavellis were not afraid to perform; not a shy one in the bunch. And their sons had probably always had the best that money could buy in instruction and education. It showed.

Chess finished the song and I, along with the other patrons, heartily applauded. Then he shook hands all around with the band, getting a hug from the tall skinny guy. But he didn't sit back down; instead with a nod of his head he indicated we were leaving. The band struck up the next song, and nodded at us as we left.

I was glad to have Chess's arm again, as by now the bottoms of my feet felt hot and tender. It was time to have my carriage turn back into a pumpkin, but before that happened I did let him know that I had been blown away by his voice, and by the song. The tune and the lyrics, and well, Chess, had latched on to my subconscious in a way I did not even want to admit to myself.

Once I was in the car, I pulled off my shoes and leaned over to rub my stocking feet.

Chess noticed. "You okay?"

I moaned. "I think I'll be paying for these shoes tomorrow."

"Ah, the price of beauty. That's what my mother would say."

I laughed. "That does sound like her."

We pulled through the farm gates and Chess parked in front of the barn. I got out with my shoes in hand, before he could do the door opening routine, and thanked him for the wonderful evening.

But he got out of the car anyway and came around to my side. "Lizzy, you're not going to walk down the barn aisle in your stocking feet are you?"

I sighed. "I am not putting these shoes on again tonight, or actually, probably ever, regardless of how good they looked with this dress."

He nodded. "Okay. Put your arms around my neck then."

I laughed. "What?"

"Put your arms around my neck."

And I did as I was ordered, feeling ridiculous.

Once I did he swooped me up, which made me spontaneously shriek. And then feel self-conscious. "Chess, you cannot possibly carry me all the way down the barn aisle."

"Lizzy, you weigh nothing, and who knows how much residual horsey fecal-matter is on those pavers."

I was about to protest that his mother's barn aisle was probably cleaner than the floors in the apartment upstairs, but let it go. I was too distracted by the completely fairy-tale evening I had just had, ending with being swooped into the arms of a prince.

Oh hell.

By the time Chess delivered me to the door that led upstairs he was, I think, ready to put me down; he *was* breathing a little hard.

And there we stood for a moment that was gradually becoming uncomfortable.

I took a deep breath. "You want a cup of tea? I have 'Sleepy Time.'" As soon as I said it I cringed.

Chess looked amused, but spared me any joking. He just said, "Yeah, that would be nice."

So he followed me up the dark staircase.

As soon as I opened the door, my little Wheezer flew out and I bent down and grabbed her before she could slip away. I hugged her close to my chest as I walked in and flipped on the lights.

"Meow, meow, meow, meow!" She was complaining loudly. And I found myself chatting right back at her.

"Wheezer, I only went out for the evening. I know, Ryder ignores you, you poor little girl. But I'm back now."

Chess pointed. "You have a kitten?"

I grabbed the teakettle and, still holding Wheezer, filled it at the sink and put it on the burner.

"Isn't she beautiful? Francesca gave her to me. It's one of the nicest things Francesca has ever done for me. She said it was for rodent control, but I think that was just a cover story in order to give me a gift. She once gave Emma a puppy. Francesca can surprise me sometimes."

Chess plopped down on the sofa. "Who named it Wheezer?" Chess suddenly looked tired. He rubbed the back of his neck.

I pulled out mugs and tea bags and then went to sit next to him on the sofa.

I was still enthusiastic, happy to share a nice story about his mother. "Francesca. I thought it was a cute name since it's a little girl kitten. There's a band called Weezer. And in the movie *Steel Magnolia's*, Shirley MacLaine's character is called Wheezer."

Chess grimaced. "When I was in grade school, the other kids called me Wheezer, y'know because of my asthma."

I frowned. "Kids can be so cruel." And then I shook my head in disbelief. "Why would Francesca name the kitten Wheezer then?"

I had Wheezer tucked tightly under my chin. She was now purring happily. Chess picked her gently up, and she protested by opening her icy blue eyes and squeaking out a plaintive little "meow."

He set her down on the floor and said, "To send me a message; to warn me away. She didn't like it when I dated Emma, and she doesn't like it that I'm interested in you. But, I won't let her interfere again. She might tell me to stay away."

And he leaned in and kissed me. It was soft and long and knocked the wind right out of me.

He had a self-satisfied grin. "But that is my reply."

And then the teakettle whistled.

# 20. Firmer Footing

*I woke up with ice blue eyes staring deep into my soul, and the sound* of purring. Wheezer blinked, and then uncurled one of her peachy striped paws to reach out and pat my nose as if to ascertain that I was indeed there. I took my index finger and touched her on her pink nose. We were both now, "plugged in" and ready to start the day. I couldn't help but feel somehow lighter this morning.

Last night, I had carefully hung up my little black dress, and rolled my Pashima like a Girl Scout sleeping bag to keep the wrinkles at bay. The shoes I had tossed to the back of my closet. I couldn't imagine wearing those torture devices again. They were slated for a return journey to the thrift store. The thought made me smile. I wonder how many round trip journeys a lot of that stuff in the store had made.

Last night, before I finally went to bed, I noticed I had received an e-mail from Marco. His e-mails had become few and far between of late. Although unstated, I understood why. I had continued to send him e-mails that were almost like journal entries. But, last night I had deleted his message without replying. Not to be mean or rude, but because the time had come at last that I could. He was too kind to push me away, but I realized I had been too needy and weak to allow him to put all his attention on the girl he carefully never mentioned, but who

I knew stood behind the camera. He did not need my permission of course, but with a touch of the delete button I gave it anyway. I had let Marco "off the hook."

Whether Chess and I were meant to be, and I was not at all sure about that, I was finding some firmer footing these days. I hoped it was not simply because a man had looked at me and said "Wow." I frowned. I never wanted that to be me. Was that me? I hoped not. But, still, that Chess found me worth a "wow" had made a difference; the equation had changed.

Last night had been fun. Chess had been fun. I had made assumptions about Chess that were wrong. He was more than an accountant who got hives when he scratched a horse on the withers. Silly, but the fact that he and Emma had dated, mattered. Not in the way that I thought it would matter either. I was not jealous, not at all. I knew Emma had moved on. She had dated a polo player in Florida, and then had moved on to who knew who out there in Texas. No, it mattered that Chess had dated Emma; someone I felt was far superior to me in every category. Should that raise my self-esteem? Was that warped? I had no idea how the world saw Lizzy. I only knew myself from the inside looking out. But, someone like Chess, who had dated glamorous Emma, was looking at me from the outside, and calling me...beautiful.

I had to stop thinking about all of this stuff. While "the unexamined life is not worth living" the over-examined life will just about kill you. I had to stop. I needed to do my job, and besides, I had a horse show to focus on. Regardless, my step was a little bouncier today.

When I emerged into the barn aisle, Ryder cut me a dirty look and spoke out of the side of her mouth. "Late night? I never heard you come in."

I happily shrugged it off. "Glad I didn't wake you."

She studied me a moment with a narrowed eye, but then seemed to lose interest and changed subjects. "Farrier's here any minute, and

Doc's coming to check on Papa sometime this morning, too, so stick around. I'm hoping to get the green light on Papa. If I don't get back in the ring right after Devon for Regionals and Finals, then this entire year has been a bust."

Ryder's tone was bossy and slightly irritated. But, I shook it off like a dog coming out of a pond. She could not touch my good mood. I actually smiled. "I'll cross my fingers for you, Ryder."

Bill, our farrier, was on his way and would be disrupting the morning's training lineup. He wanted to start with Hotstuff, because this was the last shoeing before the championships in Chicago, and he wanted to tweak a few things. That meant Margot wouldn't take her usual slot as the first ride of the day. Because of that, Margot told me to quickly tack up Winsome and we would run through the test before Deb came down for her ride on Wild Child.

I did my "lick and a promise" grooming job on Winsome and tried to remember my test. Just thinking of the test, plus having to rush, injected my bloodstream with a jolt of adrenaline, but it was eagerness, not fear, that propelled me.

As soon as I stepped into the arena, I put Winsome into gear, and rushed through the warm up. Winsome had been going well in our lessons, but after our break, when I tried to sit down and run through the test, I felt awkward. I just couldn't find my groove, and felt guilty. Had going out last night and enjoying myself messed up my riding? The second run through didn't feel much better. After only about half an hour, Deb came into the arena with Wild Child and Margot dismissed me. I left without feeling successful.

I had been grabbing the clicker after my lessons on Winsome, and building on my initial training sessions of getting Winsome through the gate. I knew the repetition was important to cement the lesson. I wanted to go out and step through the gate a few times and redeem my saddle time. Those sessions had been steadily improving, and I think it had helped to do it after my lesson when she was tired and relaxed from her workout. But today, as soon as I entered the barn after my lesson to pick up the clicker, Ryder was ordering me to get Winsome put up in a bossy tone, and I instantly understood. Today was not the day to focus on myself, and that was okay. The farrier was heating up a shoe at his forge that was set up on the end of his truck. The smell of hot iron filled the air, and the shoe glowed orange. Sparks flew as Bill hammered the hot shoe against his anvil. Our peaceful farm had the atmosphere of a factory.

Then we heard Doc's big diesel truck pulling up to the barn. It was like we had heard a dog whistle, as we simultaneously turned our heads toward the front of the barn. I hustled Winsome into the wash stall, stripping off her tack and boots in record speed. It was just going to be one of those days. Ryder tightened the girth on Papa, and nervously glanced down the barn aisle, waiting for Doc to appear. Just then, Francesca's office door opened, and the terriers burst out of the office and ran to Doc's truck, barking noisily and adding to the general sense of chaos. I am sure as soon as they got there Doc's tires would be marked repeatedly.

I heard Doc's truck door slam and saw the terriers come tearing back down the barn aisle, giving Doc an advance guard.

Instead of stopping when they got to us, they spotted the farrier, bounced once in the air, and accelerated.

They had spotted the hoof trimmings; foul smelling and indigestible, and therefore irresistible.

In a whoosh they went skidding under Hotstuff, who had his hind hoof cradled between Bill's knees while he drove in a nail.

Bill had his back to all the action, and never saw the hellions coming, although he had to have heard them.

Hotstuff jerked his head up in alarm and exploded like a bomb. He reared up and slammed his hind hoof down, knocking Bill sideways into the wall and noisily banging the rolling toolbox which went careening into the back wall.

Hotstuff plunged forward, hind legs sliding under his body; righted himself and began kicking wildly to rid himself of the loose shoe hanging by a nail or two.

Snapper and Chopper had not backed off but gamely had snatched slivers of hoof trimmings off the pavement directly under the panicking horse. They spun and dashed away before anyone could touch them, and steal their prizes.

When they left, Hotstuff froze, but was standing with his right hind held up in the air, the shoe twisted around sideways and hanging off the hoof.

Bill shouted, "Goddamn! Francesca! Goddamn it!"

Bill shook his hand and I saw blood drops fly. Those nails were sharp and Bill had not gotten the nail clinched before Hotstuff had been frightened. Hotstuff must have dragged the sharp tip of the nail across the back of his thumb. Meanwhile Francesca and Doc were oblivious, strolling down the aisle toward us, chatting.

Bill ignored the blood dripping off his hand and proceeded to get Hotstuff's hind foot back between his knees to pull the shoe. I could tell he was angry. But he worked silently. Ryder and I cut each other meaningful glances.

Doc and Francesca made it to our set of cross ties, and Doc stroked Papa on the neck, greeting the horse before he greeted any of us. "Hey, Papa."

I had to say something. "Uh, Doc, I think you should maybe take a look at Bill's hand before checking Papa."

He looked a bit surprised, but immediately turned to Bill. "Hey, Bill, horses beating you up today?"

Bill slowly straightened up, a bent shoe in his hand that would need to go back in the forge now and be straightened out. Sweat was trailing down the side of his cheek. He grabbed a greasy looking towel off his toolbox, and wiped it across his bloody hand. "Nah, this horse wouldn't hurt a fly. Francesca, your damn terriers are a menace, ran right into him to grab hoof and then high-tailed it."

Francesca feigned surprise. "I didn't realize you were here, Bill. You know I always keep them up when you're working; if they eat hoof trimmings they throw up on the oriental."

Bill grimaced. "Better go ahead and book the carpet cleaners."

Doc shook his head. "Let me get my wound care kit from my truck, Bill. Please tell me you're current on your tetanus."

Bill nodded. "Oh, yeah. I would have died of tetanus years ago otherwise."

Then Bill turned to Francesca. "When I pulled that shoe just now, I had a wet nail."

Francesca had a blank expression.

Bill continued. "That ole horse comes up lame; you tell Margot she can thank your dogs for it."

I thought I could detect beneath the frozen expression on Francesca's face a slight flush.

Francesca said, "Wet nail?"

Ryder rolled her eyes at Francesca. "Blood, Francesca; blood. Your dogs scared Hotstuff and made him yank his foot from Bill, and then he slung that shoe half off and stepped down on it, driving the nail into the sensitive tissue."

Francesca almost whispered. "Hotstuff cannot be lame, he's got a show this weekend and then we head to Chicago for the Young Horse National Championships. He's ranked number two in the nation."

No one replied, because there was no good reply. Bill just stood there waiting on Doc, with that dirty rag pressed against his thumb. It was now a dirty rag with a growing red patch.

Doc arrived with a little black case, and popped it open. He cleaned up Bill's hand while the rest of us stayed silent.

Finally he spoke. "No sutures needed. But keep this covered and clean so it doesn't get infected. Unless you want it bandaged with six by sixes and Elasticon I suggest Francesca find you some human-sized bandages from her first aid kit."

Francesca cleared her throat. "Doc, can you please look at Hotstuff today, too?"

Doc had stepped away from Bill and gathered his bloody pile of gauze and threw it in our muck bucket in the back of the wash stall.

This time Ryder said it. "Wet nail."

He raised his eyebrows. "Doesn't he leave next week for ...?"

And we all nodded like bobble head dolls.

I got my marching orders from Doc; Epsom salts and hot water, twenty minutes in the rubber soaking pail, as many times per day as we could stand to do it.

Margot walked into the barn with Deb and Wild Child just as I was coaxing Hotstuff to put his foot into the rubber tub of hot water. They were chatting amiably, until they focused on me.

Bill was now working on Lovey, and typical of Bill stayed silently focused on his work. Francesca, the coward that she was, had retreated to her office. Doc and Ryder with Papa had headed to the arena, where I am sure Margot thought she would soon be joining them, while sitting on Hotstuff.

Hotstuff, meanwhile, as soon as he saw Margot, stepped forward out of the rubber soaking pail, managing to stand on the rim and tip the whole thing over.

I wailed, "Hotstuff, give me a break!"

I looked up to see Margot scowling at the tipped over pail. Hotstuff looked pleased with himself; head held high, big ears pricked. He picked up a front hoof to beg for a treat.

Margot pointed at the pail. "Why is my horse being soaked in Epsom salts?"

Before I could answer, she turned to Bill. "Bill?"

He straightened up and threw his nippers in the rolling toolbox, shaking his head. "Best ask Francesca about that."

Then she focused on Bill's hand, which Francesca had wrapped in human sized gauze pads and white medical tape.

"You're injured?"

Bill shrugged his shoulders. "Long way from my heart and same goes for that big goofy black horse of yours. But, I can't guarantee the health of those dogs of Francesca's, least not if I can get a hold of them. But your horse stepped down on a nail, and although it wasn't near any internal structures to worry about, I still can't guarantee he won't abscess."

Deb had put Wild Child in the wash stall, but she got her two cents in. "And Francesca complains about my cats. Those dogs are hell-on-four legs."

Margot sniffed, and turned to Bill. "No need to say more. I can imagine how that little scene played out, and I'm just glad I wasn't here. I may not have been polite. All, I can say is that I'm so sorry, Bill. I trust Francesca will do better about putting up Chopper and Snapper when you're scheduled to shoe."

Then she turned back to me. "Lizzy, make up another pail of Epsom salts and get him back in the water for twenty minutes. God, I hope he doesn't abscess. I'll have you do it again tonight before bed. Now, let me go catch up to Doc. This is an important check up for Papa."

Hotstuff was a kind horse, an affectionate horse, and unusually easy going for a four year old, but trying to convince him to soak his foot was a test of my patience. I finally pulled the mounting block up and sat down, keeping my hand on his leg as if to hold it down. As soon as I stopped touching him, the foot came up, the horse either shifted forward or back, and he managed to flip the entire pail over (I finally came to think this was intentional). Meanwhile, I had basically used up an entire milk carton container of salts.

Fortunately, when Margot came back with Doc and Ryder, leading Papa, they were all smiles. "Lizzy darling, thank you. Hopefully, by soaking that hoof we can stay ahead of an abscess forming. And here is the greatest news of all; Papa can gradually go back into full work. Isn't that wonderful?"

I looked over at Ryder. I knew a large weight had been lifted from her shoulders. I hoped this meant she would relax and be friendlier. "That's great news. Ryder, I know you must feel relieved."

Ryder almost smiled. "No extensions, and mostly straight lines, but I can do that. I can start showing again after Devon."

Doc took a cautionary tone. "Just remember what we talked about, Ryder."

Ryder simply nodded.

Then Margot changed the subject. "So, now we have to worry about this one."

Doc pursed his lips and drew out his words looking directly at Margot. "Uh. Well now Margot, it could be that it's nothing. I'd give it a few days and then feel it out from the saddle, but you call me if you feel any tenderness. We'll do our best to get you to Chicago."

And Margot turned to me. "Lizzy, I leave it to you."

I noticed that she did not include Ryder in this assignment. That was okay, because Hotstuff and I were buddies, and because I was happy to do anything for Margot. While I mulled this over, Hotstuff picked up his foot and managed to tip over the pail...again.

I looked up at Margot, who was now stroking Hotstuff on the neck and cooing to him. I noticed Doc looking at Margot. I think he felt badly for her.

I repeated my instructions to Margot as I refilled the pail with warm water. "Doc said as many times a day as we could stand it."

Margot nodded then turned and glanced back at Doc. "Considering the stakes, I'd say three times then."

He nodded back before focusing on packing up his stuff.

I sighed. "Looks like I'm going to need to buy a case of Epsom salts."

Margot folded her arms. "Francesca can pick that up and deliver it to you."

And she and Doc exchanged a look.

***

I managed to get to Johnny Cash well ahead of Francesca. I had a plan. Today I brought plain old white bath towels and placed them on the arena floor. I thought it was the perfect test because it would replicate what he hated the most, changing light on the footing. I was right. Johnny didn't even want to go into the arena; balking at the entrance and bugging his eyes and snorting in alarm.

But after I had led him over each towel I got on and did our usual warm up. I had even placed towels right on the track. The first few passes he had carefully stepped or hopped over each towel, but after a few minutes he had kicked enough arena footing over them that he even stepped directly on the towels. By the time Francesca showed up he was trucking along.

Francesca leaned against the kickboards and watched silently. Being Francesca, silence meant she could think of nothing catty to say; a good sign.

I dropped the reins and walked up to Francesca. "The towels are a great idea, don't you think?"

I thought I detected a tiny smile. "I don't think they do that at the Spanish Riding School."

I grinned back at her. "Well, if they have a horse that's freaky about changing light on the ground, they can call me and I'll fix it for them."

Her mouth twisted. "Are you telling me that Johnny Cash is fixed?"

I thought that he probably was not fixed for Francesca, but I couldn't say that. So I said, "Francesca, he is more ride-able that you think he is. Get on and ride him over the towels, and imagine those bars of light and shadows that blew his mind at the last horse show."

Francesca frowned. "I need this time to practice my test. I think it's fine what you are doing but *I* certainly don't want to waste my limited saddle-time on this cowboy stuff."

I tried to sound as polite as I could. "Yeah, but, Francesca, if you want to show this horse, then you have to be able to disaster-proof yourself. You are going to have to be the one who can ride him when unforeseen stuff comes up. I can't be in the irons when the clouds part and the arena has weird shadows. You have to feel confident that you can push on in those moments. And that means *you* have to be able to ride over those bath towels."

Francesca had no reply. But she pulled on her gloves.

I held Johnny at the mounting block while Francesca got on. Then I went around and shook out all the towels and set them back down along the rail all in a row, just like the fence line of shadows at the horse show. Johnny got tall and nervous watching me, and I knew Francesca was dying to yell at me to stop scaring her horse. But, she bit her tongue.

I called out to Francesca. "Just walk him down this line and don't take no for an answer." Francesca didn't argue with me.

Johnny balked at the first towel, and Francesca, to her credit, sat up and kicked him down the line. He went, arching his neck and lowering and tipping his head to have a better look. He carefully lifted his feet over each towel. But he went.

His first trot down the line was hilarious. Francesca could barely sit him as he bounced down the line. But soon, Francesca and Johnny got into the rhythm of the ride, and Johnny was showing power that Francesca had never let out of the box.

I was almost bursting with pride watching. So, Francesca was still her stiff self, and her curb rein was way too tight, but they were cooking along a lot more forward and the towels had been forgotten.

When Francesca stopped, she was dripping sweat and out of breath. She hopped off and gave Johnny his routine lipstick kiss. Before she could leave, I fished for another compliment by giving one.

"Francesca, that's the best you've ever ridden him. You let him show off what a great motor he has."

She didn't smile. I wondered for a moment if his power had scared her. It certainly had made her sweat.

Without acknowledging my compliment she said, "Don't forget to soak Hotstuff twice more tonight."

I sighed. "Of course. But I need more Epsom salts."

She nodded. "Frank said he would drop some off at the barn."

And she was gone with her backward wave, while I pondered how she had pawned off her errand of penance on poor Frank.

\*\*\*

Frank was right behind me when I pulled through the farm gates. He was driving his moss-green vintage Jag, the black leather top was down and he had on a great pair of Ray-Bans. Frank struck me as someone who always squeezed joy out of every situation in life. But, I reminded myself, he had the money to treat himself to little presents like vintage Jaguar cars.

As I got out of my truck he was opening his door and waving to me. "Lizzy, please come help this fat old man unload his car."

I was always happy to help Frank. "I'm guessing you brought me a ton of Epsom salts."

Frank unbuckled his seat belt and swung his legs out. The car was low slung and a tight fit for Frank. He seemed to pause a second and then scoot himself to the edge of the side of the car seat before hoisting himself to his feet. On the tan leather seat next to him was a large donut box, the lid was closed, but crimped in a way that clearly showed that Frank had sampled the contents. An extra large coffee was balanced on the console, and multiple plastic grocery bags were piled on the floor.

I hadn't seen Frank in a while, and I noticed he looked tired. His jolly tone couldn't mask his apparent fatigue. Maybe it was just because I knew more than I was supposed to know about his difficulties, but I thought his eyes looked puffy and his skin almost gray.

I reached in and started gathering grocery bags. They weren't heavy so I loaded up.

Frank pointed at the bags. "Francesca told me to buy the store out of Epsom salts. She wouldn't say why."

I rolled my eyes. "I guess she's embarrassed. Chopper and Snapper got into the hoof trimmings on the floor while the farrier was under Hotstuff."

Frank grimaced. "Verboten?"

I nodded. "Oh yeah, it startled Hotstuff. Farrier cut his hand and Hotstuff stepped on a nail, not to mention the dogs can't digest it and usually barf it all up later."

Frank was still frowning. "Everyone gonna be okay?"

I smiled. "Should be. But, it's a good thing it was Francesca's fault and not one of us. I guess Francesca can't fire herself."

I felt a little guilty saying that but Frank didn't correct me.

I continued, "Hotstuff is standing number two in the national rankings for four year olds, and he goes to a show Friday and to Nationals next week, so it could mess things up if he abscesses. Epsom salt soaks are supposed to prevent that and draw out the soreness, too."

Frank shook his head in sympathy for Hotstuff, and then reached in and got his box of donuts and the couple of plastic grocery bags left on the floor. I nodded at the donuts and smiled.

"For us? I can smell them from here."

Frank winked. "You know it, baby; Old Fashioneds. I stopped for a coffee-pick-me-up and saw these things coming out of the fryer. You girls could eat your weight in these things and still burn off the calories. I did a quality control check. They were perfect. Just the right amount of crispy on the outside and soft in the middle."

I laughed. "You are a man who knows his donuts."

Frank laughed back at me in his wonderful deep full belly laugh. "Better than I should, that's for sure. But, man and woman cannot live by donuts alone. I packed one of those bags with steaks and potatoes and even bought a bag of Asparagus… enough for your Wednesday night party at Deb's. I threw in a spice rub that sounded interesting."

Frank and I walked in the barn side-by-side and I dumped all the bags of Epsom salts in the wash stall, and then pointed to the door to the apartment. "You have to come upstairs and say hello to Wheezer!"

Frank looked as surprised as Chess did. "Wheezer? What, are you kidding me?"

I laughed. "It's my new kitten!"

He shook his head. "I thought for a moment you meant Chess. My poor son got teased at school for years with that name, and it always upset me that the name stuck. He had to go off to college to lose it."

He followed me up the stairs, and I talked over my shoulder. "Yeah, that's unfortunate. But, this is the kitten that Francesca gave me. I was really touched that she gave me a kitten. Francesca was the one who named her. I didn't know it was some kind of inside joke. Chess took it well though."

Frank was silent as I cracked open the door because, of course, Wheezer was right there greeting me noisily with her incessant talking. I gently pushed her back with my boot, and pushed my way in. "Frank, you have to kind of hurry so I can close the door. She's terrible about escaping."

Frank got in and I closed the door. Up went Wheezer's tail and she trotted after us to the kitchen. I set my bags on the counter, and Frank set down the big flat donut box. Then I opened the fridge and got all the perishables put up.

I enthused, "Wow, these steaks are gorgeous, Frank. They'd cost me a week's salary. I think you should come up on Wednesday and join us; looks like plenty."

He shook his head. "Oh no. But, you enjoy."

I picked up Wheezer and handed her to Frank. "Isn't she the sweetest?"

Frank was a big guy in every way, but he took Wheezer gently from me and cradled her against his chest, stroking her under the chin. She tipped her face upwards, gazing in adoration with her stunning blue eyes, and soon Wheezer was pumping with her paws on his shirtfront and purring.

I leaned back against the counter and watched Wheezer commune with Frank, admiring his gentleness with my tiny kitten. I said, "You're a hit."

Frank almost looked bashful. He said sweetly, "I've always been a sucker for pretty little things."

He winked at me. Then said softly, "I wish Francesca hadn't named her Wheezer though."

I tried to reassure him that it didn't matter. "Wheezer didn't seem to bother Chess at all. Those drops he's taking seem to be helping. He could even pet her without getting itchy."

Frank's smile started small and then grew until he was chuckling. "Well, I'll be damned, Chess has been up here?"

Now it was my turn to try to contain my smile. And I couldn't help myself; it started small and grew until I, too, was chuckling. "Yes. Chess very kindly took me into Manhattan, since I'd never been. We used your season tickets to the St. James. I hope you don't mind."

Frank handed Wheezer back to me still smiling. "Mind? Lizzy baby, you just made my day. I've got to get going. You girls enjoy those steaks; I've still got lots to do before I sleep tonight."

And as I set little Wheezer down, I realized Hotstuff still needed two more soakings. I, too, had lots to do before I got to sleep tonight.

# 21. That Wild Ride

*I had done what I could do. But, as it turned out, it still wasn't enough.*

I could tell before he took one step that Hotstuff was doomed. It wasn't just the dull look in his eye, but that he stood (as horses often do) with one hind leg cocked, the hoof resting on the toe, not fully bearing weight. The alarms went off in my head because it was the left hind, the one I had been soaking three times a day in a warm bath of Epsom salts, trying like hell to ward off the formation of an abscess.

He hobbled to the wash stall like he had a broken leg. As I passed Alfonso he made a whistling sound and said something like "Ay-yi-yi."

I yelled back under his neck, "He's going to be fine, Alfonso! But, I'm calling Doc right now."

Anyone who has been around horses long enough will probably see an abscess sooner or later. Any injury can cause a puss-pocket to form, sort of like a pimple. And if you've ever had a splinter under a fingernail, well, you know how it hurts, but since it's inside a hoof the horse has to bear weight on it. Until that pimple has a way to burst and release the pressure, the pain is practically unbearable. Poor Hotstuff was suffering and needed relief. I just hoped Doc could give it to him.

And fast.

I got the water good and hot, and this morning Hotstuff was more than happy to gently lower his foot in the water and leave it there. He had lost all playfulness, and his eye was half closed, his mouth had taken on a tight look, his large ears, usually so floppy and to the side, were half way back against his neck. Those who don't know horses wouldn't see or recognize it, but Hotstuff's facial expression was one of stoic suffering.

I flagged Ryder down, and she took one look at Hotstuff and got the picture immediately. She leveled her gaze at me. "Doc on his way?"

I was perched on the edge of the mounting block, which I had pulled up next to Hotstuff's hind leg. "Yeah. I called him soon as I got him into the wash stall."

She sniffed. "Does Margot know yet?"

I pressed my lips together and shook my head. "Nope. I left Francesca a text though. I figure she can break the news to Margot."

Ryder shook her head and studied Hotstuff's face, then looked down at his hoof. "That horse is not going anywhere."

I sighed. I did not want to even think about it. Clearly he wasn't loading up tomorrow to go to the CDI, but surely he might still make it to Chicago. I did not want to debate it with Ryder. So, I changed the subject. "Can you get Wild Child ready for Deb? I need to stay with Hotstuff or he'll take his foot out."

She nodded, "Yeah, sure." And walked away with what almost seemed like a swagger. Maybe I was just imagining it, but I had a niggling suspicion she was glad. There is a term I had heard before... Schadenfreude. It meant taking joy in the problems of others. Ryder had missed her national competition due to Papa's lameness, and Margot had made her suck it up and go as a groom. It had nearly killed Ryder. And now it looked like Margot might miss her national championship, too. The similarity had not flown past my radar, and I knew Ryder had picked up on it, too.

Ryder brought Wild Child back to the grooming stalls and we attended to our charges in silence. But my silence was only a cover for a brewing sense of outrage against Ryder, and also concern for Hotstuff and Margot.

Hearing Doc's noisy diesel pull in gave me an instant sense of relief. And then I saw the terriers. Today the sight of Chopper and Snapper provided an additional measure of relief. It was time for the burden of care to pass from me to the good doctor and Hotstuff's owner, Francesca. And besides, they would be the ones to face Margot and deliver what might be bad news.

Doc seemed almost jolly, but Francesca's face was grim. She had to be feeling guilty as heck.

Doc reached up and stroked Hotstuff on the neck while focusing on me. "Well, Lizzy, you win some, you lose some. But look at it this way; we know that nail didn't go near any critical internal structures. This hurts awful bad, poor boy, but it's a long way from his heart. Get that hoof out of the bucket and dry it off for me and I'll get my glasses."

I did as I was told, and Doc got out his hoof knife and put on a headset thingy with magnifying glasses and a light on it. "Lizzy, look here. Francesca, Ryder, you might want to look, too. See this tiny black dot? It's not often that things are this obvious." Doc cradled Hotstuff's hind foot between his knees and pointed what looked like an ice pick at what was indeed a tiny black dot that was right inside the shoe on the sole of his foot. We crowded around Doc to have a look.

Doc continued his lecture. "So, the tract sealed over and because of that, all that soaking didn't prevent an abscess from forming. I'm going to gently pare away at this and see if I can open up the tract and drain it."

Francesca backed up and turned away. I would have stayed and watched but Hotstuff seemed to come alive. He sensed what was coming. His eyes had gone wide in alarm, the whites showing.

I went to his head and took a light hold of his halter and cooed to him. "Hotstuff, Doc is your buddy and you've got to trust that he's going to make you feel better."

From behind Hotstuff, Doc stated with enthusiasm, "Got it!" And Hotstuff jumped forward, leaning into his cross ties while holding his hind foot up in the air. Doc had a big smile on his face when he said, "Always makes me feel like a miracle worker."

Doc grabbed the foot back up and cradled it again between his knees. He managed to drain more pus while Ryder looked on with interest.

Just then Margot arrived. She knew right away, of course. She crossed her arms, and stated as a matter of fact. "Abscessed."

Doc stood up and turned, actually smiling at her. "It was beautiful, Margot. I found the tract, lanced it, and drained it. Look at his face, that horse would like to hug me right now."

And we all did turn and look at Hotstuff's face. And Doc was right. All the pain signs were gone, his ears were up, and he was looking at Margot like he expected a treat.

Doc gave the horse a scratch on the withers and then turned to me. "I'll show you how I like to put on the poultice, and then you can change it every day for the next three days. You've got to keep it open to avoid a re-infection. It'll be sore to bear weight on, so we can give him Bute for the pain and inflammation, but he needs to have some time off."

Francesca gave a heavy sigh. "I'll call and scratch him from the show this weekend. But the important question is, Doc, will he go next week to Chicago?"

His eyebrows lifted. "What day do you ship out?"

Francesca looked at Margot while she answered Doc. "Next Wednesday?"

Today was Thursday.

Doc nodded and made a *hmmmmm* sound before answering. "Then I'll be here next Tuesday morning and put on the hoof testers and watch him jog. Until then, hand grazing, Bute, and keep him poulticed. The rest of it is up to Hotstuff. And call me if there are any problems."

Doc headed back to his truck for the supplies for the poulticing, and Margot turned to Ryder. "Ryder darling, you and Nat will have to trade off the care of Hotstuff this weekend while we are at the show. I know I can depend on you. It will be touch and go whether Hotstuff and I compete in Chicago."

Ryder frowned. "Feels familiar."

Margot tipped her head. "Darling, I take it as it comes. At the end of the day, this national championship will be forgotten by almost everyone. Do you remember who won the four-year-old national championship last year?"

And we all stood there like deaf-mutes; although I knew I had watched the horse's winning rides on the USEFNetwork online. But I could not for the life of me think of the horse's name.

Margot raised her eyebrows. "I thought so." She gave a knowing smile and walked over to talk more with Doc.

***

Equus Paradiso now had just two entries at what turned out to be a big and important show in our area. Little old me and Winsome would be competing in the open division at Third level, and Deb and Wild Child were showing in the CDI at Grand Prix, which is run under FEI rules rather than national rules. FEI rules were almost the same as USEF, with some important differences that included a zero tolerance of drugs, even the benign non-steroidal anti-inflammatory drugs like Bute, as well as a veterinary inspection and restricted access to stabling.

I had been allowed by competition management to stable next to

Deb in the restricted FEI barn, which was a relief. I would have felt cast adrift and lonely away from Deb in the regular show stabling. It just meant extra security, and a neat little wristband that made me feel like a fraud. But, grooms and owners got them, too.

Ryder and Alfonso had come over the day before to set up the stalls and the tack room. It was an odd feeling to have that done for me. When we arrived, Deb and I had nothing to do but unload our horses from the trailers and put them into the beautifully set up stalls. Alfonso even unloaded our tack into the already set up tack room, and then parked the trailer and headed back to the farm.

Winsome had stepped off the trailer puffed up and light on her toes. I had put the chain over her nose for a little "power steering" and was glad that I had. I followed Deb and Wild Child into the barns, feeling like we looked important. Not only were our horses beautiful, we had 'people.'

Deb had gotten a corner stall for the Child, and Ryder had wisely put the tack room next to him, then Hotstuff's empty stall that we now used as our grooming stall, and then Winsome. That way Wild Child wouldn't be coming on to her all weekend. But it also meant Winsome was feeling separation anxiety at being so far from her stablemate. She immediately did what she had done at our last outing, which was to rear up on her hind legs and try and peer over the top of the stalls to see who she could see. She then did some laps in her stall and some whinnying. Of course Wild Child and others answered her stress call. And when they did she froze like a statue, ears pricked. It was like she had to listen carefully to see if she recognized voices. When she unfroze, she started the crazy cycle all over again. She looked unhinged, and it seemed that I had lost contact with her. She was in her horse world; no human intrusion was welcome.

And there was Deb, whistling and looking relaxed. She sat down in one of the director's chairs and was looking at her phone.

I walked over to her. "Deb, shouldn't we be doing something?"

She patted the chair next to her. "We are doing something."

I bit my lip, puzzled. "That would be?"

Deb smiled and her dimples appeared. "We are letting the horses settle."

I nodded and sat down in the offered chair. "Winsome looks totally nuts."

She smiled again. "That's to be expected. She's still new to the game, unlike my hunk over there. He has smelled every inch of that stall and peed like a dog on about five different spots. For Wild Child, this is a trip to the strip club."

I laughed. "I hadn't thought of it that way. It is like a strip club, bare-naked ladies parading all around, and although the looks and sights are stimulating ... no touchy-feely allowed."

Deb threw her braid over her shoulder and gave a hearty guffaw, then leaned toward me with a conspiratorial tone. "Let's enjoy this weekend, Lizzy. It's something we both earned, y'know? Let Ryder wait on us, and Francesca buy us stuff if she's so inclined. This is a gift, and it's really bad form to denigrate a gift in any way. I know this is new territory for you, and not something I'm used to either, but let's roll with it, okay?"

I frowned. "I promise to try, Deb. It's just that I'm nervous. I don't mean to be, but my body and my brain are practically incapacitated with anxiety. I want to be like you. You always look comfortable, no matter what. But, when I look at Winsome rearing up and down and whinnying, it makes me a little sick; my stomach hurts."

Deb did a very Margot-like thing. She patted my knee. "You know who is the most nervous show rider around?"

I shook my head.

Deb dimpled up again. "Margot. Always has been. But once she turns on, she is, she is ... well ... she's an artist, right? You may always be like Margot. You stand at the edge of the diving board scared as hell, and then you make that big leap into the air and you might as well be a bird. You can fly. That's why we train and train and train, so that you can let go and let the training take over. Both you and Winsome have that to rely on. You're both ready. Just make that leap and rely on your training. Trust yourself and your horse will trust you, too."

I thought about that for a moment. "Thanks, Deb. People always say that, and I understand it in theory. My survival instinct kicks in just like a spooking horse, and it says to run, run, run away. Meanwhile, my mind lectures me to just get over it. It's hard to perform with this stupid internal battle going on. I end up feeling paralyzed."

Deb's dimples appeared and she shook her head, amused. "You are something, Lizzy. Stuff will happen, crazy stuff, especially at horse shows. It's a wild ride, but one that you never take alone. You have an amazing partner taking that wild ride with you, right?"

I nodded, encouraging Deb to continue.

"Wild Child is one hell-of-a partner, and so is Winsome. I know the ride can't last forever, so I'm going to enjoy every moment. My ability to relax and enjoy myself does not revolve around those judges in the box. It's not about a stupid piece of satin or a silver candy dish. God, I hate all that stuff. It's about me and that hunk of a stallion in there; the two of us. But, one thing I do appreciate about showing is that I get a chance to share the beauty of it all with an audience. A great piece of music or art or dance needs an audience. Of course, there is no tougher audience than those judges in the box. Not every judge is equal, but for those I do respect, well, to earn respect from those whose opinions you respect, that's very satisfying. To be able to present to an audience a horse like that one, like your horse, too, well, that in itself should be very gratifying."

And she pointed behind her to Wild Child, who had now rolled in his fresh shavings and was swishing some of the shavings out of his tail. I laughed as he gave a good all over body shake. "Thanks for the pep talk, Deb, however it goes this weekend, I'm going to remember to be grateful. When I started this I had no idea how hard it was going to be. But, I also had no expectations. Regardless, it's all good … but in spite of all that, I'm still nervous."

Ryder came down the aisle, pulling a rolling ice chest behind her. "Hey, Frank dropped this off at the barn. It's dinner for all of us … he called it a cold-fork supper, whatever that means."

I got out of my chair, interested. "God love him, I don't know what that means either, but I know Frank only likes the best so I expect it will be delicious. I don't know how he finds the time to do all this."

Ryder nodded. "Yeah, Frank likes the best all right. If you ask me, that guy's liked the best a bit too much. He looks like hell lately. He seems tired, and I think he's put on weight. He looks … puffy, or something."

Deb stood up, too, and wrinkled her brow. "Y'know, now that you mention it, I thought his face had a weird color the other day."

I piped up, "I thought so, too. He looked sort of, um, pasty. And you're right, he seems even heavier."

Ryder and Deb both nodded.

I said, "Do you think we should say anything?"

Deb frowned and shook her head. "I'll say something to Margot. Maybe something's going on with him that we don't know about."

Ryder sneered at me. "Ask Chess, why don't you?"

Now they were both looking at me. So I said, "I will. But it doesn't mean that he'll tell me anything. Francesca's about as private as anyone I've ever met. She only shares on a 'need to know' kind of basis. I think that even applies to Chess."

Ryder was about to retort when Deb turned toward Ryder. "I'm going for our packets. I'll need Wild Child's bridle number on him before I can get on. Ryder, go ahead and put the hunk in the cross ties and tack him up for me; be sure and make the big boy glow."

Deb flipped her ponytail over her shoulder and inhaled and stretched herself as tall as five-foot-next-to-nothing could do before heading down the aisle. Ryder had not replied. Deb had ordered her about with ease, having no problem slipping into Margot's role.

That was going to be problematic for me.

After a beat, Ryder was in action. And I stood in the aisle aimless, kind of like a junior high school boy taking his girl out on the floor for his first slow dance. I had absolutely no clue what to do with my hands.

After pacing circles in the tack room, I found my "Whinny Widgets" test book, and looked back over my tests. Then I stepped into the aisle and walked through my test patterns in my imaginary dressage arena. Out of the corner of my eye I spotted Ryder watching me with a twisted smile, shaking her head. I didn't care. Winsome could work her anxiety out in her own horsey way, and I could work mine out through my human way.

Deb was a casual housekeeper, and her fashion sense was just as casual… to put it mildly. But there was nothing unkempt or disordered about our tack room and aisle or in fact her attire today. Her hair was still in its signature braid, but her breeches were clearly new and from High Horse Couture, they were a caramel brown that coordinated with Wild Child's bright chestnut coat, and her brown sleeveless polo shirt was some kind of high tech sheer fabric. It was so sheer and snug that you could see Deb's set of six-pack abs right through it. She had a new pair of brown gloves to match. Deb was wearing a pair of black patent leather boots I had never seen her wear before, and they did not have a single smudge. In a pinch you could have used them as a mirror to put on your lipstick.

Deb and Wild Child casually strolled to the warm up arena. Deb seemed unaware of the incredible sight they provided. I saw a couple girls walking along the path stop dead in their tracks, and one grabbed the shirt of the other and pulled her friend off the path to make way for Wild Child to pass. It was like Deb and Wild Child were royalty.

Deb may have been unaware, but not Wild Child. That horse had no self-esteem issues. He strutted like a peacock, even on a loose rein at the walk. He knew he was impressive and he was damn sure that if any horses were around, his swagger would signal that he was to be the unchallenged king of the herd. He made me laugh out loud to myself.

Ryder heard. She said, "What's so funny?"

I turned to see she had gathered up a bucket of supplies to have handy at ringside; a good groom. Meanwhile, my hands were still feeling empty. I had to fight the urge to snatch the bucket from her. This was going to be a weird show.

"I was just cracking up looking at Wild Child. He's so arrogant, but I love him anyway."

Ryder just made a harrumph sound and walked silently at my side to the ring. Deb had already begun her warm up when we got to the arena. As usual, Wild Child was being lazy and more interested in the other horses than actually burning calories. He should have known better than ignore the little tiger on his back. Deb had some serious spurs on and she let Wild Child feel them a couple times. His ears swiveled back toward his rider, and with a deep exhalation, he got down to business... Deb's business.

Margot arrived at my side, holding her coaching system that Deb would wear in one hand, her headset already on and the receiver clipped to her belt. She did not stop Deb or call her over. She just put her hands on the top rail of the fence and watched. When Deb passed us, they locked eyes, and Margot simply nodded. Deb kept going, and completed her warm up without Margot saying a word.

When Deb finished, she gave Wild Child a pat and a loose rein. He was relaxed and walking his huge panther walk, sneaking a peak around at the other horses in the arena with renewed interest.

Deb sidled up to the rail and stopped and leaned over for the headset, got it on, and proceeded to go back to work. She and Margot now had the ability to talk to each other in normal speaking tones. But as I stood next to Margot I was impressed at how little Margot had to say.

Deb put Wild Child together. The warm up phase was over and now Wild Child had to increase his engagement and show us his power moves. This meant gathering himself, carrying more weight over his hindquarters. It took balance and suppleness and plain old strength to work in the collection required at Grand Prix. The look Deb created in Wild Child was of a horse who had become shorter in the length of his body, with hind legs that no longer swung like a pendulum as far behind his body as under it. The front end of the horse appeared taller; the poll the highest point, his nose just slightly in front of the perpendicular line to the ground. His shoulders and front legs became lightened and free and increased the forward swing and height on their own pendulum. The moment of suspension was also increased, due to the powerful thrust of his hind leg.

It was one thing to read about it in the books, but it was quite another to see it up close and live in this stunning creature. And, of course, I knew it was another thing to feel it from the saddle and be able to guide it to more and more amplitude, and not lose control. That took not only education but feel and a sort of conviction in your own instincts. Deb had that feel, and she had that conviction. I wondered if she ever doubted herself in the saddle. As of yet, I had never seen it.

Watching Deb and Wild Child I had a very good feeling for her; for this weekend and beyond. She was indeed ready for this. She indeed had earned this. I was not so sure about myself though.

Margot looked over her shoulder at us, and then looked at her watch. "Lizzy, why don't you go get your mare? Ryder, you will need to get Wild Child bathed and braided for his FEI jog at four, so I'll need you to take him from Deb as soon as she is finished."

Ryder and I both stood up taller. No more lolly-gagging at the side of the warm up arena. My stomach did a flip-flop and I had a surge of performance anxiety.

I tried to walk back to the stables, but it felt better to jog. As soon as I got to our barn aisle, Winsome screamed at me. It was not a whinny, it was a scream. I felt she was scolding me for leaving her alone. I affected a calming tone. "Winsome, it's all right, baby girl."

I peeked into her stall and saw that she had been walking in a nervous circle. She also had deposited loose piles of manure that now were trampled and mixed into her lovely fluffy pine shavings along with what had been a flake of hay. In short, she had created a horrible mess.

I moved her into our grooming stall, which was a luxury for show stabling, but something Hotstuff's last minute scratch from the competition had provided. I clipped Winsome into the cross ties, and began the process of grooming and tacking.

Winsome was standing as tall as she could in the cross ties, on high alert. She was looking for Wild Child, ears pricked and tight as a tick throughout her body. She wanted her little herd all clustered together, and was alarmed that we had scattered. I knew when she was like this she could go off like a firecracker. My stomach was clenched, and simply would not let go. I could hear Deb's voice in my head ... the training, the training, the training. Slip into what we always did every day at home and let the training take over.

I drew a deep breath and got to it. Hooves picked, "Show-Sheen" in the tail, curry, brush, polo bandages, pads, saddle, bridle, fly spray. And for me: Boots, spurs, whip, gloves, helmet. And then one final thing: bridle number.

And it was time to get on. Just as I was getting on, Ryder came up the walkway leading a puffing Wild Child. Winsome screamed. And Wild Child, who must have been tired, answered her in a low whinny that seemed half-hearted. As I stepped into the stirrup, Winsome turned around, trying to follow her boyfriend into the barn. I aborted the mission and jumped to the ground. I patiently backed her to the mounting block and rattled the bit in her mouth.

"Winsome, get over here and stand like a statue. You know better than that." She turned her head to look at me, startled with her ears pricked. "Well, hello there, you finally noticed that I'm here."

And for some reason things got better after that. I swung up and gathered my reins and Winsome and I marched purposefully to the warm up arena, where both Deb and Margot were waiting for me. Deb held onto Winsome while I put Margot's coaching system on. And really for the first time ever, I started my warm up with my legs and stirrups feeling normal. Although Winsome was more alert than usual, and did scoot a bit left and right from God only knows what, she felt fabulous. She was putting her nerves into the work in a way that put a smile on my face. Margot's voice was low and soothing in my ear.

"Oh darling, she looks beautiful. Our little girl is growing up. I suggest you loosen her with some forward leg yields. Try this, four steps sideways and then go forward in medium trot, without shortening then go back to leg yielding. Let's see how big and scopey she wants to make them today."

This was an exercise I was very familiar with and loved. And it worked. Winsome began to let go, and show the scope, or range of motion, that nature had blessed her with. She became very workman-like. From there we did our canter-trot-canter transitions. And then we took our break. When I looked over at the rail, Deb was still there, and Francesca had joined them. Francesca never came to watch my lessons on Winsome. It struck me then that these three women, all for different reasons, had become very important to me.

I let the thought settle softly somewhere in my mind as I gathered Winsome back to me. I went through the third level exercises and patterns that I would need tomorrow in my test, and sat in the saddle in a confident way that I never would have thought possible thirty minutes ago. I thought about what I had referred to as Deb's 'conviction' in the way she managed Wild Child. That is who I wanted to be today. I seized on it. I sat in my saddle with that one word guiding me.

Margot had almost nothing to say except "good" and "yes" and the lesson was over too soon. I wanted to stay in that wonderful place. I felt confident and competent. Still, when I got back to the stable, the three women walking behind me, I found that my polo shirt was soaked with sweat and my horse lathered under the reins on her neck. Time had stopped. I was not the least bit tired.

Ryder had Wild Child in the grooming stall putting in his braids. She had set a floor fan in the back of the stall and run an extension cord, so he was also getting dried off as he was braided. He gave Winsome a low "huh-huh-huh" and surprisingly, she neglected to answer him. Winsome was back to being "my" girl.

Deb held her while I pulled her tack off and then I gathered the wash bucket and headed out to the wash rack. We were both relaxed and content. And when I returned her to her stall, it had been entirely cleaned and put to rights… by Ryder; another surprise that I reminded myself to acknowledge with gratitude. That had to have been a messy job.

The CDI horses were being called to the inspection holding area. Wild Child was all spiffed up and so was Deb, who again shocked me by showing up looking like a Ralph Lauren ad. Her hair was twisted into a French knot at the base of her neck, and she had on pressed khakis and a short sleeved brown blouse with a colorful gold and russet scarf knotted around her neck. And she was wearing jewelry; multiple leather bracelets with stones knotted into them.

We all marched behind Deb leading Wild Child in the snaffle bridle to watch him in the FEI inspection, referred to informally as "the jog." Wild Child had almost killed Margot and me the first few times we had presented him at shows. But I had made it my mission to get that little problem solved and Deb was now reaping the reward. Deb kept him busy and focused on her instead of all the 'bare-naked ladies" that were being promenaded, waiting for their turn to be presented. Instead of rearing and plunging and snapping his teeth all the way through the jog, Wild Child was lazy as all get out. I could tell he was still absorbed in watching the other horses, but he now understood that even though none of them had saddles on, he was not going to get lucky tonight. He was tethered to the fierce little tiger-woman who routinely bossed him around, and there would be no chance of ditching her. He made me smile.

Once Deb and Wild Child had finished being "accepted" in the horse inspection, we strolled back to the barn. Ryder pulled out Wild Child's braids while I helped put the barn to rights. I refused to let Deb do anything looking so elegant. I admired her bracelets and discovered that Natalie had made them for her. Margot and Francesca fished around in our cooler and opened a bottle of wine, and the three of them sat in the director's chairs and chatted amiably.

Once Wild Child was back in his stall, Ryder and I dumped the grain.

Francesca rose from her chair. "I'm off, but I'll be back for your test on my horse, Deb."

I noticed Francesca had pointed out that Wild Child did indeed belong to her.

Deb smiled. "Don't go, Francesca. Stay and share supper with us. Frank brought it, so you know it's going to be good stuff."

I saw a look of surprise on Francesca's face. We rarely included her in anything. And suddenly I wanted her to stay, too. "Yes. You should stay, Francesca. You know Frank always packs for us like we're an army."

Margot picked up the bottle of wine and started to pour Francesca another glass of wine, but Francesca put her hand across the top.

"Next time. And yes, the food is wonderful and plentiful. I know, because I suggested the menu for tonight. But, Frank and I are meeting someone for dinner." She made brief eye contact with each of us. "But thank you for asking."

And so we said our farewells.

Margot made no move to leave; she was clearly enjoying her wine. So Deb and I set the table and she looked with interest at the Tupperware containers coming out of the cooler, as we all did.

We found a huge bag of marinated and grilled cold shrimp inside a bigger bag of ice. Then there were an assortment of cheeses and pâtés along with another bag of crackers and small breads. Frank always included a selection of antipastos, too. And we found another container of fresh fruits, including grapes and cherries. I finally got what a 'fork supper' was. We could pretty much eat everything with our fingers or with a fork. We just put everything in the middle of our little table and pulled our chairs up to it. We had small plates to load, but sometimes didn't bother. We just reached, throwing the shrimp shells on the floor to sweep up after and throw in the muck tub. The conversation was light. Margot shared bits of funny stories from her early days of showing with Walter, remembering horses long gone. I could have listened for hours. It was magical.

The evening sun was low and the light slanted in, casting a golden light over all of us. After about twenty minutes Ryder excused herself to go give Hotstuff a second hand walking.

And still Margot sat there. I got the distinct impression she was getting a little tipsy.

She poured the last of the bottle into her glass and raised it, once to Deb, and once to me.

"I'm so proud of both of you."

Deb's dimples made their appearance, and she gave me a quick little wink that flew past Margot. But Margot was just getting started. "Deb darling, I am so glad you and Francesca have made your peace."

Deb's face was now impassive, but she gave Margot a nod.

Margot continued. "This is your time, my darlings. I have no doubt. And then there is Emma. That Fable horse is about to hit the scene and people will be talking. I'm telling you, Deb, you and Emma are about to hit it. I see it, and I know it. And of course, dear Lizzy, you have what it takes. Just stay the course, and in time you will be following these ladies. It's something. It's really something." Margot almost whispered, "I wish Walter could see this. He would be so proud to be a part of it."

Deb once again cut her eyes to me.

I piped up. "Margot, people will be talking about you and Hotstuff, too."

Margot did not deny it. Instead she smiled. "I hope so. I do hope so. Walter would have loved that horse. One never gives up on life with a horse like Hotstuff in your barn."

Deb reached across the tiny table and put her hand over Margot's. "And let's not forget that Pepper is lined up right behind him, Margot. Not only that, we haven't even started breeding Wild Child. Just think what we have to look forward to! As long as we have Frank and Francesca breeding horses for us, we'll always have something exciting for the future."

The golden light of the setting sun vanished, casting us into dim shadows.

# 22. Me-ow

*I had thought that one advantage of a show so close to Equus Paradiso* would be sleeping in my own bed. I turned in early, but there was no chance of getting a good night's sleep. I rode my test over and over again in my mind, and tossed and turned. And then there was the midnight attack of the ninja kitten. I had no idea what Wheezer was doing, but it included pouncing on the bed and clawing at my toes in one leap, and then batting at my head on another leap. Then she was skidding around the room banging into the walls and knocking stuff over.

I had an early wake up that seemed to come as soon as I finally fell asleep. When I cracked my eyes at the clock on my cell phone I freaked. I had turned the ringer volume down to zero yesterday at the show and forgotten to turn it back up before I went to bed. "Crap!" I said, and jumped up and grabbed the clothes I had set out and headed for the bathroom. My eyes were stinging as I put in my contacts. Then I was squinting as I brushed my teeth and gathered up my hair in a scrunchie. I was rushing so fast I almost forgot to zip up my suitcase that I had placed by the bed. I had packed all my show clothes in my rolling suitcase, putting another set of work jeans and sleeveless shirt on the top. In this hot weather I thought I might need multiple changes in addition to my show clothes, plus I didn't want to be too shabby at the competitors' party. I even packed a towel and some soap so I could clean up a bit. I zipped it up firmly this time, pulled out the handle, grabbed my purse, and dashed down the stairs. It would have been nice of Ryder to check on me. She had gotten up early and gone over to the show grounds to feed, muck, and re-braid Wild Child for his class. Since Deb went first, and my class was much later, I guess they let me sleep. I knew I had an excess of time before my ride, but still, I felt frantic.

I tossed the suitcase in the bed of my truck and hit the highway. It wasn't a long drive, but all my molecules were jittery, and that was without the benefit of coffee. Usually, as a groom, I would arrive at a show before the sun came up and be serenaded by crickets and the sound of horses stirring and asking for breakfast. Instead, I arrived at a show-ground that was already alive and bustling. This felt all wrong.

I came down the barn aisle at a good clip, rolling my suitcase behind me. Deb was sitting in the director's chair with a towel over her lap as she sipped her coffee. She raised her coffee in a salute. "There's our morning glory!"

I stopped in front of the coffee pot, and babbled at Deb. "I overslept because I had the ringer volume turned off, and then my contact lenses were stinging like crazy and nothing has gone right. I need some coffee."

Deb tipped her head, her dimples popped out, and she pointed to my suitcase. "Whatcha' got there, Lizzy?"

Ryder came out of a stall, pulling a muck cart behind her. She looked at Deb and Deb pointed at my suitcase. I followed both of their gazes. What was so special about my suitcase? Ryder figured it out before I did. I saw her face clear in a way that meant somehow she was in on the joke. My little rolling suitcase was the soft-sided kind I liked because you could load it lightly or stuff it to the brim. It worked well either way. Today it was a light load. But as I looked at it, the side nearest Ryder moved.

I put my forehead in the palm of my hand. "Oh crap."

I squatted down and unzipped the top and a tiny little peaches-and-cream face with crystal blue eyes popped out of the top.

"Meeeeeee-ow!"

Deb started to giggle. "Well, I'll be damned. That's the first time I've ever had a cat hitch a ride to a horse show. My feral cats are too skittish for that little maneuver."

And Ryder chimed in. "If cats have nine lives that one is now down two."

I picked her up and cradled her under my chin. "Wheezer, why didn't you say anything? Most of the time you meow non-stop."

Deb nodded. "I can't believe you didn't hear her on the way over."

I grimaced guiltily. "I threw the suitcase in the bed of my truck."

Deb exhaled and shook her head. "Poor little kitten. Hand her over."

I handed her over to Deb who examined her while stroking her under her chin. Wheezer started a conversation with Deb. It sounded like a list of complaints to me. But the real question was what to do with her.

I looked to our resident "cat whisperer" to confirm the next step. "I guess I should zip her back into the suitcase and run her home."

Deb got up and handed me my kitten. "Wait a sec."

I followed her into our very organized tack room and watched as she scanned her eyes around the room. Her hands were on her hips. The wheels were turning. Deb grabbed a large laundry basket filled with clean white polo wraps and unceremoniously dumped them on the woven mat on the floor. Then she grabbed another smaller plastic shopping style basket, like the ones at a grocery store. We had all our tack cleaning supplies in that one, which she dumped out, too. She put a towel in the bottom of the larger basket and then turned the smaller basket over and placed it inside the larger basket. Then she found a paper cup and had me cut it down to size and fill it with water. She went into the ice chest next and opened the container on some left over liver pâté. That also went into the laundry basket. She was a genius.

Out came the dimples. "No one mentions to Francesca who finished the pâté."

I smiled back at Deb and crossed my heart.

Deb nodded approvingly at her improvised kitten cage. "That will work if we can find some way to secure it. Kittens can be Houdinis. Oh, I know, bungee cords, we should have some in the tool kit. It should hold her until one of us has time to run her back to your apartment."

And so we pushed Wheezer into her new cage and hooked our bungee cords under the lip of the basket, ran it over the top and hooked it on the lip on the other side of the basket. It worked. Wheezer watched us through the slats of the shopping basket and meowed pitifully.

My kitten was contained. For now.

***

Ryder had put in decent enough braids and had Wild Child sparkling clean, but I couldn't help but supervise his tacking up and made sure the noseband and curb chain were just as I knew Deb liked them. I drove Ryder crazy fussing over the placement of the saddle pad and the fleece half pad that he always wore between the saddle and the pad. I had a brief moment of insight, realizing I had become just as particular as Emma had been over small details. I think I would have made her proud.

Wild Child was distracted enough by his environment that he neglected to make ugly faces or try and bite us. As much as a pain-in-the-ass as he always was, I hated sharing him with Ryder. But today, she was officially his groom, not me.

We got Deb mounted a full ten minutes ahead of schedule. Deb reached back and gave Wild Child a friendly slap on his big butt as they strode off to the warm up. He was swinging his head from left to right, ears up, taking in the scene like a king inspecting his kingdom. The rest of his troops arrived; Margot, Francesca, Natalie, and we all trailed en masse behind our king.

It was time for Deb to prove that she had the right stuff, and that Margot had made a wise decision giving her the ride.

Ryder, Natalie, and I stood near the gate of the warm up arena in a little knot, Francesca stood at the warm up fence right behind Margot, separating herself from us. The terriers sat at her feet, mouths open and tongues flopped out to the sides as they panted. Even though it was only ten a.m, the air was warm and heavy; even Chopper and Snapper were feeling it because ordinarily, they would have been straining at their leashes. But, as usual their button black eyes were bright, and they took in the busy show scene with keen interest.

Ryder set her bucket of supplies on the ground and crossed her arms, as we three turned our eyes to Deb and Wild Child. Margot was leaning her forearms on the top rail of the fence, talking softly into her coaching system, eyes intent on her protégé.

Wild Child quickly broke into a sweat, his neck wet under the reins. Deb had lit a fire under his bum. He was showing the controlled power he never gave away free of charge. It was work to ride him, but Deb was willing to pay the price to get it. Most spectators would never know or understand that cost, because when he was turned on you couldn't see it. But I knew. He had to be reminded to focus on the rider, or his mind turned to other things … stallion things.

Deb had finished practicing the trot tour, Wild Child's strong suit, and had now gone to the canter work. The terriers started to whine, stood up and strained at their leashes. We girls all turned our heads to look. An older man, tan and fit looking, was walking over. He looked vaguely familiar. He quietly positioned himself next to me and put out a hand, speaking in a stage whisper.

"I'm Dennis Walker. You're Lizzy, right? We met at the clinic with Herm Martin."

I nodded and briefly shook his hand. Dennis Walker, the Dennis Walker who had cheated on Margot with Sophie, the working student I had replaced. Yeah, I remembered him now.

Dennis Walker reached for Natalie's hand, and then for Ryder's, getting their names and flashing a white-toothed smile. Francesca clearly registered it all, but ignored him. He nodded her way, and with a low voice said, "Francesca."

Francesca made a sniffing sound, narrowed her eyes at him, and then turned to look at Margot, who was intently watching Wild Child and speaking softly into her mic, not noticing Dennis' presence. Francesca furrowed her brow.

Dennis nodded toward the arena and spoke in a genial tone. "So, Deb's riding the wonder horse these days?"

Instead of answering, Francesca rotated her back a quarter turn away from him; an intentional slight.

He exhaled slowly then turned to me. "Awfully good of Margot to give Deb a shot."

I wondered if somehow I would get in trouble for talking to him, but I certainly wasn't going to mimic Francesca and pretend he was invisible, so I said, almost apologetically, "Yes, but Deb has earned it, too. She does a beautiful job with Wild Child."

He nodded thoughtfully then added with a hopeful tone, "Do you happen to know if Frank is coming?"

I turned to Francesca and said politely, "Francesca, will Frank make it out today?"

She turned to me with narrowed eyes and said, "Who wants to know?"

God, Francesca was a piece of work. I sighed and gave up. And Dennis Walker turned with a frustrated shake of his head.

"Thank you for the conversation, Lizzy. I wish you all the best." He walked away.

I watched his retreating back for a moment and wondered. The one time I had seen Dennis Walker was at the Herm Martin clinic. Sophie was there to get help with the fancy, big, black Grand Prix mare he had bought her in Europe. Things were going badly. Of course, Dennis had intended to purchase Wild Child and had been beaten to the punch by Frank. That explained why he still took some interest in Wild Child. Considering all of this, I could understand why Francesca was giving him the cold shoulder. But, really, it still seemed so childish.

Francesca was looking at the arena, at her "wonder horse" but at the same time I knew she wasn't really present. I felt squirmy with discomfort and cut eyes at Nat and Ryder. Natalie touched her tongue with her finger, then touched her ass while making a sizzling sound; classic Natalie. Ryder was impassive.

Francesca looked at her watch and then called to Margot. "Time, Margot."

Francesca waved Deb out of the warm up arena, meaning time for Ryder to kick into gear. But I was the one who handed Deb her jacket, and rubbed off her boots. The top hat was still optional at CDI's, but we had voluntarily switched to helmets, which were the only thing allowed now at national shows; it meant we had one less thing to tote to the arena and back. Deb had managed her long braid into a low bun that was contained by a crocheted snood. Her helmet had been a splurge, paid for by Francesca and Frank. I knew it had been at least five hundred dollars. Her jacket too was clearly new and made of some new lightweight techno-fabric that stayed cool. I was the only one who knew Francesca was supposed to be cash poor, but she had to have easily dropped a grand on Wild Child for the show, and she had also generously paid my entries. I guess she probably had credit cards without any limits.

I handed Deb a bottle of water while Ryder and Natalie squatted down and rapidly pulled off the polo wraps and the bell boots Wild Child wore for warm up. We stuffed Ryder's little bucket until it was overflowing. I took back an empty water bottle from Deb and then our team headed to the show arena.

Deb kept Wild Child in motion, making small circles and little walk pirouettes until the horse in front of her made their final salute. Then she picked up the trot and powered boldly into the arena. That kind of entrance took guts. Deb had guts. Wild Child was turned on and intently focused in a way that honestly, Margot had only occasionally produced. I was so proud of Deb, and looked at the judges sitting in their boxes. If they had beating hearts, one glance at our boy should get those heart rates up. I think some experiences never get stale.

Margot was leaning slightly forward, her eyes intent on our big mean red machine, her brow furrowed. The whistle blew; Deb had 45 seconds to start her test. She halted, arranged her tailcoat, and then picked up the canter.

I rode every step of the test with her. It was a powerful test. Deb kept her foot on the pedal, and I even saw her give Wild Child a sharp little kick in the corner that made him almost leap forward. He was on notice; don't screw with the little tiger on your back. And he didn't. In fact, he did not put one foot wrong that I could see. Well, he did almost run out of room for his canter zigzags, but they had lost the weird leaning, sliding quality that they used to have.

When Deb made her slightly abrupt, but very square final halt, Natalie wolf-whistled while the rest of us applauded and whooped. I looked over to Margot and saw her wipe a tear away. And then my focus widened, and I saw him, Dennis Walker, the man who had thrown Margot over for the busty working student Sophie, standing behind her. He hovered, unsure. Margot turned, and despite a look of clear surprise, she acknowledged him with a curt nod.

He tentatively put out his hand and she politely shook it. He started to say something to her, and I heard the words 'terrific ride', but then Francesca appeared and took Margot by the elbow, escorting her toward the out gate where Deb and Wild Child were exiting in his classic panther-like walk.

Dennis stood alone, watching them leave. He and I made eye contact and he nodded and then walked away.

Margot, Francesca, Nat, and Ryder gathered around Deb and Wild Child, full of smiles and congratulations. I hurried over to join them. We all looked at the electronic scoreboard, watching for the collective scores to go up and the final score to be posted. When the final tally came up at 72 percent and change, we collectively gave another whoop. Deb had bested anything Margot had scored with Wild Child.

Deb's face was pink from her effort, her dimples deep, and her smile huge and genuine. We moved away from the arena, and Deb slid off her horse. I ran up the stirrup and loosened the girth on the near side of Wild Child, while Ryder ran up the stirrup on the other side, and then I took the reins over the head of a very tired and puffing Wild Child. I even found a half-melted peppermint in my pocket. Ryder gave my arm a gentle punch and grabbed the reins away from me, but she was smiling.

It was a wonderful feeling to be there for Deb, to do something for someone who I so admired and who had helped me in so many ways. All of us stood together around this amazing horse in a magic fairy circle of rejoicing; surprisingly, a magic circle that included Francesca. I noticed we kept reaching out and touching each other's arms, a pat, a squeeze, or a gentle slap. We were giddy; smiling, giggling, exclaiming over the highlights of the test, or Deb's skillful pulling off of the dreaded zigzags.

Natalie gathered up the overflowing bucket, Deb pulled off her coat, and Margot insisted on turning it inside out and carrying it for Deb. In fact, Deb had nothing but her white show gloves to carry as we moved as a group toward the stables. Wild Child even hung his head and walked lazily at my side.

And behind us, trailing at a respectable distance, Dennis followed.

As we approached the security guard at the FEI stabling, Dennis must have realized that he had to make a move. Dennis did not have an FEI wristband. He called out as he jogged up to us. "Margot, I wondered if I can have a moment!"

Our entire entourage came to a full stop. Francesca pulled her sunglasses up on her head and fixed him with as cold a Francesca stare as I had ever seen. But she said nothing.

Margot's tone was polite and cool, but without rancor. "Dennis, do we have something we need to discuss?"

Dennis glanced at Francesca and then at Margot. Ryder gave a tug on the reins and went into the barn with Wild Child. Deb, Nat, and I stayed put. If Deb had moved, I would have too, but since she didn't, I didn't either. Even with Dennis' tan and friendly expression I could tell Dennis was uncomfortable as we all seemed to be rooted where we stood, looking squarely at him.

Dennis finally cleared his throat and spoke to Margot directly, trying to ignore the rest of us. "I wondered if you would take Word Perfect into training. You rode her brilliantly at the Herm Martin clinic. No one else can seem to manage her."

Margot looked at him, her face impassive. "Dennis, you know that Sophie would never allow that."

Dennis bit his lip and then said in a low tone. "That's probably true. But Sophie is no longer involved with Word Perfect. Or anything else, for that matter."

Francesca's shook her head, frustrated, and put her sunglasses back down. I thought for a moment she would interject herself into the conversation but instead she beckoned for us to follow her as she strode into the barn, holding up her wristband for the guard to see. She took one last look back at Dennis and Margot, who were talking. I heard Francesa mutter, "Nervy bastard." She pulled out her cell phone and pressed a button, then said, "Hello, dear, you'll never guess who graced us with his presence just now..."

Once back in the stable, Natalie squeezed the details from me. "What's with all the drama? Who is that guy?"

I pressed my lips together and gave a small shrug. Then I whispered, "It happened before my time. Dennis was a divorced friend of Frank's, best buddies. Frank asked him to come down to Florida and golf with him, you know how Frank is, always trying to fix everybody's problems and pains. Dennis and Margot met each other and started dating, which is something she hadn't done since Walter died. And it was getting fairly serious."

Natalie had her head tipped, her freckled nose scrunched up like she smelled something bad. I continued. "But the working student, she was gorgeous by the way, I've seen her a few times, Dennis fell for her. Her name is Sophie, and she's about six feet tall, with boobs and these amazing cheekbones, and well, Dennis has a lot of money and likes to spend it. Sophie knew he was attracted to her, and she evidently took that attraction to the bank. Literally."

Natalie looked a little perplexed.

"She convinced Dennis to be her sponsor." I continued. "He bought more than horses as part of the deal. But it meant a huge fallout between not only Margot and Dennis, but with him and the Cavellis. You don't screw over the Cavellis or their friends. And so when Emma found out about the horse that Dennis had promised Sophie, she had Frank buy it and give it to Margot as a consolation prize. That horse is Wild Child. Frank felt awful about everything, since he and Dennis were such good friends."

Natalie whistled softly. "Wow. That's a lot of shit bound up in one horse."

I nodded. "Emma – you'll meet her sometime, she's great – Emma told me that Margot just gave up without a fight over Sophie's snake move. I think she was pretty depressed, and it worried everyone. She kind of went into a shell. And now Margot's given away the ride on Wild Child to Deb."

Natalie was still whispering. "Margot's a horsewoman. She wouldn't want to mix up that personal crap with the horse. Deb's the better fit for Wild Child, and we can all see it. Margot's brilliant, but Deb and Wild Child just get each other. They're 'hand-in-glove'."

I didn't respond to that, but I wondered out loud. "So, what's next, I wonder? Do you think he's trying to offer her Word Perfect to win his way back in with Margot?"

Natalie smiled broadly and slapped me on the back...hard. "Maybe. But Margot's got people around her that have money and power and care a lot about her. That's more than most can claim. She'll be all right. But, men are pigs, we know that, Lizzy. Just another reminder."

I had totally been absorbed in Deb and Wild Child, and then the drama unfolding with Margot and Dennis. It had distracted me. But then I looked at my watch and realized I had only two more hours till show time, and my stomach flopped over because I still had to braid my mare. But when I got to her stall, she was standing in the back of her stall, lower lip hanging, eyes half closed, braided. Ryder had beat me to it.

That meant my hands had nothing to do...again. So I settled into a director's chair and had the last bit of the very strong coffee in the pot. Margot came in, and she and Francesca retreated to the back of the tack stall and whispered intently with each other. I couldn't catch a single word, only the plaintive periodic meows of my kitten. I waited for the two women to come out and saw Margot put her arm through Francesca's.

Margot turned to me, "Lizzy darling, Francesca and I are going shopping, some of my favorite vendors are here. Is there anything you need?"

I smiled, "No, thank you, I'm fine."

Margot tipped her head. "I think you should try on some of the new coats, yours looks outdated."

I shook my head. "Really, I had mine dry cleaned and even had the tailor at the cleaners take it in a little."

Francesca shook her head in agreement. She said, "I think Lizzy's coat will do for the time being, Margot."

Margot made an "Hmmmmm" noise. Then she turned to Francesca. "We are going to have to find Lizzy some small gift. It will give us an excuse to shop. Come on, Francesca."

And off they strolled, arm in arm.

I sat in my chair feeling unsettled and confused. For so long I had idolized Margot. For so long I had disliked and feared and distrusted Francesca. And suddenly, instead of seeing them as my idol and my nemesis, I saw two schoolgirls walking off arm in arm to shop and gossip about boys. For some reason I found the sight disturbing.

Nat came over to me. "You going to go change soon?"

She startled me. I answered loudly, "Yes!"

And she held up a small brown bag. "For good luck." She had such a pixie face that I wasn't sure it was for real or a joke.

I opened the bag and pulled out folded tissue paper. "Should I be afraid?"

She winked at me. "It won't bite."

Inside was a leather wrap bracelet with small amber colored beads woven into it, and one silver bead, larger and longer than the others. The silver bead had etched in it one word, "Winsome."

I jumped out of my chair and started to give her a hug, but she side-stepped me. "Natalie, this is incredibly beautiful. I'll never take it off."

She shook her head, "No, don't shower in it, Lizzy. You know how that messes up leather."

I held it up to the light and the amber glowed. "Oh, yeah, okay then. Well, then it only comes off for showers. I love it."

She looked at her watch. "Go put on your show rags, woman."

I went in to the tack room and grabbed my suitcase, deciding to change in the bathroom. Natalie walked into the tack room with me and fetched the kitten in her cage. She walked back out into the aisle and put the basket up on our table, right next to the coffeepot. Then Nat undid the bungees and pulled out my kitten, putting her up on her shoulder.

I bit my lip. "Nat, please don't lose Wheezer."

Nat had started singing some song to my kitten and sort of boogie-ing around with her. The kitten looked happy, purring and bobbing her head along with Natalie. Natalie was ignoring me. So, I went to change.

When I got back, Margot and Francesca had two stock ties for me to try on. One was very trim and tailored with contrasting piping and one was poufy and frilly. Deb's voice was in my ear. Do not denigrate a gift. Francesca had paid for my entries. So, I gushed equally over both options, and was relieved as hell when the two of them decided on the one with the contrast piping.

Then the kitten was handed around, and even Francesca picked it up and remarked on her blue eyes, but then insisted the "thing" get put back in her cage.

As we were fussing over stock ties and a blue-eyed kitten, Ryder and Deb were fussing over Winsome, who was presented to me at the mounting block. The day was feeling surreal. But, as I stepped up on the block and gathered my reins to mount, I did not feel nervous, maybe a little keyed up, a little eager to get at my job, to ride that test that I had been living night and day, but not nervous. I heard Deb's words; that I needed to enjoy this, and not rush through it. This weekend was a gift. The time would pass too quickly. The good bits always did pass too quickly. I thought, "Take it in, Lizzy, take it in."

The afternoon had brought in clouds. The wind had picked up, but we did not have rain in the forecast. Still, the intense heat had lifted and the air was noticeably cooler. Winsome stepped off before I was totally settled in the saddle, but I did not correct her. She was eager to move. She seemed to know where she was going, heading straight for the path to the warm up arena.

I heard a low "hu-hu-hu" from behind me as we left the stables. Wild Child had given Winsome a send off…a good luck parting. At least that was my translation.

I had team Equus Paradiso in tow. I felt light and joyous. I gave my number to the gate steward and I entered the arena. I heard Margot in my earpiece.

"Just do as you always do, my darling. Take your time."

And I had this thought, I felt like a pro today. This was such a different feeling than when I had debuted on Rave. I wondered if my external look reflected my internal state. I gave Winsome a pat on her neck as I shortened my reins. I walked to the inside and did a few walk to halt to walk transitions, then a turn on the haunches each way. When I felt her hind legs become active and under my seat, I trotted off. I rode no preconceived line. I rode what line felt needed, keeping my eyes up and watching the traffic. If she needed to move a little sideways, we went a bit sideways. If she needed more activity behind, I asked for some power forward. I tested her reaction to my driving aids; I tested her reactions to my restraining aids. Was she swinging over her back?

Margot had few words, but let me know when I needed more or needed to be softer. The wind had continued to increase; the flags on the flagpoles were snapping and making a rattling sound. But, Winsome seemed oblivious.

We took a short break and then went through the test movements, and then it was time to go to the big arena. I walked out and stopped while my team went to work. I was handed a bottle of water that I just took one sip from, and a towel. A gust of wind blew something in my eye, and I was suddenly blinded. My left eye instantly shut.

The clock was now ticking. Deb took Winsome's reins. "What is it?" Strangely, I was still calm. "Something in my eye."

Deb was calm, too. "Take off your glove and take out the contact lens. See if that helps."

So I took off a glove, took out the lens, and blinked like crazy. Then I spit on the lens and stuck it back in. My optometrist would not have approved. But it was better. A bit blurry, but better.

Francesca was looking up at me, shooting me a death ray. "For God's sake, Lizzy, the rider before you just did her final salute. Get in the damn arena!"

I actually smiled. "Yes, ma'am."

And Winsome and I did a little jog trot through the gate. Not the power trot that Deb had done earlier with Wild Child. But we were in.

Winsome and I trotted into a headwind as we warmed up outside the little white show arena. No one was in the stands; along the side of the fence rail volunteers had been setting up for the competitors' party. Metal folding chairs in stacks were leaning up against the fencing, and big round folding tables had been set in a row. I took this in, but did not allow myself to become distracted. Winsome needed my full attention.

Somewhere on that final lap, right after the whistle blew, I realized my left contact lens had fallen out. The world would now be in soft focus. No matter.

The test began well. I knew this test inside and out, and had a plan for basically each step. It was Third level, test three, and the entire trot trip was smooth as silk. I loved how one lateral exercise flowed right into another. Winsome was swinging along in a steady rhythm, regardless of the strong gusts that seemed to push us across one diagonal while the second diagonal of extended trot felt like we were getting pushed backwards at the same time that we tried to give it all we had in a forward direction.

Our turns on the haunches went well, as did our extended walk.

Things started going south right after we picked up our left lead canter at K. I had just started my canter half pass left from F toward X, when there was a loud "BANG!" and Winsome scooted. She bolted a few steps and I got her pulled up. Then it happened again…"BANG!" She spun like a stock horse. I could only concentrate on staying on the topside of my twirling mare.

Then I heard the whistle. Somehow I got Winsome to stop. She stood in place, all four legs spread wide, head high, ears up and frozen in place. The judge was yelling and pointing, but the wind whistled past my ears. She wasn't looking at me though; she was looking at my team. I saw Deb and Nat and Ryder and Margot and even Francesca scurrying around. What were they doing? Then it registered, they were taking all those stacks of metal folding chairs that were leaning against the railing, and placing them flat on the ground.

The judge waved me over. Her voice was motherly. "Honey, wait a sec. Take your time, get steady and signal me when you're set. When I blow my whistle again, you go pick up that canter again at K, and we will start the judging from there. Deep breath, OK? Those stacked chairs fell over from the wind. This is an outside source interruption, it's not in any way your fault, it won't affect anything. Okay?"

I nodded, and gave Winsome a pat on the neck. This was the wild ride that Deb was talking about. I almost laughed out loud. Winsome and I were on this ride together. This was never going to happen again. Not in a million years. We would not pass this way again. I weirdly embraced the moment. Every rider has their war stories they liked to tell at a dinner table. Now I had one, too.

Winsome and I had a pretty tense canter trip. But she stayed on the line of travel, she did her clean flying changes, and I finished my test.

My crew cheered insanely, and Natalie's whistle was so loud it was slightly embarrassing.

I got a 66 percent, and was glad to get it. I was also grateful to the judge. Clearly she was someone who had compassion for both the horse and rider. I made a mental note to remember her name.

Natalie carried Wheezer to the competitors' party on her shoulder where Wheezer was clearly a hit. I was just concerned that someone else would take my kitten home. So I kept close tabs on her; as close as I could with half my line of vision slightly out of focus, since the spare lenses I excavated from the bottom of my purse turned out to be a desiccated unusable relic.

# 23. Horse Show Tutorial

*I was exhausted when my head finally hit the pillow. All the stress of* the day was gone, and in its place a deep fatigue. My little Wheezer was the same. She curled up behind my neck, kneading my hair and purring. There was no attack of the ninja kitten during the night.

I woke up before dawn, even before my alarm. And still Wheezer was asleep. She never spoke a word as I got up and went about my morning routine in the dim light. She was still on my bed when I zipped up my roller board. She yawned and blinked and stretched, but stayed put, as I said goodbye to her and headed down to my truck.

The gale force winds of the night before had pushed out the warm humid air, making it surprisingly cool and clear and still. I shivered, then went back up to the apartment and grabbed a hoodie.

I arrived with the sun in my eyes as it lifted over the horizon. I was early, but not as early as Ryder. Coffee was made, stalls were cleaned, and horses had long since been fed. They had finished their morning grain and were now contentedly munching hay. I greeted Ryder, knowing I would be lucky to get a grunt in reply.

"Morning, Ryder."

She nodded and then disappeared into the tack room.

I filled my coffee mug, and lifted the lid on the box of muffins and sweet rolls that had been set out, and picked out what looked like a filled croissant. I took my breakfast and moseyed over to visit Winsome.

There she was, yesterday's red-headed dragon, flat out in the stall. I whispered, "Winsome." Up popped her head as she rocked up onto her chest and tucked her front legs underneath. Her left ear and the left side of her face were covered in shavings. She turned toward my voice and wobbled her nostrils in a silent greeting.

I cooed to her. "Someone has pillow-head."

I stuck the roll in my mouth while I unlatched her door and slid it open as quietly as I could, just wide enough to turn sideways and go in. Then I sat down cross-legged next to my horse, set my roll on top of my coffee and gave her withers a scratch as a greeting. She sighed and drooped her head until her lower lip was resting in the shavings. I sipped coffee and ate my roll, with a bit of horse dander under my fingernails. The birds were chirping, and somewhere someone put on a CD of soft piano music, probably to listen to while they put in braids. But otherwise it was blissfully peaceful, the muffled sounds matching my fuzzy head.

Slowly, ever so slowly, Winsome's head sagged toward me, and finally she put her head in my lap, her eyes half closed, her breathing slow and deep. My horse, my spooky red headed fireball was going to take a nap with her head in my lap. It was a heavy head to have in my lap, but the moment was so precious that I would let her be as long as I could stand it. Never in my life had I had a horse sleep in my lap like a big dog. She was clearly one tired horse. And yet, if she were to be a show horse, she would have to summon up something for day number two. And if I was ever going to be a competitive dressage rider, I would have to do the same.

Winsome and I both snapped out of it with the sound of Deb and Natalie's voices. I wished that they could have seen us, but Winsome picked up her head, ears pricked, first coming back to her chest and then standing up with a shake. Of course, I ended up with a fine coating of shavings scattered all over me. I was still sitting in the shavings when they made it to the stall.

Nat and Deb peered in through the bars. Nat said, "Lizzy, did you spend the night in there?"

I giggled. "Nope, but you just missed the cutest thing ever. Winsome was sleeping with her head in my lap."

I got up and tried to brush off some of the shavings.

Deb shook her head. "Come out of there and I'll take a horse brush to you."

And so I was "groomed" by Deb and Nat, just like one of the horses. They actually handed me one of the horse's hairbrushes, and I used it without hesitation.

Deb and Nat were both softly laughing. Deb said, "Well, it's finally happened. You've become one of the horses."

And I smiled back at her. "Kind of a dream come true, actually."

Deb and Nat didn't look tired at all. In fact, Deb had a twinkle in her eye and a sly smile that, of course, brought out her dimples. "Nat. Tell Lizzy."

Natalie shrugged her shoulders. "It's no big deal."

Deb shook her head. "Like hell. Natalie has a commission. She's sold two more of her rabbits. A woman who bought one of them wants a larger version for her garden. I told Natalie to put a big sticker on it, and the woman didn't flinch at the price. She got out her checkbook and put fifty percent down."

I stepped toward Nat to try to give her a hug, but she sidestepped me and all I did was squeeze her arm. "Wow, congratulations. But, I'm not surprised really. You are so talented."

Nat looked at the floor. "I'm not sure how I'm going to find enough stuff to keep going. And y'know, no two will ever be the same. I hope I don't disappoint her."

Deb chimed in. "But that's the beauty of it. No two pieces will ever be alike. Anyone who buys your work will have something unique."

We were interrupted by the arrival of the rest of Equus Paradiso Farm coming down the barn aisle. That included Frank and Chess along with Margot and Francesca and, of course, Chopper and Snapper straining at their leashes; black button eyes shining bright, noses either testing the air, or inhaling the scents left on walls and flooring. Something particularly absorbing stopped them in their tracks, and Frank had to drag them away, their toenails scrabbling and scraping along the concrete as they resisted.

Deb elbowed me. "Frank's giving those dogs a free nail filing. It'll save Francesca thirty bucks at the groomers." We suppressed our giggles as Deb greeted everyone. "Man, everyone came! Wild Child and I better pull out all the stops today for team Cavelli."

Frank gave Deb a bear hug. "Baby, you and that horse are magic. I'm impressed, no matter what score you get."

Margot added, "I won't jinx you by making any predictions. But, darling, yesterday was beautiful. Now, let's look at the schedule and get organized. Chess, you can put the cooler in here. Francesca planned quite the lunch spread."

Chess came out of the tack room and had the courage to lean forward and peck me on the cheek, in front of his mom and dad. "I heard you had a crazy ride."

The kiss made me very uncomfortable, but I tried to be cool about it. "I didn't know you were coming."

Frank interjected. "I decided to give my boy here a tutorial on how to come to a horse show."

Chess looked at his dad and smiled. "Because, of course, Dad is an expert on horse shows."

Frank waggled his finger at his son. "Compared to you, Chess, ah, I am a master. Lizzy, I know my job, don't I? Chess, watch, listen, and learn from your old man."

I nodded dutifully and looked over at Chess with raised eyebrows. This would be interesting.

Chess smiled as he looked at the ceiling for a moment, and then looked at his dad, compliant. "Okay Dad, eyes and ears open, got it. Do tell, what are the rules here?"

Frank now held his finger up in front of Chess. "First, never comment on a performance until Margot tells you what you are supposed to think about it. Margot is never wrong, and will keep you from gushing when it's been a disaster. Margot will tell you when you need to be ringside and when you need to go hide somewhere until summoned."

I stood there amazed, because actually it was very good advice. Frank continued and Chess was now authentically tuned in to what his dad had to say.

"Second. Food and drink are welcome in good times and bad. You never can go wrong there. Flowers are good too, but, flowers only after food and drink."

Chess nodded and then said, "Should I be taking notes?"

Frank shook his head. "Consign this to memory, son. Third: Don't touch the horses unless they are tired; very, very, very tired. I have been allowed to hand graze them, but these suckers can go off like some kind of crazy. If they look like they have a pulse, call for backup. Instead, you can always help by emptying the muck tubs. The horses are always making more muck, and let's be honest, it draws flies. I hate flies."

We three were all smiles. Francesca and Margot had been having a confab, but now Francesca was standing behind Frank with her arms crossed, a thoughtful expression on her face. She didn't look pissed for a change. I thought perhaps Frank was looking a bit better, not so pasty. He certainly seemed more his old self. Maybe things were improving.

He continued. "Fourth and final for now, spending money is de rigueur. There are all these small vendors set up at the shows, and they need our support. I feel it is my duty to buy something while I'm here ...

small or large; plan on it. And remember, it only costs a few more dollars to go first class."

"Thanks, Dad. I have consigned it to memory."

Frank turned to Francesca. "That's our boy. He's gonna take to it just like his old man."

Francesca hooked her arm through Frank's. "Shall we go support our vendors?"

Frank winked at us before turning back to Francesca. "Platinum card's in my wallet."

When Ryder pulled Wild Child out of the grooming stall, all ready for Deb, he seemed relaxed yet alert. I, like Margot, did not want to jinx Deb with a prediction, but I too had a good feeling about their day. It was cool and bright out, the wind still. Although my mare and I were tired, Wild Child and Deb clearly were not. They looked cool and bright, just like the weather.

The Grand Prix Special was usually Wild Child's best test. He got to show off his piaffe and passage and extended trot, his strong suits, and there were no canter zigzags. He still had to do a steep canter half pass from K to B, do a flying change and then half pass the next short diagonal from B to H with a flying change at H, but it was less technically challenging for him than all those zigzags down centerline in the Grand Prix.

As a barn we trailed after Deb and Wild Child toward the warm up arena, like a line of ducklings. Natalie and Ryder and I were first in the line, Ryder holding the bucket that held a rag and a hairbrush, along with a bottle of water. Natalie had brought the show program, which she had rolled into a tube and was using as a megaphone to sing a silly song into my ear.

"Old Screwball was a dressage horse, and I wish he were mine, he never drank water, he always drank wine. His bridle was patent leather, and his bits they were German silver, and the worth of his custom dressage saddle, will never be told."

Ryder cut Natalie a wicked scowl, and then growled out of the side of her mouth. "Natalie, shut up. Your singing sucks and people are starting to stare."

Which only made Nat switch her tune. "You're a mean one, Mr. Grinch."

After that Ryder peeled off to stand by the warm up fencing, as far away from us as she could.

I shook my head at Natalie. "Why do we like torturing Ryder so much?"

Natalie grinned back at me. "She's too easy a target. I have moments of guilt over it, but they pass."

Margot and Francesca were behind us, probably taking in the working student interpersonal dynamics with interest. Behind them trailed the guys.

Deb gave her number to the ring steward as she entered the warm up, and then I saw her adjust her ear bud and nod her head as she took in whatever it was that Margot had said.

Deb and Wild Child were all business as they began to warm up. Frank and Chess and Francesca stood near Nat and me. Even Nat became quiet as she watched Deb begin.

And then he arrived again. Dennis. And without trepidation today, walked right up to Frank Cavelli, hand extended.

Frank did not appear the least bit surprised. He shook Dennis by the hand heartily and slapped him on the back. I noticed Chess reach over and also shake hands with Dennis, but without his father's enthusiasm. Francesca drifted away, making her way to stand next to Margot ringside. Natalie put the rolled up program back to her mouth, and whispered into my ear. "This just gets curiouser and curiouser."

I crossed my empty arms over my chest. "Yeah. Something is cooking. Francesca was shunning the guy yesterday, and today she is standing next to Margot, like some kind of show of solidarity. But, why is Frank being so chummy?"

Natalie looked thoughtful for a moment. Then she whispered, sans rolled up program, "You think there's a rift between the Cavellis?"

I shook my head. "Nope, never has been. More likely there's a strategy being played out. Francesca is the most conniving person I've ever met."

Once Deb began to collect Wild Child and bring him to full power, we stopped our chit chat. He was magnificent. I felt like all the railbird activity came to a full stop and all eyes focused on those two. Soon it was time to pull him out of the warm up and whip off the polos, wipe down Deb's boots and hand her the bottle of water. She and Margot exchanged parting words, and then she was on her own.

Deb and Wild Child appeared to be in their own world. Her eyes were open and looking through his ears, but I could tell she wasn't really seeing her surroundings. Deb had a small smile on her face, her dimples showing. She looked completely relaxed. The bell rang, the little board at "A" was removed by two of the show staff in lockstep military style, and then Deb headed down centerline. Deb made a crisp halt and salute, and began the trot tour. Wild Child and Deb always showed good power, but today was especially swinging and relaxed and dare I say it... happy. Wild Child actually looked happy to be in the arena. That was new. This from the horse who in the past had run backwards and reared rather than enter the show arena.

Rather than being nervous and riding each step with Deb, I stepped back. I was not nervous for her today. They had this. If I wanted to pick the test to bits, I could find things to criticize. But why not just enjoy watching? Sometimes it helped to forget all the things I now knew, and try to watch with fresh eyes, and take the same pleasure watching that a rank amateur might take. This was a magnificent animal, and he and his rider were full of joy. Margot was so right. Wild Child was Deb's ride. It was more apparent now than ever before; as if they had been meant for each other, and each had traveled a long and difficult path that led to this moment of discovering that they were meant to be together.

Oddly, the scoreboard went dark after only a few movements. When Deb turned up centerline for her final line of passage to piaffe to passage to a halt at G, Wild Child found a new burst of energy. Most horses would be showing fatigue by now, but he bounced out of the piaffe into the final passage, and halted square, standing like a statue as Deb dropped her hand in her final salute. Weirdly, we were silent for a beat or two before we remembered to applaud, and then we erupted.

Nat was jumping up and down at my side and grabbing my arm. "Oh my God, oh my God, oh my God!"

She even forgot to do her wolf-whistle. Deb strolled out of the arena as if it had been an ordinary ride, fishing a treat out of her pocket, which once out of the arena, Wild Child reached around and took from her.

The ring steward had on her exam gloves and did her bit and spur check while Deb gave us a dimpled grin. Then we swarmed her. About that time the electronic scoreboard blinked back into life. And the final score took our breath away. Deb had scored a 75%. It was the best score of Wild Child's life. Clearly, Deb and Wild Child would be leading the victory lap today in the awards ceremony. This was a game changer kind of score. An uneasy feeling fluttered in the pit of my stomach. I knew that kind of score, if she could keep delivering it, would change Deb's life. And change my life, too.

We hardly had time to untack Wild Child before it was time to groom and tack him back up with a fresh set of snow-white polo wraps for the awards ceremony. The PA called Deb's number, along with others, to collect outside the main arena for the ceremony. Margot instructed only Ryder to accompany her ringside. The rest of us were told to gather in the stands and cheer.

Of course, I, like Margot, knew that awards ceremonies were often a lot more fun for the audience than the participants. Especially when your horse tried to run away with you in the excitement, as Wild Child had done with Margot.

But, as usual, Deb did not seem concerned. She was not being casual though. She had told me that if Wild Child knew what was good for him, he would stand at attention like a good soldier and remember to say "yes, ma'am." When an honor was being bestowed upon you, you needed to bring your best company manners.

As the riders collected outside the arena, a volunteer carefully approached each horse with a long bright ribbon and hung it on the bridles, sliding the hook on the back of the rosette over the part of the brow band where the crown piece slid through. Then the three ribbon streamers were wound around the throatlatch a few times. When she came to Wild Child and the second place horse, they not only received a ribbon on their bridles, but also beautiful neck sashes, Wild Child's in the tri-colors of a champion: red, blue, and gold.

The music came on softly, and each horse was called into the arena by bridle number in reverse order of placing, and lined up facing the grandstands. When Deb and Wild Child came in I noticed Deb wisely gave herself a good buffer of space. Wild Child did stand like a soldier, with no sideways glances at the pretty horseflesh allowed.

Then the judges walked down the line, shaking the hands of each rider, while photos were taken. When it came to Deb, there was a beautiful horse blanket to hold up as part of her prize. There had also been envelopes with checks, a rare treat. I hoped Francesca would allow Deb to have that check, but I couldn't be sure. Francesca paid the entries, and it was Francesca's horse.

When the hand shaking and photos were done, the announcer asked Deb to lead off the lap of honor, and for a moment I thought Wild Child wasn't going to go. But Deb laughed and gathered her reins in one hand. Her dimples appeared, and she reached back with her free hand and gave Wild Child a slap on his butt. He walked off like a bored trail horse. She picked up a lazy canter for the first lap as she led the field, and in no way did he look like the powerhouse that had just won the Special with a 75%.

But I was not to be disappointed, because as soon as the rest of the field peeled off, and Deb passed the out gate, she looked up at the announcer's stand and gave him a thumbs up. The volume on the music rose and Deb made a transition to trot and then gave Wild Child one sharp kick, rocking him back to passage. Right to the music they passaged down the long side away from the out gate. As they turned the corner across the short side, Deb transitioned into piaffe. She kept him on the spot, not for the fifteen steps that the test required, but for about thirty.

Then they passaged around the next corner as we clapped in time to his steps. I could see Wild Child coil himself, begging to be released into extended trot. Deb was teasing him, almost allowing him to go, and then changing her mind. But finally she let him fly. It was breathtaking. Wild Child's front legs seemed to stretch impossibly long in front of himself and he ate up the ground. He was on the edge.

But she did not let it get away from her. She came back to a few steps of piaffe, halted, made him stand immobile. It was then that she delivered a big surprise. She made a quarter turn on the haunches so that Wild Child faced the stands. She took her toe on her right boot and gave Wild Child a little kick on his elbow. He pawed the ground once, and then dropped onto that knee, nose touching the arena floor. Deb was still the circus trainer, and when she had trained Wild Child to bow I couldn't imagine, but she had. The audience ate it up, Frank's laugh booming above the applause. Francesca said nothing, but I knew that she was no fan of circus tricks.

I am not sure there was anyone else in the world like Deb. And amazingly, she seemed unaware of just how gifted she was. She tapped Wild Child again with her toe, and he stood up, and then she fished out a sugar cube for him. Then, after his treat and a pat, they quietly walked toward the stables, bedecked with ribbons. The volume of the music descended slowly until the arena was silent. We just stood there a moment, even Margot did not move. Only Ryder moved, trailing after Deb and Wild Child, her head bowed, her feet dragging.

\*\*\*

There was a lot of laughing and joking and bustling about back at the stalls. Someone had already set out a row of champagne flutes on our "hospitality" table and Frank busily took the foil off a bottle, preparing to uncork it. Meanwhile Margot scolded him to open it outside where he wouldn't spook the horses. Wild Child was still in the grooming stall getting untacked by Ryder and even though Deb was still dressed in her show clothes she was in there, too, feeding him carrots. Nat climbed on the mounting block and stood on her tip-toes to hang up the ribbon and sash on the front of our tack stall. Francesca unpacked a lavish lunch spread that included roll ups of smoked salmon stuffed with cream cheese and capers. There were little crustless sandwiches and stuffed radishes and celery sticks. Then she unpacked the sweets, little petit fours and tiny puffs of pastry stuffed with custards, creams, and fruits. The Cavellis knew how to celebrate. It was a scene of happy chaos.

And into this happy scene strolled a man recognizable to every follower of "big time" dressage in America, the man in charge of finding, developing, and managing those riders at the very top, the ones being groomed to wear a flag on their saddle pad. Margot greeted him with air-kisses then handed him a champagne flute, waving her hand over our table of delights. He was all smiles.

Next, Margot wisely guided him to meet Frank and Francesca, she full of put-on grace and polish, he as relaxed as usual. And then of course, Margot gestured for Deb to join the little group. I glanced at

Ryder, pulling out the braids on Wild Child. Her jaw was set, her eyes focused on her swiftly moving hands. I knew she had to be green with jealousy. Nat cut me a look, but kept silent as she loaded her plate with an almost embarrassing amount of delicacies.

Chess sidled up to me, whispering. He had picked up on the vibe instantly. "Hey, Lizzy. Is this guy important?"

I nodded. "Very. Let's make a plate of that yummy food. I still have to ride, so not too much. It looks rich." He offered me a flute of champagne, but I shook my head and put my hand down in the cooler that held our water, fishing out a bottle.

We three went into the tack stall and sat down on top of the trunks or leaned on walls, leaving the tall director chairs in the barn aisle to the important people. I could tell that Chess was full of questions, but we spoke very little, and then only in low voices because only a few feet away great changes were being discussed regarding Deb's life and that meant our lives too. I knew that later Deb would feel free to share with me what was going down.

I felt like I owed Chess more detail, but my own understanding of how international teams were chosen was limited. I simply added, "Cream rises to the top, right? Deb and Wild Child are bound to get noticed if they can keep up those kind of scores."

I thought to myself, this could be her once in a lifetime opportunity to jump into the big league. But as exciting as it would be, to me it also felt solemn. Our great giddy celebration had dampened into a weird sort of electric buzz. Great things could be afoot...or not. Sometimes a rider has only a moment when all things seem possible, and then that door that is beginning to open is slammed in their face.

Right now, Wild Child was probably at his peak, the right competitive age. He had always been very sound. Heck, he didn't even look hard to ride to someone who didn't know any better. He was an approved stallion. His dressage riding owner, Francesca, knew she would never be able to ride her own horse. On top of all that, he wasn't even friendly. If the Cavellis needed cash, selling Wild Child seemed a logical step.

I can't say if this thought had occurred to Chess. But, when my eyes met his, I imagined his thoughts. I knew he had surely gone back in the financials to see the great sum his parents had spent to buy Wild Child. I also expected he had seen the insurance premiums on the horse. These wins would add to the horse's value. It probably looked tempting. I expected that Chess had already been considering Wild Child as an asset that could be liquidated.

Deb had indeed stepped onto a wild ride on the Wild Child. I fervently hoped, for her sake, that it was not going to be a short one.

I had finished my plate, but still hung out in the tack room waiting for the business meeting in the aisle to break up before venturing out. I still had a couple hours to kill before my class. It was my fate this day to be almost the last rider of the show.

The Under-25 Grand Prix division's award ceremony music blared over the loud speakers. Their award ceremony marked the end of the CDI divisions. I imagined Ryder was feeling that her place should have been in that ceremony aboard Johnny Cash.

Hugs and handshakes were taking place in the aisle, and the gathering broke up. Deb came in to the tack room, finally peeling off her shadbelly.

I raised my eyebrows. "So ...?"

And Natalie joined in. "Big news, I'm guessing."

Deb hung her coat up in her garment bag. "Just talk. But, still, it was encouraging."

Natalie probed. "You think that little crumb is going to satisfy us? Come on, throw us a bone, woman."

Deb put her foot up on the edge of a trunk to unbuckle her spurs and unzip her boots. "Well, to get on the A or B list of high performance horse-rider combinations I need the next CDI back here, and then we go to Devon and see if we can deliver the scores. Then it's a matter of ranking. There are two observation and training sessions, one in Florida, and one out in California. If we make the cut, we go in November to the sessions in Florida. Margot has the same goals for Emma and Fable. She's told Lu Ann and Billy they need to ship her up here to do the next CDI and then Devon. So, our little Blondie is in exactly the same boat I am."

Ryder scowled, "Blondie? Who's Blondie? Who's Lu Ann and Billy?"

Deb turned her head, "Oh, yeah, I forget that you don't know Emma. Lu Ann and Billy own her ride, Fable. Emma and I go way back with Margot. Anyway, looks like Margot will have the both of us to coach at Devon." Then Deb shrugged her shoulders, "We'll see how it shakes down after that."

I said, "Florida in November? That's early, isn't it?"

Deb smiled and answered breezily. "Yeah, but you know, 'Many a slip between cup and lip.' Margot knows better than anyone that nothing is certain. I'll ride Wild Child as long as Frank and Francesca will let me. The important thing..." and her voice trailed off as she was distracted by something. That something was Ryder coming in with a plate of goodies and a flute of champagne that she wasn't legally allowed to drink. Ryder looked exhausted.

Nat looked thoughtful, almost concerned. She lifted her chin toward Ryder. "You want to go back to the farm and take care of Hotstuff and Papa? I can help Lizzy and Alfonso get this stuff packed and back to the farm later."

I thought Ryder actually looked relieved. "Yeah. Okay. I've had about as much fun as I can stand today."

Deb piped up. "I bet you're dog-tired. Your day started in the dark both days. You did a great job, Ryder. Thank you."

I expected Ryder to make a snarky comeback. But she didn't. She sounded very matter-of-fact as she answered. "You're welcome. Congrats on the show. I thought today was the best the horse has ever gone, and I think the score can still go higher." And then she tipped the last bit of champagne in the flute delicately into her mouth. I noticed she had not eaten all the little sandwiches on her plate, but before I could rescue them, she tipped the lot into the trash and was gone.

Chess had witnessed all of this silently. His brow was furrowed, his voice soft. "I know I'm a slow study, but is there a problem here between you guys and Ryder?"

But before I could answer, Francesca popped her head into the tack room. "Chess, your father and I are going home. Shall we drop you off at the farm?"

Francesca and I locked eyes. No one, it seemed, was staying to see my ride. I felt myself start to wilt under her stare, and then I swallowed. I didn't want to look pitiful. I did not want to guilt-trip Chess into staying. Showing meant a lot of waiting, with time dragging until it was close to riding time, when the hands on the clock seemed to spin.

Chess didn't wait more than a beat or two to answer. "No, that's fine. I'll ride back with Lizzy. I am sure this crew will appreciate an extra hand for packing."

Francesca shrugged. "They have Alfonso coming at four, but suit yourself. Your father and I need to get going."

Frank squeezed past Francesca into the tack room, which barely seemed to hold one more person, especially one extra-large person. "Deb baby, one last hug. You did us proud. And I loved that bowing thing at the end of your show. Can't wait to see what happens next."

Frank lightened the mood, and we were once again all smiles. And then they were gone. Our number had quickly dwindled, the tack room providing enough room for Deb to plop onto a tack truck and stretch out her socked feet, boots standing upright next to her, bending at the ankles as if they were still filled with legs and set into stirrups.

Margot stepped into the room. "Are you guys as tired as I am?"

Deb nodded back. "Did you get any of that food, Margot?"

Margot shook her head sadly. Deb went out in the aisle in her stocking feet to look over the platters. Things were fairly picked over, and the bottle of champagne was drained. Deb waved a few flies away and brought Margot a small plate with a few crustless sandwiches that were falling apart, along with a handful of stuffed radishes, clearly the least favorite of the tasty bits. The smoked salmon and sweet puff pastries had all been consumed.

Margot frowned at the small offering. And Natalie jumped out of her seat. "Margot, I feel guilty. I mean, I ate a pile of those things. If it makes you feel any better, they looked better than they tasted."

Margot laughed. "Don't apologize, Natalie, I'm ready for something more substantial myself. Tell you what, when you guys are loaded and headed home, I'll stop and pick up some pizzas. Something loaded with meat and cheeses. I never really understood the charm of a thin little crustless sandwich anyway. We can do better for you hardworking girls."

When I grabbed the braiding box, Nat waggled her finger at me. "No way. I'm braiding Winsome for you. And I promise to put in more than my usual slack-ass number of braids. Winsome is going to look spiff."

So, I relinquished my hold on the tackle box that held our braiding supplies. Natalie swept past me, and grabbed the mounting block. As usual, she found a song to belt out on her way to the stall. "Braid my hair, baby c'mon and braid my hair. Back in the hood, feelin' good, no worries or no cares ... "

Chess chuckled. "Does she have a song for every occasion?"

I sat on the tack trunk and grinned. "Yeah. Pretty much, but don't worry, she'll have rubber bands in her mouth while she braids, and it will get quiet in there." My head felt heavy, so I crossed my legs and rested my chin in my hand.

The PA system announced the next rider into the arena, but then crackled a bit and went quiet. Our barn, the FEI barn, had emptied out quickly. Soon Wild Child and Winsome were the only ones left on our aisle. Deb had changed into her jeans and started cleaning up our stuff, wiping down the table and folding it up. She and Natalie had cleaned and packed all of Wild Child's stuff, leaving one water bucket and a net full of hay, his shipping boots set out in front of his stall. The only thing keeping our crew here was me. I felt like a drag on the day. But, I knew better than to suggest scratching my class. Margot and Deb would never have allowed it, besides; it was my qualifying class for the regional championships, and the last score I needed to fulfill the requirements for my USDF Bronze medal rider award.

My head got heavier and heavier, a fuzzy-buzzy feeling came over me, and I had a vague idea that maybe I was drooling. And then I hit that tipping point, the moment when you realize you are falling and it triggers a startle reaction. That "snap-to-it" nearly sent me off the edge of the tack trunk to the floor.

Chess stood up with a hand out in front of him, too far away to have done anything but help me up off the floor. He had a concerned look on his face. "Hey, you're exhausted. Are you sure you can ride?"

I inhaled deeply and blew out a long exhale. "Yeah, but maybe I should have some coffee."

Chess nodded. "That's actually something I can do. I think we could all use some."

Every fiber of my being wanted to sleep. And there was no good place to do it. But, I sat down on the floor on our little woven plastic floor mat. Before you know it, I was prone ... and dead to the world.

Later, Chess told me that Margot made everyone be quiet and leave me there sleeping until it was time to dress.

I registered something lightly tickling my arm, and then my cheek; Wheezer. I reached for her and suddenly realized I was not in my bed. My eyes popped open, the fog cleared. My right shoulder and elbow ached against the hard floor.

I heard Chess' gentle voice. "Hey, Lizzie. Time to wake up."

I came to a sitting position, rubbing my elbow.

"Here. It's cold, but it's still caffeine." A Styrofoam cup of coffee with cream was put in my hand. It was terrible, bitter and slightly burned, but I made a commitment to drink the whole thing for medicinal purposes; anything to feel better than I felt, which was achy and dull. I took another couple of slow, deep breaths, exhaling slowly. I did some rapid blinking trying to get my contact lenses to loosen up. They always got dry and stuck to my eyeballs if I accidentally slept in them. I think my silence was worrying Chess.

He stood over me. "Are you going to make it?"

I sighed again. "Just give me a minute."

Then I saw Margot duck her head into the stall, and looking right at Chess she tapped her watch. I turned my own wrist over and panicked.

"Oh my God! I am so late. I need to go dress." I jumped up and Chess put his hand out like a stop sign.

"Lizzy, Natalie put all your show clothes in a pile in the chair out in the aisle. You aren't late. Margot gave us a schedule and we are right on it."

I stepped out into the aisle to find Natalie buffing my boots. They shined like glass.

"Natalie! Wow. Thanks. I can't believe those are my old boots."

Natalie had her legs wide, leaning on one elbow with that same arm stuck down in the shaft of the boot, the other hand on a boot brush going at high speed back and forth on the boot.

"Secret sauce... Spit if you want to know. That and elbow grease is what makes the shine. Your horse is tacked and sleeping in the grooming stall. Time to get your show rags on."

I gathered up the coat bag and tote that held my "rags" and before I could leave, Chess had a hand on my arm. "For you." He handed me a little box.

"What's this?"

"I'm a horse show newbie, but y'know, I do listen to my parents occasionally. Mother actually helped me pick it out."

Now I was really incredulous. "Francesca? I'm stunned."

Chess had a sly smile. "Mother keeps you guessing, doesn't she? She likes it that way. But, hurry up and open it. I won't have Margot accusing me of making you late."

I pulled off the little brown ribbon and opened the box. A pair of stud earrings, lucky horseshoes with tiny little faux diamonds set into them.

"Mother said these would be perfect for showing. I liked them too, and of course, hope they'll bring you good luck."

I was now fully awake, but equally bewildered. I looked back down at my new show earrings, genuinely pleased with them. "Thank you, Chess. I love them. You know what? I already feel lucky; very lucky."

And I planted a kiss on his cheek, and then spun around and ran all the way to the restrooms to change.

*** 

Once again, I surprised myself at how good I felt in the saddle the moment I walked into the warm up arena. It was almost as if I had my own private horse show. The show grounds had almost emptied as the last classes of the show were being run. The vendors' booths had emptied. The arenas were in need of watering, but they wouldn't be watered for the few of us left. The warm up arena had room to spare.

I looked over at my loyal friends leaning on the railing of the warm up, chatting amiably with each other, relaxed and laughing. And I had Margot in my ear, encouraging me in soothing terms.

"I want you to make it short and snappy. You know how there are always scratches at the end of the show day. Let's put her together and see if we can slip in early. Just check the controls first in the walk, then a few half-steps and into sitting trot."

So, my usual rising trot warm up got scrapped. Within five minutes or so I started working transitions between and then within the gaits.

"You need to feel your way, Lizzy. Feel her hind legs step under her body. Check that she is in front of the driving aids. Does she go forward when you ask? Yes? Good. Does she stay bending around your inside leg? Is she waiting on your seat? Test her. You needn't worry about the particulars of the patterns, you know them, what counts now is that she is 100% on your aids."

Margot stopped telling me 'what' to do. But she kept putting ideas in my head as to the 'how.' She also gave me guidance.

"Lizzy, a drop more impulsion. Yes."

Or…"More left flexion. Show more bend."

And then Deb was at her elbow whispering. "Lizzy, we can go now. Ready?"

It seemed like I had only been warming up ten minutes, but Margot was right. I could go now, even though I had not done a single pattern from the test. I might as well go. I answered her. "Yes. Let's do it."

And in I went into an empty arena, a judge and her scribe sitting in their box with nothing to do. Clearly, I was filling a scratch. The judge was likely happy to see me, knowing she could have ten extra minutes at the airport sipping her latte and reading her Kindle. The thought flashed through my mind and put a smile on my face. As I passed the box in sitting trot the judge smiled back at me, and rang the bell.

I hadn't even gone once around the arena. But I turned a half circle, passing behind the judge's box to head down the long side from whence I had come. I had a bit of fun doing a few short trot steps and medium trot steps all the way down the long side, turning up the centerline in a bold forward-going trot into my halt and salute at X.

I thought of Deb, and the evident joy she felt as she rode her test. I wasn't quite there yet, but by God, I was going to do my best to imitate Deb.

I took care of every corner, just as Margot had taught me. I used my eyes to direct my line of travel, just as Margot had taught me. And somehow, I had time to think of these things and to plan each movement ahead of time. I had a lovely feeling of having time, as if it had slowed down in order for me to do this test.

I worked to keep the feeling of Winsome stepping forward under my hips, carrying me on her hind legs. And when I lost it, I was able to push her up and under with a squeeze from my leg.

When I got to the walk work I had time to think, and my thoughts were, "This is going well, but you are not done." Winsome sighed under me and stretched out her neck as we walked across the arena. She was a tired girl. I had to give her a couple taps of the whip to get her to walk with energy. Everything about her demeanor showed me she thought her job was done. There was no gas in the tank. I had the feeling that the "closed for business sign" had just gone up in the shop window. I was screwed.

It was going to take a miracle to get through the canter work. And as I gathered my reins to prepare for the canter depart, my miracle was delivered. A trailer was pulling away from the stables loaded, and a horse began to "scramble." If you have ever heard a horse scramble in the trailer, you understand that it is loud as hell. Steel shod hooves are climbing up the side of the trailer walls or stall divider as the horse loses and regains his balance.

I glanced over at the distraction, and saw my entire "crew" swiveled around looking. My back was to the judge, but I knew they were probably swiveled around in the chairs looking for the source of the racket.

Though my first disappointing thought was that this could not be happening, a second outside distraction in two days, Winsome came alive like an electrically charged wire. That "closed for business" sign got yanked out of the window. We were still open and ready to roll. She bounced into the canter right on my aid, even though she was bunched up way too tight.

I lowered her nose a bit on my outside rein and prayed I could finesse her through the movements. My little girl dropped her nose just as I had asked her to, she jumped her half passes almost too sideways and a tad behind my driving aids, but then I pushed her back out and her flying changes were up and expressive. She was settling, her initial adrenaline charge dissipating.

I finished the last centerline on an empty tank of gas, sputtering out into the final halt. Winsome was puffing, her ears drooping. The adrenaline rush was over. I scratched her withers and gave her a pat on her neck. I felt certain we had scored high enough to qualify for regionals, and to earn that USDF Bronze medal rider award, regardless of whether we had earned the blue ribbon or not. Carrots were waiting. We had made it. Our reward would be the same as the judge's. We got to go home.

# 24. Hoof Testing

*Monday was supposed to be our day off, but there was no time for rest-*
ing. Alfonso had not unhooked the horse trailer the night before because Wednesday we would need to load Hotstuff and hit the road for
Chicago. That is, if Doc gave us the green light. We all proceeded "as
if" we were going.

That meant that Ryder and I unpacked, washed, and repacked the
horse trailer. Natalie and I, who had been designated drivers/grooms for
the young horse championships, had our own packing to do. We had
gone on Mapquest, heads bent over my laptop to look at our route, and
set the GPS in the truck for the twelve and a half hour drive. If we each
did two or three hour shifts it wouldn't be so bad. Margot had told me
it was time for Nat to get off the farm for a change, and frankly I was
both thrilled and relieved that it would not be Ryder.

Francesca and Margot had taken care of plane, car, and hotel res-
ervations. Of course it was all moot if Hotstuff was still too sore to
compete. After Deb's success at the CDI, I found myself wanting this
championship for Margot and Hotstuff almost to desperation. Margot
deserved this.

As for myself, I had scored a 69% in my last test, which meant I had
earned my USDF Bronze medal rider award. I had also earned my last

qualifying score for the USDF Regional Finals in October. Those goals may not have stacked up against Margot or Deb or Emma or Ryder's goals, but for me, right now, they were more than enough. It would have been nice to have scored over seventy percent, but I was just glad to have the show behind me. I had felt much more confident showing this time around. I was proud of how my horse was advancing in her training, with two pretty blue ribbons to hang up in my bedroom, but I can't say that showing itself was a thrill. Compared to the standard that Deb and Emma and Margot had attained, I still felt like I was in Kindergarten. But, I had to remember that compared to where I was "pre-Margot," 69% at Third level was an amazing leap forward for me.

When Ryder and I finished all the unpacking, cleaning, laundry, and repacking, it was late in the afternoon. The horses had all come in from turnout, been fed, and were contentedly munching hay. I happily hid in my bedroom, enjoying the air conditioning and diving back into my novel. I began by sitting upright in my bed, Wheezer in my lap purring, her blue eyes squeezed tightly shut, but my buns went numb. Then I slunk down and read on my side, until my hip went numb. I flipped over to read curled in a ball on my other side, disturbing my kitten each time until she could reposition herself. She pumped the covers with her tiny paws, circled and settled back down with a steady thrumming purr that made me feel that all was right in the world.

My book transported me to a smuggler's cove in Scotland. I had been binge reading novels set in Scotland, and not just the Outlander series, mind you. Nat and I had between us developed a small lending library on the genre.

When my cell phone started singing a tune, I was frankly annoyed. Chess' name came up on the screen. I hesitated. Was I going to choose fiction over reality? I almost chose fiction, but then guilt seized me. I picked up the phone and forced a cheerful tone. "Hi, Chess."

"Lizzy. I hope you've gotten some rest today."

He *was* sweet and considerate. And I cringed when I remembered the good luck earrings. I couldn't believe I had almost NOT picked up. I answered, "Yup. I've been in bed reading with my kitten for hours."

"Fiction or non-fiction?"

I hesitated, but then confessed. "Historical fiction, kind of girly stuff to be honest."

His voice was matter of fact. "Oh, what period?"

I tried to also sound matter of fact. "The Jacobite rebellion in Scotland."

There was a pause. Had I sounded like a true student of history, or had I outed myself as a reader of the sort of fiction not to be found in any college syllabus? He sounded disappointed, "Not the Outlander series?"

I sighed. He was on to me. I answered defensively, "No, but what's wrong with Outlander?" I didn't wait for an answer, my voice incredulous at the notion of Chess being in-the-know. "Wait, you know about Outlander?"

There was a chuckle on the line, but he changed the subject. "Are you hungry?"

My stomach growled as if to answer, but I was in my pajamas with no intention of changing back into street clothes. But Chess, God bless him, offered to bring in food. He even offered to bring enough to share with Ryder if she chose to partake. It was a relief to stay in, and I figured I could find a big sweatshirt to pull over my PJ's. So far, manure and horse slobber hadn't scared him away, so I guess a baggy sweatshirt wouldn't either. I just did not have it in me to be a fetching "lassie" this evening.

He said, "I'm bringing Chinese, and I intend to have a book club discussion with you regarding Outlander. With all the fuss over it and the TV series, I decided to read the first one. I'll disappoint you though, one was enough for me."

So, Chess brought in Chinese, and Ryder looked bored and befuddled while we discussed Outlander.

Chess sounded earnest, almost professorial. "So, I liked the premise. I love history, and time travel would be the ultimate history lesson. Passing on history in the form of a story is as old and honorable as ancient tribesmen sitting around a fire, so I have no problem with historical fiction. Done well and responsibly, it's a great way to describe real events and lives in a compelling way. But, really, in Outlander that poor Jamie character constantly gets beaten to a pulp and yet, he can still, well, um…perform."

Ryder looked up with a sly smile. "Are you saying that's not realistic?"

Chess looked slightly embarrassed. "Let's just say I found Outlander catered to a very specific demographic that did not include me."

I raised my eyebrows and tipped my head, voice heavy with sarcasm. "Unlike all those James Bond movies with the obligatory conquests of big-chested women, who of course all desire the hero?"

Ryder repeated my words with a scowl and mock outrage. "Did you just say 'obligatory conquests?' Oh my God, who are you?"

I could tell Chess enjoyed this, and kindly ignored Ryder's jab. "Touche', Lizzy. At least James Bond doesn't pretend to be historical. And just to be accurate, not all of the women were big-bosomed. But, hey, we could start our own couple's book club. We could rotate between chick-lit and spy novels."

Ryder shook her head, clearly disgusted by both of us. "You guys are the biggest nerds I've ever met."

And she started to get up from the table, but Chess got up quicker and held up his hand. "Ryder, you girls stay put, I'll clean up, and I brought some gelato. I want both of you to relax. I saw how tired everyone was yesterday, and I know you will be back at it tomorrow."

And we both obeyed while exchanging glances. I'm not sure what Ryder's glance meant, but mine was appreciative. Chess was scoring points with me. Ryder even ate her gelato, which probably blew her calorie limit for the day.

After dinner Ryder escaped to her room, and I fetched my cat toy; a little plastic wand with a fishing line and a fuzzy lure at the end of it. Chess and I laughed to see Wheezer do amazing leaps and scoots and boxing moves as she battled with the thingy. We wore her out. And then we turned on the TV, but honestly, all I could think about was my novel. Chess picked up on my vibe, faked a yawn, and looked at his watch. "Well, I need to get back home and you need to get back to Scotland."

My face felt hot, because clearly my feelings were transparent. "I'm sorry. Dinner was great and I really was too tired to cook for myself. You were a godsend."

He leaned over and gave me a kiss, soft and tender. It occurred to me that maybe I shouldn't be so eager to go back to my novel. But it was too late.

Chess stood up. "I'll be going. I know tomorrow's an important day for you guys. Mother told me the vet comes first thing to check on the horse that's going to some important championship."

I nodded. "Hotstuff and Margot are supposed to ship to Chicago Wednesday to the national young horse championships. I'll be going, too. That is, if he's sound."

I filled Chess in on my schedule, and then with one more sweet kiss, we parted. I couldn't get into bed fast enough, and landed directly in the Scottish highlands. And stayed put until my eyes burned and the letters floated out of my reach.

*** 

In the morning, coffee in hand, I struggled to come alive. But, the familiar sound of Doc's diesel pulling up to the barn caused my stomach to clench and a shot of adrenaline to hit my bloodstream. The time of truth had arrived. Deb had decided to take Wild Child out on the hill this morning instead of in the arena, which had spared Margot from trying to concentrate on anything else but Hotstuff. It had also spared Deb from witnessing the drama, or having to witness Francesca witness the drama. I suspected the latter.

I had decided to curry Hotstuff to a high shine. He was uncharacteristically fussy and seemed tired of being treated like a hothouse flower. Even a horse as laid back as Hotstuff got nervous and edgy being caged up and only allowed to walk in hand for a week. But, he didn't get grouchy; he just refused to stand still. Some part of him was in constant motion, whether he was bobbing his head or shaking his ears or pawing or just twitching his skin and craning his neck to see down the aisle. He was a bundle of nerves.

Francesca and Doc almost snuck up on me, probably because Chopper and Snapper had been shut up. I shouldn't have been surprised about that since they were the cause of Hotstuff's initial injury.

Margot and Ryder and Nat joined our little circle as Doc opened up his leather bag of hoof tools and pulled out his "hoof tester." The hoof testers looked like a giant pair of pinchers, which was exactly what they were.

Doc picked up the left hind and wedged Hotstuff's foot between his bent knees, and then he placed the testers right on the spot and squeezed. Hotstuff jerked his foot away from Doc, which made me gasp with concern. Surely that was a positive reaction; positive meaning that spot was still tender. But then Hotstuff stretched his leg fully out behind himself, stretching his neck at the same time and moaning. Doc looked puzzled.

My body relaxed with relief. I knew Hotstuff. I laughed. "Doc, that's not a reaction to the hoof testers. Hotstuff's been too agitated to do his morning yoga routine. Wait a sec, he's not finished."

And as we stood there, Hotstuff demonstrated his morning routine of "asanas." He walked his front legs out and bowed with a dramatic yawn and an eye-roll.

Doc said, "Well, I'll be damned. That's a neat trick there, Lizzy."

I smiled. "I hope he'll show you his other move. I've seen plenty of horses stretch, but wait for it..."

And everyone stood silently watching Hotstuff. He yawned again and then did his big trick, all on his own. He crossed his front legs, using his left front to scratch the front of his right front cannon bone. Then as if he finally understood that everyone was watching him, he straightened up, his giant ears came forward and he tipped his head and looked straight at Doc.

Doc reached up and scratched him on the withers. "Shall we try this again, big guy?"

Doc picked his hoof back up and pressed the spot again with the testers. This time Hotstuff tried to swing his head around to watch, but was limited by cross-ties. He didn't seem to mind the testers or Doc. I had been right. Thank God, I had been right.

Doc put the hoof down. "Let's see him trot out on the longe line."

I had everything handy. I tightened the halter up to keep it from twisting and getting too close to his eye when I longed him, then I snapped on the longe line, grabbed the longe whip and led him out to the indoor with everyone falling in behind me.

When we got into the indoor arena, Margot pulled the heavy wooden half doors behind her. Should the unthinkable happen and Hotstuff got loose, he wasn't going to be able to go far.

My team lined up against the kickboard. There was no chatter. All eyes were on Hotstuff. I felt my grip tighten on the longe line. Hotstuff was walking, but every few strides he shook his head in a full circle, his steps too bouncy. I had a bad feeling.

Doc called out. "Okay, Lizzy. See if he'll just jog, I know he's feeling pretty tight after all his rest."

I tried to ask as gently as possible with the tiniest little cluck and movement of the whip. Hotstuff's head went straight down, shaking his big floppy ears, and then he exploded, bouncing and grunting around the circle in tight bunny hops, with his back rounded and his tail clamped. Still, he didn't try to pull off the longe line, or kick, he was just working out his kinks. I dug my heels into the ground and hung on. I looked over at Margot and saw that she and Doc were exchanging smiles and shaking their heads. Then Hotstuff came to a screeching halt, head still in the dirt, pulling on the line like a ton of bricks, and before I could stop him, he threw himself down on the ground and rolled.

I yelled, "Hotstuff, you blooming idiot!"

Now Margot and Doc were laughing loudly as I continued to hang on. Francesca was even smiling her tight smile.

I looked over at Margot and she could barely stop laughing to give instructions.

"It's okay, Lizzy. Just hang on when he gets up, because I'll bet he gets up bucking." And of course Margot was right. Hotstuff jumped up and gave a mighty fart and buck, scooted a few strides and then stopped and spun around to face me. Then he walked up to me, the vision of innocence, covered in arena footing.

Doc was shaking his head, but still smiling. "Lizzy, he managed to do everything but trot. Let's try that one again."

I pointed the tip of the whip at him and scolded him as he batted his big dark eyes at me. "Hotstuff, get back out there and trot for the doc."

He slung his head in the air and nearly pulled my shoulder out of joint as he turned and trotted away. It was not a jog, but a dragon-call snorty passage trot, with his head and tail high. Hotstuff was just not going to show Doc a jog trot.

But, the good news in all of this was that I did not see any irregular steps. The bad news was how in the heck was Margot going to ride this crazy thing in a show next weekend?

Doc called out, "Thanks, Lizzy. Let's see the other way."

Now I got trot, still passagey, but it looked just fine. Doc called out, "That's good, thank you."

Doc turned to Margot. "Margot, you can show him if you can ride him. I'm going to leave you some sole toughening paint. His soles are very soft from all that soaking. You do that twice a day this week and through the show. It's mostly formaldehyde, totally legal."

Francesca looked incredulous. "You think he's fit to compete? We can still get our money back with a vet's excuse." She sounded hopeful.

Doc blinked, then exhaled with a forced air of patience. "You ask an excellent question, Francesca. Let's put it this way, that big fellow looks sound and fit as a fiddle. I'd recommend you wear him out a bit before you get on, but I can't declare him unfit, medically speaking." He looked over at Margot and nodded. "And your rider there has a feel for these things. She's a pro. Trust her."

Margot turned to Francesca with a reassuring tone. "He'll be fine, Francesca. He's just four and that's normal behavior for a healthy four year old. All that rest has been trying for him; he's not accustomed to it. He'll be fine. I know it's a huge expense. I'll do what I can to make it a good investment for you."

Doc looked satisfied, and deftly changed the subject. "Hey Francesca, there's a new little bakery that just opened up in town that you and Frank should visit, great scones ..."

Nat walked beside me as we headed back to the barn. "Looks like you and me are going to Chicago." I nodded, and she leaned in. "I hope Margot kills it."

And I whispered back. "I just hope Hotstuff doesn't kill Margot!"

Nat guffawed and slapped me on the back, but then her voice got low and serious. "You and I, we are gonna do what it takes so this horse rocks. We'll make sure to take the edge off before Margot rides him. Besides, Margot knows what's she's doing. Francesca needs to lighten up and just trust her judgment."

I nodded back, but tactfully disagreed. "Nat, Francesca has a lot of money and pride invested in this show."

Nat listened but looked unconvinced. "Yeah, whatever. The Cavellis have more than enough of both those things. You have to pay to play."

I thought to myself that the Cavellis were currently paying with other people's money, and playing with other people's futures. But, of course I kept that to myself.

\*\*\*

Margot didn't even sit on Hotstuff on Tuesday. I longed him until he looked tired, and then he went out in the paddock for three hours. I got out the clippers and trimmed him up, pulled his mane, and gave him a bubble bath. He was a different young man by the time he finally went back to his stall. He rolled and rolled and after a peppermint, peed and then focused on eating his hay. Later, I saw him snoozing, curled up on the stall floor with his nose resting in the shavings. It was a good thing he couldn't know what was ahead of him. But of course, I did.

I fussed over every detail over leaving my animals like the neurotic caretaker I was. I made Ryder pledge to take good care of Wheezer. Deb had Winsome duty while I was away. I would miss my girls, but I knew Wheezer would be just fine, and Winsome would benefit from a week of Deb's training. Francesca had decided to give Johnny's care over to Claire Winston and have her talented young trainer Suzette ride him while we were away. I just hoped Suzette would not be sharing any updates with Ryder. But then again, what if she did? Ryder had probably been gossiping about the horse with Suzette from day one. It was out of my control.

I always felt the burden of responsibility of driving Francesca's truck and four-horse trailer, and of course, anxious about whoever was loaded in the trailer, never losing awareness of who was behind me. But I also looked forward to my drive time with Natalie who had ordered the Outlander series on audio book. Not only that, but she had made a special trip to the store to buy a boatload of junk food and drinks. There was stuff in there that I didn't even know was sold anymore. Who knew that strawberry coconut Twinkies were still made? It was like we two were heading off on a girls' camping trip. This drive would be a guilty pleasure. Since it was a twelve and a half hour drive, Natalie and I planned to leave the farm by three a.m. Crazy.

When I tip-toed down the stairs at an ungodly hour, I found a brown bag in the barn aisle with my name on it. I grabbed it up. I was fuzzy headed and could only think of coffee, which was in my thermos, ready for the road, and would have to wait.

Nat had beaten me to the barn. Hotstuff was already in the cross-ties, wearing his shipping boots, ears pricked, innocent. Nat sipped from an oversized travel mug.

She greeted me with a Vulcan greeting, right hand extended, second and third fingers spread wide. "Live long and prosper my friend."

I silently returned the greeting.

Nat pointed to my bag. "Whatcha got?"

I looked down at my bag. "I don't know? It was in the aisle."

I peered into the bag and smiled when I saw a tartan pattern. It was a tin of Scottish shortbread cookies, along with a card and note from Chess. "I have an idea what kind of audio books you two will be listening to, and thought this would be an appropriate treat. Dad sends along this loaded debit card for other essentials. He loaded three hundred dollars on it, but says to let him know if you need more since you are representing the team. Eat well and don't stay up all night reading. Love, Chess."

I kept the card to myself, but showed the cookie tin to Natalie, and told her about the debit card. We agreed that the Cavelli men were good and thoughtful guys.

Then we had to get the show on the road. I started the truck, turned on the lights and the interior trailer lights so Hotstuff would be able to see his way in. It was up to us to double-check the hitch, get the ramp down, check the hay bag, and then carefully lead Hotstuff up the ramp and back him into his slot. He was so agreeable and easy, only sniffing the ramp and snorting a bit as he checked his footing. Anyone could have stolen Hotstuff, he was such a trusting soul. I thought he looked lonely in that metal box all by himself. I even felt bad lifting the ramp and closing him up in there alone.

I took the first shift even though Natalie volunteered. She claimed to be a very experienced driver of rigs bigger than this one and I believed her, but I needed to get my sea legs. I always felt like I was pulling a cruise ship behind me when I first put the truck into gear and started to move. The first hour I couldn't listen to an audio book or eat or barely sip my coffee, I was so nervous. I reassured myself that since it was Wednesday at 3:30 a.m. it was too late for drunks to be out on the highways and too early for commuters. It was a clear summer morning with nary a soul in sight, as if we had our own private highway. Natalie and I spoke softly and at some point I began to relax, my shoulders dropping, my grip loosening a little, even though I still had my hands at ten and two. After the third hour we were ready to switch seats, and I was ready to eat Twinkies and listen from the very beginning to the story of *Outlander*.

This was going to be fun.

***

The unabridged audio version of *Outlander* is 32 hours of listening pleasure. Though our butts were numb and our backs stiff by the end of our drive, a little part of me was not ready to get out of the truck and leave Scotland and begin the work of setting up our stalls.

Hotstuff did not feel the same way. Each time we stopped to give him water and check on him, he had whinnied at us in a pitiful way. This trip would force our boy to grow up fast.

The show grounds were both beautiful and homey, its modern updates not upstaging its historical look and feel. Flowerbeds set into banks with bright yellow flowers, natural stone curved in short walls along pathways, and attractive pergolas alongside the arenas. We were lucky to be stabled in old wooden barns. No tent stabling for us. Regardless of the whinnies and the busy atmosphere that always accompany move-in day, I immediately felt at home.

Margot and Francesca were already there and directed us via cell phone to our stall. We pulled up to the barn and Natalie lowered the ramp. She was, as usual, singing. She started quietly as she strode into the trailer and unhooked Hotstuff, and then she got louder, finally belting out an appropriate tune, as she led a very tired looking Hotstuff down the ramp.

"Hush my darling; don't fear my darling, the lion sleeps tonight, a weemawop, a weemawop, a weemawop, a weemawop, the lion sleeps tonight!"

Nat winked at Margot and led Hotstuff to his stall, where he stretched out and began peeing before she could get the shipping boots and halter off him.

I said, "It looks like he's been waiting to pee since he left Peapack. Poor guy."

We stood like weird voyeurs watching him pee a river. Once the stream lost some of its force, the flow stopped and started at least twice, with the final squirt eliciting a long, dramatic, contented moan. We four girls exchanged tight-lipped smiles.

Natalie finally could chance bending over and pulling off his shipping boots. She pulled off his halter and turned him loose. He threw himself down on the ground and rolled while we filled his water buckets. When he got up he drank deeply, his ears twitching backward in time with each swallow. Then he sighed. We hung his hay bag, and watched him pull hay through the holes, the picture of a contented horse. He was tired, but looked just fine. Nat and I had done our jobs. It was time to get back to work, but I gave him one more glance, then turned to Margot and Francesca. "I agree with Nat. He's going to sleep well tonight."

Nat and I set about unloading the immense amount of stuff that travels with even just one horse. The hay and grain and extra bags of shavings, Margot's big rolling tack truck that looked like her own personal rolling closet and chest of drawers, but built like cases that rock and roll bands take on the road. It was a bitch to move around. We had also packed colored mulch and pots and pots of flowers to decorate our tack stall. Then we set up our table and chairs and our ice chest and picnic baskets of Power Bars and other snacks.

Hotstuff was not the only one who was going to crash tonight; I was beat. Nat was tiny but she was strong and tough. I was glad to have her and her muscles along. She was quick and eager and a volunteer. And she sang as she worked. Her songs and her attitude helped diffuse the tension I knew I would feel. She was worth two of Ryder.

Francesca had booked us all into the official show hotel. It meant good beds, and even a decent restaurant. Nat kept saying stuff like "sweet" and singing.

While Francesca and Margot had a dinner date with some of the other competitors, Nat and I had our debit card to order whatever we wanted at the hotel. We had the farm truck, and were free to go do bed check on Hotstuff anytime we wanted. I appreciated that Margot did not micro-manage us, and that she kept Francesca from breathing down our necks.

We got to the show grounds around ten p.m. for bed check. Nat and I were happily chatting away as we hopped from the truck, only to find a shadowy figure sitting in one of our director's chairs. We stopped dead in our tracks and the person jumped up.

"Sorry to startle you, girls. It's just me, Dennis. I just got in and was getting the lay of the land here before heading over to the hotel. It's my first time here."

I swallowed before speaking. "Oh, thank goodness it's you! I didn't know you would be here. Is Margot expecting you?"

He laughed. "Yes, of course. I told her I wouldn't miss it for the world. I've been following her ranking. This young horse stuff is interesting. I decided to donate money to the USEF Developing Young Horse program: I am now a sponsor."

I sounded like an echo. I said, "A sponsor?"

Dennis smiled, "Yes, in sport, as in other foundations, support is highly sought after and valued. USEF High Performance is therefore treating me well. I have a lovely VIP room, and I expect to receive quite a tutorial while I'm here."

Natalie blurted out, "Bet that free room cost you a fortune."

Dennis very politely laughed through his answer. "Young lady, you don't know the half of it. I expect that before the weekend is out, they'll milk me for even more, but I don't mind."

Natalie reached her hand out. "Name's Natalie. And you are?"

"Dennis Walker. We've not formerly met, Natalie, but I believe I've seen you working at the shows. Lizzy, nice to see you again."

Natalie tipped her head a bit. "I'm guessing you weren't sitting there

375

in the dark hoping to meet the grooms of the famous Hotstuff. I know we'll be famous too some day, but we don't have fans just yet."

He corrected her with a gentle laugh. "No, no. I had no expectations tonight. I just like sitting here in the old familiar Equus Paradiso chairs. I like the shows. Equus Paradiso is where I got my first taste of this stuff. So, I'm getting back to my roots, so to speak."

He offered to buy us drinks... back at the hotel. It felt inappropriate. I thought of Sophie, and how the affair must have started between the two of them... sort of like this.

Natalie and I shot each other a glance and then I politely declined for the both of us.

# 25. Churned Up

*Natalie was a terrible roommate.*

She tossed and turned and talked and occasionally even sang in her sleep. The next morning though, she was already showered and dressed when I woke up. She sat at the desk, sipping coffee and sketching, humming to herself.

She shook her head as she watched me sit up and rub my eyes. "Lizzy, man you've got the hairdo of Amy Winehouse."

I grimaced. "It's from holding the pillow behind my head all night trying to drown you out."

She winced. "Sorry. Was I snoring, singing, or giving away secrets?"

"Talking gibberish. And a song or two."

She waggled her finger at me again. "Not gibberish, my friend, I had a Gypsy tell me that I was a pirate in my past life and I've got a buried treasure somewhere. But damn it, when I'm awake I can't remember where it's buried. She said I'll only tell someone while I'm talking in my sleep. So, next time, listen up. We could use a few gold doubloons."

I rubbed my eyes again. I suspected Nat was kidding me, but you never knew with Natalie. I decided the past lives discussion needed to wait. I had to get moving.

We got downstairs just as they were setting out trays of bacon and sausage and eggs in the steam tables. We loaded our plates up and added toasted bagels and cream cheese with multiple cups of hot coffee. I was so stuffed I almost felt ill when we got into the farm truck.

The show grounds were conveniently no more than ten minutes away. Hotstuff whinnied dramatically when we walked up. His stall was a mess. He had apparently been walking in anxious circles, probably since dawn, turning his fresh new shavings into an organic mixture of pulverized poop, shavings and bits of hay. I grimaced looking at the stall and then at the fretting horse, and sighed. "He's an emotional train wreck, Natalie. He's lost his entire herd and is a stranger in a strange land; poor baby!" I sighed watching him. How I wished I could speak his language and explain to him, that we would take him right back home when the weekend was done. He would be reunited with his friends. The only way he would learn was from repetition.

We fed him his grain, but he couldn't concentrate. He wanted it, but we had hung the bucket in the corner and in that spot he couldn't keep an eye on his foreign and untrustworthy world and eat at the same time. So, I held the bucket for him at the doorway where he had a good view, and that helped. Hotstuff needed us there to settle. No horse is a loner. This one was feeling lonely and abandoned. We were part of his familiar "herd" and he wanted us to stay close.

After his grain was mostly consumed or scattered on the ground, Natalie took him for a walk and I attacked the mess he had made. When Nat tried to return him to the stall he balked at the door. So, she walked out into a sunny spot and leaned against Hotstuff while he nervously cropped the short grass. I raked and swept and then dusted, and then I made coffee and set up our hospitality table. It felt good to be clean and well ordered.

Francesca and Margot arrived. Margot nodded approvingly at Hotstuff grazing, and glanced into his stall, her voice sounding hopeful. "Did Hotstuff have a good night?"

Natalie answered before I could. "Big guy's okay, Margot."

Nat and I exchanged glances. And Margot must not have noticed since she didn't miss a beat. "Good, good. I'll ride him mid-morning then. The jog is at four. Francesca's going to be at the draw afterward to pull the number for our ride time on Friday. That test counts 40%, and then we have the final test on Sunday that counts 60%. You girls will need to walk him around and acclimate him to the grounds before I get on today. Lizzy, you judge if he needs to be longed. I'd rather not longe him if he seems okay. I want him relaxed but not worn out. The long trailer ride may have been exhausting."

I nodded. "Will do."

Natalie held him in the stall while I groomed and booted him up. We put the chain over his nose to take him for the first real tour of the grounds. The competitors' packet had a nice map of the facilities, and we knew which arena Hotstuff would be using for his championship rides, and which arena would be his warm up arena. The show had a concurrent open show going at the same time. That show had its own warm up arena and multiple show arenas. The USEF Young Horse Championships were contained on one side of the facility. It was a compact venue but still had an open feeling with easy viewing, even though the two parts of the show felt very separate.

Hotstuff had a challenging time making the walk from the barns to the arenas. He did not want to leave the stabling area to walk up the special dirt road reserved for horses. That road traveled up the backside of the arenas and was separate from the path marked for foot traffic only. I guess that way the horses couldn't endanger any pedestrians or babies in strollers or bicycles.

Hotstuff kept bumping into Natalie and swinging his head around with googly-eyes. When we had to pass the boot vendor setting up her table he slammed on the brakes and tried to run backward. I had never seen Hotstuff so terrified. Natalie hung on, and I walked up behind him cooing and was finally able to give him a reassuring pat on his butt. We let him stand and puff until he pulled himself together. I could tell this was going to be a long day. But, what else did we have to do all day?

Nat put her hand on his withers and leaned on him while he continued to have "the look of eagles." When he drew himself up, Hotstuff was really tall and Natalie never looked smaller. But she started singing softly to him. I knew the song. It was "Don't Worry, Be Happy" and I quietly joined in. We smiled as we sang. When we finished every verse we knew, we strolled to the boot vendor with Hotstuff following us and discussed her beautiful row of sample boots. Then we flipped through their catalogue while Hotstuff looked over our shoulder. We actually had to make him back up and give us more space. Then he worked on my hair with his top lip, giving me a hair-do similar to the one I woke up with.

We said goodbye to our new friend selling boots, and pulled Hotstuff behind us toward what would be his dance floor tomorrow.

Hotstuff, Natalie, and I walked our legs off until we stopped and watched the sponsor tents go up alongside the championships arena. The long side of seating between the championship warm up arena and championship show arena were set aside for "sponsors." Tents were being set up over round tables that seated eight. In the middle of each table was a centerpiece with the name of the table's sponsor prominently displayed. We saw "Equus Paradiso Farm," and right next to it, "Walker Sport Horses." Seeing Dennis now had a farm to advertise had Natalie and me lifting our eyebrows and nodding to each other to be sure it was duly noted. We also saw buffet tables at the entrance to the seating area, and a little post with the word "Sponsors" in bold letters set at the entrance, making it clear that this area was reserved. Natalie was already musing about whether we would be invited into the inner sanctum. I was sorry to disappoint her.

"I doubt it, Nat. Frank gave us the debit card so we could feed ourselves over in the cheap seats. To Francesca we're the help. We are here to provide a service and not mix with money and power."

She shook her head. "We have a table, and I intend to sit at it. We'll have so much time on our hands to watch other classes between Hotstuff's test. These are great seats because we can watch the warm up arena or the show arena just by turning around in our chairs. You know there will be food, too. It will be fantastic."

"But if Francesca..."

Natalie made a harrumph sound. "Lizzy, what? You think she'll scold me or maybe even fire me?"

"I, for one, don't want to find out," I replied.

Natalie grinned. "I got two words for you then."

I drew out the word. "Yesssssss?"

Natalie held up first one finger to punctuate the first word, and then the next finger for the second word. "Rosa Parks."

I shook my head, but smiled, remembering the Natalie I first met down in Conyers, Georgia. She was still a proud member of the proletariat, fighting the bourgeoisie and the oligarchs. But, if she sold enough of her art, she was well on her way to switching classes, though I would never dare say as much.

When we returned to the stalls, Margot was pacing like a caged jungle cat. She had her boots and spurs on. She cleared her throat before speaking. "Darlings, I was just about to call on the cell. Is Hotstuff okay? Do we need to longe him? You were gone so long."

Natalie jumped in. "He was great, Margot. We thought it would be good for him to just hang out by the arenas, to get used to all of the movements and smells. Plus, we went out to the vendor tents. You know how tents can move in the wind and all. But he was a good boy."

Margot cut her eyes to me. She wasn't totally buying it. I added, "He was nervous at first, Margot, but he settled."

She nodded but maintained her eye contact with me. "I know this is a lot for his four year old mind to cope with, so thank you for doing all of that."

I swallowed hard but kept with the script. "Absolutely."

Margot looked at her watch. "I'd better get it over with. I'm worried about this weather. I'd hate to have to do the ride in the rain, or even jog in the rain for that matter. Let's do this."

We gave Hotstuff a wipe off with the towel, fluffed out his big tail, and then put the tack on. Margot watched, looking grim faced, and then Francesca joined our little group. How she could have a shopping bag already when the vendors were just setting up was puzzling, but clearly she had been shopping.

Francesca looked over her sunglasses into the dark stall. "Did you girls use the sole toughener?"

I nodded over my shoulder. "We did it when we picked out his hooves this morning."

She sniffed. "Last night, too?"

Natalie answered. "Last night too, Francesca." Even though we both knew we had forgotten.

We held Hotstuff by the mounting block while Margot ran one last time to the port-o-let. She came out and started to get on without her helmet. I had to run and get it out of her fancy rolling tack closet. She never wore one at home, but at a competition it was a rule that could not be broken. Then of course, both Nat and I had forgotten to take the number off his halter and put it on his bridle; another rule not to be broken. We all were too edgy.

Margot looked sharp, as usual. Today she had on her burgundy boots and on top of her tan breeches, a brightly colored belt that showed off her tiny waistline. Margot always cut an elegant figure on a horse. And this horse, although not exactly a pretty boy, was tall and leggy and extravagant in his gaits. They would draw attention. Of that I was sure.

But first Margot had to get him to the warm up arena. They made it to the end of the barn aisle but when she turned him up the road, he grabbed the bit, put his head in the air, and spun around, trotting back toward Nat and me with the whites of his eyes showing. Margot growled at him, "Hotstuff!" and snatched him to a halt with a "pulley rein," (one hand up and one hand down). He slid to a stop. I grabbed a lead rope and jogged to him and clipped it onto his bit, looking up at Margot's face. Her eyes were narrowed, her jaw clenched. Hotstuff never made her angry, but she looked angry now. This was not starting well.

I didn't let her say anything. "I'll just lead him, Margot. He'll be fine once you get him into the arena. I'm sure of it."

She didn't argue. But she shortened her reins and gave him a sharp kick. I had to hustle to stay up with them as they headed back up the road. The walk past the vendors was a little dicey, but as soon as we passed them, I unclipped Hotstuff and he and Margot marched into the warm-up arena.

Natalie, Francesca, and I found a good place to stand on a grassy patch at the end of the warm up arena. Margot began her warm up in a way I now understood was typical for her first day at a show. She was tight, Hotstuff was tight. She stood at the edge of that proverbial diving board gathering herself mentally to make the leap, to let the training take over and truly "get on with it." I wished for Deb. But I also knew that Margot would get there. She had been in the arena so many times with so many horses, and yet, here she was, once again clearly doubting herself and locked up in her body.

Francesca muttered, sounding annoyed. We were soon joined by Dennis Walker. Francesca did not look the least bit surprised to see him and today didn't turn her back on him, even if she didn't exactly give him a warm greeting. He politely greeted all three of us by our names. Francesca raised one eyebrow, surprised that he knew our names, but she didn't question it. Dennis gestured toward Hotstuff. "How are they?"

Francesca shrugged non-committally, and then crossed her arms.

Dennis blinked, looking a bit uncomfortable. Francesca was still being chilly, if not still outright cold. He regained his composure, flashed a smile, and said he would see us later. Francesa watched him walk away, her face expressionless.

Natalie whispered to me, "So now it's the silent treatment. I guess in Francesca's book, that's progress."

Natalie then focused back on Margot, and changed the subject. "Margot needs to dispel some of that negative energy she's bottling up before something blows."

Margot got Hotstuff moving, though I hardly recognized him. Gone were the floppy ears and rubber band elastic movement that had characterized Hotstuff's daily work; instead he launched Margot high out of the saddle in her rising trot, all four of his legs stiff, the movement wooden and jerky.

It didn't help when a group of motorcycles whizzed down the highway that ran not far from the long side of the warm up arena. Hotstuff tucked his tail and scooted down the entire length of the arena in canter, scattering other horses around them. Margot got him back under her control, as the other riders pulled up their mounts. That wasn't Hotstuff's fault, I thought defensively. The other horses had spooked, too.

But as Margot trotted past us, she made a grimace, audibly whispering, "Something's wrong." How I wished for Deb's strong and steady presence. Deb would take them both in hand in a way that was effective and friendly. She would turn this around in no time.

I glanced at Francesca, arms still crossed tightly, a frown on her face. She said nothing.

Nat gave me a poke. "Help her, Lizzy."

I shook my head. "It's not my place."

Things came to a head when Margot sharply pulled him up in front of us. "I have never felt him like this. Something is definitely wrong with him." Hotstuff's eyes were wide, his mouth nervously chomping and foaming, his veins standing up in a fine netting under his skin. He stood still but looked ready to bolt.

There was a beat of dead silence among us. I knew everyone was waiting for ME to say something. I said, "He is totally sound, Margot, he's just scared to death. That's all."

Then Margot said something very honest. "Darling, that makes two of us I guess."

Francesca glared up at Margot without any show of sympathy. Her attitude pissed me off, given what a coward she had been at the show with Johnny Cash. When her nerves were challenged, Francesca had tucked tail and run home.

Then Dennis Walker, who I thought had left minutes before, walked past Nat and me, bravely stepped up to Margot and the agitated horse, and motioned to Margot to lean over. She did, and he whispered something into her ear. Margot laughed. And it was a real laugh. He put his hand over one of her hands that gripped the reins and squeezed it; as he let go he patted her on the thigh. They exchanged a private look; one I almost felt I should not have seen. Dennis stepped away.

Margot turned her head to look directly at me. Her glance was a request. I saw it, and quietly said to her, "What would Deb tell you right now?"

Margot nodded. "She'd say to get Hotstuff out there and 'shake his tail feathers;' to have fun; to embrace the moment."

I nodded in agreement. "Big Guy probably needs to go burn up that excess adrenaline coursing through his veins. You need to do the same."

And almost in unison my crew mumbled agreement. When Margot moved off with Hotstuff, Dennis said quietly, "Her hand was trembling; I could feel it right through her glove."

Although none of us commented, seeing the two of them together sharing a private exchange; hearing him comment on her nerves; well it softened my opinion of him slightly. Margot was not giving him the same chilly treatment as Francesca. I had just witnessed something unsettling. I had forgotten that Margot and Dennis had been a couple; they had been friends. He had broken her heart; but they shared a past. It left me uneasy as I stepped back and watched Margot pull herself together.

The transition from tension to control in Margot's ride didn't happen immediately. Hotstuff took a long time to let go of the excess energy. But it got visibly better, and each time Margot passed, I delivered one comment for her. Initially my suggestions held a question mark at the ends, like, "Maybe try trot to canter to trot transitions?" Or "Maybe more bending lines and leg-yields?"

I was terribly self-conscious knowing that Francesca was most likely thinking I was "getting above my station." But, I tried to focus on Hotstuff and Margot. I thought about how that four year old horse had almost no experience to draw upon. Hotstuff could appear much more advanced than his tender age. But, what a short time he had been on this earth. His first three summers had been spent lounging on Deb's green hill frolicking with his buddies Romp and Bounce, his momma Regina right there on the other side of the fence.

When training began, it was like he was inducted into the army alongside his mates and packed to Florida boot camp where he started his show career. He debuted with a whiz and a bang, impressing the judges. But it was his natural talent and willingness that shone through. He was still just an innocent baby. Once he qualified for the finals, he had rested on his laurels, staying home to focus on training instead of logging miles and gaining experience. And now he was here and feeling overwhelmed, lonely and frightened. I knew somehow, deep down, that he would be just fine. But, to have expected him to be his normal chilled self in this strange new environment was not realistic. He had every excuse in the world to feel overwhelmed.

Margot had finally risen to the occasion. I thought about all the insights into Margot's character that Deb had shared. Deb had been there when Walter was alive. I understood from Deb that Walter knew how to bring the best out in Margot, but that internally she always gave the credit to him, and not to her own exceptional talent. I marveled to myself that here she was, fifteen years later, having trained many horses and riders without Walter, and yet she still lacked self-confidence. She needed a Walter, or a Deb, to make her believe that she could do this. How do you get to become Margot Fanning, the Margot Fanning, and still feel that way? It was a puzzle.

Margot's fitted blouse was now soaked through and Hotstuff's black coat lathered under the reins, but they finally looked more like themselves. Hotstuff's long ears had finally relaxed to the sides. Margot finished in rising trot, stretching Hotstuff long and low, and he gratefully went there. He walked back to the stables on a loose rein, still googly-eyed, but walking in his normal huge, striding, loose way again. It was better, but this wasn't the Margot and Hotstuff that we needed if we were going to bring home the tri-color. Margot had barely looked at us as she exited the warm up, because even though she had risen to the task, despite her shaking hands, she knew they were not on their A game, not by a long shot.

Natalie and I broke into a jog after them, leaving Dennis and Francesca sort of walking together, but with a clear DMZ between them. I could not hear their words but I could hear the tone. Dennis' tones mild, Francesca's responses clipped.

We now had an exhausted baby horse. Natalie and I left Margot sitting in a tall director's chair with a bottle of water and a cool damp towel behind her neck to go give Hotstuff a bubble bath. Margot looked tiny and almost frail sitting there. I had a wave of sadness looking at her. Margot always had a happy face at home, she clearly loved her horses and derived a lot of satisfaction and pleasure from the training process, but then she went home every night to her condo, with not even a

fuzzy Siamese kitten there to greet her. This show and her ride suddenly seemed a trifling problem, and not the real problem that suddenly
seemed apparent. But work was calling.

I held the lead rope while Nat wet down Hotstuff at the wash rack
with our short curly travel hose and then made a bucket of suds. She
squirted a little soap on a sponge, dunked it in the bucket, and began
soaping him up. Hotstuff hung his head with a loose lower lip and half
closed eyes. I kept my voice low.

"So, Nat, what do you make of Dennis? I mean, he was terrible to
Margot, and now he's obviously weaseling his way back in."

She shrugged and continued soaping Hotstuff. "Lizzy, what business is it of ours? Margot knows who he is better than we do."

I nodded. "Of course you're right. It's just she always talks so lov-
ingly about Walter, and she seems so sad right now. Emma said that
Dennis broke her heart with Sophie, and yet, here he is, trying to work
his way back in now that Sophie and he are on the outs."

Natalie started rinsing off Hotstuff. When he got his face washed,
he held it up in the air like a fussy baby, the water running down Natalie's arms and soaking the entire right side of her shirt. I got a little
shower at the same time.

I handed Natalie a towel, which she used first on herself, and then
to dry Hotstuff's head.

Natalie turned to me and handed the towel back, taking the sweat
scraper. "Maybe we should reserve judgment. The guy doesn't give me
dangerous vibes, and after all this time, my meter is pretty fine-tuned."

I watched Nat flick water off of Hotstuff and thought about what
I knew about Dennis, which wasn't much. He wasn't too bright about
horses, but did that make him a bad guy? Then I thought, "Wait a minute, this was the guy that dumped Margot for Sophie!"

Natalie took the towel back and briskly toweled off all four legs. We
led Hotstuff back to the stalls, back to the little patch of short grass to

dry in the sun. Next we would give him a little napping time back in his stall while we ate lunch. Then we would braid for the jog.

Our chairs by our tack room were empty when we returned. I assumed they had gone off for a proper lunch. I knew Margot would go back to shower and change for the jog at four.

We used our debit card again to fill up on horse show food… burgers, all fresh off the grill and hot. Nat and I hunched over our plates, dunking big fat wavy fries in ketchup and conferring. I said, "Margot's in a blue funk, and there's nothing we can do about it."

Natalie was silent. That was not normal for her. She hummed a bit, then said, "I'm gonna go out on a limb here and say she's feeling a lot of pressure from Francesca."

I wasn't sure what Nat knew, or if she genuinely was guessing, and I didn't even know if Margot understood the farm's financial strains, but it was true that Francesca always poisoned the air with her own miasma of tension. I said, almost apologetically, "Francesca and Margot are friends, even though we all know Francesca is difficult."

Natalie pointed a French fry at me. "Francesca is a tee-total bitch. But I always get the impression that she uses her bitchiness in a tactical way. Margot's got to be used to it by now. You told me it's been fifteen years?" Natalie whistled, then said, "Margot's willing to pay the price in order to keep the rides on these great horses, and I know those kind of rides aren't easy to find. Just think what she'd have to give up if she gave up Francesca. But Francesca makes her job harder that it has to be."

Nat shoved the whole fry in her mouth. I nodded in agreement, "I can't imagine Margot ever walking away from her horses; never."

Nat's words were slurred by her mouthful of fries. "Yup. You gotta' dance with the one who brung ya' and in this case it's Francesca. But it doesn't mean Margot can't take a twirl around the floor with Dennis as a stress-buster. Might sweeten the weekend for her, and give her that space she needs to settle and focus."

I frowned. "But one twirl around the dance floor could lead to other stuff, and he could break her heart again."

Nat hummed a few bars of something I couldn't quite identify, then grinned, "Hey, some of that "other stuff" might be just what Margot needs. Anyway, you and I should at least be polite, maybe even chat up Dennis a little. We could tell him he needs to help Margot get some time away from Francesca. The rest is up to Margot. Gotta keep Margot happy."

Her point made, Natalie started humming again, took a sip of her coke, and then focused on her cheeseburger.

I shook my head. Natalie was so "out there" that I wasn't sure I could go along with her plan. I watched her happily eating and humming, satisfied with herself. It occurred to me then she was humming, "Summer Lovin'" from the movie *Grease*.

\*\*\*

Hotstuff was braided and groomed for the FEI horse inspection, commonly called "the jog." He had snoozed while I put in his braids. Natalie kept me entertained with funny stories while she sat in a director's chair with her sketch pad, a pencil in hand, furiously moving over the paper. She didn't let me see until I was finished. She had captured Hotstuff and me beautifully. I begged to keep it, so she signed and dated the corner and handed it to me. I knew I would cherish it.

Margot and Francesca arrived. Margot had showered and changed into a crisply tailored, sky blue three quarter sleeved blouse with a gold silk scarf wrapped around her neck. Her khaki trousers had a sharply pressed crease. She was carrying a brand new pair of sky blue riding gloves, clearly purchased to match her blouse. The sky had turned dark, and the wind was picking up. It was definitely going to rain. Jogging a horse was not something one could do with an umbrella. I looked at Margot's classically tailored outfit, her tight little blonde bun, her perfect make-up job, and thought it was all for naught. I pointed to the sky. "Where's your raincoat, Margot?"

Margot grimaced and looked upwards. "Did either of you come across a raincoat in the trailer?"

Natalie and I looked at each other, and I nodded as I realized there was one of those cheap see-through ones that are made to go over your show coat. I said, "Yeah, I'll go to the trailer and get it."

Francesca looked alarmed. "No, no, no. I know the kind and it would look terrible. I'll go buy you something more stylish, Margot. I saw some lovely all-weather jackets."

And Natalie added, "Get her a ball cap while you're at it, Francesca."

Francesca looked offended. "A ball cap? For the jog? I think not."

Natalie said, "Suit yourself. A ball cap will look better than a rain hood."

Francesca almost jogged toward the vendors.

Margot smiled. "That was a good move, girls. One thing Francesca does well is shop."

I nodded and smiled. "You don't do so bad yourself, Margot. That's a sharp looking outfit."

Margot gave a little curtsey. We put the finishing touches on Hotstuff's grooming job. He was silky smooth from his bubble bath, his tail full and fluffy. I massaged a little baby oil into his face, and then ran the towel over his coat one last time. Then we put on the bridle and he was ready to roll.

We heard the announcer call the horses to the collecting arena, but we were waiting for Francesca. She was breathlessly trotting toward us with a shopping bag. Margot had to try on three different coats in a frenzy while we yelled out "yes" or "no" for each option. We agreed on a black one that was fitted and lightweight, with a zipper. Lo and behold, Francesca had also purchased a ball cap, in black, with the National USEF Young Horse Championship logo on it. No rain hoodie for Margot. I knew the show organizers would approve of the cap and so would the photographers. Margot said that we should just carry the coat in case of rain, but she was being optimistic. The rain was already starting in smattering fits and starts. Natalie over-rode Francesca boldly and blurted out, "Put it on." And Margot complied, while Francesca scowled.

Natalie volunteered to lead Hotstuff, and I walked behind him. I had his passport tucked into an inner pocket of my rain slicker and a whip to be sure there would be no stuttering along the path to the collecting arena. It turned out to be the same warm up arena he had worked in earlier, with the path for presenting the horses to the committee set up alongside the show arena. I peeled off as Natalie joined the parade of naked horses being led around the arena in their bridles.

The rain turned from fits and starts to steady. Margot had on her new rain jacket, and Francesca was carrying an umbrella large enough that we three clustered under it. Natalie had no such coverage. She had on a ball cap, but no raincoat. She was soaked through, her jeans covered with wet and grime almost to her knees. But she seemed oblivious and kept Hotstuff walking purposefully around the arena. He was tense and uncharacteristically belting out deep-throated whinnies, but he did better than most of the four year olds who, almost to a horse, looked shell shocked, unsure of what they were doing out there. Some looked full of energy and ready to bust loose, and some just looked miserable and soggy in the rain. The newly erected tents between the two arenas began to droop with water weighing down the tops in a way that looked ominous. I wondered if they would collapse on the people huddled under them. If they collapsed, could they actually knock someone out?

While I assumed that the weight of the water was going to collapse the tents, something entirely different happened. The tents periodically and without warning gushed out the collected water, not unlike the dumping of a giant bucket, and when it dumped, the canvas snapped back with a loud crack, not unlike the sound of a thunderbolt.

All three of us huddled under Francesca's umbrella jumped at the noise. Hotstuff and all the other youngsters walking around reared or jumped too, and for a brief moment Natalie had both feet off the ground like a tethered balloon in the Macy's parade. But Nat was not going to let go of her charge, not for the world.

The rain stopped as if a celestial tap was switched off. The clouds briefly parted. Immediately following that little moment of grace, Hotstuff's number was called "on deck" and Natalie brought him to Margot.

Natalie looked like a drowned rat pulled through a sewer. But when she passed us she gave us a little performance, smiling and singing. "Little darling, I feel the rain is slowly stopping." And she pointed skyward, "Here comes the sun, nah, nah, nah, Here comes the sun, nah, nah, nah, nah, and I say… It's all right."

Margot smiled back, pulled off her ball cap, peeled off her raincoat, pulled on her brand new baby blue gloves, and with a soft, "Thank you, Natalie," took Hotstuff. I handed her his passport that I had kept safe and dry in an inside pocket. She looked ready for her close up, clean and fresh and dry, perfect smudge-free make-up. A wet and bedraggled Hotstuff jogged like a pro, and was immediately "accepted."

Francesa left us to go "draw" Margot's time for tomorrow's ride while Margot walked with us back to the stables.

Margot gave us a tutorial on draws and the order of go. She said, "Francesca has the best luck in draws, so I always let her do it for us."

Margot continued, "You see, darlings, the first day of competition is by a random "open draw" to prevent any unfair advantage. No matter the ranking, all horses start fresh once they qualify for the finals."

I asked, "Do you think there's really any advantage in the order?"

Margot nodded, "Well, judges tend, perhaps unintentionally, to leave room in the scores for a stellar performance later in the day. I truly believe judges try very hard to be consistent in the standard so that the scores across the entire country reflect the same quality. But, many things can impact scoring in very subtle ways. An open draw is an acknowledgment that order of go is one of those things. Consider what could happen if judges got overly enthusiastic by awarding a very high score early in the class? They could find themselves in the awkward position of having to give an even higher score later in the go to ensure that the placing of the ribbons was correct. In the end, they better get the placings in the correct order, or they have failed at their jobs."

Natalie added, "Wow, Margot. That could explain why I've seen scores that I thought were way too high at the smaller shows. Could it be that the judge painted themselves into a corner and had to over-score the ride to make the placings come out the right way?"

Margot tipped her head, interested. "Well, that could be. But, there are other reasons that could happen."

I said, "And that would be?"

Margot chuckled, "'Santa Claus' judges…forever delivering 'gifts.' Since horse of the year awards are decided by averaging scores, well, you can see how loved/hated such judges would become. Those scores that are 'gifts' can skew the year end averages."

Natalie said, "What about Scrooges, those miserly judges who hold back the higher scores even when they are deserved?"

Margot smiled, "Oh yes. Sometimes it's because you are early in the go. But of course, someone always has to go first. I am sure it happened occasionally that the best horse sometimes went first, and still won. But, I also wonder if when that happened, if it depressed scores for the rest of the class in order to ensure that first horse still won the class. It is a curious problem and one simply caused by human nature."

I sighed, "I'll cross my fingers that Francesca's luck holds and you get a good ride time."

Margot agreed, but added, "Well, the second day of the competition is not by draw, but by reverse score. You earn your order of go on the second day. That one is up to Hotstuff and me."

As soon as we returned to the stalls I took Hotstuff from Natalie, handed her a towel, and let her sit and relax while I pulled braids and got Hotstuff dried off and settled. Margot made a pot of coffee and poured a cup for Nat, who was filthy. Margot looked relieved to have the jog behind her and was chatty, a level of care lifted from her shoulders.

Francesca returned with the good news that she had drawn the second to last spot in the class tomorrow. We all whooped, and Francesca looked pleased with herself. Her great good luck had held. It lifted our mood.

Margot was now fully restored to her normal cheery self.

"Darlings, as soon as you finish with the dinner chores, please get a hot shower and a good dinner. Francesca and I will handle bed check duties tonight. You were grand today, but I know that drive yesterday was exhausting. I want you two well-rested."

Francesca did not contradict Margot.

Natalie and I hurried through our chores. We showered and changed at the hotel, and then asked at the front desk where we could get a good dinner. When we got to the restaurant, we passed the bar, and caught a glimpse of Margot and Francesca and Dennis, sitting around one of those little round tables with high stools. They each clutched a glass of wine, faces illuminated by one of those squat candles in a red glass globe that sat in the middle. Francesca was sitting back in her high-backed stool, but Margot was leaning a little forward toward Dennis, clearly interested in what he had to say. They did not notice us. It did not look as though Natalie and I would need to pull Dennis in as a calming influence for Margot. He was in already.

# 26. Ka-Boom

*I took my turn the next morning to hand walk Hotstuff while Natalie* cleaned his stall and tidied up. When we arrived we caught Hotstuff craning his neck over the top of the side wall of his stall, taking in the smell of his next door neighbor, a little chestnut mare that reminded me of Winsome. She in return was squealing and lightly kicking against the wall, trying to convince him to "Stop looking at me!" Hotstuff was a peeping tom.

His bedding was less trampled, and he actually ate his breakfast and left the little chestnut mare in peace. When he finished eating, I pulled him out of the stall and over to a spot, muddy from the previous day of rain, but still with bits of short grass to pick at so I could chit-chat with Natalie and try to sip the last of my hotel coffee while she worked.

I couldn't see Natalie, but I knew she could hear me when I said, "Nat, I'm still a little concerned about Margot."

We had one of those aluminum folding muck carts that Nat had pulled half way into the stall with her. She was working quickly, forkfuls of dirty shavings and fecal balls flying through the air and making a "thunk" as each forkful landed in the cart. There was an art to sifting quickly through dirty shavings, shaking the good bits through the tines while chucking the fecal balls and soiled shavings into the cart. I admired Natalie's technique.

Natalie harrumphed and spoke from inside the stall, "For such a great rider, that woman sure can be anxious. I don't see how she's been at it all these years without learning to chill more at these things."

I defended Margot. "But we all expect her to win. This whole dog-and-pony show, with all the expense, well, it's all centered on Margot and how well she can perform. If she makes the tiniest mistake that costs her the championship, then it's on her. That's a tremendous amount of pressure. I admit I want her to win in the worst way. But even if we all believe that Hotstuff is the best four year old here, and that Margot is the best rider here, some of it is just up to chance. Hotstuff has to do his part, and the judges have to agree with us. Margot is ranked number two; we haven't even watched the number one horse go yet. It might be better than Hotstuff."

Natalie grunted. "I doubt it will be better than Hotstuff. If Margot rides like she rides at home, they'll be fine. But Lizzy, if they don't win, it won't be like the earth stops rotating, y'know? When you've been at it as long as Margot, you know that. Remember what you said she told you about last year's champion? None of you could remember the name of the horse or the rider."

I sighed. "If Hotstuff belonged to Margot, if the farm belonged to Margot, it might be different. Thing is, owners and breeders want results for all the money they put into it. Margot's feeling the pressure, but if she can't let it go then she'll handicap herself for sure. She won't be able to relax until she gets her first test over with, and she has to wait all day to do it. That waiting is a killer on nerves. I should know. I had to do that last weekend. It gives you too much time to be anxious. Margot has to wait until four to ride. If something doesn't change, I'm afraid she's going to be a wreck by then."

Natalie rolled the cart out of the doorway, and went into the tack room to grab a bag of shavings. She threw it down in the stall, then pulled a pocketknife out of her back pocket and neatly and quickly cut off the top of the plastic bag in a way that showed she had done this many, many times before. She turned the bag over and then shook out the block of compressed shavings, then closed her knife and slid it back into her pocket. The plastic wrapping got shoved down into the garbage can at the end of the barn aisle and the new shavings spread with the muck fork.

She finally replied. "It's just a game, Lizzy. I love the riding and the training, and if you think of the showing as an opportunity to test your training, well, it's not too bad. But, when the stakes get high, people get crazy. They get stupid crazy sometimes. You and I, we've seen it."

We were both silent while Natalie stuffed Hotstuff's hay bag, and then took the broom to sweep back the shavings from his doorway. She finished by dumping, scrubbing, and refilling his water buckets. Then she turned to Hotstuff and me and bowed.

"Housekeeping has taken care of your room, Hotstuff. I'll be back tonight to turn down the bed and leave a mint on your pillow."

I led Hotstuff back into his stall, slipping him a sugar cube before taking off his halter. He, of course, went right back to harassing his neighbor. Natalie and I watched and laughed. We finished setting up our table and sweeping and raking. We started a fresh pot of coffee and then sat down in our chairs and took in the morning.

It was one heck of a wet showground, and still overcast. Everything we owned felt damp. We had watched The Weather Channel in the room until it got tedious. The chances of decent weather without rain were dicey at best. At least it wasn't too hot, and the flies weren't bad; all good for August.

The coffee was good and strong. I had brought a selection of the good creamers, the kind made of real cream with flavored syrups. But even with caffeine and sugar, Natalie and I had grown quiet and sleepy sitting in the tall chairs by the stall. Just the idea of the long day ahead of us made me want to conserve my energy. Nat had just pulled her ball cap low over her eyes when Dennis appeared, toting a grocery bag in each hand.

He called out, "Good morning team Equus Paradiso!"

Even the tone of his voice made me think of Frank. Natalie pulled the bill of her cap up, and sat up taller. "What'cha got there, Dennis?"

"I stopped and picked up a few things. I know Frank makes sure you ladies eat well, and he would approve that I got a few healthy things to supplement the junk food you are probably eating. I brought some fruit, nuts, and some really good cheeses and small breads; although I am pleased to see you have some of my cookies."

I was confused. "How are those your cookies? Chess gave them to us."

Dennis smiled and pointed to the logo on the cookie bag. "That's our family business. It's how I first met Frank. We're both in the food import business, or were. Frank and I are retired to the life of country gentlemen now, of course. Or, you could say, we've been put out to pasture. Frank is the one who got me interested in this horse stuff after I complained about being bored." Dennis pointed again at the cookies. "That was nice of Chess to think of me when he stocked you two with cookies. They are damned good, if I say so myself."

Natalie and I exchanged a sideways glance. Then Natalie stood up and relieved Dennis of the grocery bags. "Thanks. You're a real sport, Dennis."

I added, "Thanks for filling in for Frank, you're right, he always brings the refreshments. I wish he were here. Not only does he supply us with food and drink, well, he kind of helps lighten up the atmosphere, too."

Dennis pointed at the coffee pot. "May I?"

I jumped out of my chair and grabbed a mug, filling it. "You never need to ask. Here, and we have a great selection of creamers in the ice chest." I handed him the coffee, and he rummaged for a creamer, then a spoon. Natalie pulled another chair over next to ours and patted the seat.

"Have a seat and chat us up. We don't get out much, Dennis."

Dennis laughed, but he took a seat, and then a sip of his coffee. He nodded his head. "Good coffee."

Natalie angled her chair to turn slightly toward Dennis. I turned my chair a little, too, then sat down. We looked like talk show hosts getting ready to conduct an interview, or maybe with two on one it looked more like an intervention. If it made Dennis nervous, he didn't show it. He nodded and took another sip of coffee before saying, "I wish Frank could have made it; I do enjoy his company. Francesca, too, although I realize she can be difficult."

Strangely I found myself defending Francesca. "She doesn't mean to be. I don't think she realizes how much pressure she puts on Margot. She puts as much or more on herself."

Dennis took a long sip of coffee, one that afforded him time to be thoughtful before answering. "I was shocked to find Margot's hands were trembling yesterday. Do you girls think she's afraid of that horse?"

I had to think about that before answering. I tried to find the right words, but it was hard. I said, "Hotstuff is the kindest horse we have. But imagine what it's like to sit on a nervous four year old horse. I mean, we know what it feels like, Nat and I. Once the horse explodes, there is very little to do about it but try to stay on the topside until it blows over. We try and prevent it, and if things begin to go south we try to stop, block, and redirect. It takes nerves of steel to handle TNT without your hands shaking and your knees going to jelly."

Dennis said, "So, she was scared of what the horse might do?"

I answered, "But that's not all of it. Hotstuff is ranked number two in the country, so it's almost hers to screw up if she finishes less than reserve champion. Nat and I will most likely never know what kind of pressure that is." I drew breath, and added, "Of course, for Francesca there is the pride of ownership, and all the money that she has poured down the drain that will never be recovered, regardless of the outcome. I don't know how much Margot or Francesca think about that part of it, but for sure I do."

Dennis' smile was fatherly, and perhaps a bit condescending. He said, "Girls, I wouldn't worry about that sort of thing. Frank would never begrudge Margot or the rest of you the money he puts into the farm and the horses. He knows it makes Francesca happy."

Dennis spoke with a calm authority. If I didn't know better, I would believe what he was saying. In fact, I would be warming up to him. It occurred to me then that I was probably speaking much too freely to Dennis. But he did put me at ease.

I agreed, "For Margot, I'm guessing, the pressure to live up to expectations comes from herself as much as from others. I think it was that, more than physical fear, that made her hands tremble."

Nat chimed in airily, "Add to that, of course, the fact that you being here was apparently a surprise."

I frowned at Natalie. Good God, the girl was going where she shouldn't go.

Dennis leaned back in his chair. "Ah. Now we get down to it."

I drew another deep breath, and realized that both Natalie and I were leaning slightly forward in our seats. Poor Dennis looked surrounded. He raised his eyebrows and smiled. "Oh ladies, some information should be carried close to the chest."

I looked shocked. "I would never..."

But Nat interrupted me. "She wouldn't, but I would."

Dennis startled, started laughing, and almost spilled his coffee.

Dennis turned to get a good long look at Natalie. "You look so tender in years and sweet and harmless, but alarms are going off in my head just looking at you, Natalie. I'll bet you could be dangerous."

I involuntarily guffawed, drawing a crooked smile from Natalie. Dennis would never know the truth of his assessment. At least I hoped he wouldn't.

Natalie leaned in even closer to Dennis, eyes twinkling. "Fact is, I love this gig. I adore Margot, love Deb, cherish my friend Lizzy here, and I even tolerate Francesca. So, y'know, I'm just looking out for my peeps here when I say that we have enough drama with the horses and the emotional roller coaster that comes with competitions without dealing with broken hearts and that sort of thing." Natalie winked and leaned back into her chair to sip her own cup of coffee.

Dennis took a long breath, tipped his head, and then took another sip. He didn't look uncomfortable exactly, just at a loss for words. He had just been warned off by someone less than half his age. All in all, the man took it well. I was shocked by Natalie's lack of a filter. I grimaced apologetically at Dennis, and then shook my head with raised eyebrows at Natalie, who looked pleased with herself.

Finally, he said, "I guess I've gotten the message, ladies. Francesca said almost the same thing to me after the last show. And I realize I've got fences to mend. You'll have to take me at my word. Margot and I, well, we are adults and we'll manage this ourselves. But I can say this with confidence; Margot's hands were not trembling because of me."

I nodded and put out my hand. "I'm going to take you at your word."

He smiled a big warm smile and firmly gripped my hand. "Thank you, Lizzy."

He turned and extended his hand to Nat who held his eye a moment before extending her hand, too. She said, "So, if that's the case, how about you keep Margot laughing all weekend, and if Francesca goes cray-cray you escort Margot far, far away?"

Dennis nodded. "Yes, ma'am. I understand my mission."

Then I brightened as a thought occurred to me. "Does this mean Margot agreed to take your mare for training?"

He chuckled. "At the end of the day with you girls, it's always about the horses, isn't it?"

I ignored Dennis' remark and instead proved it true by enthusing to Nat. "You should see this horse, Natalie! She is lovely. A big black Weltmeyer mare named Word Perfect. She wouldn't do a thing for Sophie, but then Margot gave her a boot and the mare turned on like an amazing ninja warrior. It was so cool to watch."

Dennis was now laughing loudly; relieved I think that I had changed the subject. "Lizzy, you remember her! Yes, she is a warrior, that one. Wordy was almost unrideable for Sophie, spent most of her time either rearing or running backward or kicking. Sophie claimed the horse had been drugged in Europe when we tried her, but Margot blew that theory out of the water by showing off how it was done."

I encouraged Dennis to continue by saying, "Such an awesome horse."

Dennis said, "I spent a small fortune on that mare. Did you know she has three foals on the ground? One was a test breeding done when she was only four, and then the previous owner has two he produced from embryo transfer. They've all been premium foals so the mare now has her SP status. I'd just put her in the breeding shed for good, but she knows all the Grand Prix so it would be a total waste not to compete her."

I innocently said, "Oh, so that's why you need Margot?"

Natalie smirked at me. I realized my faux pas. But Dennis didn't seem insulted.

Instead he confessed. "And why I'm here, too. I started Walker Sport Horses and Wordy will be my foundation mare. With Margot in the tack, it's going to be fun as hell. She can show Word Perfect, and once we start breeding, Margot can show the offspring in these classes."

Natalie turned her gaze away from Dennis and let out a wolf whistle that almost left a ringing in my ears. She shouted, "Here come our morning glories! Wow, Francesca, I'm digging your new footwear."

Natalie had effectively prevented Dennis and me from saying another word. Interview or intervention, whatever it was, had abruptly concluded. I admit, I felt like I still owed Dennis an apology for Nat's probing, and even for my thoughtless words that made him sound purely like an opportunist. Knowing Natalie as I did, I suppose she could have said worse. She didn't accuse him of being a member of the oligarchy or using child laborers in his cookie factories.

Margot and Francesca were strolling our way from the parking lot. Francesca was wearing some cool new boots. I had just admired them yesterday at one of the vendors' tents. A kid had been standing in a tub of water demonstrating how completely waterproof they were. Clearly Francesca was doing her duty to "support our vendors" as Frank had instructed. The one thing that seemed to always make Francesca happy was spending money. It never seemed to lose its charm. In this case though, I thought she had made a good purchase.

Margot was looking "put-together" as usual, but in clothes I recognized from home. If Dennis had gotten the Frank memo on being a supportive horse show guy, he would take care of that later at the vendor tents. Would Margot take the gifts? Because in my mind, the debt Dennis owed her couldn't be paid with money. Integrity had nothing to do with money. But I had shaken his hand, knowing that in the past he had betrayed my beloved Margot. Why? I was trying to compensate for Natalie, I guess, plus, it cost me nothing to be polite. And if he did make Margot happy then who was I to interfere? At least that was what I was telling myself.

Margot and Francesca helped themselves to coffee, Francesca eyeing the stall and the tack room in a not so subtle inspection. I watched her assess the level of cleanliness and order. She said nothing. Natalie noticed and winked at me before speaking.

"Sorry we've been sitting on our asses all morning, Francesca."

Francesca just said, "Hmmmm."

Natalie added, "Won't happen again."

Margot got the message. "Darlings, it looks neat as a pin, thank you. How's our young man feeling this morning?"

I chimed in. "I think he feels much more relaxed today."

Margot nodded. "Thank goodness. Yesterday was a bit too electric. I think I'll give him a short ride this morning, feel things out from the saddle. It's clearly not enough to just have you girls lead him around. He'll feel more relaxed with some exercise to burn off the nerves."

We all nodded in agreement. I thought to myself that Margot would also benefit from burning off some nerves. I also marveled at her relaxed tone and demeanor. This was my Margot, back in charge, making a plan and working it.

We got Hotstuff ready for Margot, putting on a brand new set of fleece-lined sport boots and four new, soft, white bell boots. His giant tail combed out easily, it was so clean and conditioned and spritzed with silicone hairspray even though the damp air made it hang heavily. Our boy might look juvenile and a bit raw-boned and slight, but he was glowing with good health and care.

Margot got him to tiptoe up the path without incident. Hotstuff was big eyed and wary, but he went. He even passed the boot vendor today without stopping. He did swing his neck around to peer into the tent, but it looked like he was looking for his new friend instead of feeling afraid.

The show was going on around him today and the warm up was busy, both with horses competing and horses like us who were having a training ride. Today Hotstuff stepped obediently into the warm up arena while his entourage found our spots again on the bit of grass on the short side of the arena. The sky was steel gray, the wind gusty, but the air mild. The footing was still heavy with yesterday's rain and squished-squished under the hooves of the horses. But it still looked like it had good traction.

Margot smiled and chatted with another competitor as she gathered Hotstuff together in the walk, shortening her reins. Then she posted trot around like any other training day. There was no drama and only the smallest tension. Francesca stood to my right, Natalie to my left, and Dennis on the other side of Francesca. I glanced over at Nat, and gave her a small "thumbs up" and she winked back at me. All seemed to be right in our little world.

And then in came a snorting dragon in size extra large, a horse that called to mind Wild Child, tall and stunningly beautiful with long spidery legs and a cresty neck. Like Wild Child, he was that bright shade of chestnut with glints of gold that shimmered over his muscles even though it was an overcast day. He had four evenly matched socks and a thin blaze; a young man almost as good looking as his horse sat on him. The man had long legs, a trim physique with square shoulders, a square jaw, and sat perfectly upright. They were not dressed to show, but in training attire, schooling just like Margot and Hotstuff.

Natalie elbowed me. "Too cool for school, those two."

I was confused. I whispered back. "What's that supposed to mean?"

Nat replied, "Stallion with more testosterone than training I'm betting, and a young guy who knows too well how good he looks. Bet both of them have shit for brains."

When Natalie said that sort of thing I was speechless. So I stood back to watch what was one incredibly gorgeous hunk of a horse with his hunk of a rider. They were both fun to look at for sure. He passage trotted past Margot and Hotstuff, but was over-flexed in the neck with a wild eye. Hotstuff looked intimidated and tucked his tail, appearing to shrink in size. Our poor baby horse.

Francesca was frantically flipping through her program. Then she exhaled loudly and exclaimed, "Oh, for crying out loud!"

Dennis frowned. "What is it?"

She shook her head before spitting out, "That's him. That's the horse ranked number one in the country. His name is Rocket Socks."

Dennis looked back at the horse and rider, and I could see his jaw clench. He said softly, but loud enough that we three heard, "Let's not say anything in front of Margot about that horse, shall we? She looks so happy and relaxed today."

In response we nodded in agreement like a row of bobble-head dolls. But, oh my God, that horse was beautiful. The guy was having trouble getting the horse to focus, and riding pretty strongly, but even still, our Hotstuff looked plain and coarse next to him.

Margot rode for about half an hour, going through her normal work routine with Hotstuff. He finished soft as butter, making smooth and forward going transitions all around the arena. Margot looked relaxed and elegant too, and came out of the arena patting Hotstuff and smiling to us.

"Well, I for one am pleased."

I piped up. "Margot, he looked great." Dennis and Natalie voiced similar compliments. Francesca said, "Big improvement," and nodded sternly.

For Francesca, that was high praise indeed.

Luckily for us, Margot never asked a single question about Rocket Socks. She, like us, had never seen the horse before, and without a program had not connected the dots like we had.

Once we had Hotstuff put away for a rest period, Natalie had her thumbs working at high speed zipping around the internet on her phone to get more information on Rocket Socks than was contained in our program.

Rocket Socks had come all the way from Nevada. The stallion had been purchased from Europe by a syndicate after winning his stallion test just six months ago. The rider was a young American who had been working at a famous young horse trainer's barn in Germany. He was barely out of the young adult division, and this was his first year back in the States. We looked up all the scores for this horse, which were not much higher than Hotstuff's, and just like Hotstuff, he had only done enough showing to qualify and no more. European shows were not reflected or recorded by our Federation.

Okay, so Natalie and I agreed that Rocket Socks was impressive, and seemed to have big money behind him. But we had a great horse with a brilliant and tactful rider on his back. We were not out of the game, and we were not going down without a fight.

The four year old division of the USEF Young Horse National Championships was the largest division of the show. And Margot was almost the last ride of the class... except for one other horse: Rocket Socks. It almost didn't seem possible since the order was by random draw, but second seeded Hotstuff pulled the second to last spot, and top seeded Rocket Socks had the last spot.

Natalie and I watched some of the early horses in the class go, and even though I found myself tense and full of anxiety watching, it was clear to me that none of the horses I watched were as wonderful as our boy. Not to say they weren't good horses, they were. But most of them had a weakness that even I could identify. It's rare to see a horse with three good gaits that are not only flashy, but swing over a relaxed back. Trots can appear brilliant from tension, but that tension ruins the quality of the walk and canter. A tense horse doesn't make elastic transitions between the gaits or stretch forward and downward toward the contact without losing balance in that all-important part of the test called the stretchy circle. All sorts of things were revealed about a horse and its training in the simple test for four year olds. All in all, I gained confidence for our horse by watching the other horses.

The class wore on as the sky darkened. Natalie and I went back to the stables to finish our final preparations. Hotstuff looked content. He was munching hay, his braids tight, his coat slick and shiny under the stable lights that someone had flipped on. I was sure that in his mind his workday was done. His hay bag was full and he was as snug as a bug in a rug.

By three o'clock the rain started and my confidence began to wane. As much as possible, an entire class was supposed to compete under the same conditions. But, no one controls the weather. As long as the conditions were not deemed dangerous, which meant high winds or lightning, the show would go on.

It didn't mean any of us were cheerful about it. Margot looked grim as she approached the stall, dressed for her ride. Francesca was shaking out Margot's brand new rain jacket. Margot took a seat in one of the director's chairs and Dennis sat down next to her.

I tried to lighten the mood. "Margot, this is just like the very first test you had with Hotstuff. Remember how wonderful he was that day in the pouring rain?"

Margot made a weak smile. "Darling, yes. He *was* wonderful wasn't he?"

I nodded. "He charmed all the judges. Remember how your mascara ran? I hope you used waterproof today."

Now she smiled bigger and nodded. "Oh my yes. You don't need to remind me."

Natalie pulled Hotstuff out of the stall and pulled the stirrups down with a loud "snap," "snap." Hotstuff swiveled his big long ears around as if sending out radar scans, searching for Margot. All she had to do was say his name to get him to swing his long inelegant head around, his target located.

"Here I am, you big puppy-dog." Margot moved around and gave Hotstuff a scratch on his withers. He stretched out his neck and pointed his upper lip and wiggled it side to side with obvious pleasure. "He does look relaxed. Good boy, Hotstuff." I handed Margot her helmet and her gloves. Francesca was holding out the raincoat toward Margot and Margot pursed her lips considering her options. "Francesca, darling, I think I'll be too warm with that on. Shall I take a gamble that the rain will stay light and skip it?"

Francesca frowned. "That is entirely up to you. I plan on taking my umbrella because frankly, Margot, the radar on my phone is not encouraging."

Dennis, who had been staying quiet, put his arm out. "Francesca, let me take that up to the arena then; just in case."

Natalie was getting impatient; she tapped her watch. "Hotstuff is willing to go out and strut his stuff, but if you wait much longer he may change his mind and decide to go back in his stall and watch the show on my laptop instead."

Margot laughed out loud. "Well, I wouldn't blame him. All right, my darlings. Let's do this."

And we got her up and off they headed. Natalie and I pulled on our ball caps and our raincoats, and the rain, although light, appeared to have settled in.

We followed Hotstuff and Margot up to the warm up arena. Francesca had a huge umbrella and Dennis a much smaller one, but as soon as we got to the arenas, they peeled off and headed for the VIP section where they could simultaneously watch the class under the protection of the tents and keep an eye on Margot.

Natalie and I stood on the patch of grass that had become our station, along with a lot of other coaches and grooms. Nat carried a bucket of grooming supplies with a towel thrown over the top. We pulled our baseball caps down and the hoods of our rain slickers up, but it was hopeless. The rain ran down my jacket onto my jeans, soaking them through; my socks soaked up the water like a wick, pulling the wetness down into my clogs.

I watched Margot soldier on in the warm up as the rain came down harder, and concluded that acceptance was the only way to go. We all had jobs to do, requiring a disassociation with the physical discomfort that was part of the game. If Margot could do it with grace and style, then I needed to do the same. I glanced at Nat and saw a similarly determined expression on her face. I looked over to the VIP section to see that Francesca's arms were folded across her chest, her head tipped, as she watched Margot and Hotstuff. Dennis still had Margot's rain jacket, useless, hanging over his arm.

I turned my attention back to Margot and Hotstuff. They looked good, even with Hotstuff's beautiful full tail sagging with the weight of rainwater and the grey sand that was sticking to it. It wasn't a bad thing, as it gave him the look of an upper level horse with a lowered croup and springy bending joints behind. I knew he would get tired quickly though, carrying a tail weighted down like a sandbag. Fortunately, Margot had scheduled a short warm up since he had gone already this morning.

After about ten minutes, Rocket Socks and his handsome rider joined the warm up arena. He just about sucked all the air out of the arena. Hotstuff tried to stop and pick up his head to have a look; his eyes rimmed in white. He was clearly afraid of Rocket Socks. Natalie shook her head and mumbled, "Hotstuff, he's a bunch of bluff and bluster that signifies nothing. Go on, babycakes, go on."

And as if he heard her, he put his head back down and went back to work. The rain picked up, and the ring steward called out Margot's number. She was "on deck." My stomach turned a flip. Margot came over to us and we pulled off his wet sport boots. There was really no point in doing more. Dirt spots splattered Margot's white breeches. Hotstuff's stomach, legs, and even his chest were dirty. Natalie ran the towel over him, but it was useless. I gave him a partially dissolved sugar cube that I fished out of a Tupperware tub and offered Margot water, but she shook her head "no."

The horse in front of her headed down centerline for their final salute. It was time.

Margot and Hotstuff trotted into the competition arena boldly. So boldly that it was really a medium trot. Within seconds the judge blew the whistle and Margot now had forty-five seconds to enter the arena. Then, as if someone opened a spigot in the sky, the rain went from steady to torrential. I glanced over at Francesca and Dennis huddled under the tent and noticed that the canvas roofline was drooping with the weight of water filling it up like a woman's outstretched apron. That couldn't be good.

But I had no time to ponder that effect because Hotstuff was trucking down the centerline looking like a million bucks. He nailed his entry and halt and splashed happily through the standing water with his huge round hooves, his abscess long forgotten. He put a grin on my face as his huge ears hung to the side and flopped with each bounce. Hotstuff oozed charm.

The rain pelted down noisily as it pounded on the roof of the pavilions and the canvas of the tents. Hotstuff went through his test patterns like a metronome, keeping his head down and his ears to the side, his tail a bit tucked but otherwise looking no different in his work than on a sunny day.

And then...*Ka-BOOM!*

It sounded like the tents had been struck by lightning. Francesca and Dennis had jumped out from under their tent and now stood fidgeting nervously under the nearest pavilion, crowded with spectators. People who had been under the tents were in motion; chairs were being moved. I quickly turned my eyes back to Margot and Hotstuff; apparently they hadn't missed a beat.

Again...*Ka-BOOM!*

This time I witnessed the source of the commotion. The canvas apron had dumped its heavy contents right into the competition arena as if a dam had broken, the canvass snapping back into shape. It seemed louder than yesterday, perhaps because of the torrents of rain overloading the tent's load capacity so quickly and almost violently. Miraculously, the tents still stood. Of course, the tent apron started filling up again as the rain continued coming down in sheets.

Hotstuff finished his stretchy circle with his nose extra low, came back into the contact and finished his very smooth test.

In the downpour, even Natalie's wolf whistle was barely audible.

In the young horse classes, even though there are four judges, it is the head judge positioned behind the letter "C" who publicly announces the scores and assessment at the end of the class. The horse and rider stay in front of the judge's box to hear their shortcomings and strengths publicly critiqued. We could barely hear the judge as the rain continued to pound down, but did hear that Hotstuff had gotten a score of 10 for submission; a rarity. During the public scoring, Hotstuff hung his head down, ears flopped to the side, rested one hind leg, and appeared to be grabbing a power nap in the midst of a downpour. I could see that Margot and the judge were laughing, even though I couldn't hear a word that they said.

Natalie and I got the rain-drenched Margot off Hotstuff as soon as she came out of the arena. She hugged Hotstuff's neck, embraced all of us, then walked to the pavilion to join Francesca and Dennis. We were instructed to take Hotstuff back to the barn and clean him up before the awards ceremony.

Natalie and I had been dismissed. My "misery factor" was growing due to my wet and sandy socks that were inching down around my heels into my clogs and my saturated jeans, but I didn't want to hurry back to the stables. Nat and I gave each other a knowing glance. We dawdled in order to see Rocket Socks do his test. Natalie and I moved Hotstuff slowly past the tents, but then we pulled him to the side, out of the traffic, and peered under his neck. We noticed that most people had stayed, huddled together under the pavilions. Like us, everyone was hanging around to see the top-ranked Rocket Socks perform.

Like Wild Child, Rocket Socks had presence that could not be denied. Though I envied his rider for being able to ride such an incredible horse, I did not envy the pressure he was under. There had to be huge expectations. I didn't think for one second that the judges weren't feeling it, too. Coming into the competition ranked number one, this was the horse that they were expected to reward. The sponsors were expecting to be rewarded, too, for all the money they had invested in the pipeline of future team horses.

Hotstuff went into his "zone" after turning his butt into the wind, and lowering his head until he had tucked his nose between my knees. Now Natalie and I were looking over his neck to watch. Rocket Socks started his test well. His trot had a lot of knee action and I wondered how well he would lengthen that stride. He was close coupled, so he stepped well under himself. As I predicted, his lengthened trot didn't look any different than his working trot. I thought that should cost him points. The canter had a nice lift to the knee, but I didn't think it was better than Hotstuff's. The rain was still pelting down on us, and I glanced over to the tents to see that the roofline was sagging with water. The apron looked full to me. Something had to give.

It was in the second canter depart when the canvas roof had reached its maximum load capacity, again. I braced myself. "Ka-BOOM!"

Rocket Socks took off, bucking down the long side of the arena. Hotstuff lifted his head in alarm, jolted out of his dream-state but thankfully staying put. Natalie leaned over smiling and said, "Houston, we have a problem."

I laughed and replied, "Looks like the Rocket exploded on lift off."

We had lingered long enough. We turned Hotstuff back to the stables to clean him up, laughing at our joke and feeling hopeful about the awards ceremony. Margot and Dennis and Francesca joined us, but soon Margot would need to get back on and go to the arena for an awards ceremony in a rain that was still coming down, not quite as hard, but good and steady.

In the end it did not matter. Today's award ceremony was postponed and would be combined with the final award ceremony tomorrow.

The important thing was that Hotstuff had won day one.

# 27. The 4-H's

*Even though Natalie and I had a leisurely day ahead of us, we still* had to get up early to feed and care for Hotstuff. It didn't mean we didn't linger over our plates full of sausage and bacon and eggs and buttermilk biscuits loaded up off the steam tables at the hotel. I felt slightly ill when we climbed into the farm truck to go to the stables. We had stayed out late the night before since Dennis had treated us all to a good dinner. Nat had our debit card in her back pocket, but she sat on it all evening and let Dennis buy. I noticed Francesca sat on her credit cards, too. But no matter, it was a joyous night of victory with all the tension of the day gone. We had lingered at the dinner table with Dennis ordering a bottle of Dom Perignon to accompany our desserts. By the time the bottle was half empty, Natalie had led us in a few songs. Fortunately, by that time the restaurant was mostly empty and the place ready to close up. I could only hope Dennis left a hefty tip as compensation for our table-hogging and general rowdiness.

This morning I drove the farm truck and a very subdued Nat rode shotgun back to the show grounds. I wondered if she had a hangover. My limit on champagne was less than a glass. Nat had no such limit. I finally prodded her. "Nat? You feeling okay?"

She sat up a little straighter and then stretched and yawned. "Hmmmm? Oh, yeah. I'm coming alive. But I've been thinking."

I smiled. "Don't scare me, Natalie."

Natalie grinned. "I was thinking of Rocket Socks and the scores he got yesterday."

I sighed and nodded my head in agreement. "Are you still thinking about that ten he got for his trot?"

Natalie nodded, and said, "Yeah, that floored me. The horse had a lot of action in his knees and hocks, and lots of cadence. But, he did the exact same trot for his lengthening. Fact was, there was no lengthening. No way that trot deserved a ten."

I nodded again, and added, "I think that ten for the trot was an early gift from Santa."

Natalie sighed and looked out the window, saying matter-of-factly, "They knew they couldn't place him first after his bucking spree, but they intentionally over-scored his trot to keep him in the running for Champion on Sunday. It was a gift to the owners and the powers that be that solicit the donations. It was a promise by the judges. I'm afraid, Lizzy, that tomorrow, unless Rocket Socks loses it again, well, tomorrow they pay off the promissory note they signed yesterday."

My cheeks flushed. Natalie was too much. "Natalie, I simply don't believe that judges think like that. I mean, that's a really serious accusation."

Natalie shook her head, looking at me like I was a school child who did not understand a simple concept. "Lizzy, the pressure and influence I'm talking about is real. I'm not saying that the judges sit around and make decisions before the horses even go. But the judges are only human. They heard the buzz about this horse and the big plans that the organization has to cultivate this horse's owners into big time donors. I bet each of those judges has been online to research this horse and the scores the European judges have already awarded him, just so they have a baseline on what to score him."

I was silent as I absorbed Natalie's jarring analysis. "So, Nat, what you are saying is that the judges will be sure to over-reward that horse tomorrow so that he beats Hotstuff?"

Now she grimaced. "I wish I were wrong. But, I bet you he will get another ten on that Hackney horse trot of his that has no medium or extension in it. The judges went out on the limb for it yesterday, and they won't crawl back tomorrow."

I added, "And you think they went out on that limb in order to cancel out our horse's ten for submission?"

Nat pointed her index finger and thumb at me like a gun, and then pretended to shoot it, "Bulls-eye, babycakes."

I felt increasingly depressed. "Shit, Natalie. Are you saying that unless Rocket Socks has another meltdown, the best we can do is second place?"

I had to let that sink in a bit, then added, "Maybe we can have another rainstorm."

Nat blurted out, "Ha!"

I pulled into the show grounds and cut the engine. I was looking out on another gray day; the place, even with all the bright yellow flowers everywhere, seemed sodden and mucky and I suddenly wanted to go home. Or cry. Or cry driving home. I said, "What's the weather forecast?"

Nat had her smart phone in front of her and tapped the screen. "Rains moving out, cool air and sunshine moving in. It's going to be beautiful for days."

We looked at each other and simultaneously said, "Shit."

Nat and I stayed pretty quiet while we knocked out our chores. Natalie didn't admit it, but I'm pretty sure she was nursing a hangover. Today I mucked while Natalie hand grazed Hotstuff. I kept thinking about what Natalie had said in the truck. I would have continued the discussion while I mucked, but one thing I had learned at the first show from Emma was that the walls had ears. There were others about, quietly caring for their own horses, and what I had to say was not for public consumption. So, I waited until we had made our pot of coffee and were ready to sit. Our stall and area looked neat and tidy. I had even made a herringbone pattern in the dirt aisleway with our garden rake.

Natalie and I were sitting and sipping when I brought it back up. "I'm depressed now. Do you think Margot realizes the deck is stacked against her?"

Natalie tipped her head back and seemed to be examining the underside of the roof overhang. "Oh yeah, for sure. By this time, Margot's forgotten more about how this game is played than we'll probably ever know."

"And Francesca?" I asked.

Now she turned her attention to me. "You know better than I do what goes on inside that head of hers. But, Francesca strikes me as someone who understands how money changes everything. Francesca ought to be thrilled if her horse comes in second when all is said and done. I mean, that's her homebred. No one got a big commission selling her that horse, and I don't see anyone from the big office dancing around her, either. That's a clear sign she hasn't given any sizeable donations to the foundation. She knows if she wants to draw their attention, she'll have to pony up. The fact that no one appears to be courting her means they think it's a waste of their time."

I contemplated that. "I think no matter what you say, we all expected Hotstuff to dominate. Even you."

Natalie was quiet for a few beats then said. "Yeah. And I still think he is the best horse here. If he stays healthy and with Margot, he'll make Grand Prix one day because he has what it takes here." And she pointed to her head. "And here." And she pointed to her heart. Then she said in exasperation. "And for God's sake, his gaits are correct and big and swinging without looking like a park horse."

Then with a soft voice I added. "Hotstuff is still immature looking though, even if he has developed a lot this year. He is what he is; a tall unfinished four-year-old gelding, raw boned with funny giant ears."

Natalie nodded, "And Rocket Socks looks like a champion. He may be the same age as Hotstuff, but Rocket Socks is like an equine version of a male body builder; clearly hyped up on testosterone. We all had our hair blown back when he entered the warm up arena. You gotta admit that."

We sat in silence for a few more moments. Then Nat leaned forward. "Lizzy, you and me, we need to forget all about the drama crap and have some fun. It is what it is, and there's nothing we can do to change it; not unless you want me to pay someone to knock over a table during Rocket Socks' test."

My mouth fell open and I reached over and smacked her on the knee.

Natalie laughed and then said, "Hey, it could happen!"

I leaned my head in my hand and said, "Don't even joke about it, Natalie."

Natalie waved her hand across her face like she was shooing flies. She said, "Margot will give Hotstuff a little ride some time today, but the rest of the day is ours to watch the show. It's basically a goof off day. That's sweet, man, we gotta take it." Natalie slapped me on the knee, and it appeared that the conversation about judging and donating money and expectations was officially over.

Dennis arrived ahead of "the ladies" and poured himself a cup. "So, girls, what have you planned for your free day?"

I answered first. "We are going to spectate. How about you?"

"Well, that's where I was heading. Why don't you two come sit at my table? I paid plenty for the honor of the thing; might as well use it. I'm sure Margot and Francesca will be able to find us once our sleeping beauties are good and ready to find us."

Natalie lifted her feet off the footrest on her stool and exclaimed, "These old dogs have been barking all morning. Sounds sweet sitting in the VIP section and pretending we are one of the gentry."

Dennis looked at his watch. "The five-year-olds are about to start."

Natalie and I stood up, then Nat said, "Let's make this interesting by each of us guessing the scores and seeing who gets closest."

Dennis smiled, "Would you like to place wagers?"

Natalie winked. "Only if you insist, Dennis."

Nat tipped her head toward the tack room and said, "Lizzy, bring our programs, and dig up a few pens."

\*\*\*

It felt good to go into the reserved seating area and sit at Dennis' table. He even went and got us fresh cups of coffee from the hospitality table. Then the fun began. There was a score given for walk, trot, canter, submission, and general impressions, so we had to come up with five numbers. Although each score was interesting, the wager was won or lost by who got closest to the total.

We bet with "chits" of one-dollar value. After the fifth horse had its score announced, Nat had a stack of chits, and Dennis and I were "out." She was too good.

Dennis pulled out his wallet, and generously paid both his debt and mine. He said, "Ah, Natalie, let me guess, you've trained as a judge?"

Natalie pulled a small zippered wallet out of her back pocket and tucked the bills inside. She smiled, "I never graduated, but yeah, I did both the USDF Learner's program, and then started the small "r.""

Dennis nodded, then said, "I knew you were a ringer. Alright then, give us a play by play so we can learn something while we watch."

She agreed. Dennis and I sat watching the next horse do its test, while Natalie whispered to us things like, "walk has a clean four beat rhythm and clear over track, but could show more freedom in the shoul-

der and ground cover. 7.8" Or "Trot tempo is hasty rather than impulsive with a loss of balance on the forehand. 7.0." Or "Canter shows
promise with a good rhythm and balance and a marked jump, but could
show more scope and ground cover. 7.5."

Natalie was good and quick and sounded just like a real judge. I was
impressed and so was Dennis. At the end of each ride the head judge
took the microphone and announced the scores and the general assessment. Although Nat's scores were not always exact, they were damned
close. And the words Natalie had chosen were the same words used by
the judges.

I said to Nat, "You're a natural at this."

Natalie hesitated, and then answered. "There was a time I was going
to be a pro, and that included becoming a judge. That was a lifetime ago.
I was a gung-ho young rider. Not like our Ryder, of course. No, not like
her, but I never meant to still be a groom all these years later."

I exchanged looks with Dennis who looked interested. I said, "Natalie, you are better than Ryder in every way and you know it."

She nodded once. "Damn straight I am. Not only that, I'm also
really modest."

That made Dennis and me laugh.

Natalie never pretended she wasn't good, but on the other hand, she
had never told me she had gone through the judges' program or any
other details of her showing days. Yet she was seemingly content riding
the babies with Deb, when frankly her skill set showed she clearly had
experience and knowledge and had ridden at an advanced level. However, her experience and knowledge explained why she was so damn
good on the babies. Nat was not "still waters" but the more I got to
know her, the deeper I found those not-very-still waters to be.

Dennis asked, "So Natalie, while you might be unsatisfied with the
job of groom, I take it you no longer want to be a professional dressage
trainer or a judge?"

She finished her coffee, then said, "You got that right. I'd like to own my own horse again, and I might even like to show again…on my terms. Right now, I'm happy making my art and hanging out with you good people. That's enough for me."

Margot and Francesca did find us, just as Dennis predicted. Francesca took note of Natalie and me sitting at Dennis' table. She didn't say anything, but she narrowed her eyes at us and I found myself standing up as if to offer her my seat; stupid really. Equus Paradiso had the adjoining table, and Natalie and I were taking up only two seats at an eight top. But I had popped up like a buck private in the presence of an officer.

Margot waved me back down. "Darlings, sit and relax. This is our one day to simply enjoy the show. We'll be back to show-mode soon enough."

Francesca's mouth turned down at the corners. But she said nothing. Never had I been invited to sit with Francesca in the sponsors' tent. But here we were, of course only at the invitation of Dennis.

Natalie's show program was sitting in the middle of the table, with Natalie's scores scribbled in the margins, and the official scores filled out in the spaces provided.

Margot asked to look at the program, and we all quieted down as the next horse came into the arena. Dennis looked at Natalie, waiting for her to assess the gaits. But she sat silent.

When the horse had finished the trot work and was at walk he leaned toward Nat.

"What say you, Miss Natalie?"

I saw Margot run her finger down the side of the program, and then look back up at Natalie.

I leapt in to explain. "We've been entertaining ourselves by scoring the horses. Natalie has been spot on. She's good at this. I didn't know it but she'd started the process of getting her judge's card."

Natalie chimed in. "Not started; stopped. I dropped out."

Margot was examining the page again and then looked back up. "Natalie, darling, this is practically spot on. Why did you quit?"

Natalie chuckled and said, "Margot, I so do NOT have the temperament to be a judge."

Margot, seeming to agree with Natalie's statement, handed the program back to Natalie with a smile and a nod of her head.

Francesca said with wry amusement, "Refreshingly honest aren't you, Natalie?"

Margot smiled, "Well, Natalie, the judges' program is valuable even if ultimately you don't become a licensed judge. I'm glad to know you have such a good eye. I'm afraid we underutilize your talents at home. In the future, we'll use you to score some test riding."

Natalie shot me a look that said, "Thanks a lot."

Dennis turned his attention from Natalie and me to Margot and Francesca. "So, Margot, what do you think of this one?"

But the horse had just finished the test and the judges were finishing up talking to each other and dictating scores to the scribe.

Margot said, "Ah darlings, here are the real experts." And she motioned to the head judge who had stood up and taken the mike to begin her public scoring and assessment.

I looked over to Nat who quickly drew an imaginary zipper across her lips and fidgeted in her seat. She was ready to move.

Francesca eyed both of us and said, "Margot, what time would you like the girls to have Hotstuff ready for you?"

Margot was watching the next horse warm up around the outside of the arena, waiting for the bell. She whispered, "Not yet, Francesca."

And Francesca whispered back. "Would you like them to hand walk or graze him?"

Margot never sounded annoyed, but even I could tell Francesca was getting on Margot's nerves. "Not yet, Francesca."

It occurred to me then that Francesca just wanted us gone from the sponsors' area. Steerage had snuck into first class. I think, but couldn't know for sure, that Natalie had gotten the same signals and that's why she was looking antsy.

Dennis had the smallest smile, just enough to crease the outside corners of his eyes. He said, "Lizzy, Natalie, you girls coming to the sponsors' party tonight?" Francesca cut her eyes toward Dennis in disapproval, but she said nothing. He continued. "I have some extra guest passes and I don't have anyone to give them to, unless Francesca already gave you hers."

I looked at Margot, who also had a small smile. She nodded to me.

I said, "Nat and I didn't bring anything to wear to a party."

He said, "Oh I'm sure no one will be dressed up. We're at a horse show, for God's sake, and it's a competitors' party." Dennis pulled his wallet out and handed us each a ticket. He continued, "I wouldn't be surprised if most folks are wearing jeans. The food and drink should be decent, so, you girls come and have a good time."

Francesca spoke up. "It's a free country and I won't try and stop you two, but I expect no more than one drink each and an early bedtime. Tomorrow is a very important day and I don't want hungover grooms."

Her warning was actually a blessing of sorts. I said, "Thank you so much, Francesca; I mean, Dennis, thank you!" I picked up both tickets. Then I figured I should give Francesca what she wanted and scram. I said, "Natalie, let's go look at the clothes for sale. Maybe we could find something for tonight, if not that, at least buy some swag to commemorate the weekend."

***

There was no way either Natalie or I were going to pay fifty dollars for a shirt, which was the bottom dollar for a shirt at any of the vendor tents.

The belts and jewelry were even more expensive. I had Natalie's leather bracelet in my suitcase and I would wear that for sure. Natalie wore four different leather bracelets on her arms, along with a large faced man's wristwatch set in a wide leather band that looked like something a burly biker would wear. But it suited Nat. Natalie was tiny and small framed, there was nothing masculine about her, but it was beyond my abilities to imagine Nat in a dress, even after she surprised me with our savvy shopping trip we had made for my big date with Chess.

I flipped through a rack and shook my head. "What are we going to wear?"

Natalie shrugged her shoulders. "Jeans and a clean shirt and we wash the mud off our shoes."

I felt a wave of indecision. "I know it was nice of Dennis to ask, but do we really want to go?"

Natalie gave me a whack on my back. "Hell yes, Lizzy. First off, the food and drink will be good stuff. Second, you and I may be outsiders in this game, but what you don't get, my friend, is that a seat in the balcony is sometimes the best seat in the house. You can watch and narrate the drama without being one of the cast members. It's great fun as long as you don't give a shit."

I was shocked and I am sure she could see it on my face. "But Natalie, you do care and don't deny it."

Her eyes softened a bit. "I limit the number of people and animals I care about, Lizzy."

She added as an afterthought, "I'm not always joking, you know. Careful who and what you invest yourself in."

I nodded, "Like the results of horse shows."

"That, and the crazy-ass people who are too invested in the results of a horse show, because once the stakes get high, they get scary-nuts."

I smiled. "So, we go to the party tonight in our last pair of clean jeans, scrape all the mud off our shoes, and stuff ourselves on party food."

She grinned and slapped me again on the back. "Yup. It will be sweeeet!"

Natalie and I each bought a ball cap and a tee-shirt with the competition logo on it, just as a tourist would, to prove they actually had gone somewhere.

And we used the debit card from Frank to pay for it, which caused me some discomfort, considering what I knew about Frank's finances. But I stayed silent on the subject and thought that Frank would not begrudge me a ball cap and tee-shirt.

The day passed pleasantly enough. Margot and Hotstuff had a very casual ride. We never saw Rocket Socks work, but there was a another warm up arena nearer the barn and I had a sense that the trainer of Rocket Socks had almost worked those fancy socks right off that horse away from the eyes of any spectators. They couldn't afford another blow up tomorrow. A tired horse is usually less inclined to have a bucking fit. It was simply too much work. On the other hand, a tired horse rarely shows his maximum brilliance.

The party was held in a small older clubhouse at a nearby golf course. Dennis continued to be sweet. When we walked in, looking every bit like the grooms we were, he welcomed us loudly, waving us over to his side. He was so jolly; I thought perhaps he had already hit the bar a few times. Once again, he reminded me of Frank, and it made me miss Frank and wish he had been able to come.

Dennis got our drink orders then ushered us over to a little table with a heavily starched white tablecloth. A pretty tall blonde and another girl who was clearly also a groom were already seated there. We chatted amiably and I had an OMG moment when I realized who the tall blonde was. Famous. Deep breaths. It was like the first time I had met Margot. I still found myself star struck. When Dennis came back with our drinks, he had another famous rider in tow; this one a past Olympian. My heart started thudding and I was afraid I would start hyperventilating. I was very uncomfortable. Where were the seats in the balcony that Natalie had promised? I glanced over at Nat who was looking amused. Introductions were made all around, and I was shocked when the Olympian walked around to Natalie's chair and gave her a long hug. "Nat, this is great. I haven't seen you in forever. How is your horse doing?"

Natalie had a pleasant expression, but answered matter-of-factly, "Done. Turned out."

The Olympian seemed authentically sad. "I'm so sorry. It happens to all of us at one point or another. So what are you riding these days?"

Natalie now smiled. "Aw man, the cutest little booger with springs in his toes. I'm working at Equus Paradiso now, having a good time riding the youngsters."

Nat's Olympic friend looked thoughtful, then brightened. "Francesca Cavelli's farm?" She paused without saying another word about Francesca, then continued, "Margot is wonderful, one of my favorite people. And I hope they understand how lucky they are to have you."

Natalie's eyes twinkled as she said, "So, does that mean the next time they want to fire me, I can call you?"

She chuckled, fished out a business card, jotted a phone number on it, and handed it to Natalie. "In a heartbeat. Nat, you haven't changed a bit. I still do clinics up your way, so if you ever want to bring your little booger and ride for me again, I'll make sure you get a spot."

And Nat smiled again. "That'd be a treat. I'd sure love to."

Dennis made a few pleasantries with her, and in a minute or two, she excused herself and drifted off to mingle. Dennis turned to Natalie. "Natalie, you are full of surprises."

Nat winked. "I like to keep it that way, Dennis."

We greeted Margot and Francesca as they came in, both looking lovely, not too dressy, not too casual. Margot still wore her signature bun, and a pair of tan slacks and a blue collared sleeveless silk blouse with long multiple strands of colored pearls around her neck and a matching bracelet on her right wrist, her slender wrist watch on her left wrist. She always looked sleek and elegant without looking fussy or overdressed.

Francesca was Francesca; a little too thin, a little too much make up, and although I thought her bronze colored sheer blouse over black slacks were a bit severe, it suited her in every way. Margot was summer; Francesca was winter. Either way, they were not to be ignored. Immediately people were greeting them. Dennis hopped up and scurried to fetch them drinks. Waiters with little silver trays seemed eager to offer them tidbits, and soon people were waving them over to join little knots of people.

Natalie practically tripped one of the waiters. "What'cha got there?" He leaned down to show us his tray. "Asparagus wrapped in bacon." Natalie squinted at him. "Be honest. Is it any good?" The waiter smiled. "The asparagus is tough and the bacon chewy." She laughed. "And?" "And I'd skip the Satay chicken on skewers, too." "Anything good?" "The citrus marinade grilled shrimp is good. I like the stuffed cherry tomatoes, too. But, honestly, the prime rib is coming and I had a taste of that and it was very tender with good flavor, so save room."

Natalie slapped her knee. "You are a good man. If I had any money I'd give you a tip, but as you can see, we're lowly grooms trying to cage a free meal. Carry on, my good man."

He winked, "I'll be sure to send some grilled shrimp and tomatoes your way, but remember about the prime rib."

Someone tapped a glass with a knife and moved to the middle of the room to speak. Behind them waiters began to set up the steam tables (and I noted, a carving station). The head of the high performance league began his speech, followed by the Olympian. It was an update of the goals of the national young horse program, which was to find and develop a pipeline of top horses in the USA to develop for international competitions.

In addition, the Olympian spoke about the talent search clinics to identify horses and riders closer to the advanced level. It was impressive to hear about the USA trying to emulate the horse-centric countries of Europe. The idea was to identify not only young horses with talent, but young riders with talent. Then of course, the challenge was to see that those two pieces of the puzzle found each other. Good young horses needed talented trainers and riders, and vice-versa.

I knew that Ryder would have loved to have been in my seat at that party. She would have been eagerly fawning over the director for the rest of the evening. Both speakers did an excellent job speaking and could have done well on the motivational circuit.

A third and final speaker from the foundation rose to recognize those who had demonstrated their belief and commitment through continued financial support. Those donors were asked to stand.

Natalie elbowed me hard when one older couple stood up.

I tried to tactfully mouth two words to her behind my hand. "Rocket Socks?"

She whispered back. "Damn straight."

I noticed that in the list of names read, and those asked to stand for acknowledgement, the Cavelli name was missing. Natalie had been right about that, too.

When dinner was served, Natalie and I ignored the steam tables, and headed right for the carving station.

When the carver placed the meat on our plates, Natalie pushed our plates back at him and gave him a wink and a smile. He loaded us up. Our hot tip paid off. We stuffed ourselves on the most tender and juicy prime rib I had ever eaten.

\*\*\*

The morning of our big competition day arrived soon enough, and it was beautiful. Natalie had been dutiful about limiting her alcohol consumption. We were both sharp and ready for action. Even in the early morning hours you could tell it was going to be "Chamber of Commerce" weather. Dew sparkled on the wet grass, the air had been washed clean by the rains, the ground, though wet, had mostly drained, and the sun was peaking out from behind puffy white clouds.

Because Margot had won the preliminary round, she and Hotstuff would be the last combination to go in the finals class today. The horses went in reverse order of placings. But since the class was the first to be held this morning, whatever the outcome, we would be done before lunch. The award ceremony would be held directly after the scores were final.

Natalie was cheerful and singing loudly as I put in Hotstuff's braids. It was driving Francesca nuts, so she left to go join Dennis in the sponsors' area having coffee and whatever and watching Margot's class get underway.

Margot sat with us for a while, chatting, and then decided to rest alone in the rental car. She was settling herself for the task ahead.

Hotstuff was relaxed and more like his old self today. His crazy big ears had reverted back to their normal relaxed and floppy state rather than being stiff on high alert. He even remembered to do his morning yoga routine for the first time since we had arrived, starting with his hind legs. I quietly called Natalie over to watch. "Nat… pssst. Wait for it."

Natalie walked over to the stall front while I untied Hotstuff's lead rope from the string tie-ring I had made on the front bars of his stall. I wanted to give him plenty of room for his routine. He gave a protracted groan as he did his "downward dog," then stood up and crossed his front legs for his shin rubbing routine. It was a relief to have him back to himself. I hugged him around the neck. "There's my boy. I love you, Hotstuff." He curled his neck around my back while searching my back pockets with the tip of his top lip. I let go of him and looked into his bright eyes that were not unlike those of a curious puppy. "You are going to be stellar today. I bet you are going to blow the judges away. No matter what they think though, you are number one in our book."

I looked over at Natalie and she was looking thoughtful. She finally said, "I hope everything I said was wrong. They say, 'man plans and God laughs,' but today I hope he's laughing at Rocket Socks and not us."

We did what we could do, then we watched our clocks, each of us dealing with our anxiety in our own ways.

Margot and Francesca joined us. Dennis knew to stay away. These last few moments were always the worst. Margot sat in one of our director chairs, closed her eyes and did her visualizations, while occasionally chewing on her cuticles. I had long since noticed that under stress Margot was a nail chewer.

Francesca stared constantly at her cell phone at the scores of the other horses in the class as they went up online, her legs crossed, her foot jiggling. I stared at her bobbing foot and ruefully was reminded of her son. Thankfully, she did not announce the scores.

Natalie and I tacked up Hotstuff, checking and double-checking each detail. We hand walked him around and slowly tightened his girth. Finally, it was time. Margot waited silently on the mounting block for her horse to come to her, and I brought Hotstuff over. I held the off-side stirrup and put one hand on his bit while Margot swung up. Natalie gathered her bucket of supplies and a bottle of cold water from the ice chest, and our solemn parade to the warm up arena commenced. Even Natalie was silent.

Dennis joined us at the end of the warm up arena on the little berm of grass. Everyone around the arena was dead serious today. The air was still, the sky was blue, but no one was laughing or joking or calling out to friends. This was the last "flight" of entries to go and all of them were contenders. All of the riders appeared to be experienced and professional, and all of these innocent four year old horses were looking workmanlike as they were put though the basic exercises.

Rocket Socks looked as impressive as ever. But our boy was showing great reach and scope and today he added to that mix an air of confidence. Hotstuff, despite his giant ears and slender physique, was moving with a lot of power and swing. The FEI had made a statement a few years earlier that they were looking for "happy athletes." I often wondered how the hell they would determine which horses were truly happy, and which were simply submissive. Hotstuff today looked about as happy as a dressage horse could look. He reminded me of a puppy who has fun showing off how bouncy he could be jumping over an obstacle and how fast he could run bringing you back a spit-covered ball. Today our boy felt damn good and he was ready to show the world just how good.

Rocket Socks, having placed second on Friday, went immediately before Margot. I tried not to watch. But, of course I couldn't help but keep checking out of the corner of my eye. I thought Rocket Socks looked tired. There would be no bucking spree today. I noticed Francesca never took her eyes off him. The ring steward called Margot's number "on deck." That was our cue to focus only on Margot and Hotstuff. Margot was making a nice active trot down the long side of the warm up heading toward us, and as she passed us, Nat grabbed my arm and yelled, "Margot! Pull up!!" And Margot heard and tried, but as she drew back on the reins, the right rein popped off the bit. Margot only had the left rein, and Hotstuff obediently spun a circle to the left, nearly causing a collision with a horse that was passing on her inside. The rider cussed at Margot, who looked totally bewildered.

Nat was already darting into the arena and grabbing Hotstuff by the only rein that Margot had, drawing him over to the grassy berm. Francesca had her mouth open, and she and Margot were staring at each other. Nat took charge, just like that. "Francesca, run to a tack vendor and buy us reins. I'll see if I can fix this one."

Francesca, to her credit, took off running. I'd never seen Francesca run in my life. I didn't even think she could. But off she went at an impressive clip.

Natalie grabbed my ponytail and deftly, if a bit harshly, removed my scrunchie.

"Ouch!" I said.

She looked at the rein, making an instant diagnosis. "The hook is totally gone, like missing, I'm amazed it didn't fall apart earlier in your ride."

Margot said, "How the hell?" Then, "Get that fabric off the scrunchie or it will look terrible."

I grabbed the pocket knife out of Nat's back pocket and smacked it firmly in her open palm, like a nurse producing a scalpel for a surgeon. Natalie took it without comment.

Nat swiftly cut off the fabric, then she took the heavy rubber band and wound it around the rein, right under the stitching, put the end of the rein back on the bit, and pushed the rubber band up over the folded over leather until it was right next to the bit, then she pushed the free end back through the keeper. It didn't look too bad. She looked up at Margot. "Don't pull too hard on that right rein." And then she winked.

I pulled off Hotstuff's boots and offered Margot some water, which she declined. I thought Margot, like most riders in such a predicament, would be on edge. I was wrong. She giggled a little bit, and shook her head at us. "This is one to remember, girls. No matter what happens, I love my horse and I love my team. You two are the best! Time to turn me loose."

I wiped down her boots, and then ran the towel over Hotstuff. They looked sharp. I saw her look up at Rocket Socks still performing his test. She took a deep breath, picked up her reins, and then we really did turn her loose. She did a few simple turns on the forehand. I glanced back at the main arena and watched Rocket Socks once again go across the diagonal in what was supposed to be his lengthened trot, and once again, he did not show any difference from his working trot, just like yesterday. I could read Natalie's mind as we exchanged a glance: "hackney trot."

Francesca jogged up to us with reins in her hand. She was panting from her run. She was about to call out to Margot, but I put a hand on her arm and stopped her, "We Jerry-rigged it, Francesca."

Francesca looked surprised. "How ever did you do that?"

I opened my palm and showed her the black polka-dot fabric Nat had cut off my hair scrunchie.

Francesca hung her mouth open. "My prized horse is going into the National Championships with a hair scrunchie holding his reins together?"

"Only one rein," Nat corrected.

Poor Francesca looked winded and disappointed. She said, "For heaven's sake, why didn't you let me put the new reins on?"

Natalie matter of factly set Franesca straight, "If she were late, she could be eliminated; we weren't going to risk it, Francesca."

I whispered to her, "We put it on really tight." Francesca did not look reassured. But when I looked back at Margot, I knew the rein was already forgotten. Margot was all business.

Rocket Socks turned down centerline for his final halt and salute. It was square and immobile. The crowd erupted in applause. I looked over at the sponsors' area, and saw the owners standing right next to the head of the high-performance league, clapping madly and smiling and chatting. The head judge stood to give her scores and remarks. She was almost swooning with praise, giving Rocket Socks the same score of ten for trot that they had given on Friday. I suppose Natalie was right in that they had gone out on a limb and no one was brave enough to crawl backwards.

I double-crossed my fingers and waited for the judge to finish and ring the bell. Francesca, Natalie, and I were for once connected, side-by-side, waiting for Margot and Hotstuff and the fates above to deliver. Between rain and reins, the 'wild ride' that Deb spoke of had provided enough unforeseen challenges. It was time for victory.

Finally, the bell was rung; the head judge stood up, and Margot and our wonderful big bouncy puppy of a four-year-old trotted boldly down centerline, coming to an abrupt but square halt. Margot saluted the judge, who nodded back and took a seat. Then Margot and Hotstuff showed the world how it was done.

I rode each step with Margot and each step seemed perfect to me. Hotstuff's giant ears were hanging to the sides and gently swiveling with each stride of his trot; the bottom half of his gigantic and fluffy tail was swinging left and right with the rhythm. He did jump a little too enthusiastically into the canter transitions, and I hoped he wouldn't take off, but he settled quickly, snorting in relaxation by the time he had finished his first circle. His walk lengthening fulfilled the requirements of reach and freedom and ground cover and, of course, relaxation. It was the only time in the test where his ears came to the front and he was tempted to look around, but he never picked up his head and stayed true to the line of travel. His stretch-down circle was also just about textbook with the addition of some big snorts and trying to wipe his nose on his knee, which he sort of did without losing the tempo. Of course, to his adoring grooms, wiping his nose while he trotted in metronome tempo was just a display of his enormous charm.

When they made their final salute, we exploded in applause; Natalie blowing my left eardrum out with her whistle. Natalie and I jumped up and down and hugged each other. I didn't dare hug Francesca.

The judge stood and turned on the microphone to announce the scores. Hotstuff once again received the almost unheard of ten for submission. The head judge described him in glowing terms. When the judges announced his final score, we didn't know whether to rejoice or be sad. The scores were so close. We knew that Friday's score counted 40% and today's counted the remaining 60%. Francesca looked grim. Dennis had been keeping his distance through our crisis-mode, but rejoined us with a frown. He let us know that today's score placed Hotstuff slightly behind Rocket Socks... by a few hundredths of a percent, so we were in second place in today's standing. With that he and Francesca exchanged knowing looks. I was not believing it. Was there any chance? I looked at Natalie and asked her that question with a feeling of desperation.

Natalie shook her head sadly. She had called it. Hotstuff would not be champion. A reserve championship ribbon should be cause for celebration for almost anyone. But I physically hurt. This was wrong, and I thought that everyone, including the judges, should be feeling much as I felt. Their faces should be hot, their stomachs in knots, their throats burning hot.

If Margot felt that way, she didn't show it. We all congratulated Margot on a perfect ride. I told her it couldn't have been any better. She accepted our praise graciously, but I knew she had to be disappointed. We silently took a tired but content Hotstuff back to the stalls to put on fresh white polo wraps and a brand new set of soft white bell boots in addition to the new set of reins that we carried back with us. We brushed his tail and reapplied his coat polish and fly spray, then letting it dry a bit; we brushed and toweled him off. He would look stunning in the award ceremony and we wanted to be sure the photographer would get him at his best.

But Rocket Socks would be the one to take the solo lap of honor.

We were all quiet at the stalls as we prepared for the awards ceremony, as we had been prior to the ride. It was unstated among us, but I knew we concurred. We felt robbed.

The announcer called the numbers of the winners up to the holding area to receive their ribbons. Margot had Nat and me lead Hotstuff while she walked up to the arena on the pedestrian path with Dennis and Francesca. Since I had Natalie alone, I whispered as I walked. "Nat, have you ever had a rein lose the hook like that?"

She whispered back, "Nope. But you might as well forget about it, Lizzy. We rode in heavy rain. Everyone is going to think our stitching was rotten, and maybe it was."

And I whispered back. "And maybe we should have slept with our horse last night."

Nat just nodded in agreement.

Hotstuff got a beautiful neck sash for the reserve championships and a red ribbon for his second place finish in the final class. When it was time, Margot mounted and each rider, in reverse order, came in and lined up while the announcer did his job. The judges walked down the line, shaking the hand of each rider, and congratulating them. Then the music played and the victory gallop began. Hotstuff was full of himself, but totally under Margot's control. After one lap, Margot peeled off and exited, with the rest of the class following her, so that Rocket Socks could have the lap of honor to himself.

Four-year-old dressage horses have no special training to showcase like the Grand Prix horses often do in their victory laps. But Rocket Socks was a beautiful stallion, and easy on the eyes cantering to loud music. The handsome young man on his back let the stallion have a good gallop down the last long side, whizzing past the exit and pulling his excited stallion up halfway down the long side. Then he got the horse turned around and they exited in a bouncy trot. His grooms could barely catch up to him to grab the horse and get his rider dismounted. The press wanted a few words. Francesca waved at me. "Lizzy, you and Natalie can take Hotstuff back now. I'm sure the press will want to interview Margot, too."

Margot jumped off and ran up her stirrup and loosened her girth before I could stop her. "I've got it, Margot. You go do your interview."

Margot smiled back at me and dabbed her damp forehead. "I do hope they will interview me, because we have a good story to tell, don't we?"

I nodded, then said, "Margot, Hotstuff is the best horse here. You do know that, right?"

She smiled broadly. "Darling, I do know that. But, thank you for reminding me."

My stomach instantly felt better. Ribbons were only ribbons; stupid pieces of cheap satin. The real value of a horse like Hotstuff as a top-drawer dressage horse was only a guess, a gamble, and would be realized (or not) after many more years of training. In any case, I knew Margot would be her usual gracious self in her interview, telling the story of the mishap of the broken rein in a way that was entertaining, rather than show any disappointment in the results. Margot was a class act…always.

I did not believe Rocket Socks, with that trot of his, would be anyone's High-Performance Grand Prix horse. My guess was he would become a breeding stallion and his true worth would most likely depend on the quality of his offspring. But barring disaster, I never doubted that with Margot in the saddle, Grand Prix would be Hotstuff's destiny.

Hotstuff walked briskly toward the stables. Horses soon understand where the stables are, no matter where you go, and it seems to have a magnetic pull. A grouping of horses becomes an instant herd. I felt instinctively that he was eager to get back to harassing the little chestnut mare next door. He could not know that he was now the national reserve champion four-year-old. At the same time, despite our disappointment, he must know that we were satisfied with him. His eyes were soft, his ears flopping, his head low but nodding in time with his stride. Natalie and I had to hustle to keep up with him. I kept patting his neck, and crooning. "You are the best boy; such a good boy; the boy who should have been at the front of the line, by-the-way."

I choked slightly on the last word and felt a hot tear slide down my cheek. I darted a glance over at Natalie, hoping she didn't notice. Natalie would never let herself cry over this loss, I knew that. She did notice though, and shook her head at me. "Lizzy, let it go. It's just show-biz." Natalie's sympathy didn't make me feel better. Instead, the floodgates opened and the tears flowed down my face.

Natalie grabbed Hotstuff's reins from me and hooked her arm through mine. "C'mon, don't be such a cry-baby."

We got to the row of barns and peeled off into Hotstuff's stall, pulling the door mostly shut behind us. Nat pulled off his bridle and I pulled off the saddle. She put the bridle over her shoulder, and then pulled the saddle out of my hands. "You stay in here and pull yourself together. Pull off those polos and bell boots while you finish blubbering."

I sniffed, "Okay."

As predicted, Hotstuff sidled up to the stall wall and stretched his neck to see if he could get a peek over the top. No luck. His girlfriend was out. He then put his attention on me. I was squatting down unwinding his front left polo wrap and still sniffling but getting a grip regardless. Hotstuff started playing with my ponytail, I had found a bright red puffy scrunchie in my purse that he decided was irresistible.

At first he wiggled it around with his top lip in a harmless way. Then he grabbed it and yanked it out, along with some of my hair. I reached around to smack him, "hey!" but missed as he backed up in alarm, leaving his polo wrap halfway unwound in the stall and halfway still on his leg. I stood up, no longer crying, but annoyed.

"Not funny, Hotstuff; not funny at all; that hurt, and by the way, Francesca now owes me scrunchies." I was rubbing my scalp. He stood there with my hair scrunchie in his lips, nodding his head up and down. Then he dropped it in the shavings, immediately stretched out, and proceeded to pee. I jumped forward and grabbed my scrunchie out of the shavings before he could wet it. Now I was laughing, "You are a total nut job!"

I turned around to find Natalie and a man and woman I did not recognize standing in the doorway smiling. Natalie turned to address them, explaining. "Of course, Lizzy only means nut job in the best possible sense."

The man said back, "So, he's a clown, too? I'm not surprised. He seems like a confident and intelligent animal."

The woman added, "Hank, I think Becca would be as charmed as we are."

The man answered, "Yup. Does Ms. Cavelli happen to be here?"

Natalie answered, "She should be here any moment; Margot, too."

"It's nice to see you ladies interacting with the horse. We wanted to see him in the stall, and we're not disappointed. He's not finished maturing, but he was the best horse in that class and should have been champion. We can see that. We've been watching him all weekend, and think he'd be perfect for our Becca."

I must have looked alarmed, because the man quickly added, "I know, I know, I don't imagine you young ladies want to see him go, but we can give him a top class home. Our Becca is a great little rider with the best coaching and she already has Grand Prix experience, but the thing is it's time she brings along a young one herself. Everyone says "go to Europe" but that's not for me. I believe in buying American. So, that's what we're going to do."

The woman had put her hand on her husband's arm. And he put his hand on top of hers and stopped talking. They were looking at me. I put my hand up to my cheek to find that another tear had slid down my face; embarrassing. I couldn't think of a thing to say.

Natalie spoke up for both of us. "We're only the grooms, so we can't say whether or not he is available. You'll have to speak with Francesca. That's Mrs. Cavelli's first name. In fact, here she comes now."

Francesca came into view, walking down the pedestrian path toward us. The couple turned to follow our gaze, greeting her enthusiastically.

I heard a few bits and pieces, and then the three of them walked off together in conversation.

Natalie watched them for a long moment then turned back to me. "You better get those polos off before he steps on the loose end, trips, falls over, and breaks a leg."

I grimaced and said, "Maybe then he can't be sold."

And I felt a fresh set of tears well up in my eyes.

***

Natalie and I got on the road in the pre-dawn hours, having packed everything we could the night before. We weren't the only ones there in the dark, the parking lot was full of rumbling diesel engines, the darkness continually slashed by headlights. Many horses had pulled out the day before, but now, the ones left behind paced circles in their stalls and whinnied in anxiety.

Hotstuff had clambered eagerly up the ramp and backed into his slot, bobbing his head and poking his nose at his hay bag until it was swinging wildly around, clanking the clip against the upright support pole. He quieted as we got out on the road. Soon, the monotony would send him into road-coma. We had over twelve hours of driving ahead of us. Both Natalie and I were too unsettled to listen to our audio book just yet. We watched the sun come up and looked for a truck stop to add the magical powers of caffeine to the pathetic cup of coffee we had made in our room.

Francesca and Margot had caught a flight out the night before. Nat and I were the "roadies" with the responsibility to get our cargo safely home. I was eager to get home, too. I had thrashed around in the bed all night, pressing the button on the side of my watch that lit up the face so

I could countdown the hours to liftoff. I would have just gotten up and bagged sleep all together in favor of leaving, but I could hear the deep and steady breaths of Natalie in the other bed. Stupidly, I had cried off and on in my pillow for a good part of the night.

I loved horses. I loved training with Margot. I had even summoned the courage to get myself and my horse down the centerline at horse shows to satisfying results. But I had decided that the "business" of horses I hated. Natalie and I had kept our lips zipped the rest of the day yesterday. We had no idea if Francesca had seriously entertained the idea of selling Hotstuff, because nothing was said in our presence. We did not know if Margot knew. But, knowing Francesca and her attitude about selling Johnny as soon as she had reached her goal with him, it didn't take any great leap to see the logic. The Cavellis were strapped for cash. The Cavellis were trying to look legit as an equine business to win their appeal with the IRS. The Cavellis needed to sell something, and a live prospect had just wandered into our camp with a checkbook. Who was I kidding? Hotstuff was a goner. Poor Margot; poor Hotstuff. Every time I thought of it, it generated a fresh set of tears.

I did some venting, and Natalie listened for a while but I could tell she was getting weary of it. Finally, she said, "Lizzy, were you ever in 4-H?"

I was puzzled. "Uh, no."

She pointed to her head with her right hand and said, "I pledge my head to clearer thinking," pointed to her heart and said, "my heart for greater loyalty," then opened her palm, "my hands for greater service" and slapped her thigh and leaned toward me, "and my health for greater living."

What the heck was her point? "Yeah, sounds great. So what?"

She shook her head sadly. "It's a grand motto. But, consider this, you raise your cow or pig or sheep all year. You handle them and groom them, just like we do the horses, and then you enter the big show, and if you win the blue ribbon, guess what? Someone buys your precious and slaughters them."

That was sobering. I replied. "Wow; if you win you lose. Nice thing to do to your kid."

Natalie just made a noise that sounded like agreement… maybe, with Natalie I was never sure. We rode in silence for a few miles. Natalie leaned over and handed me a red licorice whip. I took it and gnawed on it quietly. Then I said, "I guess I should stop crying. If Hotstuff goes, at least he won't be someone's prime rib."

Nat smiled a sad smile and said, "Lizzy, that was some awesome prime rib we pigged out on. We could have been eating someone's 4-H project."

I blew my cheeks out in despair. I had devoured that prime rib. I slumped down in my seat and let the licorice hang out of my mouth.

Nat continued, "Come on, Lizzy, I hope to hell he doesn't sell. Margot has put her eggs all in that particular basket. But, if he does go, she'll still have Pepper. She doesn't own any of her rides. You actually own Winsome. That one's yours. The rest, you just do your best by them and that's enough. Margot's a big girl. She understands the business. It sucks, but there ya go."

It looked like I was not going to get any more sympathy from Natalie. So I called Chess on my cell phone. He seemed glad to hear from me.

"Lizzy! I've been thinking of you. How'd the weekend go? I texted Mother but never heard back."

I barely drew breath as I started describing the stellar ride in the rainstorm and took it from there, being sure to include the drama of the broken rein. At one point I realized I was yakking away at black screen, the call had dropped. I called him back.

"Sorry, Chess. Where did I drop off?"

"Lizzy, when you get home I'm going to make you dinner and then you can give me all the details."

I felt a little guilty. "Sorry. We have so many hours of driving ahead of us. I'll call again when we get home."

He broke in. "Don't hang up yet; just tell me how the thing shook out."

I sighed, "Okay. Hotstuff was Reserve Champion. The horse ranked number one just barely beat us."

And he said, "But Reserve Champion, that's second place, right? Number two in the country is how you went in and how you finished. Not too shabby. Was Mother pleased?"

I grunted, then said, "What do you think?"

He chuckled. "Yeah. Not likely."

I added, "But the worst part was some people are now interested in buying Hotstuff."

There was a protracted silence. I had to look at the phone screen to check that the call hadn't dropped again. "Chess?"

"Uh, Lizzy, how is that a bad thing? It could be the answer to our prayers."

I tried not to sound whiny. "But that's Margot's best and only ride right now. She adores that horse."

Again a pause. Then in tones not unsympathetic, "Lizzy, Dad's just about worked himself to death. With Mother out of town, I've been spending more time with him just to see if I can help. I don't like the way he's looking. I know you love the horses, but some things are more important. You understand that."

My throat was feeling hot, and I knew Natalie was tired of my tears. I had to get a better grip. I was tired, too. Everyone made sense, but it still felt wrong. I managed a weak excuse and hit "call end."

I needed to pledge my head to clearer thinking because my heart was already pledged too much to greater loyalty, my hands were too calloused from service, and my health was going downhill fast; so much for the four H's.

I took another red licorice whip and gnawed silently, too tired to talk. But, not too tired to think. Francesca had questioned whether she had chosen "the right girl for the job" and when I was this weary, this brittle, I questioned it, too. If I could just ride my horse, take my lessons, and enjoy an occasional horse show to evaluate my progress, then I could be at peace.

Did anyone get to live that life? Even Francesca Cavelli had her path littered with problems. The red licorice whip suddenly seemed rubbery and tasteless. Why had I reached for another? I rolled down my window and threw it out with disgust.

Natalie shook her head with a twisted smile and said, "It's bad enough that we eat that toxic stuff, just imagine what it does to the birdlife."

I mumbled something dismissive, and Natalie took her eyes off the road, narrowing them at me. She said, "You're on a downhill slide. What's eating you now?"

My eyes grew hot and my nose started to run. My voice sounded hoarse. "I don't think I am cut out for this, this, this...business." I grabbed a fast food napkin and blew my nose with it.

Natalie laughed, which seemed inappropriate. "Lizzy, if you didn't feel that way every now and then, I'd agree with you."

"What?"

"The day you no longer hate the crappy parts, the sad parts, hate it when the creeps win and the good guys lose, the day you can no longer have your heart broken, then that's the day you gotta' quit, man. If that day ever comes, you're no good for the horses or the people around them."

I put my elbow on the armrest on the door and leaned my chin in the palm of my hand and gazed at the passing landscape, silent for a moment.

Then I swiveled around in my seat and asked point blank. "Do you think I'm the right girl for the job? This job? I mean, someday being a professional?"

The way her face crinkled up in amusement, I wasn't sure she would answer me straight. I turned and scolded, "I'm serious."

Natalie's face settled into an unreadable wall as I leaned back in my seat and waited. She said in a level tone, "Margot and Francesca got lucky the day you walked into Equus Paradiso Farm. And if some days, you don't feel "like the right girl for the job" hang in there and do what it takes to become that girl, because you know down deep, this is where you're meant to be, and this is what you are meant to do. But Lizzy, that sure as hell doesn't mean that some days you won't be miserable. Goes with the territory, my friend."

Then she pointed to the bag on the floor. "Let's cleanse our palates with some red-hots."

Then in Natalie's inimitable style, she began belting out a song.

*"Country Roads, take me home, to a place I belong...*

*Paradiso, Margot Mama*

*Take me home*

*Country Roads."*

I laughed, then thought for a moment about what was waiting for me at the end of the road; the people first, the animals second.

The blue fog evaporated.

What had I been thinking? Of course I was "the right girl for the job."

I couldn't wait to get home.

# Acknowledgments

I never meant to write this many books! My original concept was to write one book about dressage in a way that both informed and entertained. My favorite books always leave me feeling that I have learned something. It doesn't matter what genre. It can be historical fiction or spy novel or a murder mystery. (I gobbled up all of Dick Francis during college.) I wanted my one book about riding dressage to accomplish that simple goal.

But, somehow, like eating potato chips, once I started I couldn't stop. I sincerely hope that riders and non-riders alike will feel that I succeeded in meeting my goal and enjoyed "the ride" regardless of the length. After having finished the fourth book, I now feel my characters are safe and happy and I can turn my back on them knowing they will be just fine. (Yes, they feel real to me because they all come from my own life in the horse world.)

I want to thank my writing buddy, Eric Johnson, who met me at Starbuck's as we exchanged chapters (he is writing a novel, too), then read every single word I wrote and made corrections and comments. He had great ideas that I seized on and used as the story progressed.

I want to thank my Sweet Briar College Vixen sister (yes, we are the Vixens), Meg Hammock. Meg had the honor of doing the final read through of books three and four. She made some great catches!

I searched and searched for the perfect photos for the two covers. Thanks to Leila Moore for the cover photo and to WAITING TO

HEAR FROM KAREN for the back cover photo. I took the photo of the bridles hanging in my tack room that I used for the spine for book three.

Thanks to Deeds Publishing for having faith in me, and for being patient while I missed every deadline we set. I followed Lewis Carrol's advice, choosing to "begin at the beginning…go on till you come to the end: then stop."

Thanks to my husband, students, and friends who left me quietly alone every afternoon while I worked. The grass got long, the house got dusty, and oftentimes the bed didn't even get made. But, of course the barn was always spotless!

Thanks to my Starbucks Barista's at Windward Commons. I felt like Norm from "Cheers," greeted by name as I came through the door, drink started for me before I got to the register. I am now having withdrawals.

Johnny Cash was a real Grand Prix horse. He was first purchased and shown by Alyssa Eidbo. He was then purchased by my friend, Elizabeth Kane. His last owner was Hannah Hewitt. He was treasured by all three riders.

Hannah was riding Johnny in a lesson when he stopped and gently lowered himself to the ground. He died with his head cradled in her arms.

Thank you to all three of his past owners for allowing me to bring Johnny Cash back to life in my pages.

Thanks especially to each and every one of my readers. Without you, I have no reason to write.

*Karen McGoldrick rides, teaches, and trains dressage at her own* Prospect Hill Farm in Alpharetta, Georgia.

She is a United States Dressage Federation certified instructor/trainer; earned her USDF Bronze, Silver, and Gold medal rider awards, all on horses she trained; and she graduated "With Distinction" from the USDF "L" program.

Karen got her first "working student" job by answering an ad in her community newspaper at the age of 12. Before, during, and after college, she worked on and off for a variety of trainers until she and her husband bought their first farm in 1992.

Karen feels that the best part of being a dressage instructor is sharing the insights, joys, and sorrows that riding, training, and loving horses have brought to her life. Writing a novel is one more way to do this.

The *Dressage Chronicles* books come straight from her heart.

*Author photograph courtesy of Alicia Frese*

# RINGS of FIRE

## BOOK IV OF THE DRESSAGE CHRONICLES

KAREN
McGOLDRICK

**Coming February 2016**

CPSIA information can be obtained
at www.ICGtesting.com
Printed in the USA
LVOW12s0737051216
515814LV00001B/74/P

9 781944 193768